Raves for the *Alien* novels:

"If you like your futuristic adventure with heapings of over-the-top fun and absurdity, Koch has the series for you. . . . A rip-roaring and outlandish romp!"   —*RT Book Reviews*

"Koch still pulls the neat trick of quietly weaving in plot threads that go unrecognized until they start tying together—or snapping. This is a hyperspeed-paced addition to a series that shows no signs of slowing down." —*Publishers Weekly*

"Aliens, danger, and romance make this a fast-paced, wittily-written sf romantic comedy."   —*Library Journal*

"Gini Koch's Kitty Katt series is a great example of the lighter side of science fiction. Told with clever wit and non-stop pacing . . . it blends diplomacy, action and sense of humor into a memorable reading experience."   —*Kirkus*

"The action is nonstop, the snark flies fast and furious. . . . Another fantastic addition to an imaginative series!"
—Night Owl Sci-Fi (top pick)

"Gini Koch has another winner, plenty of action combined with just the right touch of humor and a kick-ass storyline. What's not to like?"   —Fresh Fiction

"This delightful romp has many interesting twists and turns as it glances at racism, politics, and religion en route . . . will have fanciers of cinematic sf parodies referencing *Men in Black*, *Ghost Busters*, and *X-Men*."
—*Booklist* (starred review)

"Gini Koch mixes up the som fiction romance by adding nor tion, and moments worthy of a

ALIEN
RESEARCH

GINI KOCH

DAW BOOKS, INC.

DONALD A. WOLLHEIM, FOUNDER

375 Hudson Street, New York, NY 10014

ELIZABETH R. WOLLHEIM
SHEILA E. GILBERT
PUBLISHERS

www.dawbooks.com

To Mary Rehak and Phyllis Hemann, whose cheerful optimism in the face of any and all adversity is always an inspiration to me. Fight on, my sisters from other mothers, fight on.

ACKNOWLEDGMENTS

This book was late. Oh, not so as it would affect any of you, the readers, but in terms of when it was supposed to be turned in, which is challenging for everyone involved in the process that gets said book into your hot little hands. So, many extra thanks to my awesome editor, Sheila Gilbert, and my wonderful agent, Cherry Weiner, who remained calm, and kept me calm, as my deadline flew by. You're both the best and I'm thankful every day that I get to work with you. Oh, and your chocolate is in the mail.

Same again to my crit partner, Lisa Dovichi, who helped me get this book done, and done right, all while doing all the other million and one things she does so well that you'd never know she's a multitasker of the highest order. And of course, much love to my main beta reader, Mary Fiore, who once again had to read for errors at a breakneck pace, and still managed to find them all and remain cheerful.

Love and thanks always to all the good folks at DAW Books and all my fans around the globe. To my Hook Me Up! Gang, members of Team Gini, all Alien Collective Members in Very Good Standing around the world, Twitter followers, Facebook fans and friends, Pinterest followers, and all the wonderful fans who come to my various book signings and conference panels, I have but this to say: You still complete me and I love you all more every day.

Special shout outs to: my distance assistant, Colette Chmiel, who continues to be the only reason I get things done and the only reason I'm even sort of sane; Adrian and Lisa Payne for continuing to support everything I do, everywhere I do it; Koren Cota, Hal and Dee Astell, Thomax and Shannon Green, Blanca and Oliver Bernal, Diana Klabis, Jan Robinson, Terry Smith, and Mariann Asanuma for making and bestowing such lovely edible, wearable, and adorable gifts for and on me; author Eric Penner Haury for fun times at Tucson Festival of Books which included introducing me to his cousin, Ted Danson, who was as charming as you'd want a famous celebrity to be; author and comics artist Christopher Baldwin for help and fun times at Tucson Festival of Books; authors Terry L. Smith, Amber Scott, Shaina Hardesty, Andrea Rittschof, and Deb Haralson for fun times, help, and support at AZD—everything's better when you girls are there; "Chiropractor" Ken who saved my back during Phoenix Comicon; Lee Whiteside for always taking the best care of me before, during, and after Phoenix Comicon; Raul "Sherpa" Padron, Edward "GF#1" Pulley, Joseph "GF#2" Gaxiola, Brad "My Man" Jensen, Terry Smith (getting the hat trick!), and Jeff "BFAM" Twohig for all your help during Phoenix Comicon; fabulous authors Caris Roane, Erin Kellison, and Erin Quinn for always being there and having my back; and ever-wonderful author, BFF, and sister in crime Marsheila Rockwell, for once again helping me save my writing day while making me laugh—road trips with you are the best, babe.

Last, but truly never least, all my love and thanks to my husband, Steve, and daughter, Veronica, who continue to make the journey worthwhile. And I continue to love you both more than words can say.

IN ALL THE TIME man has been on our good planet Earth, we've stared at and striven for the stars, at least in some way.

Or so they tell me. Frankly, my experience has been that what a goodly number are doing is staring at and striving for more wealth and power. And since aliens joined us on Earth, those same people have been striving even harder to control said aliens, presumably to use them to get even more wealth and power.

I'm talking, of course, about the first time the aliens joined us for an extended stay, in the 1960s. Not the several times in the distant, ancient, and super-distant past, when a variety of aliens did flybys and, from what we can tell, evolutionary experiments here. No one was trying to control any of them. At least as far as we know.

Nope, I mean when the gang from Alpha Four in the Alpha Centaurion solar system came to live here permanently. Okay, not all of them came. Just some of them. Religious exiles, with some sympathizers and human spouses along for the ride.

They looked enough like us that they could hide and blend in. Well, mostly blend in: all of our A-Cs, as they call themselves, are drop-dead gorgeous. Maybe it's the double hearts. Having two hearts makes them all speedy and strong and quick to heal, so why shouldn't it make them total hotties, too?

Sorry, back to the more solemn recap. The A-Cs hid and blended in, known to exist only by a few Earth governments, and those with a high enough security clearance.

But, you know, the A-Cs had jobs. Math, science, medicine, killing parasitic superbeings. Mostly done in secret, because the A-Cs also have talents that allow them to alter what humans think they see—in more ways than one—but only for the safety and peace of mind of the humans not in the know. Well, most of the A-Cs were trying to keep the humans safe.

Some of them, of course, made a real love connection with other megalomaniacs, and really did their best to destroy humans and their own people seemingly indiscriminately, for whatever reason looked good on the daily menu at the Evil Super-Genius Bar and Grill.

And then I came on the scene.

In the three short years since I've discovered that aliens, and lots of them, were living on Earth, a lot's happened. I fell in love with and married one of them, we had a child, and I inherited some mutated alien genetics. I also became a superbeing exterminator and the Head of Airborne for Centaurion Division. Then, somewhat against my will, I became the Co-Head Ambassador for American Centaurion. And then, truly against my will, I ended up the wife of a Congressman and American Centaurion's Head Ambassador.

Yeah.

Fortunately, I'm adaptable.

Of course, along the way through all of this there were a couple of alien invasions that weren't as friendly as the one in the 1960s. One of them, we kept off the radar. One of them, however, changed the world. But through it all, the A-Cs were there, protecting Earth and everyone living on it. Well, you know, other than the ones who weren't. But there are a lot fewer evil A-Cs than good ones, especially since I've gotten rid of a bunch of the bad ones over the past few years.

Yet there are still those who'd rather make a buck doing terrible things to humans and aliens alike. Those who want money and power and all the perks that come with it, especially perks that let them amass more money and power.

Now, before you start to worry, I'm not anti-business. As

Oingo Boingo likes to remind us, there's nothing wrong with capitalism. Unless said capitalists are actually evil megalomaniacal scumbags intent on destroying everyone you care about and probably the Free World As We Know It. Then they need to be taken down, in the most extreme way.

But never fear, good citizens—Megalomaniac Girl is here!

Huh, you know, after the last three years, you'd think I'd be hearing a lot more clapping and cheering and lot less of the sounds of silence broken only by the quiet sound of crickets chirping. So, let's try this again. I am Megalomaniac Girl, and I have Poofs and Peregrines with me to help save the day!

Yeah, okay, that's better.

CHAPTER 1

"AMBASSADOR, would you please tell the Committee your full name?"

"Katherine Sarah Katt-Martini."

"Do you know the whereabouts of one Herbert Gaultier?"

"No." My bet was Hell, but the Committee probably didn't want to hear that.

"Do you know if he's alive or dead?"

I hesitated. I was under oath. "I think he's dead."

"Do you?" The Senator in charge of the hearing leaned forward. "Is that because you killed him?"

"No. I didn't kill him." Christopher White had killed him. But he'd had to.

"What about Leventhal Reid?"

"Nope, didn't kill him, either." My husband, Jeff, had killed Reid. To save my life.

"LaRue Demorte Gaultier—did you kill her?"

"No. Esteban Cantu killed her." Accidentally, of course, but that one wasn't on me. "Then he was arrested. And I didn't kill him, either." Other bad guys had killed him, before we could get information from him.

"John Cooper?"

"Nope, didn't do him in, either." Charles Reynolds had killed Cooper. Again, in self-defense, defending me and himself.

"Ronaldo Al Dejahl, who killed him?"

"Um, everybody and nobody. Because my bet is that he's

still alive. But lots of us have tried to kill him, and you should be grateful." James Reader had used the first guy we thought was Ronaldo for a body shield, Jeff had beaten up the real one, but he'd escaped, and my bet was he'd survived the beat-down he'd gotten during Operation Destruction, too, and was out there somewhere, waiting to strike.

The Committee didn't seem impressed. I didn't look around, but the room was huge and it seemed filled to capacity with a blur of official-looking people in politically fashion-forward suits, all of whom were giving me the Frowny Face of Displeasure.

"The entire former American Centaurion Diplomatic Corps?" the Senator in charge went on. "What about them? And Howard Taft? Antony Marling and Madeline Cartwright? Ronald Yates? And Beverly, that woman who had the most boring speaking voice in the world. Did you kill all of them and many others, including Gregory from Alpha Four, and Uma from Alpha Six, and the Mephistopheles in-control superbeing?"

Now, these were not so easy to not lie under oath about.

"Yes, sort of. Well, yes, really in the case of Beverly and a bunch of the others. I didn't do Gregory in, though." Tito Hernandez had done that. "I took out Moira from Beta Twelve, though." Jeff had handled her mate, Kyrellis. Just barely, but he'd managed it. "They were all evil and trying to destroy everyone good and the Earth. By the way, how did you know Beverly was Miz Monotone?"

The Committee looked at me derisively. "We're in your dream," the Senator in charge said. "And we agree that whoever thought it was a good idea for you to be in such a public position was an idiot."

"Can we sentence her yet?" one of the other Committee members asked. "Or at least ruin her husband's budding political career?" The rest of the Committee nodded eagerly. They were all over the idea of disgracing Representative Martini.

"Can I wake up now?"

"Do you want to?" the Senator in charge asked.

"Am I hanging out with The Congressional Grand Inquisition when I wake up?"

"Not as far as any of us know. Today. Tomorrow? Who knows?"

"That's the story of my life. By the way, as far as dream men go, none of you are what I'd like to see the next time I have a horrible nightmare."

"Who would you prefer?" the Senator in charge asked.

"Billy Zane would be a good option, he doesn't get nearly enough work. Hugh Jackman. Chris Evans. Really, anyone who starred in *The Avengers* would be acceptable. Tom Cruise, Will Smith, Nathan Fillion, pick a hot leading man of choice."

"Sorry. You already live with the best-looking people on Earth. You're stuck with us. See you next time, Ambassador."

"Can't wait."

The Senator in charge nodded. "Tomorrow night will come soon enough."

"As near as I can tell, only if I keep on killing bad guys."

CHAPTER 2

MY EYES OPENED and I looked around. I wasn't in a big room with a lot of important people looking at me while I incriminated myself and everyone else I knew. I was lying in bed.

I'd had a version of this dream pretty much every night since Jeff had become the Appointed Representative for New Mexico's 2nd District, starting right after Operation Sherlock had concluded.

Sure, people being murdered left and right and my somehow becoming the "adopted niece" of the two best assassins in the business could give anyone nightmares. But those situations never came up in my dreams. No, I got the nightly reminder of what I was really stressed over—my husband was now in a very public position and we had a hell of a lot of skeletons in our big walk-in closet.

Rolled over. Sure enough, Jeff was in bed next to me. Mr. Clock said it was five in the morning. Heaved a sigh of relief and snuggled next to Jeff.

He made the low growl that sounded like a purr in his sleep and pulled me closer to him. Buried my face in between his awesome pecs, rubbed against the hair on his chest, and let his double heartbeats lull me back to sleep. Thankfully, this time, dreamless.

The smooth sounds of Robert Palmer's "Addicted to Love" woke me up. Now Mr. Clock shared that it was eight in the morning. I really wasn't a morning person, but these days Jeff had to go to Capitol Hill most days out of the week, and Jamie liked to get up early to start her day.

However, Jeff wasn't in bed with me. Not so unusual—he usually heard the alarm before I did.

Got up and trotted into the bathroom. No Jeff. Checked in the closet. No Jeff. Went to the nursery. Happily, I wasn't having yet another nightmare—Jeff was in there with Jamie and all the animals, from Earth and Alpha Four both.

I received hugs and kisses from our daughter, snuggles from the furred and feathered beasts, and a nice good morning kiss from Jeff. Even when he wasn't trying hard the man was the best kisser in the universe.

"I hear you two have a big day planned," Jeff said as he finished helping Jamie dress and the music changed to The Pretenders' version of "I Got You Babe."

"Yep. Today's my 'be seen being all diplomatic, casual, and yet efficient' day combined with a Mommy-Daughter day."

"So, you're planning to eat every meal and snack, other than dinner, out," Jeff said more than asked.

"Yes, what's your point?" Tom Petty's "Yer So Bad" came on. This was the music mix Jeff had made for our second anniversary. He'd put a lot of thought into it, and I'd been using it as our wakeup music for the past two months.

Jeff grinned. "No point at all. I may be a congressman now, but I still know how to be diplomatic. If you hurry, I have time to keep an eye on Jamie while you shower." He swung Jamie on his shoulders and gave her what she called a giraffe ride, since a horsy ride required the "horse" be on hands and knees.

"Your sacrifice is duly noted." I took a fast shower and got dressed while ZZ Top's "Gimme All Your Lovin'", Wall Of Voodoo's "Hands Of Love", Pat Benatar's "Never Wanna Leave You", and Tina Turner's "Best" played, and Jeff and Jamie romped, assisted by all four dogs, several Peregrines, and a whole mess of Poofs. The cats and many of the Poofs chose to sit this one out and instead spent their time staring at me in the shower. Animals, they truly enriched a family's life.

In the good old days before my daughter was born, I'd

have taken longer to get ready, and not because I was skimping on the lather, rinse, repeat portions or anything now. During Operation Drug Addict some of our enemies had slipped some seriously strong, power-altering drugs into Jeff's system, which he'd then passed along to our child when I'd gotten pregnant, and she'd in turn passed along to me. We were all about the sharing around here.

So, I was now kind of half A-C, though differently from how Jamie was truly half A-C. I had the super-strength, which wasn't quite as good as the regular A-Cs under most circumstances, but was still pretty darned good for any human who wasn't nicknamed "The Rock." I also had faster healing and regeneration, which was excellent.

I also had hyperspeed. Jamie was eighteen months old, and I was just now sort of getting to a place where I could use hyperspeed for normal, mundane things without crashing through a wall or knocking myself out.

Jeff's cousin, Christopher White, had also become enhanced—though he'd done it intentionally—and he and I worked on my skills all the time. This month, the focus was on completing my personal routine using hyperspeed. So far, showering and drying off had gone well, but I used regular human for hair care because I didn't want to look like I had mange, and it was really easy to yank your hair out when you were super strong.

As "Looking Hot" from No Doubt hit my personal airwaves, I trotted to our huge walk-in closet to choose today's ensemble. A-Cs were in love with the colors black and white, and Armani, in a way that made casual obsessions—like mine for all things Aerosmith or Gollum's for the Ring—seem to be merely pale imitations of fidelity.

Therefore, my closet had a lot of black slim skirts, white oxfords, and a variety of black or black-and-white high heels in it. Happily, because I was both human—well, mostly human—and the Ambassador, I got to wear colors and other styles, at least occasionally. And because I was me, I also had a lot of jeans, several pairs of Converse, and an extremely large and eclectic set of concert T-shirts and hoodies.

For some diplomatic missions, going out to be seen all day would mean dressing up. However, I wasn't your average diplomatic bear, and it was the middle of July, ergo I was going for casual. Got into jeans, my Converse, and my newest Aerosmith T-shirt, because having Steven, Joe, and the rest of my boys on my chest ensured I would prevail over all obstacles, even if the only obstacle I could foresee this morning was picking between orange juice, cranberry juice, or a combination.

In honor of "Looking Hot," I selected a cute No Doubt hoodie, because summer back east was still nothing like summer in Pueblo Caliente, Arizona, or Dulce, New Mexico, and I could easily get chilled. Or sweat to death, if it was a high-humidity day, and a hoodie helped hide sweat stains. Plus it looked hella cute with this particular Aerosmith shirt.

"You look great, baby," Jeff said as he swung Jamie down and into my arms. He hugged both of us. "You'll be home for dinner, right?"

"I should be asking you that, but yes, we will be." Turned off the alarm clock as "Honey, Honey" from ABBA came on.

"Good." Jeff kissed us both goodbye, then headed out, holding the door open for our Embassy's Cultural Attachés, aka Naomi Gower-Reynolds and her younger sister, Abigail.

Naomi had only been married to Chuckie for about six months, so I still tended to think of the sisters as the Gower girls. They, like Jamie, were hybrids, but their human mother, Erika, was a stunningly beautiful African-American human, and while A-C genetics were dominant for all internal hybrid workings, human genetics were dominant for the outside. Like their mother and two older brothers, the Gower girls had beautiful dark skin, but when they smiled I definitely saw their father, Stanley.

Basically, the Gower girls were typical Dazzler gorgeous, which was what I called the female A-Cs, because there still wasn't one of them I'd met who was anything less than an eleven on a scale of ten. That the dumbest Dazzler was still MENSA material when stacked up against humans would have been even more unfair if almost all of them weren't also incredibly nice.

Naomi put her arms out. "Mine."

"Auntie Mimi!" Jamie squealed, while Naomi grinned.

"I resent that Sis is the favorite," Abigail said with her own grin as I handed my squirming daughter over.

"I'm the godmother. I rank higher," Naomi said as she cuddled Jamie and they did a set of hyperspeed kisses that was their personal thing. They looked like woodpeckers touching beaks at hummingbird speed to me, but they both loved it, and who was I to argue with what made my daughter happy?

Because she was a hybrid, Jamie had two sets of godparents—A-C and human. While we'd chosen the male godparents when she was born, the godmothers had been picked later. Amy Gaultier-White had won the human side based on her being one of my oldest girlfriends and also being married to Christopher, who was Jamie's A-C godfather.

Naomi had lobbied for, and won, the A-C godmother role well before she and her husband, my best guy friend since ninth grade, had really officially started dating. Since her eldest brother was the A-C's Supreme Pontifex, and also married to Reader, who was Jamie's human godfather, it seemed logical. Plus Jamie adored her, and the feeling was clearly mutual, so there was that, too.

"I love you, too, Auntie Abby," Jamie said, once she and Naomi were done being cutely nauseating in their shared adoration. "Don't worry."

Abigail gave her a kiss. "Good. Now, let's go to breakfast. You need to help us at an important meeting."

Jamie beamed and started sharing what she and her daddy had done this morning while I went and grabbed my purse. These days, I had a lot of different purses and handbags available to me, but Old Trusty, my big, black, cheap leather purse was still my go-to option. It took a licking and kept on holding everything and not falling apart. Ensured my Glock, my iPod, speakers, earbuds, Jeff's adrenaline harpoon, my wallet, a bottle of extra-hold hairspray, my brush, a scrunchie, and anything else I could think of were in it. Shoved my phone into the back pocket of my jeans.

"I'm set. Com on!"

"Yes, Chief?"

"Walter, I need the pet sitters to come on by and ensure all the animals are living large and feeling spoiled."

"So, just like every other day," Walter said.

"You got it. Tell whoever's drawn the short straws today that they're the best agents in the world and we totally appreciate them. Call me if I'm needed—we girls are going to be out for most of the day."

"Yes, Chief, Embassy is advised."

"Len and Kyle are waiting for us in the garage," Abigail said as the com went off and we headed downstairs.

The American Centaurion Embassy went up seven floors, down two for basement and parking garage levels, and then went down a lot more thanks to the hidden elevator that connected us to the Tunnels of Doom. It was a city block long and wide and, since Operation Destruction, was connected via a steel and bulletproof glass walkway on the second floors to the neighboring building we now owned, operated, and had personnel living in, which was nicknamed The Zoo.

The stairs, like the two elevators, only went down to the first floor. Then we had to cut through the first floor to either get to the stairs leading to the basement or the different set of stairs leading to the garage.

The sounds of the Embassy staff working filtered through as we walked by offices and salons. Everything sounded calm and normal as we went to the garage.

A gray limo was pulled out, idling. Officially, Len was our driver and Kyle was our bodyguard, but Len was happy to provide guarding as well. They were both former USC Trojan football players, Len as quarterback, Kyle on the line. I'd met the boys in Vegas right before Jeff and I got married, meaning during Operation Invasion. Now they officially worked for Chuckie at the C.I.A., but were assigned permanently to me and American Centaurion, in that order.

Kyle opened the door, then took Jamie from Naomi, which earned him a hug from her. We women piled in and Kyle helped me get Jamie into her car seat. Everyone in and buckled, Kyle took shotgun and we drove off and out.

"The driver is owed a hug," Len said as we pulled out of the garage's driveway and Kyle turned on the music and "Sugar, We're Goin Down" from Fall Out Boy came on the limo's airwaves.

But before Jamie or anyone else could reply, something hit the limo.

CHAPTER 3

"**D**OWN!" Kyle shouted as he slammed his fist onto the laser shield button.

Though we all jumped, there wasn't really a need for us to duck. American Centaurion limos were equipped with all the bulletproof stuff along with the aforementioned laser shielding, and many other snazzy extras. And while we'd had limos and other A-C vehicles blown up before, the bombs were put in or on before anyone got in, or they were tossed in through an open window.

Since it was summer and we had air conditioning, our windows were up. So I could see that what had hit us wasn't all that dangerous.

"Why are people throwing rotten food at us?" Abigail asked as more things hit the limo and Len floored it.

Looked around and watched those tossing crap at us scramble onto the sidewalks. "Oh. Check out the signs. Club Fifty-One is gracing us with a visit and apparently protesting that we're living here."

"Unreal," Len muttered. "Call the police," he said to Kyle.

"I'll do it." I sent a text to Officer Melville, who was the head of the K-9 department and, by now, a personal friend. "We're going to get complaints from our neighbors if those losers block the street."

"I just don't want them to hurt someone," Naomi said, as she held one of Jamie's hands and I held the other and Abigail called the Embassy and advised them that we had a problem outside and in the surrounding neighborhood.

Melville texted back. "Huh. Apparently the police are aware of the protestors and taking steps. He's a little vague about said steps, but assured me all will be well."

"So, should I take evasive action?" Len asked, as the music changed to "Everything Will Never Be Okay" by Fiction Plane, and we drove on past a lot more protestors, all of them equipped with a lot of foodstuffs.

Considered this as eggs and tomatoes hit the limo, because it wasn't a stupid or overeager question—many times, the Club 51 grunts worked as distraction for their real heavy hitters. Considering our first meeting with them had resulted in our just managing to stop them from blowing up a packed commercial jet, it was wise to evaluate our options.

"I suppose it can't hurt."

Len nodded then started off down a series of random streets. We weren't pursued, and once we were several blocks away from the Embassy, there were no more protestors.

The rest of the drive was uneventful, with all of us other than Len and Jamie taking calls or texts from Embassy personnel. We decided that a general, calm mention to our people in D.C. that Club 51 was out and about was sufficient.

I sent texts to Jeff and Chuckie so they'd know what had happened and be prepared in case the loons were protesting at Capitol Hill or around Rayburn House, the building where Jeff's office was. I received automated "in a meeting, will reply when able" messages from both of them. Oh, well, they'd see the messages when they saw them.

We arrived at our destination, which was near Capitol Hill—the Teetotaler. We'd been introduced to this restaurant by Edmund and Nathalie Brewer, right before someone tried to assassinate Jeff. A gift from the owners had inadvertently saved Jeff's life. Sadly, Edmund Brewer hadn't been as lucky—he'd been one of those murdered during Operation Sherlock.

Based on what had happened when we left the Embassy, Kyle got out first while Len kept the limo running at the curb. Kyle went inside and was in there for a good five minutes. He came out and opened the passenger door on the curbside.

"I've checked the interior, including kitchen and bath-rooms," Kyle said as he helped Abigail out. "We're clear. Rosemarie has a table set up for us that's in the back, with full visual access of the entrances to the dining area."

"She and Douglas are great." I got Jamie out of her car seat while Kyle helped Naomi out. Then he took Jamie from me and helped me out. "Len, where are you going to park?" I asked him through the now-opened passenger's window.

"Actually, I want to wash the car."

Took a good look at the outside of the limo. It was pretty much covered with rotten food and garbage. The laser shield was great for protection, but it didn't repel things that were oozy or sticky—it just didn't let them in, so to speak.

But while things couldn't get through the shield, the shield itself was dirty, and Len couldn't turn it off without essentially sharing that there was a shield on the car. "Wash the car" was code for "get it out of sight and bring it back 'cleaned' off." In a case like this though, where we'd been seen by a lot of people, the smart move was to actually go to a car wash and run the limo through.

Considering we weren't alone on the sidewalk, it be-hooved me to play along. "Good thinking. We need to get the egg off this puppy before it's too late. But I don't want you going alone."

Len shook his head. "You need protection."

"I have my Glock and we all have hyperspeed. I don't want either one of you wandering off alone. And that's an order." Regardless of how long it would or wouldn't take Len to find a car wash, or a secluded spot to turn the laser shield off and thereby lose all the crap on it, then drive back, we'd been attacked and, as far as I was concerned, that meant no one wandered alone.

Len opened his mouth, to protest I was sure, but before he could say anything, four Field agents appeared inside the limo via a floater gate and stepped out. "We'll take the limo in for cleaning," one of them said. "Just call the Embassy when you're ready to leave, Ambassador."

I opened my mouth, to argue for sure, but the agent who wasn't drop-dead gorgeous and, therefore, was the human who'd be driving, shook his head. "Mister Buchanan's orders."

"Malcolm has his own set of Field agents?" It was possible. Buchanan was assigned by my mother to protect me and Jamie, and even though he was human, he had Dr. Strange powers as far as I'd ever seen.

"Mister Buchanan suggested you get inside and off the street," the human agent replied with a smile. He walked to the driver's door and opened it.

Len sighed. "Fine." He put the car into park and got out. "I'd recommend not going to a car wash anywhere near the Embassy or Capitol Hill."

"I'll let Mister Buchanan know you and he shared the same insight," the human agent said. He and the others got into the limo and gave us all looks that suggested we move our butts. We so moved.

"Well, I'm hungry," Kyle said, as he led us inside and to our table. "So, at least we'll get to eat," he added as he got Jamie situated into the highchair already at our table.

"Yeah." Len grimaced.

"What's wrong?" I asked him.

"I don't like taking orders from him. He's not our boss— you and Mister Reynolds are."

Kyle grunted his agreement but didn't say anything.

Sincerely felt that Len and Kyle didn't like Buchanan because they saw him as proof that no one, my mother most of all, felt that they were good at their jobs. But Buchanan had a good decade and a half of field experience the boys didn't, and it had been proven more than once that Mom was right— Jamie and I needed someone with mad skills who also didn't feel that I or Chuckie were actually in a real position to give orders that had to be obeyed.

"Look at it as you're getting to protect me and Jamie instead of the car while the car is in safe hands, and it's a win all the way around. Besides, you know Rosemarie has your favorite ready for you."

Len smiled. "That's true. She's the only one who can make French toast like my mother's."

The restaurant was small, so just a few people made it seem very full. However, people wandering around with security wasn't all that unusual in D.C., so we didn't get a lot of looks. Besides, the boys were in the Armani Fatigues, so they looked as much like young businessmen as they did security or C.I.A.

We settled down, Naomi and I with Jamie between us. Our regular table had a photo hanging above it, taken the first time we'd ever eaten here. Me, Jeff, Nathalie and Edmund Brewer, Reader, Vance Beaumont, Len, and Kyle, all smiling, looking like we were having fun, which we were. Our first meal here had been a small oasis of normalcy in the maelstrom that had been Operation Sherlock.

Rosemarie had put a little black ribbon on the frame under Edmund. Looking at that never failed to give me a lump in my throat.

Naomi saw where I was looking, reached over, and squeezed my hand. "Let's order," she said gently.

"Yeah." Swallowed hard, then shoved my mind back to why we were here, which was to have breakfast and discuss our diplomatic mission's upcoming schedules.

The food here was great and the teas were even better. We tried to get here at least once every couple of weeks, which meant we were considered special regulars. The number in our party changed, but whether we had two or twenty, the Teetotaler always accommodated.

Kyle had told Rosemarie what had happened, so she was extra attentive, and brought out some special muffins and jam and two pots of house-blended tea for us to snack on while our breakfast order was being prepared.

"So, in part to avoid talking about the unpleasantness you had to start your morning with, but mostly because it's required that someone asks you the Official Question at least once a week," Rosemarie said to Naomi, "how's married life?"

Naomi grinned. "Just like last week, it's great."

"Good." Rosemarie gave Jamie a kiss on the top of her head. "Looking forward to when you bring in your baby, too." She bustled off.

Abigail laughed. "Nice to know that even casual acquaintances want to know when you and Chuck are going to get busy, Sis."

"You mean aside from everyone's parents, friends, associates, and, officially, all of Centaurion Division, American Centaurion, and probably the C.I.A.?" I asked.

"Feels that way some days. But it's okay." Naomi chuckled. "We're not quite ready to start. But soon." She winked at me. "We figure we need to get our Baby Number One before you and Jeff have your Number Two."

"We're in a race? No one told me."

She laughed. "No. But we don't want to wait too long to get started. Jeff's not the only one who wants a lot of kids, you know."

"Chuckie does?"

"We both do." She kissed Jamie's cheek. "You know how much I love my goddaughter, but she needs a girl playmate. She's got plenty of boys. It's clearly up to us to get Jamie a best girlfriend."

"Cannot argue with the logic."

We'd just finished scarfing down the muffins and jam when Rosemarie brought our food out. Muffins and jam had merely taken the edge off, for all of us, apparently. We dug in.

I'd just taken a huge bite of pancake loaded with butter and syrup when my phone rang. Always the way. Chewed quickly and didn't bother to look at who was calling. "Hello?" Hey, my mouth was full, but I could get that out sort of clearly.

"Ambassador, I'd like to introduce myself." A man's voice, smooth but also dangerous. Quickly swallowed and also checked to see who this was—my phone shared that the number was blocked. It so figured.

"Yes?"

"I'm the man who's going to destroy you and the so-called people you associate with."

"Really?"

"Really. The alien scum you've chosen to align with are going to be no more. Soon. Not soon enough, but as soon as *humanly* possible."

"Uh huh. Destroy, nasty names, alien phobia, gotcha. Don't tell me, let me guess. You're the new head honcho for Club Fifty-One."

CHAPTER 4

EVERYONE AT MY TABLE stopped eating and stared at me, looks of trepidation on every face.

Other than Jamie, who was thankfully playing with her Poof, Mous-Mous, while eating. Naomi had cut up all her food into perfect little bites, which was more proof of how much Jamie adored her. She hadn't allowed me or Jeff to cut up her food for months because she could do it herself and normally wanted to. She might only be eighteen months old, but she was advanced in a lot of ways, and this was merely one of them.

Mous-Mous came along wherever Jamie went, and since Poofs looked like fluffy balls of fur with ears, paws, and big button eyes, but no tails, it appeared that Jamie was playing with a stuffed animal. A stuffed animal that could go Jeff-sized and toothy should danger appear, but a stuffed animal at this size, nonetheless. The Poofs had been outed along with the rest of us, but even so, they tended to pass as stuffed more often than not.

My new special caller chuckled and dragged me away from the momentary enjoyment of watching my daughter innocently playing "one bite for me, one bite for you" with her pet. "That's right."

"Going to give me your name?"

"Not yet. You'll know me soon enough. Enjoy the rest of your day." With that he hung up.

Stared at my phone. "Well, that was fun. Threatening calls, they're great for the digestion."

"We shouldn't discuss it here," Abigail said. "Just in case we're being watched for our reactions."

Surreptitiously looked around. No one seemed to be paying us any attention.

"We need to finish up," Naomi said. "If they're calling you, you know that means they've got something else in motion."

Everyone nodded and we went from enjoying our meal to speed eating. The Gower girls and I didn't use hyperspeed—them because it wasn't wise to do so out in public, me because I wasn't really good with eating at non-human levels just yet and didn't feel like having syrup smeared all over my face, or hair, or worse.

We'd just finished up, Jamie included, when a group of businessmen and one businesswoman came in.

Len, who was on my other side and watching all the entrances, stiffened. "This can't be good," he said quietly.

"Who is it?"

He shot me a look I was familiar with—the "why don't you ever read the briefing materials" look. "The heads of Gaultier Enterprises, Titan Security, and YatesCorp."

"Oh. Right." Yeah, they did look vaguely familiar. "Or, as we call them, our own personal Axis of Evil. This morning just keeps on getting better and better, doesn't it?"

Naturally, said Axis were looking directly at us. They all smiled. I now knew exactly how a sea lion felt when faced with a group of great white sharks.

Sure enough, they headed straight for us.

"Ambassador Katt-Martini," the lead Land Shark said. "How fortunate that we find you here."

"Is it?" I'd avoided meeting all these people in person, but this was definitely Ansom Somerall, who was the current acting Chairman of the Board of Gaultier Enterprises. He was about six-two, average build, normally attractive. He had a full head of silver hair, but he was only in his mid-fifties.

"Of course," Somerall replied with what I was sure he felt was a charming smile. "Fortunate for me to get to be in the company of four beautiful American Centaurion ladies." He made sure to look at each of the females at the table, including Jamie.

Resisted the urge to snarl or gag, since he'd included my toddler in this smarmy come-on. Sure, my husband had used similar lines on me when we'd met—but Jeff had charm up the wazoo and Somerall definitely didn't, at least not as far as I was concerned. Rumor said Somerall fancied himself a ladies' man. Since, in addition to my husband, I knew the Ladies' Man of Ladies' Men—Naomi and Abigail's older brother Michael—I could come down firmly on the side of Somerall not having anything close to Jeff's game and being merely a pretender to Michael's throne.

Of course, when you considered the company Somerall tended to keep, perhaps he was the best choice of the bunch, which was a textbook example of damning with faint praise.

Behind him stood a taller, thin man, with thinning light-brown hair and glasses. He was sort of stooped. It made him look both somewhat unassuming and also kind of creepy. From what Amy had told me, the unassuming part was an act, but Quinton Cross had creepy down to an art form.

Cross smiled. It was, like the rest of him, both unassuming and creepy. Moved him higher up on my Latest Enemies Trying to Destroy Us list. "As Ansom said, of course it's fortunate, Ambassador. We have a mutually beneficial proposal to discuss."

"Really? And you think right now—when I'm out with my daughter and clearly already occupied with my friends and Embassy staff—is the appropriate time? Especially since I was under the impression you were supposed to be having a meeting with someone else associated with our diplomatic mission—Amy Gaultier-White."

That meeting was why Amy wasn't with us at breakfast. Wanted to send her a text and make sure she was okay but couldn't really take my focus away from the Land Sharks.

Standing just a little apart from the men was an attractive woman in her mid-forties. She hadn't seemed fazed by Somerall's come-ons, or Cross' creepiness, so either she was used to them, or they didn't bother her. Maybe both, but I figured on the former.

Janelle Gardiner had her long, dark hair done up and was in all green. Wasn't sure if she was matching her eyes today or if green was "her color." People in D.C. seemed big on the "your color" idea. Based on my experience in this town, I pegged her as the likely Brains Behind the Posturing Sharks.

These three were the power on the Gaultier Enterprises board and were the main people Amy was fighting for control of the company her father had built. If they were here, looking for me, they weren't here for a social call.

Gardiner shook her head. "That meeting was rescheduled because of this new issue. It's time-sensitive, Ambassador. We'd never disturb you without an appointment, otherwise." She smiled. "Lillian Culver would never let me live it down."

Lillian Culver was the top lobbyist for some of the biggest defense contractors, including but not limited to Titan Security. She and I weren't friends but, thanks to my "uncles" the assassins, we now had a good working relationship based on the fact that Culver knew that if she really went against me, those "uncles" would kill her and her husband, Abner Schnekedy, without a moment's hesitation or remorse. As I'd learned early, it was good to have friends in both the high and the low places.

Looked around. "Where *is* Lillian? Since you're dropping her name to get me to chummy up and all that." I wasn't asking because I liked Culver, but this was the kind of group I expected her to be at least ushering around.

"She's at the Capitol," Gardiner said. "Doing her job." Which probably meant pressuring my husband to do something against our better interests. So that was business as usual.

Managed not to ask how Gardiner knew what Culver was up to. Gaultier Enterprises wasn't a defense contractor of any kind, but their ties with Titan ran deep, and if you were in with one big defense firm, you were also in with Lillian Culver.

Of course, after Operation Assassination, Titan should have been out of business permanently. But as I'd also learned early, evil never truly died, and Titan was back in the game. They weren't quite back to what they'd been when Antony Marling had been alive and in charge, but their future was again looking bright.

And the man who'd brought Titan back from the dead and into that brave new world of financial success and government love was now stepping forward, the better to give me a friendly grin I didn't buy for a New York Minute.

Of course, him stepping forward meant that Kyle felt it was time to stand up. Len followed suit.

"Ambassador, we haven't met, I'm—"

"Thomas Kendrick. I know. We get the papers at the Embassy." And Chuckie had done his best to make sure every single person in the Embassy could recognize these people on sight. Even I, who admittedly hadn't really read these specific briefing materials, knew who Kendrick and the rest were. Sure, I knew them because Len had told me who they were just now, but now that he had, my memory had happily shared some facts.

"I'm flattered," Kendrick said politely. He eyed the boys. "I can assure you, the Ambassador is in no danger."

Kendrick was former military, and it showed. He had that crisp, buttoned-down, and above all, intense look that a lot of former military possessed. We had a lot of military working with us, and even my flyboys, who were considered the biggest jokers around, could pull off this look in a nanosecond if it was called for. Maybe it was something you learned in basic training or officer's school. But whatever it was, Kendrick had it in spades.

Kendrick's father was an American former Marine and his mother was Vietnamese, so Kendrick was also quite good looking. He'd been appointed into Titan by the Department of Defense, and that meant he might be good on the inside as well as the outside. But I doubted it. In my world—the one where people tried to kill or control me and everyone I loved on a regular basis—anyone high up in these three companies was automatically suspect until proven to be Evil Incarnate. So far, that viewpoint had never been wrong.

"Then it won't matter that we're standing up just like you, will it?" Len asked mildly. Kyle shifted so he was directly between the Land Sharks and Jamie. Noted that Naomi was texting, but other than being happy that one of us could multitask right now, wasn't sure that this was going to help.

Kendrick shrugged. "Suit yourselves. Ambassador, if we could speak with you privately, that would be best."

Wondered if Len and Kyle were having Operation Destruction flashbacks right about now and figured they were. Me, I simply braced myself for more doctored dirty pictures and forged ahead. "Would it? Then I guess you should have made an appointment. Right now, if you want to talk, we're doing it here, in front of everyone. But I do have a question— how did you know I'd be here?"

The last man standing was Amos Tobin, the person now in charge of all of YatesCorp or, as I thought of it, the House That Mephistopheles Built. He'd only recently been appointed to run things by the YatesCorp Board—they, like Gaultier, had taken their sweet time about choosing the official successor to Ronald Yates. Even before he'd joined with the Mephistopheles parasite, Yates had been a tough act to follow, especially if you were into evil plotting and so forth.

Tobin was a mogul in his own right—he'd run a variety of successful businesses, including starting several successful fast-food franchises. Before YatesCorp he'd also successfully dabbled in companies focused on publishing, music, and art. So he had the bona fides for the job.

He was a nice-looking, middle-aged black man, just starting to show some paunch around the middle. Unlike the others, though, Tobin was going for a more folksy look. Oh, sure, he was still dressed in the standard suit and tie, but it wasn't D.C. standard. He was in black on black, with a Stetson, bolo tie, and cowboy boots, all in black as well. It looked good on him, in a sort of Southern Godfather way, but I prepared myself for the inevitable bad joke.

Tobin smiled. "Ambassador, you may not realize it, but you make the news regularly. We saw you'd had some . . . unpleasantness earlier, knew you were headed here, so figured it was a good time to come see if we could help each other. You know good guys wear black." He had a faint Texas twang, and my memory shared that was his home state.

And there it was, right on cue. "Usually we add in some white, just for contrast."

Tobin chuckled. "I'm sure you do. May we join you for breakfast? My treat."

Had to give Tobin this much—at least he was trying to put this into a more friendly, normal-person atmosphere. It wasn't working, but at least he'd given it the old college try.

Of course, we'd already eaten, and the evidence of such was still on the table. So either he wanted us to eat again, he wanted us to watch all of them eat, or he was offering us a really cheap bribe.

On the plus side, or sort of, none of them sounded like the man who'd just called me. That didn't mean one of them wasn't the new Club 51 Head Honcho, but it was unlikely. This didn't mean they didn't know him, though. When we'd first run into our favorite anti-alien lunatics, Howard Taft had been the man in charge. But he'd been taking his real orders from Leventhal Reid, who'd been a Representative from Florida. Suppressed the shudder thinking of Reid always gave me. I'd seen a lot of evil in my time with Centaurion Division, but no one and nothing, not even Mephistopheles, had matched Reid.

The Land Sharks were looking at me expectantly. We didn't have a lot of options. We had no car to race off into, we couldn't use hyperspeed to run away no matter how much we might want to, and we needed to pay our bill one way or the other. Plus, we were officially making a scene in a restaurant we frequented. Yeah, they'd planned this really well.

Decided to go on the offensive. "So, you're telling me that we were on the news in some way?"

"No," Somerall said quickly. "We all have sources, Ambassador. Just as you do. Ours told us you'd been attacked by some dissidents. And while you go out on random days, when you *do* go out, this is where you tend to go."

Good to know we were predictable. That was the downside of having a favorite restaurant.

"Okay. Well, that sort of begs a question." They all looked at me with interest. Here went nothing. "Which one of you wants to tell me who the new head of Club Fifty-One is and why he's decided to start threatening me?"

CHAPTER 5

ALL FIVE OF THE LAND SHARKS looked both surprised and uncomfortable. Kendrick took the lead on this one. "They aren't a group any of us associate with, Ambassador."

"Right, pull the other one, it has bells on. How would you know we'd been attacked by Club Fifty-One unless one of them told you they'd done so and we were in motion?"

Kendrick shrugged. "We have other sources."

"Embassy staff?" Abigail asked.

Expressions said that they wished it was Embassy staff. Hoped their expressions weren't being faked. "No," Gardiner replied. "Your staff is extremely loyal. As they should be."

"True enough. So you were advised by 'sources' that we were attacked and you raced on over here to have an impromptu revival meeting. Why?"

Tobin's lips quirked. "You have an interesting way with words, Ambassador. But we're here to preach the good word, and that word is 'protection.' Mutual protection, to be exact."

Kendrick nodded. "You have an anti-alien problem. We'd like to help you fix that."

"In return for what?"

Somerall shot me what I was now certain he felt was his Charming Smile. It really didn't work on me. At all. "Favors. There are many things that your people could assist us with that would be helpful to all our businesses. And in return, there are many things all of us could do for you in return. It's what friends do for each other, after all."

"We're friends?"

"Of course," Gardiner replied.

Wondered where in the world my "uncles" were and if it would be totally wrong to drop them a friendly suggestion to come for a visit. With friends like these we didn't need enemies. "Then why are you trying so hard to block Amy's bid to take over the business her father built?"

All three from Gaultier reacted the same way—slit eyes and tight smiles. Nice to know I'd hit a hot button, not that it was a surprise.

"A multinational conglomerate isn't something to be tossed to a child who has no training in running any part of said business," Gardiner said frostily.

"Amy's a lawyer and she was raised in that business."

"Our corporate situation with her has no bearing on what we're discussing with you," Cross said. "But who knows? A mutually beneficial relationship between us could only help Amy's situation."

Wanted to argue this some more, but Naomi kicked me under the table. Considering Jamie was between us and I didn't see her move, figured she'd used hyperspeed. Decided to let this particular argument drop.

"Just what kind of 'protection' are you offering us?" Naomi asked. "Because as I understand the term, it's usually used by criminals as a way to extort money."

The Land Sharks all chuckled. "Someone's watched too much *Sopranos*," Tobin said. It was official—I didn't like his "folksy charm."

"No, someone's aware of the Mob and how it operates," I said. "It's a good question you're trying to sidestep. Unless you actually have influence with Club Fifty-One, or any of the many other anti-alien groups out there, just how do you propose to protect us from anything?"

However, before any of them replied, someone I was happy to see came in.

Cliff Goodman was the Head of Special Immigration Services reporting directly to the Secretary of Homeland Security, meaning he was the guy at Homeland Security who had the most interest in all things Alpha Centaurion. He was also one of the few close friends Chuckie had and, like Chuckie, he was brilliant.

Cliff took in the scene, made eye contact with Naomi, gave her an almost imperceptible nod, and came right over. So now I knew who she'd been texting. I'd give her the big Atta Girls later when we weren't surrounded by people we didn't like.

"Excuse me, Ambassador," Cliff said. "I'm sorry to interrupt, but you're needed at headquarters. I need to discuss some policy with you that can't wait." He flashed a quick smile at the Land Sharks. "So sorry to interrupt. Hopefully you and the Ambassador can reschedule."

The Land Sharks shot various looks of annoyance in Cliff's general direction. "I'm sure whatever it is can wait," Kendrick said.

"Not really," Cliff said politely. "It's quite urgent."

"I'm sure the Secretary would agree with us," Kendrick said a little more forcefully. "I can call her and see if she appreciates your interrupting us, Cliff."

Cliff gave him a tight smile. "If you want to disturb the Secretary, feel free, Mister Kendrick. She's in a meeting with the President, but if you think now's the right time to show her who's boss, go right ahead."

While Cliff and the Land Sharks were having their standoff, Naomi got Jamie out of her highchair and Abigail went up front to pay our bill. Len and Kyle, meanwhile, shifted so they were flanking Cliff.

I stood, slung my purse over my shoulder, and took Jamie from Naomi. "I'm sorry, but when Homeland Security needs us, we feel it's imperative we respond, regardless of the situation. Please call and make an appointment. I'll be happy to see you as soon as my schedule allows." Which would be never, but why admit that out loud?

"Thanks, Ambassador, I appreciate it," Cliff said. He made the "this way" gesture, and we headed for the door, Len and Kyle almost shoving the Land Sharks aside, in that bodyguard way where the almost-shoved knows it's move your feet or end up on your butt.

Naturally, the Land Sharks followed us onto the sidewalk.

"We could discuss our situation while we all go over to the Homeland Security building," Somerall suggested. "It's not a problem for Cliff to hear what we're talking about."

A quick look at the rest of them said they weren't nearly as sure as Somerall that they wanted Cliff listening in. However, the moment they saw me looking they all nodded enthusiastically.

"Sure," Cliff said cheerfully. "I'd love to hear what opportunities you're suggesting to American Centaurion."

"Driving or walking?" Len asked me.

"We can take you," Tobin said quickly. "We have a car across the street."

There was a parking area about a block away, and I could see a Town Car with a driver lounging against it. However, I wasn't thrilled with the idea of getting into an enclosed space with one of these people, let alone all of them, and especially not with Jamie along.

"I don't think we can all fit in that car," Abigail said. "In fact, I'm sure we can't." She pulled out her phone. "We'll get our own ride, thanks."

"Cliff, you can take some in your car, can't you?" Gardiner asked as Abigail called the Embassy and requested someone come pick us up.

"I walked, sorry," Cliff replied.

Normally I wasn't against walking, but it was hot, I hadn't put sunscreen on me or Jamie, and if we were walking we couldn't get rid of the Land Sharks any more than if we were in their car with them.

Len put his hand on my back. "We need to move," he said quietly. "All of us."

Looked where he was, which was the opposite way from the parking lot we'd all been staring at. Sure enough, there were a lot of people coming toward us, and they were all carrying signs.

"Oh goody. It's another mob."

CHAPTER 6

SURE ENOUGH, the mass of people with signs and placards were heading for us. I could hear them chanting something about God hating aliens.

"Those aren't Club Fifty-One people," Kyle said. "I think it's those so-called church people who protest at military funerals."

"Fantastic. Time to listen to Len and get out of here."

Interestingly enough, the Land Sharks didn't look pleased. In fact, they looked panicked. "You have a car coming, right?" Gardiner said as the five of them started backing toward their car.

"Yes, I think—"

"Wonderful," Somerall said, as he took Gardiner's elbow and they all started across the street. "We'll call you!"

They didn't run, but they walked with really fast purpose, Somerall motioning wildly to his driver, who flung the car doors open then got into the driver's seat. To his credit, Somerall got Gardiner into the car first, then the four men leaped in, the doors slammed, and they took off. Their car didn't peel out, but if there had been a cop around, they'd have definitely gotten a ticket for excessive speed.

"Well, one problem gone, and another bigger one's coming. It's just our lucky day, isn't it?" I hugged Jamie.

"It's okay, Mommy," Jamie said. "Mous-Mous is here."

Cliff looked worried. "Chuck's right—he and Jeff can't let you out of their sight without a problem starting. We can't have one of your Poofs, ah, activating."

"Dude, no kidding and this wasn't, and isn't, our fault."

"Argue later," Len said. "We need to get out of here."

Took another look at the mob and decided I'd let the Poof activate well before I'd let them hurt my daughter. Some of the people were waving their signs around, and it was easy to see that these really were the mentally unbalanced folks who thought their God was nicknamed The Hater. I'd read about how these people operated—they weren't going to be nice because three of us were women and we had a little girl along.

"Back into the restaurant," Kyle said. He took Naomi and Abigail's arms and started moving them inside. Len did the same with me and Cliff.

"We could use hyperspeed," Naomi suggested.

"Not good," Cliff said. "It'll get spun badly by the media. Trust me."

"But we have a car coming," Abigail protested.

"It can't get here before the mob does," Len said.

This was true. They were less than a block away, clearly heading for us, and no gray limo was in evidence on the street.

Once we got back inside, Kyle locked the door behind us while Len went to Rosemarie and told her what was going on. Then the boys took hold of us again and moved us through the Teetotaler.

"There's a back entrance," Kyle shared as we hurried past the restrooms. "We'll go out that way and the car can find us somewhere safer."

"Never a dull moment with you guys," Cliff said as we got into the alleyway behind the restaurant. "Where to?"

Abigail had her phone out. "They'll get us at any location we want."

"We can use hyperspeed, so let's go for Providence Park."

"You know," Cliff said quickly, "if you're not with me, I can probably just stay in the Teetotaler until the mob goes away."

"Don't want to barf your guts out?" Hyperspeed was hard on humans. Tito had created a nice Hyperspeed Dramamine drug that worked great for combating hyperspeed nausea. Our human agents now took some every day. However, I didn't wander around with spare pills on me, so I had none to give Cliff.

He grinned. "Not if I can help it, no. Besides, if the mob

comes in the restaurant, it'll help them if I'm there to at least tell the police what happened."

"Sounds good. Thanks for the save."

"Any time. When Mimi sends the 'we're in trouble' text, I listen. Call or text if you need me again, and let me know when you get back home safely." He hugged me, kissed Jamie, hugged the Gower girls, then went back inside.

Naomi grabbed Len, Abigail took Kyle, and we set off for the park, which was close by. It took only a couple seconds to get there and find a good spot to "appear." Len and Kyle made sure the area was reasonably clear and we all lounged casually under some trees.

"Limo will be here in five to ten minutes," Abigail said. "Where are we going, once we get out of here?"

Was about to answer when I looked down the street. "Are you kidding me? Is that seriously the same mob we just escaped from?"

Naomi squinted. "Honestly, the signs are different. I think it's Club Fifty-One."

"My God, we just rock the lucky today, don't we?"

"I don't think they've seen us yet," Abigail said.

"Give them time," Kyle muttered.

"Let's move into the foliage a bit more," Len suggested.

As we did so Naomi's phone rang. "Yes? Hi, Aunt Gladys." She stepped a bit away, which was good, because my phone rang.

The main Embassy landline, meaning it was probably Walter. "Yo, Walt, things suck here, how're you?"

"Ah, Ambassador?" The voice wasn't Walter's. And Walter always called me Chief, because I was now the sole Chief of Mission. But the voice was familiar.

"Who is this?"

"It's William, Ambassador." Walter's older brother.

"Why are you calling me from the Embassy?"

"I'm covering for Walter."

"Really. So, here's a question—what is one of our top imageers doing handling Embassy Security? Or, to put it another way, where is my Walter?"

"Walter's at a Security training session at Dulce."

"Since when?"

"Since Gladys called it. We do these periodically. Some are planned, some are impromptu. This one's both. Planned for most, impromptu for some, like Walter."

"Okay. So why is he at the Science Center for training?"

"Because there's a big dust storm around Home Base and the training session needs to be held both indoors and outdoors."

"Gotcha. And you're covering his job because . . . ?"

"Because someone needed to cover Embassy Security, and it was decided that I was the most trustworthy option."

"Cannot argue with that logic. Other than to mention that I wasn't informed of any training sessions, impromptu or otherwise, or temporary personnel switches."

William cleared his throat. "Ah, you don't need to be informed, Ambassador. Gladys handles all of that, and if she says it's time for training, it's time for training, and if she says I'm covering during Walter's training session, then I'm covering."

"Gotcha." Couldn't argue. Gladys was the Head of Security for all A-C operations worldwide. She was considered scary formidable and I concurred on the scary. Three-plus years in and I'd never seen her in person, or seen a picture of her. I was okay with this, mostly because Gladys was one of the few people around who could intimidate me, and she had sarcasm down to an art form.

"Ambassador, are you alright?"

"That remains to be seen. Why aren't you calling me Kitty?"

William laughed. "Because Walter left me very specific instructions, and it's vital to the running of this Embassy that whoever's running Security call you Ambassador or Chief. Per his very detailed page about titles and why they matter here."

"I love Walter. And you, too."

"Always good to know. Representative Martini asked me to reach you. He hasn't had a chance to look at the texts from you or Naomi, excuse me, Cultural Attaché Gower-Reynolds, but needs to have an early luncheon meeting and it's going to be at the Embassy. He'd like you to attend."

"Why did he have you call me instead of calling me himself?"

"He's been in locked-door and no-calls meetings all morning, and so has Mister Reynolds. That's why he hasn't looked at your texts. Representative Martini was able to make one phone call, and he chose to call me, so that I could make all other calls for him."

"How convenient." Though it did explain why Naomi had called Cliff—she'd gotten the same automated text messages I had from Jeff and Chuckie. "But I don't buy that as the only reason."

"He might have mentioned something about your possibly not wanting to attend because there will be other politicians in this meeting. Representative Martini told me to tell you they're all friends."

"So he figured I'd complain to you less and do what he asked without too much of an argument? And if I was mad because he hadn't replied to my texts, you'd get to hear it instead of him?"

"Yes, Ambassador, that's my take."

Huh. Jeff was getting exceptionally sneaky in an effective way. He was learning a lot from politics and other politicians, especially in terms of how to avoid listening to his wife whine. Wasn't sure if I was happy with this improvement or kind of annoyed that he'd anticipated my gut reaction so accurately. Settled for both.

"How much time do I have?"

"The meeting is going to start in about a half an hour, so you should have time to finish breakfast and get home without missing anything."

"Ah. It's not even eleven yet."

"Yes, I have both a watch and a clock here, Ambassador."

"Great. I mean it seems early to have a lunch meeting."

"Per all the best books on etiquette, lunch can start as early as eleven, and, in fact, the meeting is set to start at eleven." William was easily at an eight on the sarcasm scale and rising fast. Clearly Walter hadn't shared that constant sucking up was a job requirement. Pity. "Are you able to get to the Embassy in a half an hour or so?"

"Well, as to that . . . um, I thought we had a limo coming to get us."

"I didn't take that call, Ambassador."

"Really. Okay, if you don't get a text or a call from me in the next five minutes, assume we have a problem and call me. If I don't answer, we *have* a problem, and we're going to need help."

"Do you want me to send Security?"

"You mean you, since Len and Kyle are already with me? No. I want to see if I'm just a Nervous Nellie or not. I'll contact you shortly, William."

We hung up and I turned to Abigail. "Who did you talk to when you called for a limo?"

"Walter, why?"

"Huh." Needed to verify if William had literally gone on duty in the short time span between when Abigail and Jeff would have called. Maybe. "I'm worried that the limo coming for us may not actually be friendly."

"Well," Naomi said, as she hung up her phone. "I may have the solution. Aunt Gladys is running a Security training session today and she wants me and Sis to help her with some stuff. She's about to send a floater gate for us—and she said all of us can go there if we want, she's calibrating for multiple people to go through at the same time. She could use your help, too, Kitty, and that way Len and Kyle would get the training, too."

"As great as getting to the safety of Dulce sounds right now, I can't go. Jeff's having some impromptu lunch meeting he wants me to attend."

"The mob's found us," Len said. "We need to move somewhere, Kitty."

"We could take Jamie, let you and the guys use hyperspeed home," Naomi offered.

"Tempting." It was. Naomi and Abigail taking Jamie to Dulce meant she'd be safe, and the boys and I could kick butt if we had to. However, there was a drawback. "But if Jeff's going to be home for lunch, he's going to want to see Jamie if he can. And I don't think he'll be happy about her being at the Science Center instead of in the Embassy, no matter how good the reason, especially because we're not in actual danger."

"Yet," Kyle muttered. "But it's a matter of time, Kitty, and that time's short."

The floater gate appeared. In the olden days, I could spot them because the air around them sort of shimmered. Now that I had the special A-C Upgrade I could see the gate clearly. I hugged the Gower girls. "You two go. Two of us safe for sure is better than none. Jamie's been in a high speed footrace before, she can handle it again." Besides, a gray limo was pulling up to the sidewalk.

"I'll go make sure they're who we want them to be," Len said. "You stay with Kitty and Jamie," he added to Kyle.

The Gower girls gave Jamie kisses, then they went through the gate, doing the slow fade I always found nauseating to watch, but still less nauseating than it was to experience. The gate was still there as Len motioned for us to come on over as he opened the car's door. It turned off once Kyle and I moved toward the curb.

"Run!" Len shouted.

Looked around to see why he was stressing the urgent, so I saw what Len had—the mob was running toward us, screaming and shouting.

CHAPTER 7

DIDN'T QUESTION, just grabbed Kyle and hypersped us into the limo. Decided I'd be proud of not slamming us through the other side of the limo later, when we were safely back in the Embassy.

Len slammed our door shut and jumped into the shotgun seat as Kyle and I got Jamie into her car seat. The limo driver waited until she was strapped in before he took off. Which was good for Jamie's car safety, but not so hot for ours overall.

The mob reached us and people were literally throwing themselves on the car.

"Drive," Len snarled. "If you run them down, too damn bad."

"Len, that's not right. They may be loons but we don't want to hurt them."

"I'm not willing to run people over," our driver added. He was the same guy who'd taken the limo off to be "washed."

"The hell with your delicate sensibilities," Len said calmly, but with authority I was more used to hearing from Chuckie versus the boys. "I'm giving this order as C.I.A. You will get the Ambassador out of here, now, or I will shoot you in the head." His gun, which he and Kyle both wore in shoulder holsters, was out and pointed at the driver's head.

"Len, are you okay?"

"Yes. I'm just not willing for you or Jamie to be hurt because we're trying to protect a bunch of assholes who would kill you without remorse."

"I'm with Len," Kyle said. "And I can overpower you, Kitty. If I have to."

"Okay, no worries. Drive us out of here, damn the torpedoing lunatics, full speed ahead. And all that."

Our driver floored it and, amazingly enough, people scattered. There were a lot of them on the streets, and I noted that the church wackos were adding in, presumably working on The More Loons The Merrier Plan.

"What's your name?" I asked our driver, more to try to keep things sort of pleasant, since Len hadn't put his gun away.

"Burton Falk. I work with Mister Buchanan. I'm not the Ambassador's enemy." We weren't going that fast, but we were going fast enough that we were moving through the throng.

"Get her home safely and we'll discuss it," Len said. "With you *and* Mister Buchanan, if necessary."

"Burt, the boys are just a little tense. Being chased by mobs all over the place tends to do that to a person."

Falk turned onto a main street, and we lost most, though not all, of the protestors. "I understand. You realize that if we ran anyone over it would create incredibly bad publicity?"

"Let me explain how much the C.I.A.'s Extra-Terrestrial Division cares about bad publicity when faced with the option of one of the highest ranking A-Cs being in extreme physical danger," Len said "It's a short explanation."

"We don't give a f—, ah, crap," Kyle said.

"Nice save, Kyle. Look, Burt, the boys just want proof we're all really on the same side. So, let's get home and we can all have a Coke and a smile and laugh about this." We were clear of people with signs, which was nice. Wasn't sure if they would be waiting for us when we got home, but we'd worry about it in a couple minutes.

"Ha ha ha," Falk said. "This is me laughing in a relaxed manner."

"Wow, did Malcolm request mouthy agents or am I just that kind of lucky?"

Falk grinned. "Mister Buchanan requested agents who are able to, and I quote, 'both give it and take it from the Ambassador, who is a lot like her mother, particularly in the ballbusting category.' So, it's a request *and* you're that lucky."

"Gosh, I hope you're really on our side, because I like you already."

Falk was a good driver, though I felt Len was better. As Len had on the way out, he didn't take a direct route home. In fact, he took a circuitous route that took a good half an hour, meaning while I should have been early for Jeff's lunch thing, I was probably going to be late. It so figured. But since I'd already texted William that I was okay, I sent another text sharing that we'd be late. Then a few more random ones just because I wanted to pay him back for the sarcasm from earlier.

Amazingly enough, there were no protestors in the street when we finally got in sight of the Embassy, and we got into the garage without incident.

The A-Cs who'd been with Falk the first time were waiting for us in the garage, which was weird but I chose not to mention it because I wasn't sure I wanted to have another round of verbal sparring with Falk—Len still had his gun out.

"Mister Buchanan needs us all, right now," one said to Falk, who nodded.

"See you and 'the boys' around, Ambassador." Falk and his three A-Cs zipped off.

"Officially, on record, I don't like him," Len said as he holstered his gun.

"Me either," Kyle added as he holstered his. I hadn't realized Kyle had had his gun out, which was impressive on his part and par for my not-noticing-some-important-things course.

"You two are just transferring your feelings about Malcolm onto Burt."

"No. I don't like him for himself," Len said.

"Ditto," Kyle chimed in. "But whatever. Let's get Jamie up to daycare, where it's actually safe."

The Embassy Daycare center was on the fourth floor, so we zipped upstairs. Dropped Jamie off with lots of hugs and kisses, and filled Denise Lewis, who ran the center, in on what had transpired, while Len and Kyle went and got our pets.

Jamie insisted that all the dogs and cats had to be with her in daycare, so the cats had their own Feline Winnebago, which was a converted, enclosed, rather large red wagon. The Poofs traveled with the cats, and sometimes on the dogs' backs. I was fairly sure each dog and cat had at least one Poof they called their own. But Poofs for everyone and more Poofs for me was my motto, so it was all good.

That done, told the boys to have a little down time to relax, and I headed off to find the meeting I was supposed to be attending. Considered going upstairs and changing clothes, or at least brushing my hair, but William had said that Jeff had said that the politicians coming were all friends, and our friends were certainly used to seeing me in jeans and an Aerosmith shirt.

Realized I had no idea where Jeff was holding this meeting. It could be in our apartment, for all I knew. "Com on."

"Yes, Ambassador?"

"William, where am I supposed to find my main man and his lunchtime cronies?"

William chuckled. "In the kitchen, Ambassador. They just arrived a few minutes ago, so you haven't missed anything important, I'm sure."

"Oh, what a relief that is."

Headed down to the first floor, using hyperspeed and the stairs so that, should Christopher be in the meeting, I could confirm that I was practicing all the time, everywhere. I sometimes got tired of being chastised for having the nerve to use the elevator, and after this morning I knew I wouldn't have the grace to handle said chastising well, so chose discretion as the better part of valor.

The first floor, being the main entryway and therefore the place the most people who weren't part of American Centaurion in some way would come in, had the most normal stuff in it. Offices, dining room, kitchen, and some small parlors and salons. No one was in any of the rooms as I went by, meaning they were likely all in the kitchen. This meeting seemed a lot more important all of a sudden.

As I neared the kitchen I heard voices. ". . . been quiet for the past few months." A voice I didn't recognize. Supposedly the politicians here were all friends, but I knew our friends' voices.

"That doesn't mean plans aren't forming, it just means we

haven't spotted what they are." That was a voice I recognized without trying—Chuckie was here. Know a guy since the first day of ninth grade, know his voice at any time. "Sir, I don't want to sound negative, but you need to consider the ramifications of what you're suggesting."

Sir? Chuckie almost never called anyone "sir." Wondered if I had time to go up and change into the Female Armani Standard Issue.

Someone's head popped around the door. Jeff's head, to be exact. He smiled. "You look great as always, baby. Come on, you're just in time."

"Just in time for what?"

"Just in time to meet the head of the F.B.I.'s newly created Alien Activities Division."

CHAPTER 8

CONTEMPLATED ALL I COULD SAY. Most of my responses revolved around the idea that I was absolutely not dressed right to meet the new head of anything, let alone the head of a new division of the F.B.I. created just for us, so to speak.

However, duty called and by now everyone in the room knew I was standing in the hallway. Decided that going for what usually worked every time would probably work now. Stood up straight, stuck the twins out, and walked in.

There were several people I knew in attendance—Christopher and Amy, Paul Gower and Richard White, representing the current and former Pontifex positions, Senators Vincent Armstrong and Donald McMillan, Representative Nathalie Gagnon-Brewer, McMillan's Girl Friday and my sorority bestie, Caroline Chase, our Embassy Troubadour-at-Large, Rajnish Singh, and, of course, Chuckie, aka the head of the C.I.A.'s E-T Division. Clearly, I was privy to quite the Power Lunch.

We had one person missing who I would have thought would be in attendance—Denise's husband, Kevin Lewis. He was my mom's right-hand man in the P.T.C.U. and was the Embassy's Defense Attaché. Under the circumstances, he should have been here. Tabled asking where he was for later.

Chuckie and Gower were both doing their best not to show how amused they were by my entrance. Amy and Caroline weren't hiding their amusement at all. Christopher was, of course, glaring—Patented Glare #1. However, the person in the room I didn't know seemed appreciative.

He gave me a beaming smile as he stood and put his hand out. "Ambassador Martini, it's so good to get to meet you in person. I'm Evander Horn."

I put him at about White's age, so late fifties. He was a big guy—not quite as big as Jeff and Gower, but bulkier than Chuckie, and, like all three of them, over six feet. He had close-cropped black hair, medium brown skin, and sparkling dark brown eyes. He was nice looking—not A-C level, but a human who was definitely easy on the eyes.

Horn was also in the typical Washington Uniform, which meant either a navy or a gray pinstripe suit, coordinated shirt and tie, and fancy wingtips. He was in the gray, with a lighter gray shirt, red tie, and light brown wingtips. It looked good on him.

McMillan and Armstrong were both in the navy version of this look. All the other men, Chuckie included, were in the male version of the Armani Fatigues—black suit, white shirt, black tie, black shoes. Even before Chuckie had married in he'd adapted and worn the Fatigues. Wondered how long it would be before, or if, Horn would adapt his clothing choices.

Gave him my hand and we shook paws. "Nice to meet you, too, Mister Horn."

"Please, call me Vander."

"And please call me Kitty. Congratulations on your new position."

He smiled again. "Thank you. I hope." The others chuckled.

"Gosh, just what have I missed?" Figured I'd missed a lot, but who knew? And since no one had asked me about my morning, I knew they'd missed a lot, too. But now was, perhaps, not the time to bring up my Fun With Loons Extravaganza.

Horn sighed as he sat and Jeff helped me into a seat and sat down himself. "Not much. We were just starting to get down to brass tacks. After the incident in December, the President demanded some changes."

"You mean after over two dozen Representatives were killed off, the President wondered why the F.B.I. hadn't taken a more personal interest?"

Nathalie was doing better six months after Operation Sherlock, at least outwardly, mostly because she'd been asked to take Edmund's seat in the House and hadn't had much of a choice but to do the whole stiff upper lip thing. Amy patted Nathalie's arm and Caroline squeezed her hand.

"Yes, that's exactly what I mean," Horn said. "The President wasn't happy that the C.I.A. has been the point agency for alien activities for so long. Homeland Security at least had Cliff Goodman in place, but we at the F.B.I. had really nothing focused on American Centaurion."

"That anyone knows of, you mean."

Horn raised his eyebrow. "Would you mind explaining that?"

I shrugged. "Just because the Bureau didn't have any official division or whatever watching us, you can't make me believe that no one over there knew aliens existed on Earth, nor can you make me believe that there weren't plenty of people who wanted their piece of the alien pie. Maybe nothing was official, but I don't buy for a New York Minute that a host of someones over at the Bureau weren't chomping at the bit to get their claws into us."

"Someone didn't have enough coffee at breakfast," Christopher muttered.

Horn chuckled. "They told me you were blunt and bright. I see they weren't wrong."

"Who's 'they'?" I liked to know who was talking about me. It helped determine if what "they" had said was likely to be flattering or not.

"Cliff Goodman for one. The President, for another. Several of the Joint Chiefs of Staff."

"Bet the Secretary of Transportation wasn't one of them."

"No, Langston Whitmore isn't a fan of yours. But others are, including Colonel Franklin at Andrews Air Force Base. And, of course, the head of the P.T.C.U."

"Well, my mom is sort of required to say I'm awesome, isn't she?"

Horn laughed. "No, your mother doesn't lie on a regular basis. I believe she feels it's a waste of her time."

Managed not to mention that my mother, and father, and Chuckie, for that matter, had all felt it was a great use of their time to lie to me for years. Until I'd met the gang from Alpha Four, I'd firmly believed my mother was a consultant, my father was a history professor at Arizona State University, and my best guy friend was a self-made multimillionaire twice over and only an international playboy.

That Mom was the head of the Presidential Terrorism Control Unit, Dad did a lot of cryptology work for NASA mostly dealing with alien transmissions, and Chuckie was Mr. C.I.A. had been things I'd only discovered during Operations Fugly and Drug Addict. One day, it might not bother me that they'd fooled me so easily for twenty-seven years. One day.

"Good to know. Speaking of Mom, and Cliff, why aren't they here?" This kind of meeting seemed like one Cliff should be attending. Wondered if him coming to help us had delayed him. Then wondered if he'd been attacked by one or both of the mobs. But had a more pressing and less alarming question. "And where's Kevin?"

"Kevin's with Walter," Jeff said quickly, giving me a look that said he didn't want me talking about the Security training session.

"Cliff's on his way," Chuckie added. "He said he had a couple important Homeland Security errands to run first."

Wondered why Cliff hadn't told Chuckie what was really going on. Then realized it was the same reason I wasn't telling Chuckie or Jeff or the others what had gone on—we had a new guy in the room and I didn't know which side he was really on. Cliff knew we were okay, and he was on his way over. Tell everyone what had happened once it was clearly "in the past." He was a smart guy, after all.

"And your mother is handling other things," McMillan said. "She feels there are enough of us here to deal with the issue and keep her informed."

Would have liked to have confirmation for how in-the-know and trustworthy Horn was before I'd met him. Either Cliff didn't know or he didn't trust Horn. Made do with the next best thing to asking aloud. Looked at Chuckie and tilted my head a little to the right. He looked at Horn, then nodded. Okay, so Chuckie felt Horn was okay. Looked around the room, then back at Chuckie. Who smiled and nodded. Fine, ~~Horn could be told whatever.~~

"I still hate it when you two communicate in that way," Jeff muttered.

Patted his hand, but chose to show off my diplomatic skills and not mention that his jealousy could take the day off, in part because he'd only sounded about a three out of ten on the scale. "Okay. So, what's the issue we're all here to powwow about?"

Horn sighed. "We've identified a link between several multinational corporations to terrorist organizations."

"You mean aside from Titan Security, Gaultier Enterprises, and YatesCorp, most likely linked to the Al Dejahl terrorist organization and all of its offshoots? Because those links are seriously old news and if that's all the F.B.I. has, I think you might want to consider putting in for a transfer to another agency."

"Yes," Horn said. "But we also know that they have protection at—"

"The highest political levels. Yeah, old news. If they didn't my mother would have stopped Herbert Gaultier a hell of a long time before he, ah, disappeared." And never let me and Amy be friends, of course, so at least some good had come out of the powerful people protecting the Evil Genius Society and its entire membership.

"Yes," Horn said again. "However, the issue is that it's been identified that those who used to be in charge of these corporations have all died or disappeared under mysterious circumstances."

Did my best to look calm and cool. One thing about my recurring nightmare—I wasn't thrown or flustered by this statement in the least. "Yes, they have. What of it? Is the F.B.I. upset that the old villains aren't around any more to make a good golf foursome or something?"

Horn chuckled as he shook his head. "No. Titan was brought down, for the most part, but not completely, and it's starting to rebuild. Gaultier and YatesCorp, however, have sailed along with business as usual, with nary a hiccup, even though they lost their CEOs and then some. Meaning we have new people in old positions or people who've been around for a long time ensuring ties to terrorist organizations still remain strong. And we need them stopped."

"Is the F.B.I. aware that there's more going on with all these corporations than mere terrorist links? Because there are worse things out there than fanatics with guns, and these three corporations like to really be diverse in the kind of evil services they provide."

"Yes, we're very aware."

"So why are you coming to us?"

Horn looked me straight in the eyes. "Because I know you're the ones who took down all those people missing and/or presumed dead."

Maybe I'd been having that damn nightmare for a reason. I shrugged. "Proof would be a requirement, I'd think." Was proud of myself—my voice didn't falter in the least and I sounded close to bored.

Horn smiled. "Yes, it would be, if I wanted to bring anyone in for prosecution. But that's not my goal. The C.I.A. isn't the only agency willing to make deals in order to get things done."

"What deals are you talking about?"

Horn's turn to shrug. "We need to identify which politicians and people in power are behind these anti-alien and anti-U.S. programs. And stop them. Permanently. Preferably before the next big plan is put into action."

Asked what I felt was the obvious question. "What's the next big plan?"

"No one knows," Armstrong said. "Things have been quiet since you identified Lydia Montgomery as being the person responsible for killing off over two dozen fellow politicians."

Kept my opinion on this to myself. We'd discovered there was a Mastermind behind most of the Bad Guy du Jour plans, and he or she was working like the Sith, meaning an Apprentice was a necessity. Esteban Cantu had been one of the Apprentices, but he'd been arrested during Operation Destruction and murdered by the bad guys during Operation Sherlock. Meaning that it was Open Enrollment time for Apprentice Wannabes.

That had been what drove most of Operation Sherlock—Apprentice Tryouts. Due to evidence, some of which we were all pretty sure was planted, Lydia was incriminated for not just the murders we knew she'd committed but more besides. This had given law enforcement and Capitol Hill a nice feeling of closure. The idea that Lydia had acted alone and there was no one on the grassy knoll helping her out was a stupid assumption on their parts, of course.

However, I could confirm that while there were a lot of questions left unanswered at the end of Operation Sherlock, things had gone very, very quiet in the six months since.

Thought back to the bit of conversation I'd heard on the way in. "If things have been quiet, why are you here?" I asked Horn.

"I agree with Charles—just because things are quiet it doesn't mean nothing's going on. But I'd like your opinion, Kitty, about why things are quiet."

Looked around. "Why mine as opposed to everyone else who's here? Or is it just that you already know everyone else's opinions?"

"You've been identified by all agencies as being instrumental."

That wasn't news I liked hearing. It was accurate, sure, but that everyone in the Alphabet Agencies had me marked as their go-to girl, either pro or con, was unsettling at best. That the heads of the three corporations we were discussing had tried to have what now seemed like an end-run meeting with me only made this worse.

Looked to Chuckie again. He nodded.

"Fine. Has anyone forwarded our Mastermind theory?"

"Yes, Charles and I went over it in some detail the other day."

Made sense—Horn was now Chuckie's counterpart in the F.B.I. But Chuckie had called him "sir." Meaning that Chuckie likely both respected Horn and also thought of him as higher up the food chain. Interesting.

I'd have loved to have more time to process all this interesting, and having had a chance to sit down and regroup from all the morning's fun activities first would have been nice, too. Chose to hold off on asking where, if this was a lunch meeting, all the food was. Sure I'd just eaten a little while ago, but all the stress and such had worked up my appetite again.

"Super. Well, my opinion is that the Mastermind figured out we were onto him, and has chosen to lie low until we get distracted with something else."

Horn beamed. "That's my opinion, too."

"Why does our being in agreement make you so darned happy, Vander?"

"Because you're likely to agree with what I want to do."

Looked around the room. Had the distinct feeling that everyone else knew what Horn wanted to do and that none of them agreed with it.

"Okay, I'll bite. What's your plan?"

"I want to do a full-scale congressional investigation into Gaultier Enterprises."

CHAPTER 9

LET THAT ONE SIT on the air for a bit. Clearly I'd picked up some dream and memory reading talent, maybe from hanging out with Gower for so long. Because I could see where this plan of Horn's would lead.

"Vander, you realize that if we start congressional hearings over Gaultier, then the disappearance of Herbert Gaultier, and the disappearance and reappearance of LaRue Demorte Gaultier, and her subsequently bringing an alien invasion back with her, will be top of mind for one and all, right?"

"I don't see it as an issue," Horn said.

"Twenty bucks says you're the only one in the room who doesn't."

"I agree with the Ambassador," Armstrong said. "While I'd love to figure out all that Gaultier is involved in, and stop them, a very public display doesn't sound like it's in anyone's best interests."

Mine in particular. I'd been dreaming about how I'd handle a congressional hearing. "Not well" was my final verdict.

Horn shook his head. "We have Herbert Gaultier's only child sitting right here. She's fighting to take control of the corporation. This could help her."

"I'd love to agree with you," Amy said. "However, the Board of Directors has other plans, and has blocked every attempt to have my father listed as presumed dead. They're winning on that one in part because he's only been missing for eighteen months. LaRue's death was public and therefore public knowledge. My father's disappearance, however, was not public."

Gaultier wasn't gone, he was dead and gone. But we'd disposed of the body and that meant we had no proof. Which was good, because Christopher had killed him, and I doubted the courts were going to be excited about the fact that Amy's husband had done that particular deed. Somerall, Gardiner, and Cross, however, would be ecstatic to make that discovery.

The others chimed in with why they thought this idea of Horn's was a bad idea. But I still had a question. "Excuse me, Vander, but what you're suggesting is an idea, not an issue. Supposedly there is also an issue at hand. I'd like to know what that is."

Horn looked pleased, and it dawned on me that he was testing me. It so figured. Pulled my phone out of my back pocket and sent a text to our Concierge Majordomo, aka Pierre, and asked him to get the lunch party started, so to speak. Considering how the day was going, gave him specific requests—it'd been a stressful day so far and I wanted comfort food. He confirmed that food was coming from my favorite deli.

"The issue is that we've picked up intel that a new narcotic is about to hit the streets," Horn said.

"Not to sound callous, but why is that our concern? Unless, of course, and I'm just spitballing here, this drug is a lot like Surcenthumain or what they hit Malcolm with." During Operation Sherlock, the bad guys had given Buchanan a shot of a suspended animation drug. It had worked really well, but we'd thankfully found the antidote. Surcenthumain was why Jeff, Christopher, Christopher's "lost aunt" Serene, her son Patrick, Jamie, and I were now officially Extra Special with a Side of Mutated.

"We don't know what the drug is," McMillan said. "However, the information at hand does indicate it's likely to be a drug we wouldn't want on the streets. And by that I mean it's a drug likely to permanently alter the persons taking it."

"I can't buy why they'd release Surcenthumain just randomly," I said, as Pierre came in, followed by some A-C Field agents, who started to set the table and get food onto it.

Refrained from telling them they were all my heroes, but it took effort. "It's too powerful a drug. That's something you sell to the highest bidder, not hand out to the local pushers."

"That's why I want to launch the investigation into Gaultier," Horn countered. "They're the most likely source of the drug."

The others started talking again. I got a nice, frosty Coke, snagged a toasted bagel and—while I loaded on the cream cheese, capers, lox, and onions—observed.

Everyone was fired up about the drugs and the suggested investigation. Everyone was also coming up with alternative ideas for what to do. And if I'd spent a relaxing morning having fun with my friends and daughter before I'd been thrust into this meeting, I might have been, too.

However, I was still revved up and more than a little paranoid from being attacked at literally every turn, and I hadn't been prepped for this particular situation. Therefore, I was willing to sit back and occupy my mouth with chewing and swallowing my food, while my eyes and ears paid attention.

Horn was observing, as well. He was active in the conversation, but he let the others do most of the talking now, though he made sure to keep on coming back to the idea that the only option was a full congressional investigation. I wasn't up on all the ways to take down Big Pharma, but going before Congress usually was a last resort, not your opening gambit.

Horn hadn't been moved into the position he was in because he was a moron. Since Operation Destruction had outed us to the world, the President and other world leaders had made some temporary changes. No new elections until the next cycle, which meant anyone in office when the Dino-Birds From Space attacked was sticking around for, as of now, at least another eighteen months. Appointees and special elections to fill seats opened by death or disablement only, which was why Jeff and Nathalie were both new congresspersons.

This was one reason there were so many anti-alien groups out and active right now—Club 51 was just the one we knew the best, so to speak. But many of these groups were protesting the suspension of our constitution, and for others, it was just a nice moral outrage issue they could hide their bigotry and xenophobia behind.

However, the F.B.I. had been given the direction to add on an official division just focused on aliens. Okay, no surprise—all the other agencies had the same. The question was, though, why had the F.B.I. waited so long? The first wave of A-Cs, which had included White, had come in the 1960s. That was a hell of a long time to wait to put someone in charge of paying attention to what the nice aliens were up to.

Meaning they hadn't waited.

So, what the F.B.I. was doing was now "creating" a division they'd probably already had working clandestinely. And if they'd put Horn in charge, it was likely that he'd either been in charge of the clandestine section or he was incredibly in-the-know and experienced.

My phone was out, and no one was actually paying attention to me. I did a search on Evander Horn. He popped right up. Scrolled through to find the pertinent information.

Amy was passionately arguing that we had to come up with a better plan than the congressional hearing when I found what I was looking for—Horn's undergraduate degree wasn't in Political Science, Communications, or even Business. His degree was in Psychology.

"If we give any of the Board any indication that we know for certain they're up to no good, they'll destroy evidence faster than you can blink," Amy said with conviction.

"There are ways to avoid that," Chuckie said. "Search warrants being served by a plethora of law enforcement, for example."

"Maybe." Amy didn't sound convinced. "Ansom Somerall may have become the Chairman of the Board, but Janelle Gardiner and Quinton Cross are still both trying to take control. However, they're all happily working together to oppose me and anyone else who might want to have a say in the day-to-day or overall goals of the company and if—"

"Ames, everyone, let's relax and take five for a minute." Hoped the others would catch on that my interrupting Amy mid-sentence was intentional. "Have some sodas, juice, or Pierre's special iced tea, eat some food, it's all fresh from the deli." Turned to Horn. "I'd like to ask our new bestest friend here one important question no one else yet has."

Horn smiled at me. "What's that?"

"Well, first off, I'd like to say something. Impressive use of reverse psychology, Vander. You have us all hysterically trying to come up with anything other than what you keep on suggesting. But we're busy people, and I, personally, have already had a hell of a busy morning, so let's cut to the chase. My question is simple: What the hell do you actually want us to do that we will somehow think is our own idea, not yours?"

Horn stared at me. "That isn't my intention at all."

"Bullpookey, pardon my French. You want us solving your little problem, and you want us to think it's our idea, too. I want to know why." Looked at Chuckie. "I also want to know, immediately, if Mister Horn here is really a human being or if he's got that special something inside him that makes him keep going and going and going."

"I'm not an android," Horn said.

"Glad you can read my mind and all, but we have a saying in Pueblo Caliente—prove it."

CHAPTER 10

FOR THE FIRST TIME, Horn seemed uncomfortable. "I really don't think that's necessary." He didn't sound cool or suave—he sounded defensive.

"You're on American Centaurion soil, and, news flash, I'm the highest ranking American Centaurion on premises. Here, I outrank even the Pontifex." Noted that Reader, aka the Head of Field for Centaurion Division, and therefore the only person who could outrank me in the Embassy, wasn't on premises. Figured Gower and Chuckie had told him to stay home for a reason. Revised my opinion on why Chuckie was calling Horn "sir."

"I'm not challenging your authority," Horn said. "I just see no need to prove that I am who everyone here knows I am."

"Sucks to be you, because I'm saying that you're going to be proven to be one hundred percent human, or I'm calling in the National Guard, which in our case, means you're going to be handled with extreme prejudice by Centaurion Division."

"It's a non-intrusive test," Raj said calmly. The tension in the room ratcheted down. Troubadours, they had a lot more power than the empaths and imageers wanted to admit. "Our staff physician performs it routinely on our personnel, or friends," he nodded toward Chuckie, "who tend to travel in the more dangerous circles. Think of it as an odd custom and a formality that will allow American Centaurion to fully accept you and your new position."

White nodded. "I've taken the liberty of asking Doctor Hernandez to join us and perform the test while we're all here. He'll be with us shortly."

Horn didn't look much happier. "You won't have to remove your suit jacket, let alone any other piece of clothing," Jeff said gently. "No one here will be seeing anything you don't want them to see."

Horn visibly relaxed. "If it's truly non-intrusive," he said, but he still didn't seem comfortable or even close to in control of the situation. Looked at my phone and scrolled through his bio again, a little slower this time.

Tito arrived, quick introductions were made, and then he pulled out what looked like one of the wands security used at airports to do the closer body frisks, only with a lot more blinking lights on it. A-Cs seemed to take a lot of their design cues from human airports, God alone knew why.

While Tito slowly ran the Organic Validation Sensor over every part of Horn, I looked for possible reasons for why Horn had gone from Smooth Dude In Charge to Freaked Out Paranoid.

Found it, and suddenly felt kind of bad. "Oh." Looked over at Horn. "Sorry. I get why this just freaked you out. But, honestly, you're freaking me out, too. We've been fooled before, and you were manipulating us. Next time, don't play games with us, and we won't put you into a situation that makes you feel emotionally unstable."

"Mind telling us what you're talking around?" Christopher asked.

"Once Tito's given us the okay or the shoot-to-kill signal."

Horn managed a weak chuckle. "I'm certainly hoping I get the okay."

"You do," Tito said. "Anyone else I need to check while I'm up here?"

"No, I think we're good, unless everyone else wants to be wanded to show solidarity with Vander."

"I'd like proof we should be feeling that solidarity," White said. "Under the circumstances, that is."

"That's fair." Horn looked around the room. "Actually, the Ambassador is right. I was manipulating you. I know some of you, but not most, and I've heard stories. I wanted to see what you'd come up with when faced with a situation all of you wanted to avoid."

"Nice," Jeff said, sarcasm meter starting to rise. "However, as Kitty said, we prefer people actually telling us what they want, instead of trying to play us."

Horn shot him a quick smile. "I understand."

"You want to explain why asking to be proven to be a human instead of an android worried you?" Amy asked. "Or should we have Kitty do it?"

Horn grimaced. "It's not for the reasons you think."

He was going to pussyfoot. I hadn't had enough Coke to feel like letting him. "He doesn't want to take his clothes off." Everyone stared at me. "Seriously, it's in his profile on the government websites, at least, it is if you read between the lines. A drunk driver caused a horrific several-car crash about twenty-five years ago, which included Vander and his family. He lost his wife and young children, but he was a hero, because he dragged every single person out of their cars, many of which were on fire, his included. He's the reason anyone lived through the accident."

Horn looked down. "I have burns over seventy-five percent of my body," he said in a low voice. "Miraculously, not my head, face, or hands."

"The drunk driver lived. That you didn't murder him with those unburned hands is more of a shock to me than the fact that you took damage. But I think I speak for all of us in the room—those scars aren't going to look hideous to any of us. They're going to look like medals of honor."

"Thank you." Horn cleared his throat. "The drunk driver spent ten years in prison. When he got out, he drowned himself in a bathtub full of vodka. He paid his price." He sighed. "And the next thing I'm sure Kitty is going to mention is that I've spent a lot of time with the research arm of Gaultier Enterprises, looking for a better cure for burn victims. That's my cause, understandably. But it means I have links into Gaultier."

"So do we," Chuckie said, nodding toward Amy. "That doesn't mean we're the bad guys, and I think it may be safe to say the same for you." He looked at me. "And before you ask and berate me, yes, I knew all this. And," he grinned, "let's also just say that Vander wasn't the only person manipulating this situation and let it go at that."

"Oh, Secret Agent Man, you move in sneaky, mysterious ways."

"He does," Jeff said, sounding slightly pissed off. "But I'd like to know why."

McMillan shrugged. "Isn't it obvious, Jeff? Charles wanted everyone's cards on the table, Vander's in particular. He has a very effective weapon in your wife that he knows how to use."

"Thanks, I think." I was a weapon?

Chuckie laughed. "She's like Mel Gibson in *Lethal Weapon*, but with a different kind of crazy."

"Wow, the compliments keep on coming." Had to admit, Chuckie was probably right. "So, before anyone else chimes in on my special kind of crazy, let's get back to the real situation at hand. We don't want a congressional investigation, and, Vander, I really don't think you do, either. So, what is it you want us to do? Trust me when I say that we're a lot more willing and effective when we know what the actual goal is than if we're flailing around in the dark."

Horn nodded. "I'm willing to believe it. Fine. What I want, and I believe you all want as well, is to get to who's really running things, the bad things, at Gaultier, YatesCorp, and what's becoming the new Titan. The latest narcotic is what I believe is going to be the tip of a terrifying iceberg."

"And you want us to melt that sucker down so the good ship USA doesn't turn into the Titanic, right?"

"Right." Horn laughed. "I like how you think."

"Someone has to," Christopher muttered.

I was going to tell Christopher that I'd hurt him later, when my phone rang. It was Buchanan. "Excuse me a moment." Got up and stepped away. "Hey, Malcolm, what's up?"

"Missus Chief, I remember something."

"Good, good. Memories are great and all that. Why are you calling me about them?"

He made the exasperation sound. I got that a lot from Jeff and Chuckie; nice to know Buchanan had joined that team. "I mean I remember something from when I was drugged."

"Oh. Okay, I'll take the 'duh' on that one." The drug Buchanan had been hit with was experimental for long-range space flight. It put the body and brain into suspended animation, and also slowed the aging process.

The downside to it was that the drug's recipient would have memory loss of the thirty minutes prior to the drug's injection, give or take. Memory loss of the time after the injection, when the subject was slipping into suspended animation, was also a given. Since Buchanan was our only known human test subject, we didn't have a lot to go on beyond this, though Dulce and NASA Base had been working on it these past six months.

"What do you remember?"

"I'm pretty sure Colonel Hamlin is alive, or was the last time I saw him."

CHAPTER 11

COLONEL MARVIN HAMLIN had been the head of An-drews Air Force Base before Jeff and I had been assigned to the Embassy. He was anti-alien, but all described him as a good man. He'd disappeared right at the start of Operation Destruction, and had been assumed to be one of the "Cap-tains" in charge of a section of the supersoldier projects.

However, at the start of Operation Sherlock, Hamlin had arrived at our Embassy to share that he'd disappeared not when everyone believed, but actually much earlier, right be-fore Jamie was born. He'd run because he'd discovered there was a Mastermind behind the majority of the conspiracies going on, and the Mastermind had sent assassins, and lots of them, after the good Colonel.

Hamlin was, in part, why we believed in the Mastermind theory. Buchanan had been taking him to get proof of the theory and, if proven, to a safe house, when he'd been at-tacked and drugged by the now finally really and truly late and mostly unlamented Clarence Valentino. Clarence's corpse was being dissected every which way by a team at the Dulce Science Center, because he'd taken a huge dose of Surcenthumain, which meant he was finally a person of use and worth, at least in the realms of medical research.

"We need to get you here for a debrief." Not that I wanted Buchanan to share this with Horn, or even the rest of the politicians in attendance.

"I am there, Missus Chief. Waiting for you in Mister Former Chief's office."

Didn't even bother to ask how he'd gotten in or how long he'd been here. Buchanan had those Dr. Strange powers and moved in ways even more mysterious than Chuckie's. Those ways had saved my life, and Jamie's, more than once so far.

"Gotcha. We'll be there in a flash. So to speak." Hung up and rejoined the others. Shot everyone a bright smile. "I'm so sorry, but can I pull all my menfolk away for a minute or two?"

Got a variety of looks. None of them were enthusiastic, most of them were suspicious. Always the way.

Jeff sighed and nodded. "I think we'll be brief." He looked at the other A-C men. "Eat fast." Turned to Chuckie. "Bring your plate. Everyone else, enjoy the luncheon portion of our meeting."

Jeff then proceeded to finish his food using hyperspeed. The other A-C men were doing the same. Chose to not risk it and try to finish up eating using hyperspeed—smeared cream cheese on my face wouldn't be much better than smeared syrup.

However, I was still hungry. Made two more lox, bagel, and cream cheese sandwiches, grabbed another Coke, got a glass of iced tea balanced on my plate, and headed for Jeff's office. Proving he was indeed the smartest guy in any room, Chuckie had done the same.

We reached the door at the same time Jeff, Christopher, White, Gower, and Raj did. We were a well-oiled machine. At least, that was how I was choosing to look at us at the moment.

Buchanan was lounging at the edge of Jeff's desk. Put my Coke down, handed him the iced tea, and put my plate down between him and my Coke. "One of those is mine, one is yours."

He grinned as Jeff muttered quietly. "Missus Chief, I appreciate the thoughtfulness."

"Want to tell us why you couldn't walk down the hall for your lunch?" Jeff asked, sarcasm knob heading toward ten.

"Because what I have to tell you is classified and something we don't want shared with random politicians. Or do you think your wife and I are trying to have a sexual tryst in front of all of you?"

Chuckie snorted a laugh. "He tends to think like that, yeah."

"Hilarious." Jeff sighed. "Fine, sorry, it's already a tense day and it wasn't supposed to be."

"Yeah, and you don't even know what my group went through."

"I do," Buchanan said. "And I think I'm about to make the day tenser." He took a sip of the iced tea. "This is really good. I need to spend more time inside the Embassy."

"You have something for us?" Christopher snapped. "Spill it or I'm going to join Jeff's team and assume you just wanted to get Kitty alone."

"Alone with five other men. Yeah, that sounds like my kind of party." Buchanan's sarcasm knob was already at eleven. He shot me a look I was familiar with, in part because I saw it from Chuckie all the time, too—the "are these guys for real?" look. He took a bite of his bagel. "Delicious. Thanks, Missus Chief."

"You're welcome. And, not to worry—everyone's testy, perhaps from eating too fast. Chuckie and I are still consuming, so we're not as tense. Anyway, Malcolm has information I foolishly thought you'd all want to hear firsthand. If you don't, go back to the kitchen and Chuckie and I will handle it."

Jeff rolled his eyes. "Pardon me. What's going on?"

Buchanan took a bite. "You first, Missus Chief."

"Fine." Did a very high-level recap of my morning. "So, there you have it. Fun times had by all."

Jeff ran his hand through his hair. "I'm sorry I wasn't able to take your texts. Even more so because of this."

"It happens, and we're fine."

"Your turn," Christopher said to Buchanan.

Buchanan took another bite. Got the impression he was pissed about Jeff and Christopher's bad attitudes and contemplating when and how much to share.

"We have information that a new drug is about to hit the streets," Raj said, troubadour tones definitely on Soothe. "Which is what we were discussing when you called. This was after the new head of the F.B.I.'s Alien Affairs Division got everyone riled up by suggesting congressional hearings. He did it *to* get us upset, as near as we can tell, so let me apologize for all of us if we're not being as receptive as we should be."

Buchanan laughed. "The smartest thing Mister Former Chief's ever done was to keep you on staff here full time." He looked at Jeff. "I've had a long night and a very active morning, so I'm not in the mood for your jealousy crap. I'm never really in the mood for it, but I'm less so today. Keep in mind that the people I'm assigned to protect aren't actually you. I don't care if you like having me around or not. My boss, who is your mother-in-law, is ready to rip you a new one if I mention your attitude problems to her again. And yeah, that's a threat."

I wasn't used to seeing Buchanan this openly aggressive toward Jeff, especially over such a small jealousy reaction. Sent Tito a text.

Jeff stared at him for a moment. "Oh. Sorry. You okay?"

"What?" Christopher asked, speaking for all of us.

Buchanan shrugged. "Tell them. Let's see if you're right."

Jeff ran his hand through his hair again. "Ah, in addition to breaking up and arresting various mobs of protestors, he just had to beat down and arrest about a dozen people last night and this morning. They were setting bombs around the Zoo."

"Bingo," Buchanan said as he finished eating. "You are as good as Missus Chief always says. Now, do you want my information or do you want to piss me off some more?"

Tito came in with his Wand of Power. "I want to check you first. Per the Ambassador."

Buchanan shook his head with a laugh. "Sure, why not?" He looked over to me as Tito ran the OVS over him. "Sorry I'm not in the calm, cool, and collected mode you're used to."

"Just want to be sure it's really you."

"Not a problem."

Tito nodded. "True enough, there's not a problem, in that sense. This is really Malcolm." He cocked his head at Buchanan. "I want you coming up to the infirmary after this meeting, before you go anywhere else."

"Why?" Seemed to me there was a problem if Tito wanted Buchanan at the infirmary sooner as opposed to later.

Buchanan grimaced. "He thinks this could be a drug reaction."

"It could be," Tito confirmed. "I want to run tests. If the

latent side effect of what you were hit with is increased irritability or aggression, that's something we need to know now, in part so we can figure out how to counter it in you."

One of the many side effects of Surcenthumain was to make the person taking it far more aggressive and more than a little paranoid. Christopher had handled that side effect better than Jeff or Serene had, possibly because he'd shot up willingly.

However, the drug Buchanan had been hit with had come out of the original project that had created Surcenthumain. Buchanan had no superpowers that we knew of, but if the aggression effect came later on, maybe those would as well.

"I'll be there when we're done," Buchanan said. "Unlike some people, I don't object to medical care."

Jeff opened his mouth, then shut it. He looked worried, not angry or jealous. Which meant I was now officially worried.

"Malcolm, are you feeling okay?"

He heaved a sigh. "Somewhat. As you well know, Club Fifty-One is active again, and they've upped their game. I have teams assigned. I was hoping Reader or Crawford would be here. I need to discuss security issues with them."

"They're in Dulce," Gower said. "There's a Security training session going on they need to be a part of."

"And we didn't want Reader here in case Horn, our new F.B.I. best friend, tried anything," Chuckie added, confirming my earlier theory. "You want to tell us what you want put in place and we'll make it happen?"

Buchanan nodded. "You need agents put into every building in this area, embassies in particular. At least three Field teams per building."

"Why? Club Fifty-One is all over the idea of blowing things up, I get it, and they're seeming to live for mob protests, but that seems kind of excessive."

"Missus Chief, I don't do excessive. I do necessary. And it's necessary."

"Why?" Jeff asked. "Not arguing. Asking."

Buchanan sighed again. "Because Club Fifty-One just got a new set of friends. One of them's the Secretary of Transportation. And one of them's the new head of Titan Security. Meaning your most coordinated enemies are being funded and given some really good weapons."

CHAPTER 12

LET THAT ONE SIT ON THE AIR for a moment. Buchanan was full of fun facts, and we hadn't even gotten to the relevant one that had brought us to this meeting.

"So Kendrick lied." Not a shocker, really. "I'd bet the rest of the Axis of Evil are involved as well."

"Maybe," Jeff said.

"We don't know for sure, but it's a damned safe bet," Chuckie said.

An additional fact insisted I share its presence. "That's why Horn asked for the meeting this morning, isn't it? He knows, and he wants . . . what? Us to be ready? To see if we have a clue? To know how we're going to counter?"

"All of the above," Chuckie said. "When did you discover this?" he asked Buchanan, voice tense.

"Last night. And if the F.B.I. knows and you don't, then we have more problems. Because I truly had no idea until last night, and Angela didn't, either."

"That's why Mom isn't here."

"Correct." Buchanan shrugged. "And there's more, which is why I actually called Missus Chief. I'm pretty sure I remember something from when I was attacked. I'm sure I left Colonel Hamlin alive."

"That's good news," White said. "Can you tell us what memory has come back to you?"

"Not enough. The memory's choppy, sort of like things you remember from when you were very young. Images, mostly. But the feelings associated with the images are pretty strong. I can see Hamlin getting out of my car, which means we were in it before I was hit with the drug."

"That's incredibly helpful," Chuckie said. "Because it means we can start putting a timeline to the disappearance. Anything else?"

Buchanan nodded. "I feel that I'd believed him, so that could mean he'd given me the proof necessary to show we had a Mastermind working."

"Also helpful," Gower said. "Because we can stop wondering if we don't. Not," he added dryly, "that we've spent much time worrying about *not* having one."

"True enough. I also have an image of a door closing. It's a door that's familiar, but I don't know why."

"Could it be one of your safe houses?" Chuckie asked.

"Could be, but I think I'd recognize the door more if it was. And I don't."

"We checked your safe houses already," Christopher mentioned.

"And I checked the ones I didn't tell you about," Buchanan said with a grin. "He's not at any of them."

"Maybe he's at his." Everyone in the room stared at me. "Oh, come on! Hamlin was in hiding for over a year when he came to me. He hadn't left the country, because if he had, why come back to ask me for help? How would he know what was going on, as much as he did, if he was elsewhere? He wants to find and stop the Mastermind, or else he wouldn't have come to us. So, he's here, somewhere in or around the D.C. area, hiding out, keeping an eye on things."

"Why would he take someone else to a safe house?" Gower asked. "That seems dangerous, especially if he's trying to hide."

"He didn't take a 'someone,' he took Malcolm. I'd bet because he had the information there and Malcolm would be someone who he'd be likely to trust." I'd told Hamlin to trust Buchanan, point of fact. "And Malcolm would want to make sure Hamlin was somewhere safe, right?" Buchanan nodded. "So, Hamlin refuses to hide out at one of Malcolm's safe houses, probably just in case. Hamlin, like Malcolm, has to have more than one safe house or he'd have been killed before we ever met him. So, Malcolm takes Hamlin to one of Hamlin's safe houses."

"But that means we have no way of really knowing if Hamlin's still alive," Raj said. "Someone was following Mister Buchanan. It seems a safe bet that they followed him to this safe house."

"Not if it was close." Closed my eyes and did a timeline. "Let's say that Hamlin's hiding out somewhere very close to us. I mean, he walked to our Embassy, didn't he? No one ever saw a car or a cab, so that means he walked."

"I'd agree," Raj said. "I was the one who answered the door, and I saw no vehicle with him or pulling away."

"Okay. So, he and Malcolm drive off to see the proof." Opened my eyes. "If they drove, they didn't leave the Embassy via the front door *or* the Tunnels of Doom. They left through the parking garage."

Buchanan nodded. "I definitely parked inside the Embassy on the night of the party."

Decided not to mention that this insight of mine would have been better had it come to me six months ago. Better late than never, right? Chose to forge on lest someone, Christopher most likely, point this out.

"So, they drive off, and Hamlin's safe house is close. Malcolm does the 'be sure we're not followed' thing, gets the proof he needs, and leaves Hamlin in safety, probably with the promise to come back to take care of things. Maybe to contact him the next day, even."

"Then what?" Christopher asked. "Oh, and the whole car thing would have been more helpful six months ago."

"I hate you sometimes. Just want that on record." Christopher smirked. Decided I preferred him glaring. Chose not to share this. "So, anyway, then Malcolm does . . . what? Comes back to the party?"

"No," Buchanan said slowly. "I'd go to prove whatever Hamlin showed me."

"I found him unconscious in the tunnels under Gaultier Research," Christopher said. "We assumed this before and I think it's still a good assumption now—I think you headed there."

"Maybe." Buchanan sounded doubtful. "I don't know that the timeline would have worked out."

"We've never recovered your car, and the P.T.C.U., C.I.A., and several other agencies were quite determined to find it. So maybe you went elsewhere, and that's where your car is or was, and where Clarence hit you."

Raj cleared his throat. "Ah, if I may, what if Mister Buchanan headed to Titan?" Everyone in the room's turn to stare at Raj. He smiled. The full room's attention didn't seem to be a bother for a troubadour. "It would make sense from a timeline perspective, and also logic. We all know Titan is rebuilding. Per Mister Buchanan, they're supporting Club Fifty-One. Colonel Hamlin had identified that Titan had actions running against us. Maybe he'd identified more, and Mister Buchanan went to check those out."

"So they dumped me under Gaultier to, what, throw the blame onto them?"

"Seems possible to me," White said. "Precedent exists for actions like that."

"Or they're working together and decided the Gaultier tunnel section was easier to hide you in. Or they wanted you found. These companies were in bed with each other before; it's not a shocker that they'd be in bed again. And based on my morning, the five heads are tight, so I think it's a good bet it was a joint action."

"I agree," Chuckie said. "And it makes logical sense. So, we know what Horn wants, and it's now coinciding with what we want. So what do we want to tell him when we go back to the main meeting?"

"Nothing about Hamlin or Malcolm. In fact, I'd like to tell him nothing at all about this meeting. Of course, that means that Chuckie and I will tell whatever lie we come up with and the rest of you will smile and nod."

For the most part, A-Cs couldn't lie to save their or anyone else's lives. There were exceptions to the rule. White and Raj were both pretty good in the short term, as were a few others on staff. The best liar in the A-C community I knew of was Camilla, who was undercover at Gaultier right now, under Chuckie's orders and direction.

Chuckie shook his head slowly. "I'd like to mention the Club Fifty-One activities, if only to see how Horn reacts. However, I realize that would mean we'd have to tell him all about your morning and explain how we got word of the rest of it, and that we want to avoid."

"Why not say that one of our personnel was ill?" Tito asked.

"Why did I need every guy in the room with me who wasn't a politician?"

"I'm a politician," Jeff said morosely.

"You're special."

"Yeah, thanks, baby. Why don't we just say we were called away on official Centaurion business, smile, nod, and go on with our meeting?"

We all looked at him. "Um, will that work?" I asked finally.

Jeff shrugged. "As I've had the 'pleasure' of learning, it works on Capitol Hill every damn day."

White and Gower both nodded. "I have no issue with that story," Gower said. "Especially since it's true."

"Then it's settled. Malcolm gets to hang out with Tito and we get to go back and play mind games with the F.B.I. Today's just continuing to get better and better every hour, isn't it?"

Gower chuckled. "Yeah, Kitty. Routine."

CHAPTER 13

HAPPILY, Jeff was proven right and the "private meeting, it's all good" explanation was accepted without argument.

We got back to the issue at hand, which was how to find out what Gaultier, Titan, and YatesCorp were up to, beyond the presumed assumption, based on a lot of precedent, that said "horrible evil."

"We have an agent infiltrating within Gaultier," Chuckie shared. "However, I won't share that operative's information with you, Vander, for a variety of reasons."

"No argument," Horn said, looking like he'd like to argue but already knew he'd lose. "Do you have anyone in Yates-Corp or Titan?"

Chuckie shook his head. "Titan's involvement with the assassination attempt at last year's President's Ball meant we had full access into the company. However, the E-T Division was removed from control, and I was told to leave Titan alone."

"And you did?" I found this hard to believe.

Chuckie shrugged. "The order came from up high. There are times to do what you're told, and this was one of them."

"Does that mean we need to look into whoever gave you that order?" Horn asked.

"I honestly don't know," Chuckie replied. "Angela's aware, and she may have someone on it already. The P.T.C.U. didn't relinquish jurisdiction on Titan, since they posed a terrorist threat. They also coordinated with Homeland Security, which turned it over to the Department of Defense. Bottom line is that I stopped worrying about it because the right agencies and divisions were working together."

"What about YatesCorp?" Nathalie asked. "Is anyone there?"

"Not from the F.B.I.'s side," Horn said.

"None that I know of from the C.I.A., either," Chuckie said. "We were all told to back off a long time ago." He shot me a look that said to shut up and not ask the question I wanted to.

So I didn't ask him why he'd obeyed that command. Because his look told me that Chuckie had indeed ignored it. However, he didn't want to share that with present company, and I was in agreement with that mindset.

"Amos Tobin is the new guy in charge," Amy said. "Though it took forever for him to get appointed."

"The Board of Directors did take their time," Horn agreed. "However, I believe it's because there's an unusual stipulation within the incorporation documents, and in light of your fight to reclaim Gaultier Enterprises, I believe it's relevant. If a blood relative of Ronald Yates is found, and proven to be a blood relative, that person can assume a seat on the Board at any time, with full membership and voting rights, and with a salary commensurate with the rest of the Board. There's no limit to the number of blood relatives who can do this, by the way."

Didn't look to see which of our A-Cs were clearly showing they were Yates blood relatives. Figured at least three of them were. Instead I focused on Horn. "How many have stepped forward?"

"None so far," Horn said. "Ronaldo Al Dejahl had sent a letter to the Board of Directors two years ago. However, he wasn't confirmed as a blood relative before he, ah, disappeared."

"And just how do you know this, Vander? I'm asking because you seem to know a whole lot about these things, and I'm wondering how long you've been digging into these corporations before you came by for this informal little stress fest."

Horn smiled at me. "I was in our White Collar division before I moved over to Alien Activities. I know a great deal about most of the Fortune Five Hundred."

"Has the Board searched for any Yates relatives?" Amy asked.

"No." Horn chuckled. "YatesCorp isn't in any hurry to bring on some untried Yates relative just for the thrill of them throwing a wrench into the smooth working of a multinational conglomerate."

Ronald Yates had made Hugh Hefner look like a choirboy. We already knew of two illegitimate children—Ronaldo Al Dejahl and Serene Dwyer. Both of them were the younger siblings of White, and therefore of Jeff's mother, Lucinda, and Gladys "Scary Chief of Security" Gower. Jeff and Christopher were therefore Yates' grandsons. And Jamie and Patrick were his first official great-grandchildren.

Within the A-C community alone we had enough people to take over any Board. But the A-Cs weren't the problem. The rest of Yates' illegitimate children out there were the problem, because they'd be hybrids, and likely powerful hybrids, or full blood A-Cs, also likely to be supremely talented. And we had no idea how many there were, where they might be, or if they were already on the side of evil or not.

"Yet they've publicized the Relative's Clause in the incorporation documents?" Raj asked.

Horn shook his head. "No. I only know about that because I was digging into YatesCorp when they were making their decision on Amos."

Interesting. Horn was on a first name basis with Tobin. Hoped that didn't bode badly for us, but since I was now supposedly on a first name basis with all the Land Sharks, I wasn't one to judge too harshly.

"How long have you known about this clause?" Chuckie asked.

"Not too long." Horn shrugged. "I didn't really think it would be too relevant to Centaurion." Either he didn't know who Ronald Yates had really been to the A-Cs, or else Horn was lying like a wet rug. Had no bet either way. Chuckie didn't look happy, though, and half of the room looked uncomfortable.

"So, what's the situation on the Hill?" Raj asked, smoothly changing the subject. "Is there positive reaction to the news of this new F.B.I. division?"

As the conversation shifted, I wondered if Raj and Chuckie practiced handling issues in meetings or if Raj was just that good. Bet on just that good.

Unhappily, the conversational shift meant the meeting continued on, only focused on what was going on at Capitol Hill. It was the usual political blah, blah, blah now that Horn was assumed to be on our side. None of it was that specific to American Centaurion or our interests, and I was bored out of my non-policy-loving mind within minutes.

Fortunately, just before my eyelids closed and my head hit the table, my phone rang.

I stepped away as fast as possible to take the call. It wasn't from a number programmed into my phone, but at least this number wasn't blocked, so maybe that meant whoever was calling wasn't about to threaten me. "Hello?"

"Chief?" a voice whispered.

"Walter?" I whispered back. "Why aren't you calling me using your Embassy cell?"

"Chief, we're in trouble. Big trouble. We need hel—" And with that, the phone went dead.

CHAPTER 14

NOTHING LIKE A CALL FOR HELP that's cut off mid-word to wake me right up. However, I didn't want to share the news that Walter might be in trouble with half of the room's occupants.

On the other hand, I wanted the other half activated. Then again, Jeff had to go back to Capitol Hill, and congressmen weren't supposed to go into action. And then again, I had support elsewhere in the building.

"Would you all excuse me a minute?" I asked. "Minor household emergency."

Jeff shot me a look that said he didn't believe it. "Let me know before you go out, baby. Chuck, too."

Dang, he'd done the old emotional and mind reading thing. Well, probably for the best. "Will do. Nice seeing everyone." With that I headed for the infirmary.

I was distracted, so used human speed. I called Walter's Embassy cell phone on the way. "This is Walter Ward of the American Centaurion Embassy. I'm unable to take your call at this time. Please leave a message and I'll return your call as soon as possible."

So much for that. Decided that I got bawled out a lot for not calling Alpha Team, so I called Reader. "You've reached James Reader. I'm unavailable." Wow, Reader's voicemail sure had changed from the good old days.

Tim was next, and after the last couple of calls, I expected what I got. "This is Tim Crawford. I'm busy fighting crime and saving the day, so can't take your call at this time. Leave a message and I'll call you back when I have some breathing room."

Gave it a try with Kevin. "This is Kevin Lewis. Leave a message and I'll get back to you." Apparently he and Reader weren't big on chatty voicemail recordings these days.

I reached the infirmary while listening to Lorraine and Claudia's perky cell phone messages. Per Nurse Carter, Buchanan was still here, just finishing up. No worries, I had Serene to call. "This is Serene Dwyer. I'm so sorry I've missed your call. Please leave your name, number, a detailed message, and I'll get back to you just as soon as possible."

I was about to try the flyboys when Buchanan and Tito came out. "What's up, Missus Chief? You look tense."

"I am. Walter just called me from an anonymous number to tell me he was in trouble. Or rather, 'we' were in trouble. I've called everyone on Alpha Team, other than Paul, who's here, and all their phones went to voicemail. I'm officially worried."

Tito and Nurse Carter looked at each other. They both pulled out their phones. "I'll call Dulce, you call Airborne?" Nurse Carter said.

"Yep." Tito looked at me. "Call Home Base."

It was nice to work with people who didn't question when the weird or scary started, and instead began handling it immediately. Buchanan pulled out his phone while I tried calling Nellis Air Force Base, better known to the rest of the world as Area 51.

"No answer," I said, at the same time Tito and Nurse Carter said the same. They both dialed again.

Buchanan grunted at his call. "You're sure? Okay. Thank you." He hung up. "I just checked with the Pentagon. They show no disturbances of any kind at or near either the Dulce Science Center or Home Base."

"Well, no one's answering their phones." Sent a group text to everyone we were trying to reach, flyboys included. "Alpha and Airborne, maybe they're busy. Perhaps Dulce's in lockdown. But Nellis Air Force Base should be answering their phones or the Pentagon should know the reason why."

Nurse Carter shook her head. "I've tried at least a dozen numbers at Dulce. The Medical Center isn't answering, nor are any of the different research sections."

"Interesting," Tito said to whomever he'd actually reached. "Yes, please monitor and let us know if you find anything. Thanks." He hung up. "I just called Alfred. NASA Base doesn't show anything as being wrong in Dulce or Home Base. And, neither he nor I know if this is relevant, but Brian called out today, so he's not at NASA Base, and Alfred thinks he was home, in the Science Center."

"Where's Michael Gower?" If one of the astronauts closely associated with Centaurion Division wasn't where he should be, I wanted to check on the other one.

Tito grimaced. "He called out too, and he's supposedly with Brian."

"Fantastic. Naomi and Abigail went over there earlier, too." Sent texts to both of them. No response came back.

"Excuse me, Ambassador," William's voice came on the com. "Representative Martini is asking for the four of you to join him in the kitchen and to tell you that the outsiders are gone."

"On our way, William. Keep the com on us and patch us in to the kitchen. And try to reach Walter, please." The four of us went to the elevator, because the three full humans didn't want to have to deal with my hyperspeed prowess unless they had to, and I knew it.

"What's going on?" Jeff asked via the com as we waited for the elevator.

"William's here because Walter's supposedly at Dulce for some Security training thing. But they aren't at Home Base because of a dust storm. Walter called me to share there was big trouble, and he was cut off mid-word."

"No response from Walter, Ambassador," William said, voice tense. He'd already lost one brother—I knew he didn't want to lose another. I didn't want him to, either.

Elevator arrived, we got in. "We've tried calling everyone, Jeff," Tito said as we headed down. "Only your father at NASA Base and the Pentagon answered their phones."

"That includes Gladys," I added.

Heard a variety of impressive cursing from the kitchen.

Decided Amy's was the winner, though Caroline's came in a close second.

"Let me make it that much better. Per Jeff's dad, Brian and Michael both called out today—which you'd think would be odd for astronauts to be able to do just like a normal person, but whatever. We can't reach them, either, and Alfred thought they were both at Dulce."

"Michael didn't tell me he'd be there," Caroline said. Since they were engaged, she'd be the most likely person Michael would give his itinerary to. "He didn't spend the night last night, though, so maybe he was doing something with Brian."

"Kitty, what's your guess for what's happening?" Chuckie asked.

"I love that you're asking her for a guess before she has any information," Christopher snarked as the elevator doors opened.

The four of us ran to the kitchen. "Oh, you're just jealous because I usually guess right. Megalomaniac Girl reporting for duty. And I think the dust storm that prevented everyone being at Home Base is related to whatever's going on. And I think we're going to hate what's going on."

"But that's all the information we have," Buchanan said. "Unless Missus Chief is holding out on us."

"Sadly, no. I've texted everyone—no one's replied. Including Kevin, Brian, and Michael." I cleared my throat. "And also including Mimi and Abby. They went over to help Gladys."

"You told us before," Chuckie said. "I've tried texting Mimi, but I thought maybe she wasn't replying because I hadn't answered her texts from this morning."

"Where's Patrick?" Jeff asked, worry plain.

"With Jamie and the other Embassy, Alpha, and Airborne children," William replied. "On site, in the daycare center. I've advised Denise that she shouldn't release the children to anyone at this point in time. Doreen and Irving are there as well. I've also requested that Len and Kyle go to and stay with them and the children. They're there, as are all the Embassy animals."

"All?" We had four dogs, three cats, twelve mated pairs of

Alpha Four Peregrines, and more Poofs than anyone other than Rain Man had a hope of counting. All was a big number.

"*All*," William confirmed. "Doreen said to tell you that their Peregrines sort of herded her and Irving to the daycare center. Denise said to tell you the animals look stressed and ready."

"Shields up, William!"

"Already done, Ambassador. I activated the shields as soon as you told me to try to contact Walter."

"Good man." Effective thinking ran in the Ward family. "So, all we know for sure is that whatever's going on, the only person who tried or was able to tell us anything was Walter."

White looked thoughtful. "Missus Martini, correct me if my memory's inaccurate, but wasn't Walter one of the few who held out against my 'younger brother's' mind control?"

"Yes, he was." White and I looked at each other. "You don't think that's it, do you, Mister White?" I really hoped he was going to say no.

"Sadly, yes, I do, Missus Martini."

"Think what's it?" Caroline asked.

"I hate what you two just jumped to," Chuckie said. "But with what we know, it's a good hypothesis."

"Which is?" Christopher asked.

I answered. "We think Ronaldo Al Dejahl is back in business."

CHAPTER 15

"WILLIAM, patch us in with Hacker International, will you?"

"She means the computer lab," Jeff added.

"Yes, Representative Martini, I know. Walter left detailed instructions, including the Ambassador's nicknames for everything and everybody. Hacker International is connected. Have taken the liberty of putting them on-screen for you, Ambassador."

After Operation Sherlock, Jeff had decided that if we could find a way for him to never have to visit with Hacker International in person, he wanted that way installed immediately.

So, we'd done an electrical remodel and added big screen monitors with video cameras built in into every room where we had meetings or might want to have meetings. This was most of the general rooms in the Embassy and the Zoo. Since it had been done by A-Cs, it had taken an afternoon. Just one. Hyperspeed was the greatest.

The interior of the Zoo's computer lab came onto the big screen in the kitchen. It showed five men—Stryker Dane, aka Eddy Simms, from good old Pueblo Caliente, Arizona, Big George Lecroix from France, Dr. Henry Wu from China, Ravi Gaekwad from India, and Yuri Stanislav, aka Omega Red, from Russia. They were all busily at work at their computer terminals, but I wasn't sure if that was because they were aware that Chuckie was in the Embassy. Chuckie was essentially their boss and he had them in a constant state of alert fear. Jeff really appreciated this, and told Chuckie so often.

They were the best hackers from their respective countries, though each one had his own specialties. In addition to hacking, Stryker was also the author of the very successful *Taken Away* series wherein he recounted his "totally true" tales of being kidnapped and probed by aliens. Needless to say, Stryker wrote fiction.

He made the most money of the team, therefore, because he had the extra income source to add into all the other income sources. He also had the strongest personality, so he was Team Hacker's unofficial leader. Sadly, he still had man-boobs, an appearance you could charitably call "slovenly," limited personal hygiene, and long, unkempt hair that, if cleaned and brushed, would be his only attractive feature.

Big George was tall and thin, but still had the Uber Geek look going. Henry was small, balding, and timid in looks as well as actions. Ravi was pretty normal looking and he was engaged to a Dazzler, so he'd fixed up his look a little bit. Omega Red was blind and buffed out, making him the total Hacker International anomaly. I wasn't sure if he knew that the others never lifted anything heavier than a Big Gulp cup, or if he just liked lifting weights, but he was the only one of them who'd be worth anything in a physical fight.

They were dressed pretty much alike in khaki cargo shorts, sandals, and T-shirts. Today's group T-shirts were commemorating the *X-Files*. They had a nice selection, no one duplicating the other's image choice. This was done because I'd made a joke about them having assigned Geek T-Shirt Days and instead of them dressing nicely for a change, they'd instead created a Shirt Rota Chart. With pride.

Chuckie had ferreted out Stryker's "bunker" when he and I were in high school and, despite the age difference of about ten years, they'd become friends. So I'd known Stryker since high school, too. I'd known all the other guys by the time I was out of college. They'd joined us as a group, however, during Operation Destruction and had never left. Not a day went by that Jeff didn't point this out to me. Unhappily. But I found them useful. And fun to bait. Though the baiting would probably have to wait. We had an emergency.

"Eddy! How's it going? Actually I don't care. You and the rest of the wacky gang need to roll into action."

"Already on it, Kitty." Stryker sounded tense and he didn't look away from whatever he was working on. "Ravi was talking to the reverse engineering team at Dulce and was cut off. We've been trying to reestablish communications ever since. It's definitely not our side."

"Jennifer and Jeremy were at the same training session as Walter," Ravi added, sounding worried. Understandable—Jennifer Barone was his fiancée. She and her brother were a Field team assigned to us permanently during Operation Destruction. Jennifer was an imageer and Jeremy was an empath.

"Why were they there?" I asked.

"Gladys said they performed security here, so they needed the training," Ravi replied.

"How long have you been trying to make contact with Dulce?" Chuckie asked before I could ask why Len and Kyle, my C.I.A.-assigned bodyguards, hadn't been requested. Not that I wasn't glad that they'd been with me this morning, but if Gladys had asked for the Gower girls and the Barones for this security thing, why not the boys, too? But the boys being here was, all things considered, likely to be a very good thing, so I chose not to question aloud.

"Twenty-three minutes so far."

"That times out about to when Walter called me."

"Have also checked with Home Base," Big George said. "No response. On any line."

"And we had the system auto-call every line, too," Henry added.

"What's the weather like around Area Fifty-One and the Science Center?" I asked.

"Clear," Omega Red replied. "Why?"

"Because there was supposedly a huge dust storm at Home Base earlier today, which sent training exercises to Dulce. Do you have any record of such?"

They were all quiet, and every one of them was typing. "No, weather services show nothing," Stryker said finally. "As I know you know, it's monsoon season in Arizona and parts of New Mexico, but there are no storms in either state today."

"Caliente Base. Someone try to reach them, right now."

This was the base in my, Chuckie, and Stryker's hometown. It wasn't as big as most of the others, but it was of decent size, and it also housed a great majority of the A-Cs under thirty, due to my having declared them political refugees during Operation Drug Addict.

"Caliente Base is online," William said. Felt the whole room relax a little. "They can't raise anyone at Dulce or Home Base either. They want to know if they should investigate."

"No. Tell them we'll be there shortly. I don't want anyone going in until we have all areas cleared. Check the Dome. And every other base worldwide."

"Yes, Ambassador."

We waited. Couldn't speak for anyone else, but I was certainly praying that the Dome, which was the main gate hub for the entire world, was secure and still in communication with us.

"The Dome and all bases worldwide other than Dulce and Home Base reporting in," William said. "All bases on High Alert. Dome is locked down. All personnel have been told to wait for your order, Ambassador."

"Why oh why is Kitty somehow in charge?" Christopher grumbled. "The power goes straight to her head."

"With Alpha Team inaccessible, she and the Pontifex are the highest ranking individuals available," William replied. Could've sworn that, despite the situation, he was trying not to laugh. At Christopher, I hoped.

While Jeff and Christopher both tried to look like they didn't hate hearing that, and also tried not to look like they desperately wanted to go back to being the Heads of Field and Imageering, Gower cleared his throat. "Kitty, I need to talk to you, alone, just for a moment."

"Sure, Paul." We stepped out and went down the hall to Raj's office. Gower closed the door. "Paul, if this is about ACE, I know."

Gower looked shocked. "What do you mean you know?"

"Jeff, Chuckie and I know that ACE isn't . . . around right now. We haven't told anyone else, and we won't tell anyone else. If ACE needs us for anything, we'll all do whatever we need to, but we know ACE isn't here to help us."

Gower's shoulders slumped and he sat down. "How long have you known?"

"Chuckie's known the longest. Jeff and I found out at the start of Operation Sherlock."

He heaved a sigh. "I wish I'd known you all knew. It's been hard to pretend to talk to ACE without him inside me."

"We think he's still there, Paul. Per Jamie ACE is still . . . around somewhere."

"I don't feel him, and I haven't since a few weeks after the invasion."

"Right when the tunnels went back to impenetrable?"

"Yes, right then." He rubbed his forehead. "We're clearly under attack of some kind. Someone's going to ask where ACE is and why he isn't helping us."

"Specifically why he's not saving James." Reader was Gower's husband. ACE had helped save his life before, and if something bad had happened to Reader, we were going to have to deal with our enemies knowing ACE was gone at the same time as grieving our hearts out. Which sucked.

"Or Serene. Or anyone else. Such as everyone at Dulce and Home Base."

"We'll deal with it. I'll spin it in some way, Paul, don't worry. Chuckie and Jeff are ready to follow either one of our leads on what's going on with ACE. The four of us will handle it. We can't let ACE being on sabbatical stop us from figuring out what's going on and saving our people right now."

"I know." Gower heaved another sigh and stood up. Shoulders squared, expression of calm confidence on his face—back to the religious leader of an entire exiled race. Good. We needed him on his A game. "I'm going to officially give you full control of the A-C population when we're back with the others."

"Super. Why?"

"Because I can't give it to Jeff, or rather, Representative Martini. I can't give it to Christopher, or rather, the husband of the woman fighting to control Gaultier Enterprises. And I can't in good conscience give the reins to Chuck because he's C.I.A. and we don't want them running us, nor do we want the F.B.I. and Homeland Security demanding their fair share of us. So, you're our leader."

"Thanks for the vote of confidence, there, Paul."

He grinned. "And besides, when the evil madmen plans arise, as I'm sure we're facing right now, there's no one better at the helm than Megalomaniac Girl."

"Ah, you do love me and respect the skills."

Gower laughed. "Kitty, when it comes to someone figuring out what the crazy people have going on, there's no one who's your equal." He hugged me. "And, as James would say, you'll always be our girl."

I hugged him back. "So, does this mean you two are willing to go bi and add me into the marriage?"

"I think Jeff should be worried about how hopeful you just sounded."

"I think I'm still waiting for your answer."

CHAPTER 16

WE REJOINED THE OTHERS. "So, you're still willing to be my wife?" Jeff asked, sarcasm turned to only about a six on the scale of ten.

"Since Paul insists that he and James aren't ready to go bi yet, yeah."

Gower shook his head with a laugh. "No matter what Kitty insinuates, she loves you best, Jeff."

Jeff put his arm around me. "A man can hope, anyway. So, what's the plan?"

Gower cleared his throat, all levity gone. "William, please send this through to all bases and facilities."

"Ready, Pontifex Gower."

"To all Centaurion Division and American Centaurion personnel, as Supreme Pontifex I'm declaring that, until we know the status of the majority of Alpha and all of Airborne Teams, and the status of Home Base and the Dulce Science Center, we are officially in a state of emergency. Full leadership will reside with our Ambassador and Head of the Diplomatic Corps, Kitty Katt-Martini, who will now be considered as acting as the Head of Alpha Team until the state of emergency is removed. Please obey her orders as you would anyone else from Alpha Team. Kitty, to you."

Fortunately, I'd been prepared for this handoff. "I'd like all bases and facilities to remain on high alert. If we have Field teams out, I want them brought in unless they're dealing with a superbeing. In which case, they need to contain it as fast as possible and get back to a base."

Superbeings weren't nearly as common as they had been, in large part because we'd taken the ozone shield down on Alpha Four, and in other part because we'd eliminated the in-control Mephistopheles superbeing. That Mephistopheles had been joined with Ronald Yates was just the kind of fun that we associated with Centaurion got to have on a regular basis.

"What about other threats or the return of missing personnel or communications?" Jeff asked me quietly. "Who will personnel report to in case you're not available?"

Resisted the urge to hug him. He wasn't asking because he was curious. He was asking in this way to ensure I covered all the leadership bases. He'd been the Head of Field for over a decade, after all. And he'd been training me, in that sense, since we met.

"Advise the Embassy immediately of any other threats identified," I shared in my Official Giving Orders Voice. "But barring an immediate threat such as fire and the need to evacuate a facility, don't take action without it being approved by me, Richard White, or Rajnish Singh."

Got a lot of shocked looks for that one, other than from White and Raj. Christopher opened his mouth. I put my hand up and he shut it.

"I want as complete a roster of missing personnel as possible. We have a lot of people who went to Dulce today who aren't there normally. If you can't verify that someone's where you think they should be and can't reach them to verify their well-being, that information needs to be sent to us immediately. By the same token, should personnel presumed missing turn up, let us know that immediately as well."

Time to shoot for the rosy outlook. "The moment anyone establishes contact with either Dulce or Home Base, or any individual known to be at either location, determine situation as fast as possible and advise the Embassy immediately." Okay, so not rosy so much as hopeful. Whatever. "Let's keep calm, carry on, figure out what's going on, and stop it. Embassy out."

"You're back to just the Embassy Complex, Ambassador," William said.

"Great. I need a team to assemble so we can head to Caliente Base. We'll gate over there, then take jets to see what's going on at Dulce and Home Base."

"What do you mean 'we'?" Jeff asked.

"I mean me and the rest of the team I'll be taking. Which won't include you."

"Then you're not going," Jeff said firmly.

Everyone in the room gave him the "really?" look. "She's the Head of Field Operations right now," Chuckie pointed out. "Kitty essentially has to go lead whatever action she wants to initiate. And she's right—you, as a representative, can't go."

"You have to act like nothing's going on, Jeff. So that our enemies don't know for sure that we've figured out that something *is* wrong."

"Something's more wrong, Kitty," Stryker said. "We're being hacked." As he said this, all five of them, even Omega Red, leaped up and started pulling plugs out of the walls and flipping switches.

"The Embassy?" Chuckie asked.

"All of Centaurion Division," Stryker replied as he and the rest of Hacker International continued to run around the computer lab hysterically.

Raj and White both zipped out of the room, Tito right after them. Decided not to ask where they were going. Hopefully to pull plugs out of walls and such.

"I think it was triggered by the search for personnel," Ravi added as he leaped over a desk and yanked two computer towers out of the wall. Henry, Big George, and Omega Red were working on getting the big servers unplugged. We had a lot of them, though.

But happily Raj appeared momentarily on screen, then suddenly all the machines in the room were clearly turned to the "off" position.

"William! Send me to all bases again."

"Go, Ambassador."

"This is Ambassador Katt-Martini. We're at DEFCON Bad. Everyone unplug everything electronic and computer based—our system is being hacked. Pull the stuff out of the wall if you have to, turn off any Wi-Fi or Bluetooth devices, get off the 'net at the fastest hyperspeeds possible, whether humans are watching you or not."

"Reports coming in, Ambassador," William said. "All bases are affected, including NASA. Determining extent of damage now."

"Take me off the all-speak or whatever."

"Back to Embassy complex only, Ambassador."

"Thanks. Now, what the hell? Eddy, how can *we* be hacked? You guys installed firewalls and all that jazz, didn't you?"

"The best there are," Big George shared. "You already had a top-of-the-line system in place when we joined you. But we made it better."

"We made the Centaurion system impenetrable," Henry added.

"And our firewalls and defenses are being cut through like a light saber cuts through Qui-Gon Jinn," Ravi said. He sounded freaked out. This wasn't good.

"I recognize the signature," Omega Red said. He sounded frightened. We moved from "not good" to "really scary."

"Whose is it?" Chuckie asked.

"It's not real," Stryker said firmly. "There's no way it's real."

The hackers started arguing amongst themselves while still furiously doing things. I caught some of it, but nothing they were saying made sense.

"Dudes! I want answers, and I want them now. And I want them in this order—can you stop it, how bad is the damage, and who the hell is it Yuri thinks is responsible?"

More hacker snarling but finally Stryker shared. "We can't stop it. The 'it' was a virus that infiltrated our systems, stole our files and then destroyed them."

"At the root," Ravi added. "Meaning we can't get them back."

"What about backups? Surely we back things up? I mean, I back up my iPod, surely you've backed up our systems."

"We did, all of Centaurion has a massive backup system in place." Stryker's voice was clipped. "We're off the 'net, so

I can't be sure yet, but it looked like all backups were affected, too."

"How? Aren't the backups housed somewhere else?"

"Yeah, they are," Chuckie said. "They're housed at Area Fifty-One."

"It gets better. Super duper, so, while we wait to hear what we've lost and what horrible things have also been done to our systems, who's behind this? And I don't want to hear the 'it can't be' line, because ten minutes ago you'd have said Centaurion Division couldn't be hacked like this."

Stryker sighed and, for the first time looked right at the camera in the computer lab. He looked angry and freaked. "It's a myth, okay? But the myth is that there's a super-hacker, almost like a hacker god, and he's responsible for all the really big, insidious hacks that happen. But this one person doesn't exist."

"He does exist," Omega Red said, with more than a hint of stubbornness in his tone. "Because the only one who could have hacked through all of our defenses and into a system that's more secure than any government on Earth is Chernobog the Ultimate."

CHAPTER 17

"WHO?" JEFF ASKED, speaking for most of the room. "I love the names you guys come up with for your- selves." This earned me a dirty look from all of Hacker Inter- national.

"I'm with Stryker," Chuckie said, eyes narrowed. "Cher- nobog is a myth. He's been rumored to have been around since the nineteen-eighties. He's never been found, never been caught, and never been proven to actually exist."

"How hard did you look for him?" I asked Chuckie.

"Not as hard as I looked for some things," he admitted.

"Because Chuck didn't need to waste his time on a myth," Stryker said.

"He's real," Omega Red said, stubbornness more appar- ent. "Just because none of you can believe that the best of the best is Russian doesn't mean he's not real."

Raj and White returned. "Systems are unplugged all throughout the Embassy complex," Raj shared.

"I'm certain we were too late, however," White added. "At least if the message on any and all active computer screens was indicative."

"What did it say, Richard?"

"I have no idea, but I'm fairly certain the characters are Cyrillic." He handed me a piece of paper. There were letters on it, but I didn't recognize them. Handed it to Chuckie. Who held it up to the camera on the viewing screen that let Hacker

International see us. "Someone get this into Yuri's Braille system immediately."

Henry did as requested. Omega Red's expression of stubborn belief went to nova levels. "Chuck, it says, 'Now you see it, now you don't.' I guarantee that's from Chernobog. It sounds like him."

"You mean it sounds like someone who wants us to think it's him would sound," Stryker said.

Decided to nip the argument I could see starting in the bud. We didn't have time for Hacker International to go into one of their famous group fights that ended up as group sulks.

"I don't care. Whoever it is has just hacked into what you all feel is the most secure system on the planet. I don't care who it is, but whoever it is, we need to stop them. It's easier to call this mysterious hacker Chernobog than He Who Is Scary Evil, so to speak, so let's just make Yuri happy. Oh, and that was an order, by the way."

"See?" Christopher asked of no one in particular. "She's already on a power trip."

Tito returned at this point—saving me from having to come up with a cutting remark for Christopher—carrying his laptop. "I wasn't hooked into the system, Kitty, so all my data is secure. I checked."

"No special message on your screen?"

Tito shook his head. "Just the test results I was reviewing. I checked, and my external hard drive is also secure."

"Not that I mind, especially not today, but why weren't you hooked in?" Wanted to ask if Tito was hitting the extreme porn sites or something, and then decided that was probably not a question befitting the current pseudo-leader of the entire A-C population. Score one for learned decorum.

"I'm doing that . . . special research we've discussed." Tito was shooting me the "really?" look.

"Oh. Right!" Memory shared that Tito was searching for what we called the Yates Gene, meaning he was studying blood and DNA from Jeff, Christopher, Jamie, Serene, White, and a few others. As such, his research—the project itself along with the results—was restricted to him, Emily, and Melanie, Claudia and Lorraine's mothers. Who were also likely at Dulce and therefore in extreme danger. "Good job, Tito. Okay, gang, we need to get our strike team over to Caliente Base pronto. Are the gates working, does anyone know?"

"NASA Base has tested," William shared. "Gates seem to be in order. However, the agents who tried to get to Dulce via a gate were, ah, bounced back. Alfred decided not to try with Home Base, in part because by then you'd given the order for everyone to stay put, Ambassador."

"Good, because that bouncing back thing sounds dangerous." And nauseating. Going through the gates made me sick to my stomach. Going through and then immediately being tossed back sounded like a surefire way to pray to the porcelain god for me.

"They weren't harmed," William said.

"Which makes no sense," Jeff said. "Why would our enemies gently return our agents back to where they started from?"

"Maybe it wasn't our enemies. Walter had enough time to call me, and he used to run gates at Dulce. Maybe he flipped a switch or something."

"It's a good theory," White said. "One we can't confirm from the Embassy, however."

"I'm with you, Mister White. Jeff, you're going back to work. Enjoy pretending everything's okay on the congressional floor. Chuckie, you stay with him. Raj, you're in charge here—coordinate anything that's actually diplomacy-related with Doreen, and keep me advised of any information. Paul, Amy, Caroline, Magdalena, go join the rest of our little flock in the daycare center."

Gower shook his head. "You need my help."

"No, we need to keep our Pontifex, or, rather, one of our most likely targets, safe and sound. Per you, I'm in charge, Paul. You're on guard my daughter and the other kids duty."

"What am I going to be doing?" Christopher asked testily.

"Going with me, Malcolm, and your dad."

"Just the four of you?" Jeff sounded ready to freak out, though Christopher perked up considerably.

"While I'm sure the four of us can handle anything, no, of course not. What do you take me for?"

"I'm going, too," Tito said. "For all we know, we're going to need medical there."

"Works for me. And no, Jeff, before you complain again, that's not all. William, I believe our royal guests are across the street visiting the Romanian Diplomatic Mission. Can you call them and get them back here, please?"

"Yes, Ambassador. Per Walter's notes, I should tell them they're about to go into battle, is that right?"

"You got it."

"Seven of you still doesn't seem like enough," Jeff said, sounding more than a little worried.

"You can't go, Paul can't go, Raj needs to stay here, I want Chuckie with you because, news flash, I don't want this to turn out to be some plan to get you into a position of vulnerability. I'm open to ideas, but I really don't want to throw Field agents at this until we actually know what's going on."

Before I could take another breath, we had more people with us. Princesses Rahmi and Rhee, from Beta Twelve of the Alpha Centaurion system, or, as I preferred to call it, the Planet of the Pissed Off But Getting Happier Amazons.

Rahmi and Rhee had been sent to us during Operation Sherlock and, without ACE around and with the unrest we'd sort of been told about in the Alpha Centaurion system, we had no idea of how to send them back. So they were living with us, which was fine for all concerned, because it never hurt to have two of the best warriors in the galaxy hanging around waiting to be of service.

All the Amazons were shapeshifters. In their normal forms, the princesses looked like all the rest of their clan— limbs slightly elongated for humans, larger and more muscular build, larger oval violet eyes, spiky hair, and really badass attitudes. Rahmi was a brunette and her younger sister Rhee was a blonde, but otherwise, it was clear they were sisters, and Queen Renata's daughters.

However, we required that the princesses look like humans while they were with us. This wasn't a hard request for any shapeshifter to achieve, but over the past six months they'd altered their looks just slightly and now had chosen to look like a combination of their mother and, per everyone else in the Embassy, me. It was flattering in a really weird way, but I'd gotten so used to weird over the past few years that it barely registered on my Weird-O-Meter.

The princesses weren't alone, however. Adriana, the granddaughter of the Romanian Ambassador and his wife, was with them. Adriana was a pretty girl, but she was also being trained in the old ways of the KGB by her grandmother, Olga, who was a former operative and a literal fount of knowledge. I was particularly appreciative of this, since Adriana had saved my life during Operation Assassination.

"Grandmother said I should go along to help," Adriana shared, proving that, as always, Olga likely knew what was going on, or at least some of it.

Adriana was dressed in her form of butt-kicking clothing—cargo pants, long-sleeved T-shirt, Doc Martins, and backpack, carrying who knew what, but all of it likely good for covert operations—all in black. In other words, she fit right in with the A-C Color Scheme of Choice.

"Awesome, Olga rocks and glad to have you along. I'm calling this team good because I want Len and Kyle staying with Jamie. Jeff, can you handle your part, as in, go off and pretend nothing's wrong?" The man couldn't lie, but hope liked to spring eternal.

He heaved a sigh. "Yes. I'll be monitoring you. I'll know when things go wrong."

"*When?* They could go right, you know, Mister Polly Positive."

Everyone other than the princesses snorted laughter. "While you race off into danger without me, I'll see if I can come up with when, if ever, things have gone right all the way through a situation," Jeff said, sarcasm meter heading toward eleven.

"Glad you've got a new hobby. My team, let's get the eight of us to Caliente Base, get our people, and kick some bad-guy butt."

CHAPTER 18

GOWER TOOK TITO'S LAPTOP and escorted Caroline upstairs while Chuckie called Cliff and told him to cancel coming to the Embassy and instead meet up with Chuckie and Jeff at the Capitol.

Rahmi and Rhee went and got their battle staffs, which looked like the lovechild of a javelin and a light saber. Sadly, they only had one each. Dulce had been working on making replicas, but hadn't yet been successful, possibly because we didn't have the right materials on Earth.

Amy and Nurse Carter came with us to the basement to say goodbye to their men. A-Cs tended to keep the gates in their homes and such in the bottom floor, preferably the basement, if one happened to be available. Either that or in a bathroom. Or both. Aliens were weird. But again, this was now down on the low end of my Weird-O-Meter Scale.

The Embassy's gate was indeed in the basement. We also had a stationary floater gate in the computer lab, which was less of an oxymoron than you might think. I still felt that there had to be another gate, a hidden one, somewhere in the Embassy. But no one had found it, and even Chuckie thought I was just being a crazy paranoid about it. But my gut said there was another gate, and my gut also said that I needed to find it before our enemies used it against us.

However, now wasn't the time. While the two White couples did their goodbyes, Jeff pulled me into his arms and held me tightly. "You know I'm not happy about this, baby."

"I know. But you'll know if I'm in trouble." A thought occurred. "Speaking of which, can you pick up anything emotionally from anyone who might be at Dulce?"

"No, and I've been trying. I'm betting that means there's an emotional blocker or enhancer, or many of them, over there." His brow furrowed. "That could mean I won't be able to feel you when you're there."

"We'll manage. I promise to call for help if we need it."

Jeff put his finger under my chin and tilted my head up. "I'll hold you to that." Then he bent and kissed me. Like always, his kiss was amazing—sensuous and arousing. And also like always, I was ready to go to bed by the time he slowly ended the kiss. He chuckled. "Nice to see your laser focus on the priorities is still intact."

"Always." I hugged him tightly. "We'll be fine. I promise."

"Prove it to me by coming back quickly and in one piece. You know, do you want me to take you through the gate?" he asked, just a little too casually.

"Nice try. Do I need to call Chuckie down here to do his Vulcan Nerve Pinch thing to keep you under control?"

Jeff sighed. "No. I just thought I'd offer."

White kissed Nurse Carter goodbye, came over, and took my hand. "I'll handle my partner, Jeffrey. You go off and handle the things we can't."

"Fine, fine." Jeff didn't budge.

"William, are you on the com?"

"Yes, Ambassador. I've advised Mister Reynolds. He's heading downstairs now."

Jeff rolled his eyes. "Fine! I'm going, I'm going. We're all going." He ushered Nurse Carter and Amy before him and they all headed for the stairs. Jeff looked over his shoulder as he started up. "Just remember that the main military base we call on for support is most likely under siege, and that means any real firepower will take a lot longer to arrive."

"We will do, Commander." This earned me a grin, then Jeff headed upstairs. I heard him and Chuckie start kvetching at each other. Well and good, they were taken care of.

"Nice to see he thinks we're completely incapable," Christopher muttered.

"He just wants to go with us. Mister White, if you'd do the gate honors."

White spun the dial and calibrated the gate for us to go one at a time to Caliente Base. "Dad, you go first, I'll go last," Christopher said.

White shot a look over his shoulder. "Missus Martini?"

"Sure, I guess. We're going to a base we know is secure. Mister White, then Malcolm, Rahmi, Tito, Adriana, Rhee, me, and Christopher. Sound good?"

"Yeah," Christopher said. I wondered if this was some holdover thing for him from when he'd been Head of Imageering.

"Great. We'll get weaponed up once we're all there."

One by one everyone stepped through. As Rhee did the slow fade that was like a nausea appetizer to my stomach, I steeled myself for the trip. But before I could go through, Christopher put his hand on my arm. "Kitty, I need to tell you something."

It dawned on me that I hadn't asked Christopher what he could see of our people. Considering his Surcenthumain boost had given him the ability to see beings in the Alpha Centauri system—both externally and, in that creepy-but-good way we seemed to attract naturally, internally—this was an oversight on my part.

He looked worried and serious, and my stomach knotted. "What can you see from over there? Are our people okay?"

His shoulders slumped. "That's what I wanted to tell you. I . . . I don't know."

"What do you mean you don't know?"

Christopher shook his head. "For the past few months my abilities have been . . . diminishing. Once all the chaos was over and Chuck and Naomi were married, I tried to see Alexander and the others on Alpha Four, to see if I could tell what was going on. And . . ."

"And?"

"I couldn't. I couldn't see anyone. I tried everything, but came up with nothing. I could still see people on Earth, though. But that's been fading. My range has gotten less and less. Right now I can only see inside someone if I'm touching them. Otherwise, nothing."

Had no idea what to say. "Wow," seemed to about cover it. Congratulated myself on keeping the "that totally sucks" and "well this day just keeps on getting better and better" comments to myself. This diplomacy gig was good for something. "What about your speed?" In addition to his expanded imageering talents, Christopher had become the fastest A-C in the world due to the Surcenthumain.

"That's still there. I don't know why, but that hasn't been affected at all. But I can't tell if anyone's alive or dead at Dulce or Home Base. Or anywhere else for that matter."

"Who else knows?"

"No one. I haven't even told Amy." He swallowed. "I don't know if the regression is done or not."

"We'll have Tito test you later. Are you okay to go on this mission with me?"

"Yeah. The rest of me is fine. I can still read and manipulate images, and do everything else I could before I took the drug."

"That's good. Let's get over there. You want to tell your dad or you want me to?"

He grimaced. "I don't really want to tell anybody. I didn't want to tell you, but I figured you were going to ask me to check on something somewhere along the line."

"Yeah, I would have. There's no shame in it, Christopher."

"Yeah?" he said as he made the "after you" gesture, meaning it was time for me to head through the gate. "The only positives from my taking the Surcenthumain were my expanded powers. Now I've lost the majority of them. So where does that leave me?"

I patted his cheek. "Back to where you started. You know, at the awesome level."

CHAPTER 19

DECIDED THAT CHRISTOPHER AND I had both stalled enough, took one for the team and stepped through the gate. The usual feeling of moving very slowly and very fast at the same time ensured the usual additional feeling of overwhelming nausea.

But, as with all gate transfers, it didn't last too long and, happily, I wasn't bounced back. I stepped forward quickly, so Christopher wouldn't run into me, and took a look around.

Caliente Base was like a miniature version of the Dulce Science Center. If the word miniature could be applied to a huge complex that went down ten stories and was who knew how wide. Someone knew, of course, that someone just wasn't me. I'd decided early on not to sweat the small stuff and the various bases' dimensions definitely fell on the "small stuff" side of the house for me.

We were in the main gate level for Caliente Base, which meant that, if memory served, we were one story under ground level. This level didn't have as many A-C bells and whistles as the rest of the base, but the impressive display of gates, computer banks, and Field agents made up for the lack of snazzy, high-tech equipment.

In the olden days of six months ago I'd have been worried, with good cause, that Rahmi and Rhee would have attacked the men. However, the princesses were actually fast learners, and they'd adjusted well to the fact that we had a lot of men around and most of them weren't evil or in need of a beating.

I let out the breath I'd been holding—there were a lot more than our team here. To a person, every face I could see looked worried. There was a face I wasn't expecting to see here, though. Said face was chatting with the princesses.

"Dad, what are you doing here?" I trotted over and gave him a hug.

"I was with Alfred when the trouble started," Dad said. "I asked to come with the agents who verified Caliente Base's gates were functional."

"And Alfred let you?"

Apparently I hadn't kept the shock and disapproval out of my tone, because Dad chuckled. "There was no risk, kitten."

Chose to refrain from explaining that there was likely a lot of risk. Dad was here, in one piece, and the troops needed me focused on the matters at hand, not to be asking why my father had suddenly decided he was Action Professor.

"No worries, Dad. When Jeff and Chuckie arrive, then you can tell them to go back home, and you can go back home with them."

"You told them to go to Congress," Christopher pointed out.

"I did. And did you notice that Jeff only argued a little and Chuckie didn't argue at all? I hope you don't think either one of them has actually decided to be a big boy and trust that I can handle things on my own, because that would be a ridiculous assumption on your part."

White laughed. "I noted that Charles passed a little sign to Jeffrey."

"I missed that, but good catch, Mister White. I made my assumption based on years of experience. Anyway, Dad, I expect them to give us a few minutes and then show up. Please let them know I'm not happy that they're here any more than I'm happy that you're here."

"Will do, kitten," Dad said with a sigh. "What's your plan?"

"I want to see if we can get to Home Base via a gate."

"I'll test it," Christopher said before anyone else could. "I'm the fastest and if the bounce back is what I expect, my speed will make it less of an issue. And if we have hostiles there waiting, again, I'm the fastest and they'll have the hardest time hitting me."

Chose not to argue. I didn't want Christopher hurt, but it had to be an A-C testing the transfer, and if there was a problem he was indeed the best guy for the job. Plus, he'd been a Commander for over a decade. "Go for it, just go with a weapon at the ready."

"And your phone on," Buchanan added. "Wear a Bluetooth and be in contact with us." He handed Christopher an earpiece.

"Where'd you get that?"

Buchanan gave me the "duh" look. "From the hackers. They've already paired the devices with everyone's phones." He slipped one on and handed out identical headsets to the rest of our team.

"Good thinking," I said as Buchanan gave me mine. Decided not to ask when he'd gotten these. Could have been while we were all talking, could have been days prior. Buchanan worked in those mysterious ways and I didn't have time or mental bandwidth to worry about said ways right now.

Christopher shot Buchanan Patented Glare #3, but acquiesced and put on the earpiece. My phone rang and I answered it. "Hello?"

"It's me," Christopher said, joining Buchanan in the Duh Experience. "Your bodyguard wanted me on with you, remember?"

"I was just being polite, geez. Carry on, and let's hope that whatever's on the other side isn't faster than you."

The gate was calibrated and Christopher stepped through. "I'm here," he said a second later. "No issues."

"We'll come over, then," I said.

"Wait and let me check the entire base out." We waited. I counted. A whole fifteen seconds went by. "No one's here. It's completely deserted." Good to know Christopher hadn't been wrong about his speed still being all that and an extra-large bag of chips.

"We're all coming, then. See if you can find us a jet that will hold the full team."

"Do I have to?"

"Yes. Would you rather run across a state to get there?"

"You're the only one around with a pilot's license. So the answer is 'yes.'"

"Ha ha ha, you're hilarious. Find a jet and be sure it's got a full tank of fuel. That's an order."

"Oh, yes ma'am. Hope your head can fit through the gate."

"Wow, I can't wait to get over there and hurt you. Stay on the line, just in case. And so you can hear me disparage you to everyone."

"You'd better hurry if you want to beat Jeff and Chuck."

He had a point, and we were both bantering because we were stalling. Decided to act like the Head of Field again and get the next phase of our plan going. "Okay, my team, let's get over to Home Base."

"What are you expecting over there, kitten?" Dad asked.

Saw no reason to lie and figured the troops here should probably know what was going on. "We think Ronaldo Al Dejahl is alive, well, and back in business. Clearly he has a hacker on staff now, because I don't buy that we got hacked at the level we've just experienced in a random coinkydink. And, since none of the weather services or military bases or NASA picked up a sandstorm big enough to make everyone at Home Base feel security training had to move to Dulce, he's probably also got someone who can create some seriously impressive illusions."

"I'm coming with you," Dad said. "And before you argue or order me to stay here, I need to remind you that there were only a few people who could hold out against his mind control, and I'm one of them."

Dad had a point, much as I didn't like it. Al Dejahl had expanded talents—he was an imageer and could create the illusion of being someone completely different, just like a shapeshifter. He also had troubadour talent and, as Dad had mentioned, he was really good with the mind control.

"Your father makes a strong argument," White said quietly. "Most of our team, you and me included, are untried against my 'brother's' mind control."

"We will guard him," Rahmi said. Rhee nodded enthusiastically.

I could argue and tell Dad to stay here, only he'd just convince someone to send him right behind us, my orders to the contrary or no. Or he'd wait and convince Jeff and Chuckie to bring him along. Better he was with me. If I chose to look at the term "better" to mean "lesser of a whole lot of evils."

Gave it one last gasp. "I don't think Mom would like it."

Dad chuckled and showed me his phone. He had a text from Mom. "Be careful and remember that Kitty's in charge. So be extra careful."

"Oh, Mom is just *hilarious*. Fine, fine, Rahmi and Rhee, protect my father, please and thank you. I guess that'll be eight more to head over to Home Base now," I said to the A-C doing gate duty.

He nodded. "We're ready, Commander. Do you want anyone else accompanying you?"

I'd been thinking about this. "No. But I do need to give instructions to whoever's in charge over here."

The A-Cs nearby looked at each other in an uncomfortable way. "Ah, the Base Leaders are all at the security training, Commander," the gate agent admitted finally.

A niggling worry crawled up. I looked at White. Was pretty sure he was having the same worry experience. "Okay," I said slowly. "So, when they're gone, who covers the leadership role? You're set up like every other military group on the planet, ergo, there's always someone in charge."

"Not really," Buchanan said quietly. "If you consider our military, once you have the officers out of commission, the enlisted men fracture into their groups under their sergeants."

"Sort of like *Under Siege*, got it."

"Under what?" Christopher asked in my ear.

"An old Steven Segal movie."

"Great. You're going to use that as your blueprint, aren't you?"

"Maybe." Totally. "Okay, I want whoever is in charge of the gates, whoever is in charge of military actions, and whoever's in charge of science and medicine within Caliente Base here in less than five seconds. I realize you're all thinking that said individuals are over at Dulce right now, so I want you to all either choose your representative or whoever's been doing the job the longest to show up."

"What about weapons?" Christopher asked.

"Request whatever you and Malcolm think we need. I've got my Glock in my purse, so I'm good."

While Christopher and Buchanan discussed armaments, three A-Cs appeared: two men, one woman, all extremely young. Not that A-Cs would, since alcohol was deadly to them, but I wasn't sure that these three could legitimately buy a drink, let alone enter a bar without being carded. To a one, they looked uncertain and like they didn't feel they should be hanging with me.

The Dazzler, who was typically gorgeous with long, curly, light brown hair and a perfect hourglass figure, cleared her throat. "You wanted us, Commander?"

"Names, ranks, serial numbers, please and thank you."

"Viola Sciacca," the Dazzler replied. "I'm in charge of the sciences right now." She didn't add, "I think", at least not out loud, but her expression said it plainly.

"Carmine Giordano," the taller male A-C said. As with all the clan, he was incredibly handsome, with a darker Mediterranean look going. "I've got Security, which includes the gates, Commander." He didn't look or sound nearly as uncertain as Viola, had, but he didn't sound ready to take charge, either.

"Romeo Ruggero," our last A-C shared. He was about Christopher's size and build, but unlike Carmine, he was on the fairer side. "I've got military actions right now, Commander. So to speak."

"What were you all told, when everyone else went off to the Security training?"

The three of them looked at each other. "Nothing," Viola said finally. "Just that everyone would be back later today and to carry on with our regular duties."

"None of us are actually in charge," Romeo added. "But our teams felt we were the most appropriate for who you were asking for, Commander."

"Gotcha. Okay, well, as of right now, you three *are* in charge here. Adapt your thinking and actions accordingly. You're the nearest base to where we're going, and therefore to where I expect a lot of bad things to be happening. Romeo, what's our military status here? As in, do we have jets, tanks, or weapons?"

He nodded. "Yes, but only a handful." He cleared his throat. "We don't have most of our human personnel, Commander. They were all sent to Home Base for the training."

A-Cs had reflexes that were so fast they couldn't safely operate human machinery. Meaning that a base without human personnel was a base that couldn't actually use any of its military vehicles.

Worry coalesced into certainty. I looked at White. "They chose their first target very well, didn't they?"

White nodded. "I think so, Missus Martini. But I don't know how they got to her."

"I don't either. But she gave in to Ronaldo's mind control last time, so it's not a leap to assume it's happened again." Looked at my three new Heads of Whatever. "Someone get me accessed to all our bases worldwide."

Carmine made a fast call. "You're on, Commander. Just speak normally, all personnel can hear you."

"This is Commander Katt-Martini, with an All Bases Alert. As of right now, you are to consider that Gladys Gower, the Head of A-C Security Worldwide, has been turned or captured. Repeat, as of right now, please consider Gladys Gower to be Centaurion Division Enemy Number One."

CHAPTER 20

THE COLLECTIVE GASP from the majority of the people around me was impressive. Figured the same was happening worldwide. Having Gladys compromised wasn't quite as bad as having all of Alpha and Airborne compromised, but it was close, and since they were all in trouble, we were officially at the definition of DEFCON Worse.

I carried on. "Do not respond to any of Gladys' directives. If you are responding to one right now, cease immediately and advise me and the Embassy of what said action was. If she, or anyone saying they have her authorization or orders, contacts you, you are to not respond or reply and to advise both me and the American Centaurion Embassy immediately."

William's voice came into my headset. "Ambassador, Mister Buchanan asked that I be hooked into your call with acting-Commander White."

"Good call." Chose not to comment about Christopher's new old title. For all I knew, I was going to have to reactivate Jeff, regardless of his current position within the U.S. government.

"Kitty, I could hear your announcement over here at Home Base," Christopher said, sounding worried. "Which means there's a good chance it was piped through to Dulce."

"No," William said. "I was on prior and coordinated, Commander White. I sent the directive to you at Home Base, but prevented it from going to Dulce."

"You rock, William."

"Thank you, Ambassador. Would you prefer that I call you Commander?"

"Nah, titles matter a lot more to Christopher than they do to me. Did you want to tell me something or just let me know you'd taken over being the Voice in the Sky?"

"I wanted to ask something and tell you something. Is the rest of your strike force on their headsets, Doctor Hernandez in particular?"

My team all verified they were on the group chat. "What do you need, William?" Tito asked.

"What Centaurion information do you have on your laptop, Doctor Hernandez?" William sounded like he was working to keep his voice very calm and measured. Which boded.

"Not that much, just medical information that relates to my job or the research I'm doing. Why?"

William cleared his throat. "Because if what's coming in from our bases is correct, we've lost all our data. And when I say 'all,' I mean every scrap of information we've had since we arrived on the planet."

"Today's just going to keep on sucking until it can't suck any more, isn't it?" I asked of no one in particular.

"Apparently," William replied. "Any orders, Ambassador?"

"Yeah. We need some humans who can fly things over at Caliente Base. I'm hesitant to pull in regular military help, mostly because we're so unclear on what's actually going on. But if my team needs backup, I'd like it to arrive via means other than a gate."

"We're unable to provide personnel status right now, Ambassador. We're still essentially offline."

"Fabulous." Contemplated my options. They seemed remarkably slim. "Okay, please ask Luke Air Force Base to get prepped and ready. Same for Miramar—we may need some Top Gun pilots again."

"This is sounding a lot like when you first joined us," Christopher said.

"Isn't it, though? William, please advise Colonel Franklin of what's going on, but ask him to refrain from sharing the information with anyone else. Same with my Uncle Mort. I'd like the Marines standing by, but not deployed as of yet."

"On it, Ambassador."

"Good man. My team, start heading through the gate and join Christopher. Viola, Carmine, Romeo, get together who and what you can to support us. Romeo, that's going to fall on you the most, but I expect the other two to help you. You three need to work like a team, and I don't care that you probably haven't had to do so previously. We thrive on on-the-job training around here."

The three of them nodded. "We've gotten the weapons request from Mister Buchanan," Romeo said. "Sending over to Commander White right now."

"And I have whatever else we wanted here," Christopher added.

"What about Field teams?" Viola asked.

"I really don't want to throw more of our people at the problem until we know they won't be affected by whatever's going on over at Dulce. Get them prepped and ready, but as with human military, they're on hold until we ask for them."

Everyone other than White and Buchanan were through the gate. "Anything else, Ambassador?"

"Yeah. Pull in Mister Joel Oliver. Have him, and Len and Kyle if necessary, see what he can get out of Olga."

"Grandmother told me I was needed, but not much else," Adriana shared. "I believe she will want Len and Kyle to visit along with Mister Joel."

Chose not to mention that she was now on a sort of first name basis with our favorite investigative journalist. Oliver had been bumped up from the ranks of the Loser Paparazzi to Our Man With The Insider Knowledge after Operation Invasion. He still wasn't used to the love from the general populace, but he was one of the few people I knew we could trust. Apparently Olga felt the same way.

"Super. Oh, and William, please ask our friends at the Israeli and Bahraini Embassies to also be on standby." Who knew if we'd need Mossad or Bahraini Royal Army support? Besides, they were all human and that meant they could all operate the machinery. And they were our friends. Had a strong feeling we were going to need all our friends shortly.

"Ready, Missus Martini?"

"Born that way, or some such, Mister White."

White headed through the gate. "William, get Viola, Carmine, and Romeo onto our group-speak. Malcolm, after you."

He shook his head. "No." He looked at the gate agent. "Calibrate for two." The agent did so, then Buchanan put his arm around me and held me tightly. "Mister Former Chief may not like it, but we can't afford to have you tossing your cookies right now."

With that, he stepped us through.

It only took a second, but I began to gag almost immediately. Buchanan held me tighter. It helped. My foot hit terra firma and the nausea started to subside. "That was awful," I said when I could finally talk again.

We were in the middle of a big hangar that doubled as Home Base Command Central. As Christopher had said, we were the only people here. There was an impressive pile of weapons and ammunition nearby. We were armed for a lot of bear. Of course, they were probably armed for a lot of us, too.

Buchanan ignored Christopher's glaring. "William, we need whoever can verify gate functionality. The Ambassador's weakness with the gates is known, especially to those higher up the food chain. The transfer felt . . . stronger to me than the one from the Embassy. Assume the gates have been tampered with, and don't allow any other personnel to go through them until we have confirmation they're all working properly."

"Really?" I asked. "The Dome is secure."

"But the person who would give the Dome orders is believed to have been turned," Buchanan said patiently.

"He's got a point," Christopher said, as my stomach finally settled and Buchanan let go of me. "The gate felt a little odd to me, too. Only the one coming into Home Base."

"Great, more good news. Anything else?"

"I've found a plane. I want to be on record that I hope either Buchanan, Tito, or Adriana can pilot it."

"I can't," Tito said calmly. "I've taken a few lessons, because Tim insisted, but I'm a last resort."

"I can fly, but Missus Chief has a higher pilot's ranking than I do. Or than Adriana does," Buchanan added with a grin.

She nodded. "I am with the doctor. I'm a last resort, not the first choice."

"Four jets would give us a better chance," White said thoughtfully.

"You expect us to get shot down again?" Christopher asked.

"Yeah, your dad's right, I think it's a possibility."

Christopher zipped off and was back laden with what looked like parachutes. "Put these on. Regardless of who's flying the plane or planes."

They were parachutes. I wanted to be offended, but the intelligence behind the idea was too strong. "Good plan."

"This isn't a plan, Kitty. This is a hope for survival."

"You say tomato, I say tomahto."

"Let's call the whole thing off," Dad chimed in, as he put his parachute on. "I'm flying with you, kitten, whether we're in one plane or four."

"Why don't we go in two?" Buchanan suggested. "I'll take Doctor Hernandez, Adriana, you go with the Ambassador. And before you ask, Missus Chief, I'm the best pilot after you."

"No argument, Malcolm. But I have a better idea."

"Really? I'm sure you and Former Pontifex White are correct—they're going to attempt to shoot us down."

"They might. But not if they can't see us coming."

CHAPTER 21

EVERYONE STARED AT ME. "Mind explaining that?" Christopher asked. "There are no stealth fighters on base, at least not that I found."

"Stealth planes only hold, at most, a crew of two. However, if we have a plane that's set up for either air or desert camouflage, that would work."

"I'll look again, but I didn't see any," Christopher said.

"Not a problem. William, please contact Colonel Franklin and ask him where Home Base keeps their painting supplies."

"You've got to be kidding," Christopher said. "We can't paint a plane."

"Why not? You, your dad, and our princesses all have hyperspeed. It doesn't have to be a perfect paint job, just enough of one to give us a little extra time."

Tito held out his phone. "I've looked up what it should look like. I think we should go for air camouflage, since once we're on the ground, it's a different set of problems."

"This is unreal. Why didn't you have this done before we got here?"

"By you alone, Christopher? I'm giving you a painting team. That's efficiency, that is."

Buchanan gave Christopher a look I could only think of as derisive. "How did you manage to get anything done before Missus Chief arrived? Or did you argue with your cousin's decisions a little less than you do hers?"

"William's advised me of where the painting supplies are stored," White said, hopefully preventing a full on fight between Christopher and Buchanan. "I'm sure the princesses and I can manage without you, son."

Christopher threw his hands up. "Fine! Far be it for me to suggest we need to hurry up."

"We'll be back in a flash," White said reassuringly.

"Take me along," Tito said before they could leave. "I'll oversee the paint job."

"I wouldn't miss it for the world," Dad added.

"Works for me."

"Of course it does," Christopher muttered as he shot Patented Glare #2 at all of us, me and Tito in particular.

"Take all our impressive guns and rocket launchers and stuff with you." This earned me Patented Glare #4 from Christopher, but White and the princesses picked things up, and Christopher followed suit. They all zipped off, came back, got the rest of the supplies and zipped off again.

When they returned, White was holding a couple of books. "I found the manuals for the plane Christopher's chosen. He and I can read them after we're done altering it to your specifications, Missus Martini." Then Rahmi took Tito's hand, White took Dad's, and the six of them disappeared.

I'd have been worried about the hyperspeed effect on Dad, but he'd started taking Tito's Hyperspeed Dramamine, too. Along with everyone else who worked with us, including my mother and all of the P.T.C.U., Mr. Joel Oliver and Adriana also had their own prescriptions, because, as Olga put it, they preferred to be prepared. Everyone was all for dramatically reducing the barfing your guts out part of the Human Hyperspeed Experience.

"Is Once-Again-Commander White always that much of a pain in the ass?" Buchanan asked me.

"Only when he's really stressed and trying not to show it." Adriana laughed. "Men."

"You said it. Present company excepted, Malcolm."

"Thanks, Missus Chief, I'm touched."

Rhee returned, smudged with some blue and white paint. "It's ready. The Great Tito's example was easy to follow and, as expected, he ensured all was done perfectly."

Rahmi and Rhee had the biggest case of hero worship ever recorded, all focused on Tito. We still weren't sure what their mother had told them about us in general and Tito in particular, but whatever it was, both princesses insisted on referring to him as either the Great Tito or Tito the Great. I found this cute and funny. Tito found it embarrassing. The other men found it jealousy-inducing, simply because Tito was the only male who never had to worry about how our resident Amazons would react around him.

Considering they'd finished in less than two minutes, I doubted Tito had done much other than crack wise at Christopher, but discretion was still the better part of valor and I chose to keep this to myself.

Rhee took my hand, I grabbed Buchanan, he grabbed Adriana, and we zipped off.

The smell of wet paint announced we'd reached our aircraft. Just hoped we wouldn't all get high from the fumes. But sacrifices had to be made, and the reward was going to hopefully be worth the risk.

Jerry Tucker, my favorite flyboy and flight instructor, had made sure I could fly any and every airplane available within Centaurion Division or housed at Home Base. Therefore, I could fly the aircraft Christopher had chosen.

Unfortunately, due to the number of people with us, he'd had to choose an aircraft made more for carrying things than maneuverability.

"Is that a B-Fifty-Two Stratofortress?" Adriana asked. She sounded underwhelmed.

"Yes. Or, as I know you know we call it, a BUFF." It wasn't the sleekest aircraft in the world, but it looked great—big, blue, white, and gray, not nearly as fugly as the flyboys all insisted these planes were.

"Buff?" Christopher asked.

"Big Ugly Flying Fugly."

"It looks slow," Christopher said. "And not all that maneuverable. But it was all I could find that would hold all of us."

"And Christopher and I have both read the operations manuals while we were waiting for Rhee to retrieve the rest of you," White added. Hyperspeed was great for so many things. "So while we can't operate anything, we can advise."

"Excellent and good thinking, Mister White. Additionally on the plus side, I can fly this puppy. And it looks better with the paint job, too. So it's at least three for the win column. Let's get in and get our flock over to Dodge. We have a shoot-out of some kind I'm sure we're late for."

CHAPTER 22

BUCHANAN WAS ACTING AS MY COPILOT, with Dad sitting in as navigator, Tito filling in as bombardier, and Adriana covering the electronic warfare station. I'd flown a BUFF before, so I didn't need White and Christopher's help, so they were backing Tito and Adriana.

Wasn't sure that we'd need to drop bombs or deal with threats in the air, but the bombs were already loaded into the B-52's belly, Tito and Adriana seemed calm about their assigned roles, White and Christopher appeared to actually have understood everything they'd speed-read, and I figured we might as well go in armed for bear.

Buchanan and I couldn't wear our parachutes while we were in the pilot and copilot's chairs. They were nearby, on either side of my purse, but if we were hit, he and I would have to move quickly. Chose to believe we wouldn't be hit. Told myself I'd grab the parachute first and my purse second. Was glad Jeff wasn't nearby to call me a liar.

Unlike the takeoff I'd had to do way back when, this plane required taxiing down a runway. Also unlike that first takeoff, I was in good shape with this one.

"Why are you plugging in your iPod?" Dad asked, as I handed my musical gear to Buchanan.

"Really? Because it's me and I fly better with tunes going. Under the circumstances, we're going with Mötley Crüe. Malcolm, roll their *Saints of Los Angeles* album."

Christopher joined us as the rocking sounds of my favorite L.A. band filled the airwaves. They weren't Aerosmith, but sometimes a girl needed a change. "Seriously? Music? Now?"

"You want to pilot this puppy? No? Then go back and help Tito and Adriana."

"We're going to die, you know," Christopher said.

"Not today." Well, not if I could help it. "William, you still with us?"

"Yes, Ambassador."

"We're all about to turn our phones off. When Jeff and Chuckie try to follow us, be sure they take a maneuverable jet, okay?"

"You're certain they'll be going there?"

"As certain as I am that the next few minutes are going to redefine the term 'bumpy ride.'"

"Signing off, Ambassador. Call if you need us."

"Okay, gang, phones and earpieces off, headsets for the plane on. Let's strap in, we're heading for Dulce."

The takeoff wasn't my best ever—I hadn't flown anything for a while—but it was like riding a bike and came back to me quickly. Of course, when you fell off a bike you only went a couple of feet and usually weren't likely to die. Did what Jerry had taught me and focused on the positives, even though "Face Down In the Dirt" was on. We'd be fine.

"Kitten, should your head be bobbing like that?" Dad asked.

"It's called head-banging, Dad. And, again, I fly better this way."

"That's open to debate."

"Everyone's a critic."

"We're at cruising altitude," Buchanan said calmly, as I leveled us off. "Well done, Missus Chief."

"See? Someone took the Washington Wife class and understands that support is necessary and helpful. Speaking of helpful, Dad, a little navigational support wouldn't be turned away."

"Hmmm . . . head east."

"No, really? Head east where? I need a heading and so forth."

"I can navigate us, Missus Chief."

"Thank God."

"Has Kitty gotten us lost already?" Christopher asked.

"I don't recall saying we should have the group communications line open."

"I thought it would be better, kitten."

"Thanks ever, Dad."

"Focus," Buchanan said calmly. "You're letting the nose drop."

"It makes the ride more interesting for those of us in the back," Tito shared. The rest of the crew, princesses included, took this as their cue to add in. It was a party on our airwaves in record time. The only positive was that Adriana shared she was fairly sure she'd figured out how to activate the various jamming technology at her disposal, thanks to White's instructions.

"It's a good thing I can handle a lot of distractions while flying a big plane loaded with weapons and bombs."

"That's why you're the woman for the job, Missus Martini."

"Thanks, Rick honey. Remind me to hurt you later." So, bickering, complaining, and joking, we headed for Dulce, accompanied by the Crüe's "White Trash Circus."

The weather was great, so we hit no air pockets. Jerry had trained me to handle them, but the B-52 was a lot bigger and heavier than the jets I'd spent more time in, so the less stress the elements gave me, the better.

The BUFF wasn't supersonic, but Dulce wasn't that far from Home Base, so we arrived in good time. Of course, once you were in the air, it was relatively easy. Takeoffs were hard, but they were nothing compared to landings. Landings were hard in the best of circumstances. I knew without asking that I wasn't going to have the best circumstances available when I wanted to put us safely on the ground.

"We're closing in," Buchanan said. "Are you able to control the aircraft if we're lower?"

"Yeah." Jerry had prepared me for all eventualities, including flying low under the radar, so to speak. I dropped our altitude, but carefully. There were only a few complaints from the peanut gallery.

From the air, Dulce looked like a very boring installation

doing nothing in the middle of nowhere. I'd learned early on that the more boring and inconsequential a building looked, the more likely it was to be housing things of the most supreme importance and secrecy.

As I'd also learned early on, Dulce had ground-to-air missiles. Camouflaged or not, our jamming systems working correctly or not, I had to figure someone was going to fire on us soon. However, there were other things of interest on the ground.

"Kitty, I see what looks like a dust devil forming," Tito shared.

"Yeah, we see it, too. I think dust giant might be a more apt description though."

"There's no way that's natural," Dad said. "The formation is wrong and there are no signs of high winds."

"Someone back there in the bombardier area see if you can identify who or what is causing the dust storm that looks more like a tornado."

Tornados were so uncommon in Arizona and New Mexico as to be almost unheard of. This combined with Dad's correct observation about the lack of high winds and the prior knowledge that a "dust storm" had moved everyone from Home Base to Dulce pretty much ensured this was man-, or more likely, alien-made.

Which begged another question. "Is it real, can anyone tell? I was thinking that someone on Al Dejahl's team might be creating an illusion."

"There are desert plants being pulled and shoved in a way that indicates there are real winds down there, Missus Martini."

"So, they have a weather witch on their team?" We were the X-Men. If there was a Storm character hanging about, by all rights she should be on our side. Of course, that was the comics and this was my real life. Of course the bad guys had a weather witch, or warlock, on staff.

"Not sure," Christopher said. "But I agree with my dad, it looks very real, based on what's happening around and because of the dust storm."

Said dust storm was definitely coming at us. I tried to fly around it, but it caught up quickly. Wasn't sure if that was normal, but since I'd outrun a few big dust storms in my Lexus IS 300, which, while fast, wasn't up to airplane speeds, had to figure the dust storm was unnatural and definitely out to get us.

The outer edge of the dust devil hit us. Sure enough, it was real enough to toss us around. I managed to pull up and away, amid a lot of cursing from the back, along with a tremendous amount of bickering. "I think we've figured it out," Tito said finally. "Glad Adriana's along and that Richard is a speed-reader of the highest order."

"That last shake you gave us really helped," Rahmi said. Apparently the princesses were learning sarcasm. Had no idea who'd been teaching them that skill.

"I'm not positive, but there is what appears to be a tank," Adriana shared. "I believe someone is standing on it. The dust storm's activity suggests it's emanating from the same area as the tank."

"What kind of training do you have?" Buchanan asked. "The Former Pontifex and Commander having read the manuals or not, I'm impressed any of you can work this equipment."

"She's gone to a really good espionage school. Probably the same one you went to, or close to it, Malcolm." Contemplated our options. "I wish I knew, for certain, if the tank had all hostiles in it or not."

"We're at war," Buchanan said quietly.

"But I don't want our side hit by friendly fire."

"Kitty, stop worrying about that!" Christopher sounded stressed. "It's now exactly like last time—somehow, that dust storm is firing on us."

CHAPTER 23

"WHY IS IT NEVER EASY?" I asked of no one other than the cosmos. "Adriana, in the words of one of my favorite rappers, bombs away." Considered asking Buchanan to switch the music to B.o.B.'s "Bombs Away," but decided the Crüe's "MF of the Year" was plenty good enough. I was quick-thinking that way.

"You have to help," Christopher said. "Get us over the target."

"What *is* the target?"

"The center of the storm," Buchanan said, as a huge hunk of dirt splattered onto our windshield. "Are they firing dirt clods or actual artillery?"

"Both," Adriana shared.

"We need to hit the tank, then, Missus Chief."

"The tank is still within the tornado," Adriana confirmed.

"Great. Enjoy the upcoming turbulence."

While more interesting and impressive cursing emanated from my crew, I focused on both getting over our so-called target and avoiding being shot down. Always easier said than done.

The BUFF wasn't made for a lot of fancy maneuvers. It was made to go long distances carrying a lot of firepower. Also, flying this close to the ground gave me less safe maneuverability.

"Firing," Tito said. "Hold on."

The bomber shook a little. "Malcolm, up higher or land?"

"Higher. The tornado's heading for us again."

"So are more projectiles," Christopher shared.

I pulled back hard on the stick and took us up. The interesting cursing increased. Our team was really well-versed in swearing. While I was clear on the words the menfolk were using, I wasn't sure what the princesses or Adriana were actually saying, but they got the gist of it across clearly.

"We missed the tank, but hit close enough that the tornado has stopped," Tito shared. "So we affected whoever was creating the dust storm. We didn't drop a nuclear warhead, by the way."

"Um, does that mean we have a nuclear warhead with us?"

"Several," Tito replied.

"Fantastic."

No sooner was this out of my mouth than things got more fantastic. The BUFF shook and the sound of rending metal hit our airwaves.

"We've been hit!" Christopher shared, as the plane started to shake and tried very hard to pull the stick out of my hands.

"Somewhere in the back," White added.

"Shot came from the tank," Tito confirmed.

"Apparently the tank is very well made," Dad said. Calmly. Someone had to be calm. Was glad Dad had volunteered. That way I didn't have to pretend I was the calm one.

The BUFF was, unsurprisingly, having problems. Getting hit with whatever tanks hit you with wasn't easy for anything. As I tried to get the plane back under control, the dust storm returned. So whoever we'd knocked down had gotten right back up again. Always the way.

We were encircled within moments. The wind was trying its best to spin us around, while the dirt and sand and flying flora were making it close to impossible to see. I was trained on using the instruments, of course, but seeing was a nice addition, especially when there were mountain ranges nearby and while trying to land.

"The tank is firing again," Tito said.

"Dive left," Adriana ordered.

Managed it, but not because of any great flying skill. The dust storm happened to whip us the correct way. Didn't figure that was going to happen a second time. "Time to land! The captain requests seat-backs and tray tables up."

"Where are we going?" Buchanan asked.

"Down, out of this storm, and away from that tank. We can use hyperspeed to get back if, you know, any of us survive the landing."

"The warheads aren't armed," Tito said. "Should we bail out or can you land us, Kitty?"

"Do we want to parachute out in the middle of a tornado?" Christopher asked.

"I'd love to land." In part because this was a hella expensive plane and I didn't want to see what the repair bill would be. On the other hand, it was replaceable and the same couldn't be said for anyone on board. "But, tornado or not, you'd better bail out."

"You need to bail out, too," Buchanan said sternly.

"We all do."

He shook his head. "I'll take it from here."

"Malcolm, are you insane? I'm the best pilot in the plane, you said so yourself."

"Yes, but you're also not going to be able to land this thing." He looked at my father. "Help me get her out."

"We all go," Dad said firmly. "Angela wouldn't want you to die in a fiery plane crash, especially since that would mean you weren't around to protect Kitty."

"There's a weird logic in all that. Everyone needs to bail while we're high enough up that the parachutes have time to open." Managed to escape the storm. "Okay, gang, the windshield's filthy but I can see well enough to land us or continue flying so everyone can jump. Decision time right now."

"Too late," Tito shared. "We're too low. I can see the ground too clearly, and we can't risk taking another hit. Kitty, you need to land the plane."

"Everyone strap in! Assume crash positions!" I barked the orders but somehow felt calm. There was now no option to jump out, so the heck with that idea. And this way, I wouldn't lose my iPod.

My crew were talking, saying goodbye, ensuring they were all strapped in. But I ignored them and instead channeled Jerry and pretended I heard his voice in my ear. As

"Going Out Swingin'" came on, I relaxed and focused on the basics.

Landing gear down, wings as steady as possible, altitude in a controlled drop. The desert around Dulce was basically flat, so no worries about finding a landing strip.

We got closer to the ground and the plane started to shake even more. But I had enhanced strength these days, and I could keep the stick under control.

"I love you, Kitty. Any last words?" Dad asked. "Just in case."

"I love you, too, Dad. And, yeah. Once we're down, I'm going to find whoever shot at us and seriously kick their ass."

"Interesting last words," Buchanan said.

"Like those?" I asked through gritted teeth as the ground rose up to meet us. "Got a couple more for you. Everyone hold on!"

CHAPTER 24

I HEARD JERRY AGAIN, clear as day. Telling me to keep control of my big bird, to pull back gently on the stick while I applied the brakes, and all other sorts of relevant flying dos and don'ts.

The wheels hit first, which was a wonderful thing. Of course we bounced, because there couldn't be a landing of mine with someone else in the plane that was smooth and uneventful. I only scored perfect landings when I was alone and had no witnesses anywhere nearby.

We bounced a lot and the BUFF didn't seem to actually want to slow down. I had to be careful about braking, however, because if I broke too hard we could flip.

From above the ground had looked completely flat. Now that we were skidding along it, flat wasn't really the operative word. Bumpy was much more accurate. I tried to ignore all the cacti we were running over. Figured any desert animals had already scampered off when they heard us coming.

After what seemed like an eternity, the plane started to actually slow down. Which was good because that was when I saw the outcropping of rocks we were headed straight for.

Tried to turn the big beast, but it wasn't having any of that, meaning the tank had probably damaged our rear fuselage. We hit the rocks, and while we were going slower than we had been, we were at a rate fast enough to ensure that when we slammed into the rocks, they slammed us right back.

"What just happened?" Christopher shouted as we did a

big bounce and, landing gear messed up, started to skid and spin.

"We fought the rocks and the rocks won." I was speaking through gritted teeth still because I was now fighting to keep us from flipping again, this time side to side. We'd lost part of the landing gear, but, based on the fun tilt we had going, at least one wheel on the left was still intact.

The BUFF decided that, with one wing up and one wing down, going into an uncontrolled spin sounded like the most fun ever. There was a lot of noise coming from my crew. Hoped Tito wasn't hurt because it sounded like others were.

The wing that was brushing the ground hit those damn rocks again. They were sharp, evil, desert rocks that had apparently been waiting for us and honing their rock skills since the time of the dinosaurs. They sheared the tip of the wing off. So much for my hope of returning the plane intact. Went back to hoping I'd return all the passengers intact and call it good.

We spun for a few more long, excruciating seconds. Then I could tell the BUFF's speed was slowing. Oh sure, we hit the rocks a few more times, ensuring the clipped wing was also now bent and something ugly had again happened to the rear, but still, we were slowing.

In what seemed like forever but was really only about a minute later, the plane came to a lazy stop. We were facing Dulce, meaning our butt was on the rocks. Good. Wondered if there was a way to make the BUFF do a plane-fart onto my newest inanimate enemies. Figured I'd have to table that goal for a while.

I knew we were looking toward the Science Center only because I could see a dust storm in the distance and took the location as a given. The dust storm looked far away, but it also appeared to be heading toward us.

"Let's get out of this plane, just in case," I said as I took my headset off, grabbed my iPod, shoved it back into my purse, and put my purse strap over my head. I felt shaken up, but not hurt.

Buchanan helped Dad up and out. Miraculously, they both seemed unharmed.

We joined the rest of the crew in the bombardier area. The

exit was blocked due to our landing position, naturally, but the princesses activated their battle staffs and used the glowing laser ends to create a new door by slicing through the side of the plane.

Everyone out and in the sunlight, Tito did a fast medical inspection. There were a few cuts and bruises, but really, everyone looked remarkably okay.

"Well, any crash you can walk away from. And all that."

Christopher graced me with Patented Glare #5. "Why is every flight with you like this? Actually, I take that back. You landed better the first time than you did now."

"Again, I point out that we're alive and well and reasonably unscathed. Why so tense, Christopher? Too much caffeine?"

"I think we need to pay attention to the storm," White said, pointing toward the dust. The wall of dust. It was definitely heading toward us at a slow but steady rate.

We all stared at it. "Um, gang? I have a great, new idea. Let's get back in the plane."

"Can we fight whatever's causing this from inside the plane?" Rahmi asked.

Refrained from making a snide comment. Beta Twelve was a warrior planet, and their natural, instinctive response was to fight. Wasn't sure if any of them even had a flight response, but if they did, it was low on their reflex totem pole.

"It's pretty hard to fight blowing sand and dust. It tends to win, while it's removing your skin and blinding you."

"The rate of speed of the storm indicates the storm's creator is in or on the tank," Buchanan said.

"They are undoubtedly not out of ammunition," Adriana added.

"Meaning we'd be sitting ducks inside the plane. But we're just moving targets outside of it, and I'm sure the tank's carrying more than just its cannon. The more to shoot at us in exciting ways kind of thing."

"We should be able to outrun it," Christopher said. "At least, I can. I can take the rest of you along with me."

One of the nice things about hyperspeed was that you only had to be holding onto the person with it in order for it to carry you along as well. The downside of Christopher's extra-speedy with a side of fast hyperspeed was that it affected A-Cs just like regular hyperspeed affected humans, and the Hyperspeed Dramamine wasn't any help, either. Wasn't sure that throwing up was the best plan to fight whoever we had to face. But maybe we could throw up *on* them, and that would be a good start.

"Malcolm, what do you think?"

"I think there are weapons in this plane that can be used against us."

"Um, super. Does that mean we leave it or defend it to our dying breaths?"

"You're the one in charge," Christopher snapped. "Make a decision."

"A wise leader always considers her options," Rhee said, shooting Christopher a look that shared she was willing to fight him to prove this point.

"This leader would like to get some actual advice. Someone feel free to chime in." Before anyone could, my phone rang. Dug it out. "Jeff, now's not a super-duper time."

"Leave the plane. Whoever's after you is feeling remarkably triumphant. They're after you, not the weapons."

"I knew you and Chuckie weren't really going to do what I told you."

"I officially reinstated myself as part of Alpha Team. Congressional decree and everything. Pierre, Chuck, and the jocks were witnesses."

"Fabulous. Where are you?"

"At Home Base. Using a floater gate to get to you. I'd rather get to you on the other side of the sandstorm."

"Gotcha. I'll call you back." Hung up and dropped my phone back into my purse. "We're doing Christopher's plan per Commander Martini."

"You going to put your husband back as Head of Field?" Buchanan asked.

"He's already done it himself, so yeah. Besides, I'm more used to hearing his orders and disobeying them than the other way around."

"We may have a challenge getting around the storm," White said. "The dust storm seems to be expanding."

This was true—the storm was a lot wider than it had been

only a minute earlier, and it wasn't simply a trick of perspective. Whoever was creating this stuff had some serious skills.

"We can run through it as easily as around it," Christopher said. "We should be fast enough that we won't be hurt as long as everyone keeps their eyes closed."

"Should be?" Tito asked. "I don't have enough medical with me to handle being flayed alive, and we can't expect help from the Science Center."

"Real warriors understand the risks," Rhee said timidly. The timid was only because she was arguing with The Great Tito. Had Christopher said the same thing, Rhee would probably have already started kicking his butt.

"There's smart risk and dumb risk," Tito said. "We want to be sure we only take smart risks."

"Being inside the plane would mean we have protection," Adriana said. "But it will also mean we're trapped."

White disappeared but was back quickly, loaded with weapons. "We'll need these, I'm sure, whether we stay or go."

While White went and got another few armloads of our available weapons and the rest of us armed ourselves. While White and Christopher put back anything we weren't able to take along, I contemplated our options.

Staying with the downed plane was the right choice if we were in the middle of nowhere and were hoping to be rescued. Jeff and Chuckie were on their way, so rescue was possible. However, they'd specifically requested we get closer to the Science Center.

Christopher was the fastest thing on the planet, though the dust storm seemed to be trying to make it to the Number Two slot. Made the executive decision. "We're going to go for it, gang. But first, Mister White, we need a parachute."

He took off the chute he was wearing. "Yes?"

"We need sizeable strips so we can wrap our faces and any exposed skin." Cocked an eye toward the impending storm. "And we need do to all this fast."

"Good thinking," Dad said proudly, as White and Christopher ripped up a parachute as requested and Buchanan had the princesses use their intact parachutes to wrap themselves up. The *Xena: Warrior Princess* look was one everyone from

Beta Twelve favored, especially when going into battle, but it wasn't a great choice when running through a sandstorm.

"Everyone ready?" I asked as I wrapped my parachute around my face, leaving only a small slit where I could see.

Got the requisite replies from everyone other than Christopher. "Son," White said patiently, "you need to cover up, too. Speed may just mean our skin flays off that much faster, yours included."

"That's an order," I said before Christopher could argue. "And I still outrank you, so just do it. Remember to wrap everything, nose and mouth, and most of your eyes, too."

"The material is thin enough that I think we can wrap our eyes and still be able to see," Buchanan said. "And we should do so, even if we can't see, because if we get hit with too much sand there, there won't be anything Doctor Hernandez can do to bring our vision back."

"Wrap your hands, too," Tito added as he did so. "Not so much that you can't hold on, but every little bit of exposed skin being covered is going to help."

The storm wasn't too far away when the team was finally fully wrapped. Buchanan was right—one layer of the parachute was thin enough to see through, so to speak. Veiled eyes or not, what was headed for us didn't really look like a storm. It looked like a wall, a very thick, impenetrable wall, of dirt, sand, and God knew what else.

Of course, if I ignored the situation, the rest of what I could see was fairly humorous—we looked like we were trying out for RuPaul's Mummy Drag Race, Rahmi and Rhee especially. Adriana looked the best of all of us, but that was a perfect example of damning with faint praise. Chose not to mention any of this. Morale was bad enough already.

"Join hands, don't let go of your partners no matter what, and remember to keep your eyes closed. We're going to go a lot faster than any of you are actually prepared for."

I zipped up my hoodie and put the hood on, grabbed Buchanan and my dad, the rest of us formed a daisy chain with White at the end, and Christopher took off.

CHAPTER 25

WHILE I LOVED THE RESULTS, and anything was better than going through a gate, hyperspeed had never been my favorite thing to experience as a full human.

When I'd become a sorta A-C, I'd figured hyperspeed issues were a thing of the past for me. But that was before I'd run around with Christopher going at his I'm The Real Flash, Baby level.

Doing this speed made regular A-Cs like White sick to their stomachs. Doing this speed with eyes closed was exponentially worse.

"Keep your eyes shut!" I managed to shout. I wanted to open my eyes, so had to assume everyone else did, too. Figured the next sounds I'd be making were those related to barfing my guts out.

"And your mouths," Christopher called. "We're about to hit."

Hit was absolutely the accurate word. Sandpaper isn't fun to rub against your skin. I was incredibly thankful we'd wrapped up. Looking like mummy fashion victims was worth not having desert sand imbedded in our skin forever.

We were still moving nauseatingly fast, but the sand just wasn't going bye-bye. Took a couple of small rocks to the stomach and broke my own rule and opened my eyes a bit.

To see something dark and metallic in front of me.

We were still in our daisy chain formation, but that didn't mean we were running single file. Based on both experience and what little I could make out in my peripheral vision, such as it was, we were more serpentine, with me in the middle, and with no one actually behind Christopher. Meaning he had no idea we were near the tank.

I'd always had good reflexes and being on the track team all through high school and college while also doing Kung Fu had helped hone said reflexes. Reflexes could get you into trouble, of course, but there was a lot to be said for not taking the time to think in certain situations.

I shoved Dad one way and Buchanan the other, as I let go of their hands. "Get out of the way!" I shouted, so they'd be clear that I'd done this on purpose. "Christopher and Richard, keep moving!"

Momentum ensured I was still moving forward at a rapid pace, meaning I had two options. Slam into the tank in front of me, or jump. I jumped.

As with many other physical abilities, A-C's had improved jumping from humans and my track coaches had ensured all of us could do pretty much every event. I'd been okay with the high jump, which was good. The tank's cannon being right above me wasn't that great, but I managed to grab it as opposed to slam my head into it, so I counted that for the win column.

Used the still-existent momentum to swing up and onto the top of the tank. Almost fell off, but grabbed a hold of the person who was already there and used them to steady myself.

Whoever it was, they were as surprised by me as I'd been to see the tank in front of my face.

"Ack!" It wasn't the most terrifying war cry, but it did confirm that the person, who was in a buff-colored cloak-burka combo and was far better wrapped up than any of my team, was most likely female or a very young male.

The positive of scaring the hell out of my opponent was that the sandstorm stopped immediately. The positive of all of this scaring the hell out of me was that my nausea was kept at bay. Another one for the win column.

Wasn't sure where my team was, but I hoped far away and not under the tank's tread. Being under the tread was possible because the tank was still moving. Whether this meant there was a driver inside I was going to have to deal with, or whether the thing was on its version of autopilot, I had no guess. Decided to deal with the enemy I was holding onto and worry about the rest later.

Slammed my fist into what I hoped was her gut. "Oof!" She was big on the one-syllable responses, but that worked just fine for me.

Decided to go for the gusto and slammed her head into my rising knee. Grabbed her head, or at least the fabric covering her head, and hit her again.

She was sort of down but not, unfortunately, completely out. She grabbed my leg and pulled. I fell backward. Tucked my head as I went down so it didn't hit the metal. My opponent jumped on me and tried to do ground and pound. Well, tank and pound.

Grabbed her arms at the wrists and held her off. Wished Tito was near enough to shout coaching instructions. But he was either still running or barfing his guts out, meaning it was up to me to get this chick under control pronto.

Kicked my leg up while I shoved her back. Slammed my knee into her back and, because I'd shoved her arms back sharply enough, her head fell back into my toes. Wished my Kung Fu instructors were around to see this performance, because it was hard and rare to pull this move off. But, of course, when I was really showing off the awesome skills, the only witness was the person I was using said skills on.

She fell forward onto me, but I managed to shift to the side, so she slammed onto the tank. By now, if someone was inside, they'd had to have guessed there was a fight going on outside. Since the tank was still moving, hoped this meant it was on autopilot.

Managed to roll on top of her and take her back. I wasn't particularly great with the various choke-out techniques available, but the old arm around the neck and tighten ploy seemed to be working.

"Kitty," Christopher shouted. "Get off! The tank's heading right for the plane."

Looked up to see that, yes indeed, we were going to hit the jet very soon. In fact, the tank was likely going to hit the jet's fuel tank. Which was likely to redefine the term "very bad."

Let go of my opponent and got to my feet. Dragged her upright and, holding onto her, jumped us both off. Sure, I used her as my soft landing, but still, that seemed only fair. Plus it ensured that, finally, I knocked her out.

Christopher dragged me to my feet, we each took an arm, and ran like hell. He wasn't using the fast hyperspeed. In fact, he wasn't really using hyperspeed at all, meaning he'd potentially burned himself out. It wasn't a long trip from super-duper power level burnout to total burnout, as my time with Jeff had amply illustrated. Wasn't sure how Christopher would react to an adrenaline harpoon to the hearts, and sincerely hoped I wouldn't need to find out.

I heard the sound of rending metal behind me. Runners, sprinters in particular, are taught early on not to look behind them during a race. The runner who looks behind is the runner who *is* behind. Chose to speed up and use my hyperspeed.

Almost flew by the others, but managed to stop reasonably close by. They were near to, but not quite at the doors of, the Science Center.

"Everybody down!" Christopher shouted.

The team didn't argue. Everyone hit the dirt, literally, with Buchanan covering my father while White covered both of them. Christopher covered me as I covered our prisoner, Rahmi covered Tito, Rhee covered Adriana, as the tank went fully into the plane.

Results were immediate. They weren't the results I was hoping for, but they certainly were immediate.

CHAPTER 26

THE JET AND TANK EXPLODED. Which was impressive. Thanked God that we hadn't armed the nuclear warheads. No mushroom cloud was good.

Debris, however, was not good.

The last time something big had exploded nearby, I'd had Jamie's stroller with me and Mr. Joel Oliver had activated the laser shield button. Come to think of it, that wasn't the last time, merely a time.

But whatever time it had or hadn't been, for that and all the others we'd had either A-C laser shielding or ACE helping protect us. We had neither now. And while A-Cs and Amazons healed quickly, which was why they'd covered all the humans, it's hard to recover from flaming pieces of jet hitting you, no matter where you're from.

The person I was lying on shoved up on her hands, hard. Christopher and I tumbled off, as she got to her knees and put her hands out. A wall of sand and dirt, easily a hundred feet high, went up between us and the debris. Chick had some serious skills.

The wall of dirt fell over, toward the explosion. I'm sure there's a more technical term for it, but visually it truly fell, just like a wall can, straight over.

We all stood up. Christopher and I grabbed hold of our prisoner, just in case. "How did you know the tank was aimed for the jet?" I asked.

"You'd gotten yourself lost in the sandstorm. I was looking for you."

"Aww, that's sweet. Thanks."

The air near us shimmered and Jeff, then Chuckie, then Gower appeared. "Are you all alright?" Jeff asked, worry plain. "There were issues with the gate and Chuck wouldn't let me run here."

Took this to mean Chuckie had intelligently used his Vulcan Nerve Pinch move on Jeff, because I doubted that Jeff would have listened to reason when he knew we were in danger.

"Why are you dressed like . . . that?" Gower asked.

"He means like mummies," Chuckie added, in case we weren't clear that we all looked like bizarre fashion victims.

"We had to run through a huge sandstorm and we wanted to keep our eyes and more tender organs. Yes, we're fine, thanks for actually asking, first in no thanks to and then because of her." I indicated our prisoner, and pulled her headgear off. Was indeed a chick. Wanted to interrogate her, but there was a more pressing question.

"Before Missus Chief goes on or asks, allow me," Buchanan said. "Why are you here, Pontifex Gower?" Glad to see the question had been pressing for Buchanan, too. "You're undoubtedly a target, and were told to stay in the Embassy."

"I may be," Gower said, jaw set. "But my brother and sisters are here and I'm not going to hide in the Embassy when they need me. And I was one of the few who could hold out against the mind control. You need me, and my sisters and brother need me."

"Speaking of targets, Sol, what are you doing here?" Jeff asked.

"Long story," Dad said cheerfully. "I'm happy to be along for the ride."

"Someone should be," Christopher muttered.

"You know, I'm wondering if all of this, and them having Michael, Mimi, and Abby in particular, is simply to get Paul here."

"Maybe, but whatever their goal, they have my wife, every adult hybrid other than the Pontifex, most of Alpha Team, all of Airborne, and most of Centaurion Division Security, along with all of Centaurion Division's information, and who knows how many other hostages."

"Succinctly put, Secret Agent Man. Any ideas?"

"What's our weapons situation?"

Buchanan and White shared our small but mighty arsenal. Adriana's backpack was nice and full of useful things as well. "That's all you brought?" Gower asked when they were done. He sounded more than a little shocked and peeved.

"We brought plenty more."

Jeff, Chuckie, and Gower looked around. "I don't see them," Gower said finally. "Are they cloaked?"

"Ah, no. They're still in our downed plane. I think, anyway. I mean, realistically, they've blown up. Just like the plane. And the tank."

The three of them stared at me.

"Blown up?" Jeff asked finally.

"Why?" Gower added.

"Is there anything left of the plane to salvage?" Chuckie asked. "Or the tank?"

"I mentioned a sandstorm, right? The person Christopher and I are hanging onto used a sand tornado and dirt clods, along with tank artillery, to shoot us down. Then she rammed her tank into our plane. Then she dumped dirt on all of that to prevent the explosion from killing us. I guess anyway. Anything to add to that?" I asked her.

Either she was a shapeshifter, an imageer with image overlay talent, or she wasn't a full-blooded A-C, because while she was okay to look at, she wasn't Dazzler gorgeous by a long shot.

She was taller than me by a few inches, with long, light brown hair and average features. Her build was slender—not that you could tell since she was still in what now kind of looked like a Jedi robe, but having just fought with her, I could confirm what she'd felt like.

Her one exceptional feature was her eyes—they were bright green. They were also glaring daggers at me. She didn't reply.

"Okey dokey. Well, why we went down is because it's hard as hell to fly a Big Ugly Flying Fugly in the same way you handle a super-maneuverable jet. However, while there was damage, the BUFF wasn't totally destroyed—there was plenty of it left, along with all of its contents, until our 'friend' here blew it up. And we left most of the weapons there because Jeff said the person creating the dust storm wasn't after the plane or its contents and we were in a hurry."

"Kitty did a masterful job of keeping us all alive and landing safely," Dad said, oozing parental pride and support. Considered the benefits of always having Dad along for the ride. Figured they couldn't outweigh the risks of him being in danger, let alone what Mom would do if he got hurt while along for said rides. Chose to bask in the glow of someone thinking I'd done a good job for as long as it lasted.

"Kitty's crash landing took a lot out of us," Christopher added.

Basking glow lasted all of two seconds. Potentially a new world record.

"You were a Commander for over a decade," Chuckie pointed out. "I'd kind of expected you to be, I don't know, helping Kitty in some way."

"Everyone's a critic. You want to harangue someone? I give you Sand Chick."

Chuckie looked at our prisoner. "Good point. Who are you and what's your role in all that's going on?"

"We'd like your full name," I added. "And then we'd like to know if you ever knew your father."

"Or mother," Chuckie added.

"Right, or mother."

"You're all going to die." She had an accent. It was vaguely familiar, but I couldn't place it.

"What part of the Middle East are you from?" Chuckie asked. Unsurprisingly, he could place it. Realized it sounded familiar because I hung out with the Bahraini and Israeli Diplomatic Missions quite a lot these days.

She didn't answer.

Gave her a little shake. "Your name or your country of origin. Pick one, or better both, and share the information we want. Now."

She remained silent, with a look of pride. Clearly she'd been told that her holding out on us was of paramount importance for The Cause.

Buchanan selected a gun from our recently dissed but still darned well good enough for government work arsenal, cocked it, and casually aimed for her head. "She's the nice one. I'm the hired, trained, amoral killer, and I'm hired by someone who will be just fine if I say I chose to kill you because you represented a threat. Keep that in mind for the rest of your time with us, however brief a time that might be."

"Mahin Sherazi," she replied quickly, as I noted Adriana giving Buchanan a look of impressed admiration. Olga would undoubtedly be getting a fun earful when we all got home.

"That's a beautiful name," Dad said, falling naturally into the Good Cop role. "It means related to the moon, right?" She nodded. "And your last name means your family comes from city of Sheraz, located in southwest Iran, correct?" She nodded again. "So, are you Iranian?"

"Yes." She said this like she was admitting something as opposed to confirming what Dad and Chuckie had already figured out.

"Great, we get it, death to America and all that jazz. Here's the thing . . . despite the burka you don't look Middle Eastern. You sound it, but you don't look it. At all. And yes, sure, I've seen the picture of the beautiful Afghan girl on the cover of *National Geographic* and all that. You're not her. So I'm just going to go out on a limb and say that your mother wasn't actually Iranian."

"I don't care about death to America. I care about death to my father's killers."

It so figured. "Your father, the one who impregnated your mother, was Ronald Yates?" She nodded. We'd all assumed as much, but it was nice to be sure.

"Kitty's right, her mother was an American reporter for one of the many divisions of YatesCorp." Chuckie was looking at his phone. "She covered some stories in the Middle East, met an Iranian man, fell in love, got married, had a child. Only one. At least, only one that was acknowledged. There could be more, of course."

"How'd you find all that?"

"They may have taken us down, but they didn't affect the cellular network and Google lives on."

"Ah, good to know. So, Mahin, when did your mother tell

you who your father really was? Or did you discover it when your half brother showed up to recruit you into the great cause or whatever?" She'd identified using the name of the man who'd undoubtedly raised her, so that could mean she was new to the whole Al Dejahl Cause.

"I have always known."

"Your mother told you that the man whose name you have wasn't your real father?" Chuckie didn't sound like he bought this one. I didn't, either.

Buchanan smiled. It was quite a nasty smile. I wasn't used to seeing him pull this one out, but good to know he had it handy. "Missus Chief, you and the other Reappointed Commander step away. Don't want to get you two all blood-splattered."

"Fine," Mahin snapped. "I've always known I was different. Other children played in the dirt. I made the dirt play with me."

Missed ACE a lot right now. ACE had never mentioned other hybrid children, but that probably only meant that the information fell under the "too much interference" heading. Wished it had occurred to me to ask about them before right now.

"Did you ever hear a voice in your head, telling you how to control your power?"

"Yes. My father watched over me."

"That wasn't your father." The words slipped out before I could stop them. There was nothing wrong with this particular sentence, other than the fact that Gower couldn't pull ACE up to share the truth.

Mahin gave me yet another dirty look. She had a variety of them. The Yates Gene certainly had its privileges. Glaring was Christopher's Olympic Event; dirty looks were clearly what Mahin had focused on in her training. "As if you would know."

Chose to let discretion be the better part of keeping my mouth shut and hoped no one else would decide we needed to bring Mahin up on the ACE situation. "Whatever. Are your mother and father good with your being with the Al Dejahl terrorist organization? I mean the man who raised you, not your sperm donor."

"My parents are dead," Mahin said, voice tight. "However, they always encouraged me to do what I felt was right."

"And you took that to mean buddying up to terrorists was the way to go? Interesting choice. So, when did you join up with Ronaldo Al Dejahl? Before or after your parents died?"

She didn't reply.

Chuckie sighed. "We can force you to tell us, you know. Why make it difficult on yourself?"

"I will not betray my family."

"Your parents are dead, so you can't actually betray them, other than to be someone they wouldn't be proud of. Don't know what their views were, so I have no idea if you're winning Daughter of the Year or not. And, as Chuckie said, we don't see a record of any siblings."

"I am an only child," she admitted. "My parents didn't have other children and not acknowledge them."

"Good to know. But here's the thing." Pointed to White. "He's your family, too. As close to you as Ronaldo is. So are they." Pointed to Christopher, Jeff, and Gower. "They're all related to each other and to Yates. More of your relatives are in the Science Center."

Mahin's eyes flicked away from me, then back. It was over in a flash, but I'd spent the last three-plus years with people who really couldn't lie well. Everyone had tells, and I was fairly sure I'd just seen one of hers.

"Chuckie, Malcolm, Adriana, are you all thinking what I'm thinking?" Figured it was a safe bet they'd seen the same as I had. They were all trained or being trained to look for tells from those in their custody or similar, after all.

"Absolutely," Adriana said.

"Yep," Buchanan concurred.

"Yes," Chuckie said, making it a full hand. "I'd like a good way to make the determination, though. Because it could be a fake."

"Something's fake, I'll give you that."

"Determine what?" Gower asked. "What's fake?"

"This situation is fake, Paul. And what we need to do is determine where everybody we're trying to rescue actually is."

CHAPTER 27

I TENDED TO THINK BEST when I was running my mouth. Continued to so run while watching Mahin carefully. "Here's what I think has happened. Our people were indeed taken and herded into the Science Center. But I don't think they're there any more."

"Why not?" Tito asked. "Why try to keep us away if they're not there?"

"The usual bad guy reasons, distraction most likely."

"Or they were anticipating our response," White pointed out. "They were able to do so before."

"The Science Center didn't fire on us," Christopher said.

"And there was only the one tank," Adriana added.

"Good points." The first time the Al Dejahl terrorist group had taken over the Science Center they'd absolutely shot at me and Christopher. One tank, while a good start, wasn't likely to take out A-Cs, simply because they were so fast. And the baddies had certainly anticipated most of our reactions during most of Operation Confusion, after all, and that was when Ronaldo Al Dejahl first came onto our collective radars.

"I agree with the logic, but I'm not convinced," Chuckie said.

"Fine. Home Base is deserted. I'm not sure what Ronaldo's mind control range is, but he didn't execute this plan all on his lonesome. He has his newly recruited terrorist grunts with him, I'm sure. Why not leave a couple of them at Home Base to shoot or capture us?"

"Because the Science Center is easier to lock down," Jeff replied.

"Yes, it is. And it's locked down nice and tight. But I know from personal experience that anyone inside during lockdown can get out easily. And Ronaldo knows we can do that, even if he didn't have Gladys under his control, because we did it when Jamie was born."

Jeff's eyes narrowed. "Are they after her again?"

"I'm sure they are. There had to be a reason all the Embassy animals were with the kids."

"We need to get back." Jeff looked ready to run all the way to D.C. Couldn't blame him, really, but that wasn't going to be a wise plan.

"Yes, but I don't think they're making their move against the Embassy just yet."

"Why not?" Christopher asked, sounding almost as worried as Jeff. "They got all of us out and here."

"Not all of us. But I think they left Mahin here to keep us extremely busy while they continue on with the rest of whatever their plan is. Regardless, we need to verify if anyone's still in the Science Center or not."

"We need to go back to the Embassy," Jeff said urgently. Only, he didn't look all that urgent.

Remembered that he'd been able to feel Mahin's emotions. "Well, I think we should go to Gaultier Research."

"Why?" Chuckie asked.

"Just a feeling. Or, maybe Titan Enterprises."

"Where's the relevance, Missus Chief?" Buchanan was obviously speaking for most of our group.

"Could be very relevant. Or, there's always good ol' YatesCorp."

"Maybe we should search Home Base again," Jeff said. By now we were getting the "you so crazy" looks from just about everyone.

"How about Caliente Base?"

"Or the Dome," Jeff suggested.

Saw the realization of what we were doing dawn on Chuckie. "Oh, I think we need to check C.I.A. headquarters. Or the F.B.I. Maybe Homeland Security, too."

Jeff didn't look like he'd gotten what he was emotionally

searching for yet. Decided to branch out. After all, Al Dejahl was in charge, and that meant I needed to think about the times we'd tangled with him. "Paris."

"Or Paraguay," Chuckie added.

Another idea nudged. "Tunnel system." As I said this Jeff nodded. "They're really in the tunnels?"

"Yes." Jeff smiled at Mahin. "Thanks for your help."

"I didn't help you at all," she snapped.

"You mind telling us what the hell you're going on about?" Christopher asked.

Chuckie shook his head. "You've been out of fieldwork too long."

Buchanan looked like he'd caught on. "Want me to take our prisoner away, Missus Chief?" I was still holding her arm and could feel Mahin tense up. Good.

"Yes, please and thank you, Malcolm. Just far enough so she can't hear us."

He nodded and took her from me and Christopher. "Understand that if you try anything, anything at all, I'll kill you. And no one will be near enough to us to tell me to stop. Nod if you understand."

She nodded. "You're all murderers."

"Nope, not all," Buchanan said cheerfully. "But I am for sure, so don't test the depths of my human kindness, because I don't have any." He led her off, being rather rough, a good hundred or so feet away.

"Should I go with him, just in case?" Adriana asked me.

"Yeah, good call. We'll fill you both in once we know what we're doing." She trotted over to Buchanan and Mahin.

"They should be far enough away," Jeff said in a low voice. "And I don't know whether to be insulted or not that none of you could figure out what Kitty and I were doing."

"I presume you were using your empathic talents to determine what Mahin knew and identify where our enemies are or are headed, Jeffrey."

"Then why did you look so confused, Mister White?"

He shrugged. "I wanted to ensure our prisoner felt you two were acting like idiots versus emotionally interrogating her."

"Is everyone else going to jump on that bandwagon?"

The rest of the team shook their heads. "I just thought the two of you had lost it," Tito said, clearly speaking for everyone else. Presumed he was speaking for Buchanan and Adriana, too, though I decided we could live without the confirmation.

"And this is why I say again that Richard is really the best Field agent we have."

"I'm touched. However, the tunnel system is intricate and worldwide. Were you able to determine anything else, Jeffrey?"

"Before you answer that, are you sure she wasn't fooling you in some way?" Chuckie asked Jeff.

"And are *you* sure Buchanan's not going to shoot her in the head?" Christopher asked me. "Or Adriana? She's got a gun out, too, now."

"If she tries anything, he'll kill her without a thought," Jeff replied. "However, all that 'amoral killer' crap was just that, crap. He'll kill her because she represents a threat to Kitty, but he won't enjoy it. Same with Adriana, she'll shoot if Mahin becomes a threat, but otherwise, she's just there to give Buchanan company and support. And, seriously, I'm an empath. If someone's not wearing an emotional blocker, and both of them aren't, then I can read them."

"Sorry," Christopher said. "I mentioned that the crash landing took a lot out of us, right?"

"Out of you, at least." Hey, I was getting tired of the complaints about my skills.

Jeff rolled his eyes and went on. "As for Mahin, I'm pretty sure about her reactions. She's absolutely not wearing an emotional blocker. If she's using an emotional overlay it's impressive, because I could feel more than just a few emotions. She wasn't as easy to read as Kitty is, but she's pretty close."

"Is she human?" Everyone other than Tito stared at me. "Really? I think the android question is one we should always ask, particularly since they have all the human emotions and can fool Jeff."

Tito opened his medical bag and pulled out an OVS. "I agree, and I've taken to carrying this with me any time I'm leaving the Embassy. I can wand her whenever you want, Kitty."

"And this is why bringing Tito onto the team is still probably my proudest recruiting achievement." This earned me a grin from Tito and a nice version of Patented Glare #1 from Christopher.

"Presuming she's not an android," Jeff went on, clearly choosing to ignore the opportunity to praise my recruiting skills, "she's not used to hiding her emotions from anyone. She might not even have been told that she should try. I don't get the impression she's known any of the people she's now associated with for very long."

"What's her dominant emotion?" Chuckie asked.

"Not what you'd expect, especially under the circumstances."

"And that is?" I asked for all of us.

"Loneliness."

"Interesting," Chuckie said. "That's probably how Al Dejahl got her hooked in. It works for most cultists. But does that mean we can turn her? Because if we can, she'd be an asset. But if we can't, she's another dangerous liability."

"I'm more concerned with where everyone is and what's going on," Christopher said.

"Has anyone tested to see if we can get into the Science Center?" Rahmi asked. "I realize you say it's locked down, but an attempt should be made."

Jeff shrugged. "Not yet. You two," he pointed to the princesses, "and Christopher, come with me." He took Christopher's hand, confirming that, for now at least, Christopher was out of hyper-juice.

They all zipped off. They were back almost immediately. "No way in," Jeff said. "In addition to everything else, the shields are up."

"We bounced off the walls and doors," Rhee added.

"So, what are our options?" Chuckie asked. "We don't have enough firepower to blast our way in."

Nostalgic memory waved. "Christopher and I know a way in that doesn't require blowing things up."

Christopher shook his head. "You and your mother both had security measures put up on the old drainage pipe. Gladys knows about that; she's the one who ensured it was handled."

Considered this. "We should try it anyway."

"Why?" Chuckie asked.

"Because we can determine how far under Ronaldo's control Gladys really is," White replied.

"Mister White, it's like you read my mind. Exactly. If the pipe's open, or we can get in with relative ease, then Gladys took off the security somehow and is fighting back. If not, then we know she's fully under Al Dejahl's mind control."

Jeff looked thoughtful. "It might not prove anything, either way, but the whole excuse used to get our people herded here and captured was Security training. So maybe the guards normally stationed in that area won't be there. Either by accident or design."

"But I thought we were assuming the Center is empty," Dad pointed out. "Should we spend the time?"

"Yes, because, if nothing else, we'll be able to get into the tunnel system close to where Al Dejahl and the others did," Jeff replied.

"So the question is, should we try the drainage pipe to verify the Center is empty?" White asked. "And, if so, should all of us attempt the entry?"

"How sure are you that no one's inside the Science Center?" Chuckie asked.

"Our captive is sure," Jeff said. "If she's not an android and not fooling me, then there's no one in there that she knows of."

"That she knows of . . ." Closed my eyes. "Wait, wait. Don't say anything. Let me think. How likely is it that Al Dejahl has hooked back up with the same gang he used to run with, or at least their new counterparts?"

"Why are you talking if you're thinking?" Christopher asked.

"Three plus years together and you have to ask that? Chuckie's right, you've spent too long on non-active duty."

"I'm going to say something since you asked and answer your question," Chuckie replied. "My guess would be extremely likely."

"Okay, we know that Jeff couldn't feel anyone at the Science Center earlier today, so it's a safe bet that they have emotional blockers somewhere in the facility, maybe all over it. Probably at Home Base, too."

"That's a safe assumption," Jeff said. "Where are you going with this?"

"Why can you feel Mahin?"

Opened my eyes to see Chuckie nodding. Jeff shrugged. "They didn't give her a blocker or overlay, or hers are broken. Or something like that."

"Or Al Dejahl expected you to read Mahin and think no one's there. Sort of like in *The Princess Bride*." This earned me a chuckle from Dad, blank looks from everyone other than Tito, and an exasperated sigh from Chuckie. Wanted to call Buchanan back, but figured he'd have sided with the Exasperated Sigh Team.

"So she was told what they wanted Jeff to read and us to know," Chuckie finished quickly, presumably so I wouldn't describe the scene from *The Princess Bride* I was referring to for the others' enjoyment.

"Which is par for their course. Ronaldo wasn't the brains of Operation Confusion, but he isn't an idiot and LaRue was obviously a good teacher."

"So, what does that mean?" Christopher asked.

"It means they want us on a wild goose chase. Looking in the tunnels, racing back to the Embassy. They don't actually want us here."

"Meaning we want to get into the Science Center," Gower said. "So that would mean all of us go to the drainage pipe."

"No. It means we need to do exactly what Al Dejahl wants."

CHAPTER 28

GOT THE BY-NOW-PREREQUISITE WTF looks from most of my team. "You mind explaining that?" Jeff asked.

"Really? I mean all of us need to very obviously go away. So they see us going away and know that their clever plan has fooled us yet again. So that we can sneak back in. Loaded for bear. To catch them unawares. And all that."

"We don't know if we can get in," Christopher said, patience clearly forced. "What's our plan if we can't use the drainage pipe? Blasting in? Coming up through the tunnel system?"

"They'll expect that," Dad said. "At least based on what Charles and Kitty are saying, which makes sense to me. They've told Mahin that they're in the tunnels and that she's to stall and stop us here and not give up their location at any cost, I'm sure. So while we may fool them into thinking we've left, they'll have guards on any tunnel access points, just in case we decide to try to access the Science Center that way."

"We use a gate." Now I got the WTF looks from everyone, other than Buchanan and Adriana, but presumably only because they were too far away to hear me. "Look, the agents were bounced back by whatever when they tried to use a standard gate that was in a base. However, I don't think there's a way to flip a switch and turn off all floater gate activity."

"No, there's really not. It could be done from the Dome, but nowhere else," Jeff confirmed. "The trouble we had getting here was more of a security issue—making sure that no one could track the floater's signature."

"Great. And I know there's a way to use the gates when the shields are activated, because we do it all the time."

Jeff nodded. "Yes and no, but I'm willing to discuss intricacies later."

"Then let's obviously leave, taking Mahin with us, and use a floater gate to get inside."

"What if someone can read our emotions?" Tito asked. "Or if they have the imageers watching us?"

"The beauty of the emotional blockers and overlays is if they're active, they can't feel us any more than I can feel them," Jeff confirmed.

"No way to tell on the imageers," Christopher said. "But if we stand around long enough, I'm sure someone will come up with the idea."

"I agree we need to move, but I want Mahin searched for bugs," Chuckie said.

Knew without asking that this task was going to fall to me. Always the way. But we couldn't trust the princesses with it, mostly because they could miss something that just didn't seem suspicious to them. We shouldn't have one of the men do the search, because it was going to have to be a strip search. Probably a cavity search.

"Tito and I will do it." He was a doctor, he was used to searching cavities.

"Bugs or trackers could be internal, and that means a strip and cavity search," Chuckie said.

Tito heaved a sigh. "What's wrong with all of you? I have an OVS with me. It looks for anything suspicious, both organic and inorganic. She doesn't have to be stripped, or have her cavities searched. While I'm verifying if she's an android or not I'll verify if she's carrying something we don't want as well."

"The emotional blockers and overlays are cloaked with a substance our equipment doesn't pick up," I reminded him.

"If Jeff can read her, those aren't on her person," Tito reminded right back.

"Works for me, I just wanted to point it out."

"Good. I'm going to go either put our minds at ease or have Malcolm and Adriana deactivate an android with extreme prejudice." Tito trotted over to our other little group and started wanding.

"Uh, one question." Rahmi sounded hesitant, which usually indicated she was about to counter something I or, more likely, Tito might have said. "Why are we taking this Mahin with us?"

"She's a prisoner of war." Figured I'd put it in terms the princesses would understand immediately.

"Yes, I understand that. But, we have determined she is being used."

"That's right," Jeff said. "At least we believe she's being used. She might see the light and join our side, but she might not, and we don't want to let her go back to rejoin our other enemies."

"Do you normally take your prisoners of war with you?"

"Yeah, we do . . . oh. Wow. Good call, Rahmi."

"You've lost me," Jeff said with a sigh.

"The princess makes a good point," Chuckie said.

"What point is that?" Christopher asked. "That we don't kill our enemies immediately or just let them wander off to attack us again?"

"No," Chuckie replied. "What Rahmi means is that we take our prisoners along all the time, it's something we do regularly, meaning it's something that can be anticipated. Kitty tends to grab whoever she comes across and drag them into her wake. Tito's a great example, but he's not the only one."

"The Planetary Council, for another example," White said. "And since we know Ronaldo and LaRue attended the Martinis' wedding reception in secret, it would seem a safe bet that he is anticipating our once again attempting to turn an enemy into a friend."

Tito returned. "She's human. So are Malcolm and Adriana, in case anyone was feeling paranoid. Mahin has no bugs or implants or anything else dangerous like that on her. She did have a few weapons hidden, but Adriana searched her and found them all."

"So, what do we do with her, then?" Christopher asked. "And before we suggest that someone takes her off somewhere, I need to point out that we have no idea what the extent of her talents is. She could be a lot more powerful than we've seen."

"And that could mean they're also expecting us to take her somewhere and then she becomes an infiltrator." This was really like the poison scene from *The Princess Bride*. What a pity I hadn't spent years taking the poison antidote so that the choice didn't matter. Decided I was still technically the one in charge, so made the Executive Decision. "We take her. No one can read her any more than they can read the rest of us. If she's going to try something, better with us, where we can stop her, than somewhere else where she might get the drop on whoever's guarding her and thereby actually infiltrate."

"So, where are we going?" Gower asked. "Exactly?"

"First to the wreckage of the plane and tank. Then via floater gate to Home Base. Then back to the drainage pipe."

"Why the bouncing around?" Jeff asked.

"No, that's wise," Chuckie countered. "It should at least give us a hope of confusing our enemies if they're actually in the Science Center and watching us. Gladys may have given them everything and guessed what we're going to do, but it's worth a shot."

"Then let's get this show on the road. It's now at least a couple hours after my last meal and I'm starving."

Jeff heaved a sigh as he took my hand. "Only my girl."

CHAPTER 29

JEFF HELD MAHIN while I took Buchanan and Adriana aside and shared the plan with them. In addition to Adriana's weapons search and seizure, they'd spent the time tying Mahin's hands behind her back using some of the ripped-up parachute.

"We got nothing out of her other than the fact that she thinks we're all murderous pigs, me most of all," Buchanan shared when we were done.

"She's not fond of me, either," Adriana said with a smile. "I believe Grandmother would be able to get information out of her though."

"If only we had the time to bring Mahin to Olga. Or knew that it was safe to do so."

"Which we don't," Buchanan said. "However, I think she'll talk to your father. He did the Good Cop role well and he doesn't give off the same vibes the rest of us do."

"Good to know. I don't want her alone with my dad anytime soon."

Buchanan gave me a wolfish grin. "I like being Bad Cop, so no worries."

"I see that. Can't argue, I prefer the Bad Cop role myself."

Buchanan and Adriana had no argument with our plan, such as it was, so we all linked hands, Buchanan and Jeff each holding one of Mahin's arms, and then we took a leisurely hyperspeed run to the remains of the jet.

Since said remains were pretty well covered with sand

and such, we didn't linger long. Mahin, being a hybrid, had no issues with the hyperspeed, which was good in that we didn't have to watch her throw up. Chuckie texted in the coordinates to Colonel Franklin so the military could do cleanup, then Jeff called for a group floater gate.

We all stepped through together and exited at Home Base. Christopher and the princesses verified there was still no one there but us while I made my stomach settle down. Mahin had no negative reactions to the gate. Decided I might need to hate her.

"Do we keep the mummy look going?" Tito asked as Christopher and the princesses returned and Chuckie put handcuffs onto Mahin while Buchanan removed her parachute bonds.

"No," Jeff said. "You all look ridiculous, and while the element of surprise is one thing, I don't think we can reasonably count on all of our enemies falling down laughing when they see all of you. Some of them, yes. But not all."

We stripped off the impromptu parachute fashion wear. Happily, we were all intact and reasonably unscathed. "Scoff if you like, but I say any fashion choice that allows you to get through a sandstorm without major injuries is a good fashion choice."

"Last chance to change our minds," Christopher said, once we were all devoid of parachutes and Mahin was officially in C.I.A. custody, or at least C.I.A. handcuffs.

"Unless you've had a genius moment, we're rolling with what we have." This earned me Patented Glare #2, but no snide comments, so took that to mean Christopher hadn't come up with anything better. "I do have one request. Dad, I want you going back to Caliente Base."

"Absolutely not," Dad said calmly.

"We don't know what we'll be facing, but people shooting at us would be a safe bet."

Dad shrugged. "I realize you and your mother do this sort of thing all the time, kitten. And I don't. However, you're my daughter and I'm here and, therefore, I'm not leaving to let you go off and get shot at without me along to do my best to protect you and the rest of our family and friends."

"We don't really have time for this argument," Jeff said.

"Our family, friends, and co-workers are in danger, held hostage or worse, and we have to go. Now. Sol, just stay in the back."

Wasn't thrilled, but didn't argue. Because Christopher argued for me. "Jeff, think for a minute. Where we're going, ah, echoes. And we have to be single file for a while." He grabbed me and Jeff and pulled us aside. "I think we're going to have a problem, more than one, if we try to take our prisoner along."

"It was hard enough when it was just me, Christopher, and three of the flyboys."

"I don't know that we can control a hybrid in there, and she'll have ample opportunity to shout her head off," Christopher went on. "Sure, we can gag her, but we still don't know what she can do. What if it's a lot more than we've seen?"

Jeff ran his hand through his hair. "Fine, I know where you're both going with this. I'm fine with Sol staying behind with Mahin, but he can't possibly handle her on his own."

"But we have someone with us who can." I motioned for Buchanan and Chuckie to join us and we quickly explained the situation. "I want my dad somewhere safe, and I want Mahin guarded by someone who's nasty enough to kill her if necessary but smart enough to avoid it if at all possible."

"I'm the man for the job, and your mother would agree that with the Reinstated Commanders along you're probably well covered," Buchanan said. "However, Mahin's a hybrid. The moment the rest of you are gone, she's going to try to overpower me, and she probably can, handcuffs or no handcuffs."

"That can also be handled," Jeff said. "Where do we want all of you going?"

"Guantanamo," Chuckie said without missing a beat.

"That's fine, as long as I can get a floater to get myself and Mister Katt to all of you, or out of there, depending. It's not someplace I think your enemies would expect and it's heavily guarded."

Jeff and Chuckie made the calls while I explained the situation to Dad. "Pump her for information," I said in conclusion, in part because he was likely the only one who had a shot, and in the other part because I knew he was disappointed to be sidelined, especially right after Jeff had told him he was coming along.

"Will do, kitten. Should we send you whatever information we have as we get it? Or will that cause a problem?"

"No idea, Dad. I'd say if it's vital, send no matter what. If not, save it for when we contact you guys."

The floater gate appeared, hugged Dad and gave him a kiss, then he and Buchanan each took an arm and stepped through with Mahin. Got a text from Buchanan about a minute later saying they were there, all was well, and Mahin was shackled and being taken to a cell designed to hold a bull elephant.

Waited for Chuckie to get confirmation from Guantanamo that our prisoner was secured and that Dad and Buchanan were just fine, and then, confident that we had at least a little part of the problem contained, Jeff called for a new floater gate.

It appeared and the rest of us stepped through. While Jeff didn't carry me, he did have his arm around me and held me tightly. It was a nice feeling in amidst the nausea and stress.

We exited in a patch of desert I was familiar with—the wash that the Science Center's old drainage pipe had emptied into.

This location was great for several reasons beyond no one really thinking about it much. For starters, it was about a half a mile away from the back of the Science Center, so not easily seen in the first place. The wash was a big one, wide and deep—the bottom was a good eight feet lower than the main plane of the ground around this area. And the drainage pipe and the area around it were additionally hidden by a variety of cacti and desert scrub foliage.

On the downside, the pipe now had a nice metal grate attached to the opening.

Rahmi and Rhee started to pull at the grate with Chuckie and Tito giving them direction, I pulled Jeff and Christopher aside.

"Christopher, before you and Jeff go help the princesses wrench that grate off and then we all get onto our hands and knees, I have a question."

"Only one?" Christopher asked, sarcasm knob definitely heading for eleven. "If it's 'how are we going to get that grate off without alerting the entire Science Center to our presence,' I have no idea."

"At the present time I only have the one question, and that's not it. When we used this way back when, there was a fork in the pipe. We went to the right. What would we have come to if we'd gone to the left?"

"The reclamation system."

"Awesome."

"Why is that awesome?" Jeff asked.

"Because the only thing that anyone's paid attention to as far as I know is this outer opening and the opening on the fifteenth floor by the Lair. And while Mom and I cared about the pipe and its security breach, I don't think anyone else, Gladys included, really did. So I'm willing to bet that no one's done anything with the left fork, including block it off or put security on it."

"Assuming we can get this new grate off, how does that help us?" Jeff asked.

"Simple. It gives our second team the true element of surprise."

Jeff and Christopher stared at me, then spoke in unison. "Second team?"

CHAPTER 30

"THE SECOND TEAM, or the stealth team if you prefer, will go down the left fork, and get into the Science Center through the reclamation system."

"I thought we were all supposed to be stealthy," Christopher said.

"While the others do what?" Jeff asked.

"Go down the right fork and hopefully get into the Science Center that way."

"But you expect the first team to get caught," Christopher said.

"Not entirely. But I do expect that team to have to fight. Which is why I'm going to make you two happy and head up the second team."

"Oh, yes, that makes me feel so much better," Christopher snapped.

"Who do you want with you?" Jeff asked.

"Richard, Paul, and Adriana. Chuckie needs to be with your team so someone who can lie believably can do most of the talking. You'll also have Rahmi and Rhee, who, let's face it, are worth about ten Field agents each when it comes to fighting."

"Which team is Tito on?" Jeff looked worried. "I'm not saying I agree with this plan, but I do want to hear all of it."

"He'll need to go with you. When push comes to shove, he's the only man the princesses are going to listen to."

We argued some more, but I won, mostly because Jeff

could see the wisdom of splitting our team and he wasn't fully convinced anyone was in the Science Center, Mahin's tell and my brilliant hypotheses or not.

The others didn't have nearly as many issues with the two teams idea as Jeff and Christopher had. Chuckie, in particular, felt it was something our enemies wouldn't expect.

It took Jeff and Christopher as well as the princesses, but they were finally able to rip the grate off the pipe's end. The pipe still had a thin layer of old, icky water in it. This was good and bad. Good in that it indicated I was right and no one had given this pipe more than the cursory "look, we took care of it, happy?" treatment. It was bad because we were going to have to crawl through it to get anywhere.

We had the fun business of deciding who would go first and last. After a lot of whining and arguing, it was decided that Christopher would lead and Jeff would bring up the rear, presumably to have our best fighters and the guys who knew the intricacies of a pipe with one fork in it leading and protecting our rears.

However, because the pipe wasn't really someplace anyone would want to have to lie down so someone else could crawl over them, our order going in actually mattered.

After much discussion, it was decided that the princesses would follow Christopher, with Tito and then Chuckie behind them. White would be behind Chuckie, with Gower, Adriana, and then me.

Way back when, during Operation Fugly, Matt, Chip, and Jerry were with us when we'd crawled this pipe tunnel, and they'd had flashlights. Turned out the only flashlights we had this time were with Adriana, whose backpack looked nowhere near to being as stuffed as my purse, but which contained so many more useful items. Thankfully she had two, so Christopher took one and White took the other. Those of us not near to those two would get to crawl in the dark.

Truly felt Jeff had insisted on me going next to last so he could be the one staring at my butt for this part of the journey. His grin when this occurred to me was pretty much confirmation. Decided it was cute and flattering and definitely preferred him focused on my butt than, say, Adriana's, so it was all good.

"Attack" order determined and our two flashlights in the hands of each "team lead," then it was the fun business of crawling on our hands and knees. Wished we'd left our parachute wrappings on, but hadn't had the foresight so everyone instead got the fun of crawling through ick.

Jeff gave me his standard great kiss while the others started in. "You be careful, baby," he said when he ended the kiss.

"I'd rather be in bed."

He grinned, his eyes smoldered, and his eyelids drooped. "Nice to see you remain focused on the priorities." He looked, as he so often did, like a jungle cat about to eat me. I loved this look. That I wouldn't get to see it in the pipe or however long it was going to take us to solve our latest crisis was just another one for the Hate The Bad Guys column.

It was finally our turn. Jeff helped me down, patted my butt, and then I followed Adriana into the pipe, Jeff right behind me.

We could have used hyperspeed to get through, but Christopher didn't want us racing in. I wasn't sure if this was because he was burned out and hadn't regenerated yet or was actually based on cautious wisdom. However, I agreed that conserving our strength for the battle or battles ahead was wise, so hadn't questioned this.

The downside was that stagnant water with extra special "don't look and you'll be happier" additives and the fact that the pipe seemed endless, though I knew it wasn't. It was just a lot slower going with ten of us versus five of us.

Wasn't sure if not being able to see what we were crawling through was better than knowing exactly what we were sloshing around in or not. Especially since A-Cs had better vision than humans, and, once in for a couple of minutes, everyone's eyes adjusted. Meaning we could make out more than just blackness. Decided not looking was probably the best course.

"You doing okay?" Jeff asked quietly.

"Yeah, just glad I have hand sanitizer in my purse. Be sure to take the time to wash off if you're able."

"I can only hope we'll have time to clean up before we have to fight. If not, hopefully whoever attacks us is a germaphobe."

We went on in silence. I listened for the sound of someone

behind us. After all, the last time we'd used the pipe to get in, Ronald Yates had followed us. But I didn't hear anything out of the ordinary, other than quiet sounds of cursing or someone being grossed out by whatever they'd just put their hands in.

Finally reached the fork. The old baseball mitt Jeff and Christopher had played with when they were little boys was still here. We'd taken the bat and ball, and used them, too, during Operation Fugly. Took the mitt. Couldn't shove it into my purse, but I brushed it off, shook it out, and put it on my head.

"Seriously?" Jeff whispered.

"Yes. We might need it, you never know."

"Only my girl. By the way, I can't feel you now, so we must be within the range of the nearest emotional blocker."

"That's good, I guess. If you can't feel us, neither can anyone inside."

"Let's hope. Be careful, baby, and never forget that I love you."

"I love you, too, Jeff. Be safe." I crawled to the left and caught up with Adriana. Heard Jeff go off to the right.

There was more light in here. At first I thought it was because I was closer to White, then remembered he was still about the same distance from me as before. Looked around and realized this part of the pipe was getting a little larger.

Neither Jeff nor Christopher had mentioned this. Would have liked to have confirmed if it was just that they hadn't remembered or if it meant that this side wasn't as forgotten as I was counting on.

However, the extra space was appreciated. There was less stagnant water on this side, or else the extra width of the pipe meant the water was more spread out and so dried up more quickly.

After what seemed like forever, I bumped up against Adriana. "We're here," she whispered. She also stood up, offered her hand, and helped me up.

We'd exited into a metal room. Plenty big enough for the four of us, with room to spare. It wasn't huge, but after the pipe it felt incredibly spacious for a rectangle—Jeff and Chuckie would have been able to stand upright, but anyone taller would have to hunch over.

"It's nice to stand up."

"It is," Adriana agreed. "But there seems to be a problem."

Resisted the urge to say that of course there was, but it took effort. "What's wrong?"

"Richard can't open the hatch," Gower said.

Gower was holding the flashlight, which meant I could see better now. He handed it to Adriana, then went to help White try to wrench the hatch open.

Not that I was some sort of expert, seeing as I didn't spend my days in pipes or small metal rooms attached to pipes, but this metal seemed different than I remembered the metal on the other side being. There was more rust, for one thing. And there were handholds near the hatch. In fact, there were handholds all over this room.

There hadn't been anything like that on the other side, either a room or handholds. Christopher had wrenched the grate off, but it had come off more easily than the grate had today. He'd said the metal was a special alloy, too. But this metal just looked like iron.

The hatch made a creaking sound. "Almost got it," Gower said through gritted teeth.

I got a very bad feeling. Maybe it was instinct. My gut. Feminine intuition. It was more likely that I'd seen a lot of movies and TV shows and I was fully aware of the way our luck ran.

"Richard, Paul, make sure you're holding tight onto one of those metal handles nearby. That's an order. Adriana, you too," I added as I made sure my purse was closed and securely over my neck, and followed my own advice. I put the mitt onto my free hand.

"What do you expect, Missus Martini?"

"I expect us to not like whatever happens when you get that hatch open."

"What if nothing happens?" Gower asked.

"Then we can laugh at my overactive imagination. Adriana, try not to lose the flashlight."

"I'll do my best."

"Super. Then go for it, guys."

White and Gower pulled, and, as they'd expected, the hatch finally opened.

And as I'd expected, we didn't like what came out.

CHAPTER 31

WATER GUSHED FORTH. Prayed there was nothing "extra" in it, but I was a lot more focused on holding on.

The water's force shoved the hatch fully open. This was great, only Gower was trapped behind the hatch now. And White's grip on his handhold was slipping. We were in the process, as we so often were, of redefining the term "really bad."

"Kitty, catch!" Adriana said, as she threw the flashlight at me.

Taking the mitt was proven to have been prescient. Adriana's toss wasn't accurate, but the mitt gave me just enough extra grabbing reach and power that I caught the flashlight. Barely, but I caught it. There were benefits to having been, as Jeff would have put it, a jock for all of high school and college.

Adriana caught White as he lost his grip. There were a few frightening moments when it wasn't clear if she was going to hold on, or if they were both going to slip. If they did, they'd knock into me and take me with them back down the pipe.

If we fit, that is. But if we didn't fit, we'd get knocked out. Heck, we could get knocked out whether we fit through the pipe or not. And if a body got knocked out and blocked the pipe, then the water in this metal room would fill up fast.

But White was able to grab a metal handhold. This jostled Adriana enough that she lost her grip. White hauled her back. They went back and forth with this for a little bit. It had the potential to be humorous. When we were out of here and dry. Maybe.

Meanwhile, I had a flashlight held precariously in a baseball mitt, Gower was trapped, and the water wasn't slowing down.

The only saving grace was that we weren't all on our hands and knees, trying to breathe the water. This was mitigated by the fact that there was a lot more water coming out than the pipe could send through all at once. Our heads were above the water line—for now. How long that lasted was going to be dependent upon how much water was going to come out of whatever we'd opened and how long it would take for the smaller pipe to send it all out into the wash. I didn't need Chuckie here to tell me that things weren't looking rosy.

White and Adriana finally both got a firm hold on separate handholds. They held onto each other still, just in case. Couldn't blame them. Sort of wished I was near enough to Gower to be holding onto him and vice versa.

Of course, as I thought of it, I had no idea if Gower was drowning or not. The way I had the flashlight held, the light was pointing toward the ceiling near to where White and Adriana were. I could try to move the flashlight toward where I thought Gower was, but I was barely holding onto it as it was. Didn't think I could manage moving it without losing my tenuous grip.

Went for the next best option. "Paul! Paul, can you hear me? Are you okay?"

"Sort of," he called back. "I'm pinned. I can breathe, but I can't move."

"Pinned is better than drowned. Everyone just hang on. This can't go on forever." I hoped.

"Based on water flow, I believe we'll be underwater soon," Adriana said. She sounded fairly calm. Which was good. One of us should be.

There was nothing for it. We could hang around here and potentially drown, or one of us could try becoming a salmon and give swimming upstream the old college try.

If Jeff was with us, I'd have honestly suggested he be the one to try, because he had the Surcenthumain boost and was the strongest. Plus, based on when I went swimming in the

Potomac during Operation Assassination, he could hold his breath for a long time.

I knew if I mentioned my plan White would suggest he be the one to try. He was awesome and all, but he was still Christopher's dad. I didn't want to have to tell Christopher I'd told his only remaining parent to swim into whatever the hell was on the other side of the hatch, especially if that sole remaining parent didn't make it.

Gower was trapped, Adriana was a full human. That really left only me.

"Adriana, can you grab the flashlight?"

She reached out, White still holding her. "No. You have to toss it back to me."

"Be ready." The mitt was on my left hand, and I was right-handed. However, I couldn't swim and take the flashlight with me. And if I mentioned what I was going to do, White would, for sure, leap off to go ahead of me.

Let this be like firing a gun from a moving vehicle. I focused on relaxing, on becoming one with the movements, choppy though they were. Then, once it felt like I wasn't really moving, that it was Adriana who was bobbing back and forth, pinpointed where I wanted the flashlight to land and lobbed it over to her.

She caught it, which was definitely a big one for the win column. "Shine it slowly around the part of the room without water, and then at the hatch," I told her.

Adriana obliged. There were plenty of handholds, but it was going to take me a while to get from one to another in order to get to the hatch. It was hard to be certain, but the water didn't appear to be stopping, meaning I probably didn't have the luxury of wall climbing over.

"Mister White, if I'm not back in about two minutes, then and only then can you or anyone else come after me. I'm saying this as the Head of Field and all that jazz. Top girl order sort of thing."

"What are you doing, Kitty?" Gower asked.

"Something you won't like that has a ton of risk but could save the day."

"Ah. Routine."

"You got it, Paul. Adriana, keep the light on the hatch,

please and thank you." With that, took a deep breath, held it, and shoved off against the wall, down and toward the hatch.

Track was great for improving lung capacity and my life-style ensured I somehow always ended up running with scary people sporting guns or worse chasing me. The strength I'd reverse inherited from Jamie came in just as handy, though—the water pressure wasn't letting up and I needed to use a lot of effort.

Those regular Adjust To Being A Super workouts with Christopher were really paying off. Normally I had to be en-raged in order to really get the A-C skills going. I wasn't enraged right now, and scared really didn't do the trick for me. But I'd worked on my abilities enough that I could bring forth the hyperspeed and use it for swimming. Or as I was thinking of it, running in the water.

Managed to get down and grabbed the lip of the hatch's opening. I'd kept the glove on, and it was working like a re-ally big water wing. My purse was a hindrance, but there was no way in hell I was going to let it wash away. Some of its contents might be salvageable and for all I knew Jeff would need his adrenaline somewhere along the way.

Once through the hatch, the real issue was if I could find the top, or an air pocket, before my lungs exploded. Kicked up hard, keeping the mitt above my head, just in case I hit something. I had to keep on kicking to go up—the water wanted to suck me right back down and through the hatch.

The will to live is strong. The will to ensure that I had a sliver of a prayer that my iPod was still going to work was stronger. Flutter kicked like I was in the Olympic Trials and was rewarded with seeing what looked like light above me. Far above me, but above me nonetheless. So either that was where the air was, or the golden light was calling me to Heaven. Figured it was air, and kicked harder still.

Had to let the air out of my lungs slowly in order to make it, but managed to surface just before I had to take a breath or die. After some serious gasping for a couple of seconds, realized I was in a big tank. The water had been clear, so was hopeful I was in the clean water tank.

I also wasn't alone. There was someone at the edge of the tank, standing on a metal platform, looking at me.

"A little help?"

He shrugged.

"I have three friends who are probably drowning or about to in that little metal room down below."

"Shouldn't have come in the back way, should you?"

Several things were registering. He was good looking, but not A-C gorgeous, with an unruly mop of brown, wavy hair and a scruffy goatee that looked good on him. Green eyes, but not green like Mahin's or Christopher's. Green like a cartoon character's. He had a devilish expression, but in the cute guy way, not in the red lobster suit with horns way.

He was also extremely short but his torso and head looked perfectly normal, meaning he was most likely a dwarf. And he had an accent. As with Mahin's it was familiar, though nothing like hers, but I couldn't place it.

"Look, charge us with breaking and entering later. I need to ensure that the current and former Pontifexes and one of our friends all don't drown to death. I'm the current Head of Field, and I'm giving the official 'save our butts' order."

He smiled. "Oh, I know who you are. You're the one who likes to ask for twenty different obscure types of soda pop while you're in a jet at thirty thousand feet. But not to worry. Can't have you losing both the current *and* former Pontifex on my watch." With that he snapped his fingers.

White, Gower, and Adriana appeared on the platform next to him, gasping.

I said the only thing that came to mind. "Who the hell are you?"

CHAPTER 32

"**MY NAME IS UNPRONOUNCEABLE** to any of your races," he nodded toward White and Gower, "but you can call me Algar."

I swam to the edge of the tank. "You're not an A-C or from their solar system? And you're not a human?"

He reached a hand down. "You're asking or telling?"

"Asking." I put out my hand and he grabbed it above the wrist.

"No." He pulled me up. Easily. More easily than Jeff could have. Set me down gently as well. "Interesting choice with the baseball mitt." He smiled again. "But that's why I like you. You always make interesting choices."

Took the mitt and my purse off and put them down while my mind raced. I could think very quickly when I had to, and the feeling of having to was quite strong. "You're the Operations Team? You're the Elves?" As I said this, I realized his accent sounded Irish.

Algar grinned. "That's me. You're a bright one. Even if I did give you a hint. Lassie." Got the distinct impression the accent was being faked for my benefit and Algar's amusement. He patted White on the back. "Come on, there. Time to breathe. You too," he said to Gower, as he patted his back as well.

"Wait, you're really an Elf? Or a Leprechaun? Or whatever?"

Algar gave me a look I was used to—the Prove You're Smarter Than You Sound look. "What do you think I am?"

"Not from around here." He grinned, but didn't say anything else. Got another distinct impression—this one was that we weren't leaving this area without Algar's approval. And that was likely dependent upon me figuring out what he wanted me to. Always the way.

I looked around. We were in what I was fairly sure was a small reclamation plant. It didn't stink, for which I was eternally grateful, but it didn't look like someplace anyone would just hang out for the fun of it, either.

We'd indeed come up through clean water—I could see almost all the way down to the hatch, which was now closed. Our tank was connected to two other tanks, both filled with what looked like clean water. The water level in "our" tank was high and seemed constant, though it looked like one of the other tanks was low and slowly filling back up. Assumed this meant it had been emptying into "our" tank as "our" tank had emptied into the holding room, meaning we'd never have lasted until the water had fully drained out of the pipe.

It was an impressive system but what it was doing was the question. If this actually was a reclamation area, the water needing to be cleaned and filtered appeared to be missing. There were other things missing, too. And there were things here that made no sense, including what looked like a bed off in a far corner of the room, mostly hidden behind the third tank.

"I thought this was water reclamation, but you're not reclaiming anything, at least, not that I can see."

Algar shrugged. "I'm reclaiming it. Just because you can't see it happen doesn't mean that it's not real."

"You sound Irish, but there's no way you are. Your eyes are wrong for any human or A-C. You're too strong, and that snapping the fingers thing would make me think you're magic, only I don't think you actually are."

"So, what do you think I am?"

He'd nodded his head toward the others on the platform when he'd told me his real name was unpronounceable, no one had ever mentioned a race of short, strong, people with really bright eyes over in the Alpha Centauri system, and he had powers that seemed unreal. But then again, as was so often said, the higher the technology, the more like magic it appears.

"I think you're from far, far away. My guess is the galactic core, but that's only a guess." After all, the Ancients and Mephistopheles had come from near the core, and they were all extra-special as compared to those of us out here in the boondocks part of the Milky Way.

This earned me another smile from Algar. "Correct." Wondered if he knew Olga. He'd love her if he didn't—they were clearly cut from the same Make You Work For It cloth.

"And you're here to save us from drowning how and why?"

"You were just lucky."

"I doubt that. So, how is it that you're the Operations Team? I've been told that team works via a spatio-temporal warp using black hole technology."

Algar nodded. "I do."

"You, one dude, are the entire Operations Team? You're not the Elves but the Elf?"

He shrugged again. "It's a dirty job, but someone's got to do it."

"I call shenanigans. I've been told, nay, *lectured*, about how there's this whole team of A-Cs dedicated to the cleanup cause. Pierre said he's met them, too."

"Pierre may think he's met 'them,' but yet you've never met a single one of them, have you?"

This was true enough. I'd never met anyone who'd ever said they'd ever been on the Operations Team. Nor had anyone ever mentioned that their dad or mom was, say, on the Operations Team. "You're saying that everyone's lying to me? People who have, for the past three-plus years, proven to me on a daily if not hourly basis that they can't lie? They've been aware you're around and lying like time-tested politicians?"

Algar chuckled. "Oh no, not everyone. Not most, really. It's rather the other way around. Most believe, truly believe, that there's a full Operations Team in place." He helped White and Gower to their feet. "Just a small handful know of my existence. Only those with a right or a need to know."

"We're in the middle of a huge attack right now. Any chance you can fix things up with a snap of your magic elvish fingers?"

"Absolutely not." Said with the calm coolness a person would use when passing on the offer of a refill of Coca-Cola.

"And why is that?"

"Would you like me to explain it for you?" White asked.

Algar shot him an amused glance. "You enjoy the pussy-footing as much as I do."

"Not when our people's lives are at stake."

"They're always at stake. That's what makes you all so interesting." Algar turned back to me. "Yes, I'm an alien race. We're immortal, or close to it. I'm faster than you can conceive, faster than any A-C could ever hope to be, even if they were born in a Surcenthumain petri dish. My people are Black Hole People."

"You mean your planet became a black hole?"

"No. I mean our planet is within a black hole. We exist within it. Believe me, it's a great boon to many things. Speed, strength, and immortality are just part of what comes with being part of the Black Hole People."

"So why are you here doing everyone's laundry?" Algar suddenly seemed very interested in helping Adriana into a comfortable sitting position. "Oh, come *on*. Time, it's of the essence. And all that. Richard, you feel like sharing?"

"Only if Algar wants to hear my particular spin on his existence."

Algar rolled his eyes as he turned back to me. "No, I've heard it. When you're immortal, things get dull. So, I . . . journeyed around the galaxy. Stumbled onto Alpha Four back when they thought they were Alpha One and Only. Their king was a good man, trying to get a planet organized and headed into what you'd call their Renaissance Period. Those are always interesting times, so I stuck around and struck a bargain."

Wanted to ask why a being as powerful as Algar appeared to be needed to bargain with a far less powerful race, but chose to hold the question.

"In order for the people to focus on the important tasks at hand, I agreed to be the one who handled all the grunt work chores, so to speak. In return, I get to hang around and watch. I don't interfere, and no one but the ruler actually knows I'm here."

He stopped talking and gave me a pleasant smile. I waited. Nothing more was coming from Algar.

"Really? I'm supposed to buy that line of doublespeak?"

"What do you mean?" Algar sounded mildly offended. Decided not to care.

"No one just hangs around doing the dishes and picking up the poo-poo undies for the hell of it. The only people who do so tend to be parents, and they do it because they love the people they're picking up after. Or they're hired to do a job and do it. For pay. Not for grins and giggles. And while I can buy the whole 'with great power comes great responsibility' line, what I can't buy is that you've been around for what sounds like hundreds of years without letting on that you *are* around."

"Closer to thousands. And a few know," Algar admitted.

"Because they don't look shocked out of their minds, I'm betting Richard and Paul know." They both nodded. "Because you were and are the Supreme Pontifex, right?" More nods. "I want the real story, guys, and I want it now. Official order, and all that," I added to Algar.

"Algar doesn't wish to be found," White said. "So, we provide him with an interesting world to interact and partake in, while he provides us with useful services."

"Gotcha. You're a wanted man, a criminal. You're Loki. Or the Q. Or some combo of both."

Algar grinned. "In a way, I suppose."

"Wow, you got those references?"

He nodded. "I watch every show on television, have seen every movie, read every book."

"Every one?"

"Every one. The good ones, the mediocre ones, the bad ones, and the terrible ones. I'm faster than you can actually conceive and boredom is always a threat."

"So cleaning up for the A-Cs is, what, a thing you do to pass the time?"

"Pretty much. You're right, I'm hiding out. However, the crimes I'm accused of are well past your comprehension. They're crimes of an immortal. And before you waste time trying to figure them out, to make it something you *can* understand, I disobeyed our Prime Directive more than once.

And no, you don't get to know what that Prime Directive is. Just as with any other accused, I don't believe what I did was wrong and I don't feel the punishment will be just. Eternity is long, especially if your prison will be one of sensory deprivation."

"So how did you come to Earth?"

"Ah, good question. The bloodline had thinned, over time. Power made Adolphus a lunatic, and I don't enjoy the company of lunatics. Alfred was a good man, and I expected him to bring Alpha Four back to what it should be. However, when Richard and the rest were being exiled and Alfred chose to go with them, I chose to go with *him*."

"Adolphus let you go?"

"He had no choice."

"I can believe that and can't argue with either your assessment of good old Kitler or Alfred. So Alfred knows about you?"

Algar shook his head. "No. Only the actual ruler knows. Alfred was named for me," he added with a touch of pride. "But he doesn't know that, either. It was his grandfather's wish, as a way of thanking me and keeping me tied to the bloodline. However, fond as I am of my namesake, once here on Earth, it was apparent that Richard was the true leader. As you've said more than once, Richard led the people's hearts and minds. And now Paul does. Though your husband is far more of a king than he would ever want to admit. But until he *is* king, he won't know about me."

"So, you're also like Santa Claus and see us while we're sleeping and know when we're awake?" Contemplated how likely it was that Algar had his own porn channels and they consisted of everyone, all the time. Wondered if I'd ever be able to have sex again. Considered that Algar was basically a hottie and figured I'd find the will to go on and let Jeff keep on giving me the Orgasm Buffet on a regular basis, hunky voyeur or no hunky voyeur. Hey, girls like the bad boys, after all.

"Yes, I can." He grinned. "I don't watch you having sex. That pastime got boring a millennium ago. A-Cs aren't that inventive and humans are worse."

So much for that fantasy. Ah, well, probably better all the

way around. If Algar was telling the truth, which I had no real way of knowing. "Wow, considering what's out there, I'm sort of surprised to hear that."

He shrugged. "Trust me. It gets old when it's always the same old things. And it's always the same old things. But you all keep on enjoying the same old things, so I can understand why you keep on doing them. Now, you have some grand rescue or something to get back to. Don't let me detain you."

"Wait a minute. You're just shoving us out? How do you know we're not going to run and share that you're here?"

"We won't," White said quietly. "And Algar knows this."

"Why won't we? Who knows besides you and Paul?"

"Gladys. And only Gladys."

"Hard to keep the Head of Security out of the know," Algar added. "On this world, anyway. On Alpha Four 'because I'm the king and I said so' worked pretty well."

"Yeah, humans are a lot less willing to not ask the big questions than A-Cs, I guess. But this means that if Gladys knows then Al Dejahl knows."

White shook his head. "We can't actually share the information, knowingly or unknowingly, unless we're in his presence. Algar has . . . ways of preventing it."

"Memory wipe kind of ways?"

Algar shook his head. "Not a wipe. Similar to how the A-Cs use the gases natural to Earth to manipulate human memories. I can just do it to anyone and don't need to use anything else beyond what's inside me. I don't do it often. It's part of my agreement."

"The agreement that prevents us from sharing that Algar is here," White added.

"Makes sense." How we could share something if Algar was as powerful as he seemed was a question I didn't want to ask, lest it had somehow never occurred to anyone else, Algar in particular. "So, why won't you help us?" I asked our personal god in the machine instead.

"You have a superconsciousness hanging around and you have to ask me that?"

"Yeah, I do. ACE was created and programmed. The way he was created, he's close to a god. You're not a god."

Algar snapped his fingers and he and I were somewhere

else. In fact, we were out in the middle of space, in a bubble. "If I take away the bubble that's protecting us, you die and I don't. Tell me I'm not a god now."

I was scared, but a different kind of scared than I'd been in the water. I was the kind of scared that did for me what most fear did for me—it pissed me the hell off.

"Screw you. You're stronger than me, more powerful than me, but you're not a god. Gods create and protect, they don't just destroy."

Algar snapped his fingers and we were back with the others. I got the impression they weren't even aware we'd been away. "You're right," Algar said, as if we hadn't moved. "If I did what you wanted me to, though, then I'd move that much closer to god status. Maybe not in your eyes, but in the eyes of most."

Considered all that I'd just learned, including the fact that Algar was a little bit of a jerk. Maybe more than a little bit. "This isn't about us as much as it's about you. You don't want to do anything too showy because if you do, they'll find you."

He jerked. "What do you mean?"

"You're hiding out. If you helped us, really helped us, that would send up a flare to the people hunting you down. They'd come and take you, and if you could fight them, you'd have done that already, meaning either they're stronger than you or there are just so many more of them that you don't stand a chance against them. That's why you aren't helping us beyond doing something that everyone but, what, three people thinks is being done by regular old A-Cs. You're hiding in plain sight, in that sense."

He smiled slowly. "Of all of the cute little apes who've made good on this planet, I can say with confidence that you're my favorite."

"And of all the Mötley Crüe songs out there, I can say with confidence that the one that fits you best is 'MF of the Year.' "

White and Gower both winced. Perhaps telling the most powerful being around that you thought he was the jerk of jerks wasn't all that wise.

But Algar threw his head back and laughed. "The start of a beautiful friendship."

CHAPTER 33

ALGAR LAUGHING WAS PROBABLY a lot better than Algar threatening to space me again, so I tossed this into the win column.

Noted that for all of this, Adriana hadn't moved or reacted, other than when Algar had put her into a sitting position. As I looked carefully, she wasn't breathing, or moving, or blinking, but she didn't look dead. "What have you done to her?"

"Nothing. She's in stasis. She won't remember any of this. You'll have saved everyone and she'll go on about your mission with no memory of me or this situation."

White looked as if he'd like to leave, so took that as a sign we should get moving. But I wasn't quite ready. "So, what will you do if Al Dejahl wins? If all the people, Alfred included, are mind-controlled or destroyed?"

"I'm not like the thing you call ACE. I'll just leave. Find another group of interesting beings and hang out with them for a while."

"Will those interesting beings allow you to hide as well as we do?"

"Can't see why not."

"Can't see how. While about half of the Alpha Centauri system has humanoids on it, you probably can't pass for any of them. But you could walk outside right now and pass for a human. Other than your eyes, which I'll wager a really good pair of contacts could fix."

"What's your point?"

"You won't do anything that can show you're here to those hunting for you, I get it. But you're going to be hard-pressed to find a planet so easy to hide on, especially since you'll have to go closer to the galactic core. And I know you could tell us something, anything, that would help."

Algar nodded. "I could. And then, the next time, you'd come to me again, and you'd harangue me some more, beg, plead, threaten, whatever. And maybe I'd do it again. And then, after a very short while, it becomes a habit. And instead of doing for yourselves, suddenly you're hailing your great god Algar and your free will and my anonymity are things of the past."

"We don't do that with ACE."

"Ah, but you do. By all rights, the Z'porrah invasion should have destroyed this world, certainly the main city under attack. And yet Washington, D.C. and all the rest of the world still stand. And the humans didn't nuke each other in the process. You didn't prevent any of that—ACE did. Because of you. It got involved, and it gave itself away."

"Is ACE in trouble?"

"Not as you'd understand trouble, but yes. Because all stronger, immortal beings of all kinds have a form of Prime Directive."

"That's what you did, your crime. You interfered."

He snapped his fingers again. Nothing changed. Other than, as I looked around, White and Gower seemed as immobile as Adriana. "No." Algar reached up and patted my cheek. "No, that's what I chose not to do."

"So you're a good guy?"

He shrugged. "Good is in the eyes of the beholders. Is it good that I've allowed not one or two but hundreds of planets and civilizations to destroy each other and themselves? Is that a moral choice?"

Algar wasn't asking lightly or rhetorically, so I thought about my reply before I gave it. "I guess it depends on whether or not you value free will."

"That's one way of looking at it, yes."

"Were you one of the race we call the Ancients?"

"No, but we knew of them. That's why I wandered out this way. Followed their paths, in my own way, of course."

"Of course. The Ancients interfered."

"Yes, they did. And both good and bad came of it. But they weren't immortals."

"I don't see the difference, honestly. Short life or a long one, why does that affect your moral code?"

He sighed. "Let me give you more perspective, and more food for thought. Most Black Hole People remain within the Black Hole Universe. Your science is eons away from determining that all the black holes are interconnected, particularly how they're connected. We have a rich, full universe that provides us infinite work and entertainment. But some of us are chosen to leave."

"Were you chosen or did you run away?"

"I was chosen. I was in charge of a solar system. My third, by the way. Billions and billions of souls in that system. I chose to let them have free will. All of them. And while there were many leaders, on one of the planets eventually one leader was more strong and charismatic and powerful than any before him. And he destroyed his world, sent a bomb more frightening than your worst nukes right into his own sun. Billions died, all at once, not just on that planet, but on the others in that system. There were eight planets teeming with life in that solar system, wiped out by one power-mad individual's free will. Was my allowing that to happen a 'good' moral choice?"

"Um . . ."

"Let me make it more complicated. Or maybe easier. That took place in the system one over from the system the beings you call the Ancients came from. They chronicled the event as a warning to others, and did their best to spread their good word."

"I knew they were missionaries!"

"Yes, and your ability to make those kinds of leaps is why we're having this conversation right now."

"I'm not the only one who can so leap."

"No, but you're the one who was at the right place at the right time and made that leap *when* it mattered. Timing and luck count much more than most humans want to believe. Anyway, the beings on the one world, the world responsible for the destruction of its entire solar system, survived. In a sense."

That very bad feeling from earlier returned, sharing that I wasn't going to like the next things Algar said.

"You call them parasitic superbeings. I was on Alpha Four when the man you called Ronald Yates was banished to Earth. I might have even suggested it."

"Why?"

"Being helpful. It was clear he was a danger. Along the lines of that other leader, the one who destroyed his entire solar system. He was very like the one I'd allowed to destroy every living thing he could."

"Why didn't you kill Yates, then?"

"Because there is a chasm larger than the Grand Canyon between 'might,' 'will,' and 'did.'"

"Ah, the *Minority Report* defense. I'll allow it."

"*So* glad." Algar definitely had a sarcasm knob, and apparently it flipped to eleven easily. "Because of what I can do, I saw when the leader who'd destroyed his own solar system arrived and joined with Yates."

He paused, presumably waiting for a reaction from me. I didn't have one. Well, not one I could verbalize. Maybe that was Algar's point.

"So, consider that I'm the reason Mephistopheles ever existed on your planet. And yet I did nothing then and still do nothing now to either stop or hinder either him or his offspring. *Now* what are your thoughts about free will and passive noninterference?"

Thought long and hard before I replied. And looked at White while so thinking. "Some of his offspring are good and some are bad. And one side will win. You *are* on the side of good, so to speak, because you help us, and I don't think you're doing Ronaldo Al Dejahl's laundry, for example."

He chuckled. "No, I'm not."

"So you aligned with the good guys as an active choice. Because you could have chosen either side when you came here, couldn't you? Or no side at all and just wandered off like you say you will should we annihilate ourselves."

This I didn't buy. Algar was attached to the A-Cs, more than he seemed willing to admit. Or maybe he told himself he wasn't attached so that when he did nothing it didn't bother him as much.

"Yes. Alfred is still unaware that I exist and I could have chosen to not let Richard know."

"You said I couldn't comprehend your crimes. But I can."

Algar shook his head. "I've explained this in simplistic terms, as if, for my people, you were a little child. There's always more going on than you see or are aware of, including the true nature, effect, and ramifications of choices. Layers and twists upon layers and twists. That's how the universe works. Even when you win, somehow, you can still lose. You know that from experience."

"True enough. So why tell me all this? Will I forget it the moment I'm away from you?"

"No, but your thoughts about me will be shielded. As for why?" He shrugged. "As I said, you're my favorite."

"Why?"

He smiled slowly. "You always say please and thank you. You've never taken what I do for granted. And I find your offers of gifts of milk or money in shoes to be somewhat . . . endearing."

"So I not only actually called it, in that you're more like the A-C Elves than a confusing scientific answer, but you also like me because I'm polite? Wow. Mom and Dad would be so proud. If I could tell them about this. And Christopher. I'd love to tell Christopher about this. I might even be able to do it without a lot of gloating."

"Which you can't. I'd say sorry but I'm not. You won't be able to talk about me, not even with Richard or Paul, unless you're with me and I allow it, such as I have now."

"Or Gladys," I added. "She knows about you, even if she can't tell Al Dejahl about you. Which is good. But I can talk to her about you once she's okay. I mean, we brought her back from under Ronaldo's mind control before. We can do it again. You could do it, if you wanted to."

Algar snapped his fingers. White and Gower were breathing again. Or we were back from whatever time hold Algar had put the two of us into. I wasn't sure and doubted he'd give me a straight answer if I asked.

"Well, about Gladys. There's more than a little problem with Gladys."

"What problem is that?" Gower asked.

Algar shook his head. "You'll get to find out."

"But you're not going to tell us?" Figured he wasn't, but also figured I should ask.

"No."

"You *are* just like the Q." I'd never liked the Q, because they were pompous, capricious, all-powerful jerks. Algar had the potential to make the Q look good. And he knew it, too, and clearly wanted me not exactly liking him. Why was the question.

"In a way, I suppose. But your situation is much less like *Star Trek* and much more like *The Mummy*." With that he snapped his fingers and the four of us weren't in the water tank area anymore.

CHAPTER 34

WE WERE STANDING IN A ROOM that had the faint odor of sulfur and sewage along with small tanks and equipment that said "Reclamation" and "Reclaimed Water: Do Not Drink" all over them.

We were all also completely dry. The baseball mitt was on my left hand, my purse was over my neck. Opened my purse. Everything in there was dry, too.

Pulled out my iPod and earbuds. Put them in and pushed play. "MF of the Year" came on. It'd been playing when we were in the plane and the iPod wasn't on repeat. So Algar had a sense of humor. And, I guess, wanted me to know I hadn't been dreaming or hallucinating.

Left the earbuds in and the music playing low enough that I could still hear everyone and clipped my iPod to my belt. Needed the reassurance of tunes right now for some strange reason.

"I'm glad we finally got that hatch opened," Adriana said. "But I'm gladder your imagination was just overactive, Kitty."

"Ah . . . right you are." I wanted to ask Gower and White what the hell had just happened but I couldn't. I also wanted to ask what had happened to the water tanks, and why there were water tanks in the Science Center in the first place. Wished I'd asked Algar when I'd had the chance. Maybe next time. If there was a next time.

"I'm just relieved none of our enemies were here in the rec-lamation system," White said, as if everything was totally normal. Figured I'd better follow his lead. He'd been living with the knowledge of Algar's existence for a long time, after all.

Took the mitt off and tucked it under my arm, then dug my Glock out of my purse and made sure a full clip was in. "I'm ready to move on, then, Mister White. I think we need to find Gladys."

"We need to ensure that the Science Center is clear," Gower countered. "If you're right, everyone's here somewhere, Gladys included."

"Yes. Back to the excitement of being under siege, Missus Martini."

They were right. More to the point, they were trying to tell me to forget about Algar. I didn't call on the Elves for help with anything other than food, clothes, and cleaning, and that was how it had to be. My clothes and belongings were all nice and dry. Looked down. My hands were clean, and so were my pants. Decided not to point this out.

Gower did a hyperspeed check of the reclamation area—it was clean, so to speak. Other than the hatch, which White closed, there was only one door in or out of the room. Managed not to mention that the hatch had been closed already. This spatio-temporal-black-hole stuff really messed with your head.

Had to get my head back in the game. The music changed and "Saints of Los Angeles" came on. Let the music rev me up. A few bars was all it took. Headed for the door.

I didn't open it right away, but listened at it first. Didn't hear anything. Opened it slowly, ready to slam it shut or open, depending, but the hallway it opened to was empty.

Realized we weren't on the lowest level, where the room I'd dubbed Martini's Human Lair was, where we'd lived for my first year or so with Centaurion Division. We were on the second level, the one right under ground level.

All A-C bases went down. The Science Center went down fifteen floors. Main Operations, or what I called the Bat Cave Level, were on the third floor. The ground level had the main launch area, motor pool, main gate area, and other logistical sections.

The second floor where we were had human medical. Other than when I'd had to bash in Beverly's head with a baseball bat to prevent her from killing or sterilizing Jeff, I hadn't spent a lot of time on this level. Possibly because it was also where a lot of standard maintenance happened, so it made sense that the reclamation equipment was here.

What didn't make sense, any more, was how the left fork of the pipe could take us to the second floor, but the right took us to the fifteenth, and yet never went down. And none of us had noticed or mentioned it—not Jeff and Christopher when they were little; not me, Christopher and the flyboys when we crawled through the first time; not Gladys and Security; and not even my mother when she was told about how the pipe that emptied onto the equivalent of just under ground level led to the hallway just outside of where I was sleeping fourteen floors below.

Clearly Algar was in control of that pipe in some way. Maybe the pipe was still here because it *was* the spatio-temporal-black-hole, or its machinery.

Chose to absolutely not mention this aloud. Not because I wasn't sure if I even could or not, but because I had to figure that Algar had put us here for a reason. He might want to say he was just a helpful observer and wasn't involved, but he was indeed involved. Perhaps only like an observer at a baseball game, but he was involved. And he obviously had a favorite team.

While White zipped through the floor to see who or what might be around, I shoved this newest wrinkle away, hard, and ran through our past experiences. The first time the Science Center had been under siege everyone other than Jeff and a few others had been herded to the top level. But when Al Dejahl had taken over he'd done it in the Research area, in the library, in fact, which was below us.

I truly had no clear idea of how wide the Science Center actually was, but I was pretty sure it was much wider on all four sides than the ground level would indicate. I always related to rats in a maze whenever I had to find my own way around here.

However, hyperspeed meant White could search it, vast or not, in under thirty seconds. "All clear," he said when he rejoined us.

"Up or down?" Gower asked.

"That's the hundred thousand dollar question, isn't it? A

part of me thinks Ronaldo will go for the library again, but another part says he'll try somewhere else. So, up, I guess? It's one floor to search if no one's there and then back down."

White nodded. "I'd hate to discover they were on the top floor after we'd searched all the way down." He took my hand, Gower took Adriana's; we headed for the stairwell, and went up.

We reached the stairwell door. Nothing and no one. We zipped through. This stairwell was back off the main floor, so we were actually hidden by a wall. White stopped walking and shoved us against said wall "We're not alone," he said in whisper.

We slunk up to the doorway in the wall. As with the first time I'd found people up here who shouldn't be, there were a lot of folks in camouflage. They weren't doing anything much, just standing around with assault rifles.

"Do we round them up or kill them?" Gower asked, keeping his voice low.

"There are too many," Adriana replied. "We would need to use explosives."

"We can get those easily enough," White said.

"Wait." There was something wrong with these people. They were literally just standing there. Sure, they could be on duty, but they weren't at attention or even seeming to be paying attention. "Wait a second."

Scanned the terrorist crowd. Based on the body structures, there were a lot of women in this group. Sure there were women terrorists—Mahin was one, after all—but this many in this particular organization didn't seem statistically likely.

Searched for a face, any face. Was finally rewarded to see a couple people who were more or less facing us. They were both incredibly attractive, ill-fitting military garb or not.

Pulled everyone a few steps back. "I'm pretty sure those are our people, as in, A-Cs, and probably humans who work with us."

"Why?" Gower asked.

"Presumably so that if anyone breaches through the shielding somehow they'll either kill our own or our own will kill them." This was a rather impressive bad guy maneuver. After all, if we could have gotten in when we were dealing with Mahin, we would probably have shot first and asked questions later.

"So what do we do?" Gower asked.

"We still have to find Ronaldo and everyone else. The people on this level don't account for even a tenth of those who are missing."

"Library again?" White asked.

Was about to reply when the song changed to "Just Another Psycho." Should probably nominate it to be our official Bad Guy Theme Song.

But none of the Megalomaniac League thought they were ordinary. So, would Ronaldo do a repeat? And if he was, why? He'd wanted Jamie last time, and this was the last place where she'd be. She'd lived all but about a week of her life in the Embassy.

It dawned on me that Algar had told me that he watched every TV show and movie, read every book. Probably read every magazine, too, and listened to our music. So, he could have used any pop culture reference when telling me what we were about to face. But he'd picked *The Mummy*. Why?

There was only one reason I could come up with—to give me a clue.

There were different versions of the movie, but I'd really only seen the one starring Brendan Fraser. I'd seen it a lot. The heroine was a librarian, so maybe that indicated everything was once again happening in the library.

But if that was the case, why not use *Groundhog Day* as the clue? Why specifically choose *The Mummy*? Sure we were trapped in an underground building in the middle of the desert that contained a lot of valuable stuff along with a lot of people who wanted to kill us. And we had two teams inside. Okay, so *The Mummy* made sense. But not enough sense. At least, not yet.

"Why *The Mummy*?" I asked aloud, being sure to keep my voice low. All three of them looked at me blankly. "Really? No one's seen that movie?"

Gower shrugged. "Why go see a movie about someone in a sarcophagus? I'd rather visit a museum and see the real thing."

Stared at Gower for a long moment. "I know what level we need to go to next."

CHAPTER 35

"YOU'RE SURE?" Gower asked, as we approached my least favorite area in any Centaurion Division facility.

"Yes." I was nervous because I hated this area and was already expecting something to jump out at me. Switched my music to my Action Rock mix and put it on random. Proving that we were really one with the Crüe, "Primal Scream" came on.

"It makes sense," White agreed. "This is where everything changed for my half brother the last time."

"Mister White, why do you call him your half brother? I mean, I know he is, but it's not like you were raised together, clearly, and he's not exactly brimming over with brotherly love."

"I say it to remind myself that even though he's my enemy, he's still my blood. He's not a random individual—he's someone who, if we'd known about him, found him when he was young, might be a very different person today."

It was never confusing to me, how White had kept the A-Cs on the path of right, why Algar would choose to tell White of his existence, or why our enemies always somehow had White in their sights—he was, quite frankly, the moral ideal, and that meant that he was a target.

Gower, by having worked and learned under White for years and now being the current Pontifex, was also a target. The wisdom of storming the Science Center with two of the most likely Bad Guy Targets Du Jour was in question. However, presumably everyone was a target right now. So, better to storm with two guys who knew what the situation really was than not.

Minor leadership dilemma over, we reached what I thought of as The Chambers O' Doom but was commonly referred to as the Isolation Area.

The isolation wing was large, in part because we had a lot of empaths, and Jeff wasn't the only one who would push too far and then basically collapse. Also, while the empaths and imageers both used blocks—mental and medical—to keep from being inundated by the reality of their powers, the on-slaught of human emotions was a lot harder to deal with than the information gleaned from an image. An imageer could choose not to touch a picture. An empath couldn't choose to not feel the people around them.

The Science Center being the size it was meant it housed well over a hundred isolation chambers. The empaths, and sometimes the imageers and others, were put into the chambers to regenerate in a safe place.

According to Jeff, who spent more time than anyone in isolation, the isolation chambers were wonderful safe havens. To me, who usually spent my time in an isolation area on the outside looking in, they looked like a cross between an Iron Maiden and a sarcophagus, with a lot of extra tubes and needles added in just for fun. The Science Center's isolation area always reminded me of a cross between Franken-stein's lab and a haunted Egyptian tomb.

"I don't hear anyone," Gower said quietly as we listened at the stairwell's door.

"This level is quite soundproofed," White said. "Though I hear nothing as well."

I didn't either, but I was sure Algar wanted us down here. "Paul, the last time, you held out against the mind control. You and the others who could were locked into isolation chambers. What are the odds that's happened again?"

"I'd think high," White said.

"But that was a last resort," Gower said. "And he was keeping us in there to use us. I don't know that we should count on our people being safely locked away."

"True enough. Though it was hard as hell to get you guys out because Gladys changed all the security codes. Which she's probably done again."

"We'll deal with it as we have to," White said.

"I have a question," Adriana said before we could do anything else. "Why haven't we been intercepted yet?"

"How do you mean?"

"No one has come to stop us. If the facility is under siege, where are its guardians? Are the only guards the ones we saw at the top level? That seems remarkably . . . trusting, and I doubt these enemies are trusting. And where is our other team?"

"Maybe our other team has already handled everything else?" Gower asked. He didn't sound like he thought that was a real possibility, but the hope was definitely there.

Considered this as "Bite the Bullet" by Motörhead came onto my personal sound system. It wasn't the same listening to them at low volume, but I did kind of have to be able to hear what my team was saying. "Or the bad guys know we're here and know we're coming, and are lying in wait, not making any sound."

"You're really sure this is the place for a standoff?" Gower asked.

"I'm really sure that Ronaldo almost won last time, in this area, and that Jeff beat the crap out of him, in this area."

"And you made your first decision as Pontifex in this area," White added softly. "I'm with my partner—we should be prepared for attack the moment we go through the door."

"Let's weapon up, gang. And remember," I added as everyone pulled out guns, "the majority of the targets are going to be our own people being mind controlled. We have no idea who's under control or not right now, and Ronaldo Al Dejahl is a strong enough imageer that he can change to look like anyone he wants to. We can't shoot to kill, even if we want to."

"We'll shoot to wound then," Adriana said calmly. "If needed."

"Let's prepare for the worst and hope for the best," White said. He nodded to Gower, who grabbed Adriana's hand while White grabbed mine.

"Ready, ladies?" White asked.

"As we'll ever be, Mister White. Let's go see what bizarre form of Mexican Standoff we're dealing with this time."

With that, White opened the door.

CHAPTER 36

I WAS AMAZED we hadn't heard anything. Because there was a hell of a fight going on, albeit farther into the floor. Apparently Isolation had the best soundproofing of any A-C facility, including the Embassy. I'd never be willing to have sex here, regardless, but it was good to know.

The fight, in fact, was going on exactly where Ronaldo and White and then Ronaldo and Jeff had fought before. Meaning this spot had been chosen on purpose. And also meaning that we were expected to come inside. Decided to table what this might mean in terms of Mahin or not for later.

The fight was going on at hyperspeed, but thanks to being enhanced, I could see it. Adriana couldn't, and neither could any of the other humans in here. Though most of them looked down if not completely out.

Spotted all the flyboys, all looking decidedly worse for wear. Same with Tim and Kevin. All of them were down and looked unconscious. As I looked for him, Reader came flying backward through the air, slammed against a wall, and joined the rest of the humans in unconsciousness. Chose to believe they were all unconscious at least. Gower growled. Couldn't blame him.

Jeff's team was still up and active. Tito and Rahmi were attacking together, while Chuckie and Rhee were teamed up, the princesses shouting instructions to their respective humans. It was remarkably effective, and, of course, both Chuckie and Tito had fought A-Cs and others with hyperspeed before. Of course, so had the other guys. They were taking on a lot of Field agents, and most of Security, based on body size. It wasn't an even fight.

"I'm going to help Charles and Princess Rhee," White said to Gower. "You take our good doctor and Princess Rahmi. Missus Martini, I'm sure you'll be going to assist your husband. Adriana, my dear, stay here at the door and don't let anyone through."

With that he and Gower took off. "I thought the Pontifex was not supposed to get involved in these kinds of brawls," Adriana said.

"They're not, but you can't really blame them." There were a lot of random Field agents. They chose to pay attention to us. "So much for you merely guarding the door."

"Do you truly want me at the door or helping?"

"Actually, you might want to go through it and stay on the other side."

"No, I will stay to help you. The coming fight looks quite unfair."

"Can you actually see to help?"

"Grandmother has been working with me on the skill. And I believe the medicine Doctor Hernandez created to help humans handle hyperspeed has a side effect of helping the eyes 'see faster.' So somewhat."

"It'll have to do." We were out of time—the random A-Cs had reached us.

Rage tended to be my friend. I didn't have a lot of "flight" in my makeup. I seemed to always be on the side of "fight" for that particular reflex option. As I'd been learning every day since giving birth to my daughter, rage was vital, because rage meant I was in full command of all the A-C bells and whistles I'd inherited.

Rage was easy to achieve right now for some reason. The Crüe's "White Trash Circus" came on again. Worked for me—it had a good beat to fight to. And I was going to fight.

Shoved the Glock into the back of my pants, kept my purse over my head, had a weird idea, and put the baseball mitt on. Would have preferred a bat, but improvisation was my middle name.

The agents were on us. And I started spinning, fast.

I wasn't doing this move merely to get dizzy. I was using the mitt as an extension of my arm, so that I could keep the agents just a little farther away. It had the advantage of being quite old, and therefore not exactly supple.

Leather, if not kept up as it ages, tends to get hard. This mitt wasn't up to solid wood standards, but it had been left in a pipe for twenty-plus years. It was pretty hard, made to feel harder by the speed I was going.

It was also effective, at least if the grunts of pain I was hearing from the men I was hitting were any indication.

The only downside was that I wasn't tall enough to hit most of their heads. Had to solve that problem, and quickly.

Found a shorter A-C of the group attacking me and stopped spinning. Jumped on his back instead. He started trying to get me off and, happy day, decided that spinning around was a great plan.

Rage being what it was, I was actually stronger than the guy who I was using as a stepladder. So I was able to get onto his shoulders and lock my legs around his back. As long as he didn't watch MMA and therefore realize that if he just fell forward I'd be screwed, we were good.

Apparently he wasn't a fights enthusiast, because he just kept on spinning to try to shake me off. This was great, because while we were going slower than I had been, I was now higher than the guys I was fighting.

Adriana saw what I was doing. I knew this because as I slammed the mitt into the head of the nearest A-C, she used a low kick to knock him off his feet. In fact, she was using the Iron Broom Sweep, where she stayed low, had her leg out, and spun around in a 360 as she swept the legs of the A-Cs near us. This was an impressive technique. Which meant I had to knock more heads in order to keep up. Worked for me.

She was slower, of course, but that gave me more time to hit agents, slam their heads together, and so forth. My unwilling partner was actually a great help. He kept on trying to hit me and I kept on slamming his arms away from me, meaning he ended up hitting someone else around us.

We flailed around like this for what felt like a long time, but which I knew to be less than three minutes, because

"White Trash Circus" was still going when the last A-C around us hit the ground.

While Adriana slammed heads into the floor to ensure the agents were out and stayed out, I dealt with the guy whose shoulders I was riding. Decided the easiest way was to just hit him until he stopped being ornery.

Slammed the mitt into his face a few times while I tightened my thighs around his neck and head. This was working, but not fast enough. Decided to go for the impressive option. But it would require tag-teaming. "Adriana, need that Iron Broom move again!"

Leaned forward, looked him in the eyes, albeit upside down, grabbed his arms and kept them off my thighs, then flipped myself backward as hard as I could, while pushing against his back with my feet and lower legs and pulling his arms back.

Adriana, meanwhile, both heard and answered the call. She swept his legs as I went back. I let go with my legs and hands and did a backflip. I landed on my feet and my purse didn't hit me in the face, so I was definitely counting this one as deserving of at least a 9.0 for Olympic Trials. He landed flat on his back. His head slammed into the floor, but Adriana did another slam on him anyway.

"I approve of the double-tap."

"Good." Adriana got to her feet. "I hear women fighting."

Grabbed her hand. "You lead, let's go see."

We took off and, sure enough, we found some women fighting all right, behind a big set of isolation chambers. Claudia, Lorraine, and Serene were fighting back to back against the rest of Security. Speaking of unfair fights. Sure, the one Adriana and I had just had had been unfair, too, but this one looked worse. The girls were seriously pissed and the Security team looked pretty bad.

Remembered what the fight Jeff and Christopher had been having looked like. They hadn't been doing nearly so well as the girls. "I think I need to go help Jeff."

"I'll stay here." Adriana pulled some rope out of her backpack. "I have a plan."

"I'll let you run it. Hoping you're conscious and unhurt when I get back." Zipped off to where I'd seen the guys. Sure enough Jeff and Christopher were fighting one person. A woman. A small woman. If she was five feet tall that would be pushing the boundaries of measurement. And they were losing.

They were losing in part because they weren't trying to kill this enemy and in fact weren't really fighting as hard as I'd seen both of them do before. Was pretty sure that was the case for everyone else on Alpha and Airborne who was down and out, as well as those still fighting. These were our people, under mind control, and our side knew it.

As I arrived, this one tiny opponent sent Christopher flying, similar to how someone had done with Reader. Christopher slammed against an isolation chamber door and went down. Then she turned back to Jeff. She was older but still Dazzler gorgeous, with short, black hair. But I could see familial resemblance, more to Lucinda than White, but still, there.

I had a damned good guess who this was, and I also knew one thing, clearly—the gloves had to come off. And there was only one person here who could do that. Me.

She wasn't my aunt or sister, she wasn't someone I worked for, and, more to the point, she wasn't someone I'd ever actually met in person. And I was tired of her intimidating me. That was so last Operation ago. Right now, as she slammed a fist into Jeff that doubled him over, slammed her knee into his head, then tossed him aside and onto the floor, I wasn't intimidated—I was enraged.

When Jeff didn't get up, I quickly went from enraged to supernova rage levels. I had one thought, and one thought only, and it wasn't how to subdue my opponent without hurting her.

"Hey Gladys, got some news for you." Took my purse off and tossed it near to Jeff. Hopefully someone would be able to give him an adrenaline shot, because I was betting that he needed it. Kept my earbuds in and iPod on. Tunes were always my friends.

She turned to me. "What's that? You're quitting Centurion because you've never belonged here in the first place?"

"Nope, something much simpler. Bring it, bitch, 'cause you're going down."

CHAPTER 37

AS THE SONG ON MY IPOD CHANGED, I was now certain Algar was controlling my playlist. Because the new song was "Kill Your Idols" by Static-X. A fine song to kick butt to, good, fast, angry beat, helpful lyrics. Put it on repeat.

Gladys did that creepy crack your neck just by tilting your head really hard thing. Was pretty sure she did it to *be* creepy. Chose to look at is as a challenge, to see if I could crack her neck a whole lot harder.

Unlike most of my opponents over the years, she wasn't talking. That one insult seemed to have been it. Instead of chat, she launched herself at my legs.

I jumped up and did the splits. She flipped into a forward roll and as I came down and spun around, she tackled me, hitting my stomach with her head.

"Ooof!" I sounded like Mahin. And figured I knew how she'd felt when I was kicking her butt. I went backward, Gladys on top of me, straddling my chest, all the better to do her version of ground and pound. Her version sucked, and by sucked I mean hurt a lot.

Still had the baseball mitt on. It was working great as a defensive tool—I had it in front of my face for protection and absorption of blows.

"Defend your head!" Tito shouted. Ah, my MMA coach was watching on the sidelines. Or, more likely, coaching while he was also kicking butt, which was a standard move

for him. For this I was grateful. I'd personally thought the
mitt was handling the defensive end, but I put both arms up,
bent in front of my face.

"Knee her back! Knee her back and work to get out!" Tito
was full of good advice.

I'd pulled it off earlier when no one was around. Might as
well give it a go here, in the presence of witnesses. Besides,
Gladys was tough but she was also small.

Shifted my hips so I rocked her, slammed my knee into
her back as hard as I could, while I shoved my arms at her
with all my strength.

Gladys went back as my leg went up. The move worked
perfectly again. The only problem was that Gladys was a lot
shorter than Mahin. I did hit the back of her head, but with
my shin. Which hurt like hell.

It stunned her, though, which was what I needed. Used the
mitt to hit her with a slapping left and she went off of me to
my right. I rolled to my left and scrambled to my feet.

She ran toward me again, and I decided it was time for my
favorite Kung Fu technique—Crane Opens a Can of Whup-
Ass.

Jumped to the side onto the leg whose shin wasn't hurting
with my other leg up. Blocked her with my nice pointy Crane
Hands. Side blade kick to her knee. Okay, to her hip, she was
really short. Two palm strikes to her head, another to the face,
and a fourth to her floating ribs. Okay, to her damn shoulder.
No wonder she was considered so formidable—she was hard
as hell to hit correctly.

However, I was definitely rocking her. The next move was
another kick to take out her knee. Gladys, seeing this, tried
to swerve out of my reach. No worries. Crane Has Long
Wings wasn't hard to do from this position, either.

I chopped the back of her neck with the side of my right
hand as hard as I could. She stumbled and almost lost her
balance, but recovered and ran on. Into an open isolation
chamber behind me, which I saw as I spun around to supposedly hit her with the second Crane Wing.

She came out with a hypodermic. Not this again. "What
are you going to threaten to do to Jeff or Christopher this
time?"

She looked at the hypo in her hand then back at me. "Nothing. I'm going to stab this through your eye. And there won't be a single thing you can do about it."

"I think there are several things I plan to do about it." Thought madly about what weapons take-away forms I knew. Crane said this was not in the rules and requested a knife or a gun, since Crane and I actually knew how to take both of those away. Needles were long, sharp, pointy, and yet small, making them hard to stop. Crane said it was out of ideas. Baseball Mitt shared that it was ready to take whatever it had to for the team.

Gladys smiled. "I doubt they'll work. ACE isn't around to help you any more."

Figured part of the problem with Gladys that Algar had mentioned was that she'd figured out somehow that ACE was indeed on hiatus. Not good. I needed a weapon. I could pull out my Glock and just shoot her, but that seemed extreme at the moment, and not in any small part because I didn't want to blow away White's sister in front of him. That just seemed so horribly wrong to do to anyone, let alone someone I cared about. I just wanted to knock her out—potentially into a bloody pulp, but still "out" was what I was shooting for.

Should have kept my purse on. Could have gotten the harpoon out without looking. Oh well, so much for that. Could always grab my own hypodermic out of the isolation chamber—they always had tons in there—but that seemed both scary and ridiculous, even for me. Plus that would mean my back would have to be to Gladys, and even for a second that didn't sound wise.

She ran at me, hypo held like a knife, slashing as she got closer. She slashed and stabbed, I dodged, using the mitt to block.

Wanted her away from the people who were unconscious, my husband especially. So I started backing up.

"Running away so quickly?" she sneered.

"This? This isn't running. When I run, you'll know."

More thrusts with the needle from her, more dodging and blocking from me. At this rate one of us was going to get tired, and it was a fifty-fifty chance it might be Gladys. Not the best odds. Time for something offensive.

Technically, she was so tiny I should have been able to just pretty much use my longer reach and smash her. But she was fast, skilled, and waving that needle around. Fighting Uma the Bitch Leader during Operation Invasion had been a lot easier. But I'd had an Amazonian battle staff to use then.

"Tito! I need a distance weapon of some kind!"

Something sailed through the air. "Kitty," Rahmi shouted. "Catch!"

Put my right hand up and caught Rahmi's battle staff. They were weighted more like a javelin—one end heavier than the other—but both ends glowed. The staff was activated which was nice. Activated, it resembled a double light saber, allowing its wielder to totally get their Darth Maul on.

"Gladys, just a mention. This staff can cut through you like butter. Don't make me want to do that. You know this isn't you. You're being controlled by someone you happen to despise."

"How would you know what is or isn't me?" she asked. "Or who I despise?"

"You're Richard's sister. You telling me that you're choosing Ronaldo over him?"

"Richard's dead," Gladys said. "I saw him die."

Couldn't risk looking around. "Mister White!"

"Here, Missus Martini. Essentially right behind you. Gladys, it's me."

She looked right at him. *Right* at him. "I have no idea who you are, but you're not my brother." She looked around. "And before any of you try to claim kinship with me, I don't know who you are, just that you're not who you say you are." She looked back to me. "Other than you. I know who you are."

"And just who is that?"

"You're the reason Richard and the rest of my family are dead." She said it calmly, as if it was longtime common knowledge. "You infiltrated us and destroyed us. And for that, you have to die."

With that, she lunged toward me.

CHAPTER 38

MY MIND LIKED TO WORK FAST in situations like these.

First off, it casually pointed out that there was no way Gladys was this convinced that no one she'd known all her life were her family, at least not over a few hour period. Meaning Ronaldo had probably been working on her for a while. Or else she'd been having problems ACE had nicely been covering up or helping her with.

Both options said the same thing—she wasn't going to stop.

As I put the staff up into a defensive position, my mind then shared that both Option #1 and Option #2 had issues. My mind had a challenge believing that Gladys had turned. No one from White, to Jeff, to Walter, would buy this, long-term mind control or not. And if ACE had been working with her, he'd have told someone, Gower for certain.

Ergo, perhaps, and hopefully, this wasn't the real Gladys. Tito had an OVS, and it might be a really good time to use it. Because Option #3 said we had a lovely new android in our midst, and, awful as that was, I was kind of praying Option #3 turned out to be the case.

But in order to verify which Option was our Big Winner of the Hour, I had to take her down. But not down permanently, in case Options #1 or #2 were what was going on.

Gladys closed the gap and Thought Time was over. I was really being tested on my long-term muscle and skills memory. Hadn't fought with a Beta Twelve battle staff since just before my wedding, but thankfully the skills liked to show up when I needed them most.

The Skills would have preferred to have my left hand free and open, but Baseball Mitt said that it was, so far, the only thing really helping me, and the rest of the Peanut Gallery could chill. Had to agree. And I knew how to use a staff one-handed.

As it turned out, Baseball Mitt had called it right. Blocked Gladys with the staff and slapped the hypodermic out of her hand with one awesomely altered Crane move. Crane felt that it deserved second billing in the fight and was hanging about, waiting to offer help as needed.

Crane suggested a front ball kick to whatever part of her body I connected with. Did the move, got her right in the sternum. Go Team Sanity!

As Gladys fell back, I took a moment to listen. Didn't hear the sounds of fighting any more. Hoped that meant that more than White were still standing up. Of course, if they were, a little help would have been nice.

Then again, I wouldn't want to get near the active end of a battle staff, so perhaps the others were just showing wisdom.

Or else they were leaving room for Rhee. Who came up behind Gladys and slammed the length of her battle staff against the back of Gladys' head.

A normal person, human or even A-C, would be down now. Gladys wasn't down. She shook her head, reached back without looking, grabbed the staff, and wrenched it out of Rhee's hands.

Baseball Mitt, Crane, The Skills, and I all agreed. "She's not Gladys, I think she's an android!" Hoped this would get someone verifying with the OVS.

A blur ran past and around us. "Kitty's right," Christopher called. "Per the OVS, whoever Kitty's fighting is not fully organic."

"Android, ninety-nine percent confirmation," Tito said. Heard some worried muttering. "No one ever gets a hundred percent, Kitty, android or organic. Clothing, fillings, and so forth."

"Awesome."

Gladys went into a staff-fighting stance then launched herself at me.

I could fight with a staff one-handed, but it wasn't easy. She used her staff to knock mine out of my hand. It went flying. Decided I'd had enough and I went for my Glock.

Blocked her staff with the mitt. We were very close to each other. I'd been practicing and was able to flip off the safety with one hand. Did so, slammed my Glock into the side of her head, and fired.

She was definitely an android, and I knew this not simply due to the fact that we'd been fighting all this time and she hadn't tried to get the gun out of my pants, but because she didn't die or stop trying to kill me.

No worries. Mom had worked with me on rapid-firing techniques and, like Christopher, she didn't really ever say, "Good enough, we can stop training now." Shot several more rounds into her head, which staggered her back a bit. Then did a line of fire from her head straight down.

Clip emptied, Android Gladys was still up, but clearly malfunctioning. At least I took her jerking around like she was having a major seizure to be a malfunction, since I doubted anyone had created an android that would try to do the shimmy as either an offensive or defensive technique.

Rahmi and Rhee got back into the act. Rhee grabbed her staff and retrieved it from Android Gladys while Rahmi grabbed Android Gladys' head. Never let it be said that the Amazons weren't hella strong. She ripped Android Gladys' head off her body.

Finally the body dropped. "We need to get that head to a lab for study," Tito said.

Considered everything that was going on. "Oh, crap. Rhee, take the other end of the body." I grabbed the feet. "Rahmi, keep the head. Come with me, as fast as possible!"

Adriana had the door open, meaning she'd made the same leap I had. We were closer to the bottom levels than the top. And the top had our people milling about waiting to kill us. But I doubted Algar wanted this in his pipe system.

However, the fifteenth floor also housed major incarceration. And if we lost one cell, it was better than losing people or isolation.

Headed down at the fastest hyperspeed I could manage. Found the first open cell, we tossed the body and head in, and I slammed the door.

We were just in time. Because the android parts exploded as the door closed.

It was a hell of a big explosion, and it blew the door out. Which blew the three of us back.

I wasn't a fan of slamming into a wall. It hurt like hell. Unlike the guys, it didn't knock me, or the princesses, out. But the wind was definitely knocked out of me. From what I could tell, it was the same for Rahmi and Rhee. And I'd only heard one explosion and frankly expected two.

On the plus side, my earbuds were still in and my iPod was still playing. So I had that going for me.

Thankfully, someone had followed us. Three someones. Serene picked me up, Claudia took Rahmi, and Lorraine grabbed Rhee.

As they ran us to the stairwell the second explosion went off. Couldn't be sure but it sounded bigger than the first. It definitely rocked the girls, but all three kept their feet and didn't drop their cargo. As part of said cargo, I was particularly grateful.

Hoped I hadn't destroyed this entire level, particularly because the Lair was on this level. But better the level than all of us.

"Go girl power," I said as Claudia slammed the stairwell door shut and Serene put me down.

"That's the best android yet," Lorraine said without preamble. "Because it was around all of us and no one thought that Gladys was acting odd or anything."

"Until, you know, she went crazy," Claudia said. "But Al Dejahl was in the building and we just figured she was mind controlled again."

"It's nice to know that our luck just stays consistent, isn't it? I see the League of Evil Geniuses has regrouped and re-formed and is back, bigger and better than ever."

"You don't know the half of it," Claudia said. "You up to going back upstairs?"

"Sure. Princesses?"

They confirmed they were back in fighting form, so the

six of us zipped up. Perhaps not as quickly as we'd zipped down, but still, we were zippy and not dragging, or blown up, so I felt I could toss another one to the win column.

Arrived to see Tito wanding everyone and having Adriana wand him as well. Gave us the "over here" motion, so we six went and got wanded, too.

"Thankfully, everyone on this floor is who we think they are," Tito said.

"That's a lot of people."

"I started checking as soon as we identified Gladys as an android."

"Good thinking." Looked around. One person was conspicuously missing. Looked around again. Make that two. "Where are Jeff and James?"

CHAPTER 39

"I'M RIGHT HERE."

I spun around to see Jeff looking beat up but otherwise alive and well. Wasn't the right time to throw myself into his arms shouting, "You're alive!" But I wanted to.

He gave me a small smile. "I'd like it, but yeah, not the right time."

"Thought emotions were blocked here."

"They are. Read your expression."

"Go you on the good husband points. Where's James?"

"In Security Main. Where we need to get back to."

"You need adrenaline."

"Not right now."

"You're a liar about the need for speed."

"Probably. But that needs to wait. We have other issues."

"Jeff, can you hear me?" Reader's voice was on the com.

"Yeah, James."

"I've got the shields down. I'm calling in containment units from Caliente Base. What floors do we need contained?"

"Just the ground floor."

"You cleared the others?" I asked.

"The lower levels were empty."

"But when we got to this level and found Gladys and the rest of her team waiting for us, we couldn't exactly keep on going up," Christopher said. "If you cleared the facility down to here, though, we should be good."

White and I exchanged a look. "We didn't," I admitted.

"Why not?" Jeff asked.

"We knew where to go," White replied. "Your wife's instincts."

"Fabulous," Jeff groaned. "We need those levels searched and cleared, then, James."

"James, everyone on the top floor is armed with an automatic or semiautomatic weapon. Most of them are A-Cs."

"Got it. Agents from Caliente Base coming in riot gear. I have a floater aligning near you, stay out of its way."

"Tell them they need to disarm and bang heads," Jeff said. "Literally."

"Why are we banging heads?" I asked.

"I second the question," Reader said.

"To try to clear the heads of those of our people who are still under the mind control," White said. "Apparently, as Adriana showed us, heavy blows to the head dislodge my brother's mind control."

"Ah, the Hawkeye Technique. Or maybe it should be called the Black Widow Technique." Wasn't willing to call Ronaldo Loki. Loki was a compliment I wasn't willing to hand Ronaldo.

"I have no idea what you're talking about, baby."

"Really? You saw the movie. With me. But anyway." Trotted over and retrieved my purse. "Chuckie, can you verify that my purse isn't containing things it shouldn't?" Handed him said purse.

"Oh, yes, ma'am. Anything else? Foot rub? Latte?"

"Numbers to your Swiss bank account."

He laughed as he pulled a small black rectangular thing out of his pocket. It was similar to the Alien Things Finders he'd had during Operation Invasion, only sleeker. Presumed this was a newer, special model, or else this was for bugs and such only.

He ran it over my purse. "You're clean. So to speak."

"What's that supposed to mean? I feel fine and I'm sure I look no worse than anyone else here."

"Really? Trust me, don't look in a mirror."

"Thanks ever." I honestly didn't feel awesome, but the faster healing and regeneration that A-Cs had was the best thing ever. Even my shin didn't hurt that badly right now. And, frankly, if the worst pain I had after all of this was a banged up shin, I should probably head to Vegas and put some money on double zero.

"James, we could use medical support," Tito said. "Thankfully we have no dead, but we do have injured."

"On it. Floater is live," Reader said. "Stand back."

Normally no one cared about keeping out of the way of a floater gate. Figured Reader was just on edge. Until I saw the number of Field agents pouring through. Had a feeling we'd pulled in more agents than just those at Caliente Base.

In addition to the sheer numbers, no one would want to get in the way of this particular exiting horde. I'd never seen an A-C in anything other than the standard Armani Fatigues. These guys all looked like S.W.A.T., minus guns, but with the clear riot shields police use. They were also all wearing headphones.

"You've chosen to go my way and have everyone listen to tunes while fighting?" Took the iPod off repeat. "It's Not Over" by Daughtry came on. And now I was certain Algar was controlling my iPod, because that song wasn't on this particular playlist.

"No, they're sending white noise type of signals," Reader replied. "It's a way to prevent them from being mind controlled."

"How'd you come up with that?"

"Your mother," Jerry replied with a grin. The other flyboys also seemed to find this funny.

"Seriously?"

Hughes grinned even wider than Jerry. "Yeah. Your mother's been teaching all of Alpha and Airborne how to block mind control, hypnotic suggestion, or brainwashing."

"Oh. Great." She hadn't taught me, but perhaps that was because she felt I was already able to resist all of those things. Or else she didn't feel the need to share her special techniques with her only daughter.

Walker laughed. "Don't look so hurt, Kitty. Your mother said she hasn't bothered to teach you because you can't concentrate on anything for too long anyway."

"Wow, I feel the love."

"Medical arriving now," Reader shared. Sure enough a variety of Dazzlers came through with gurneys and med kits. Knew for a fact they were from NASA Base, mostly because they all nodded to or hugged Serene as they trotted past to get to the wide variety of injured, banged up, headachey Field agents.

Some Field agents dressed normally, but wearing the headphones, arrived and fanned out. "We'll ensure all personnel transfer to Caliente Base, sir," one said to Jeff.

"Agents reporting personnel in housing," Reader said. "Limited resistance. Jeff, I want Alpha, Airborne, and Embassy teams in Security with me now. That includes you, Doctor Hernandez."

Tito shrugged. "They can use me here."

"We're going to need you more elsewhere," Reader said, voice tight. "Seriously, get in here. Now."

"Where is Security Main anyway?"

Everyone stared at me. "You mean you don't know?" Tim asked finally.

"Dudes, seriously, it's me. This place is like the biggest rat maze ever. And before you point out that I lived here, let me point out so what? Mazes aren't my thing."

"Trust me," Jeff said. "If you blindfolded her and put her anywhere in the Science Center, she'd have no idea where she was. If, on the other hand, you blindfolded her and put her in a room with a bunch of her CDs, she could tell you which was which, what band, what year, and do a comparative analysis."

"What's your point? And, more *to* the point, where's Security actually at?"

Jeff shook his head with a sigh. "It's the other half of this level."

CHAPTER 40

LET THAT SIT ON THE AIR A BIT. "Is it?" I asked finally. "And has it always been?"

"Yes," Gower said. "There are maps on every floor, you know. Security is clearly marked."

"Maps. Really?"

"Really," White said, obviously trying not to laugh. "The information was in the briefing books you got when you first joined us, as well."

"Was it?" Maybe it was. I'd finally clawed my way through those gut-busters after Operation Destruction, but since I wasn't living at the Science Center any more, I'd skimmed the chapters on it, which had meant I could skim a good third of the reading matter. I hated being near isolation, so I rarely ventured here. Even when Jeff was in isolation, I tended to stay away—my stress levels always rose and he was powerful enough that he could feel me, even isolated, when I was that close.

"And you thought she read those?" Jeff asked.

"I did. Just not, you know, every single word."

"I'd bet on every third word," Christopher said. "But James is waiting for us. We should go give Kitty a tour."

"I know where it is," Chuckie said as Christopher headed off through the Isolation Chamber Maze and the rest of us followed him. "And I never lived here."

"You slept over. I think."

"I did. But not as often as you slept over."

"Blah, blah, blah. This from the guy who had to basically lead me around our high school all freshman year?"

"Good point. Mazes aren't your skill. Neither are floor plans."

"I'm ignoring you. Anyway, I'd have thought Security would house higher up. What with the need to broadcast to all facilities and whatnot." I was blithely ignoring that, yet again, I hadn't paid attention. It hadn't mattered until right now, anyway.

"We have our ways," Gower said, sarcasm knob only at about a six on the scale.

"I see that. And, from what I'm seeing, they are dark and creepy ways." Christopher was heading toward the far end of the isolation area. I'd never ventured this far—this level creeped me out too much, so I never wanted to be in it any longer than I had to.

This part of the level wasn't well lit. In fact, it was downright dim bordering on Scary Street Corner in a Really Bad Neighborhood Dark. The far wall had an opening that you could easily miss because everything was so dark. Naturally, that was right where we were headed. The creepiest point in the creepiest level. Because it would disrupt the cosmos if we were heading to a bright, cheerful place for any reason at any time.

"Get into single file," Christopher tossed over his shoulder. I was the only one not already moving into formation. Jeff took my shoulder and gently put me behind Chuckie, with Jeff behind me. Chuckie was behind White.

"Why?"

"Security isn't as easily accessible as the rest of the facility," White said as Chuckie and Jeff both heaved the Exasperation Sigh. "It's based on full body scanning, so that someone can't pretend to be someone else to get in."

"Like take their hand or their eyeballs and fool the system?"

"I wouldn't have put it quite so graphically, but that's part of your charm, Missus Martini. And yes."

"I can see the wisdom."

"Can you?" Jeff asked. "I'm not sure."

"Hilarious. And here I was, all worried that you'd been

hurt." We walked through the darker opening in the dark wall. Shockingly, the corridor was also dark. A-Cs had better vision, which I'd supposedly gotten along with regeneration, but I could barely make out anything. "Who designed this place? Wes Craven or Stephen King?"

"It's set up this way to discourage people from coming by to chat or hang out," Jeff shared. He kept his hand on my shoulder, which I appreciated.

"Yeah, well I can bet that works extremely well." The corridor wasn't all that long and then we reached another opening. It looked like there was nothing else, just blackness in front of us. "Another way to repel visitors?"

"Yeah. And it's the entrance. It's a special kind of gate. You walk through it, the system confirms you're not carrying bombs, and that you're someone authorized to enter Security Main. And before you ask, baby, yes, you are. You've been authorized since you joined up."

"I'm honored. Sorta. And, is it black on both sides? As in, we can't look in, and they can't look out to see enemies are at the door or not?"

"Correct."

"Wow. Are you guys trusting. And weird. But I'm already on record for the weird part. And probably the too trusting part, too."

Chuckie walked through. It wasn't a slow fade like with a regular gate. He was just sort of swallowed up by the blackness.

Jeff and I were the last in line. "You can't carry me through this?"

"No. One at a time. It won't make you sick. I promise."

Heaved a sigh. "Fine. I'll be a big girl." The song on my iPod changed to "Out Go The Lights" by Aerosmith. Really wondered how much of a galaxy class jerk Algar actually was. He was enjoying his audio jokes, I knew that for certain.

Jeff kissed my cheek. "That's my girl," he murmured in my ear.

Reminded myself that this wasn't a good time to stop and suggest we do the deed right here. The corridor was dark enough that we could, but it wasn't the right time and this entire level was never going to be the right place.

Stepped into the black. Jeff was right, it didn't make me sick. Felt a very slight, almost pleasant tingling all over, and then I was through. "Wow. And I thought the Bat Cave level was impressive."

The room I stepped into was well lit, and loaded with a ton of monitors, switches, microphones, and other impressive-looking apparatus I couldn't name all over the place. This looked like a much bigger version of Walter's Mini Command Center in the Embassy, which made sense. We had over twenty people in here and it seemed remarkably uncrowded.

As with Walter's set-up, living quarters were attached. These rooms looked just like the rest of the Science Center's housing—a combo of really nice hotel with some Industrial Boredom touches here and there.

There were four rooms like this. One was larger than the other three, and it didn't take genius deductive reasoning to figure that Gladys had the biggest quarters and her three right-hand folks had the others. Which explained how Gladys appeared to be awake 24/7—the others took shifts, too, and alerted her for any issues. She probably didn't get a *lot* of sleep, but more than I'd thought.

"Why aren't there video screens in here? I mean, I get it; we don't film our own people. But someone has to keep an eye on what's going on outside, don't they?"

"Yes, but that's normally taken care of at Imageering and Field Central Command, or filtered through from the top level," Jeff said, as he joined the rest of us. "If the Heads of Field or Imageering, and now Airborne, are unavailable, U.S. military at Home Base makes most of the 'fire or don't fire' decisions."

"What about some focus on the stairwells? We use those all the time, at least during ops like this one. And we were on a floor with maintenance and medical, meaning I'd believe there has to be some Security there."

"We use people, we don't use cameras," White said. "We do at the Embassy, but not really anywhere else."

"Why not?" Adriana asked. "It seems useful and remark-ably trusting, as Kitty said."

"Until the last few years, we weren't focused on internal

threats but external ones. Frankly, until Missus Martini joined up, none of our bases had ever been infiltrated."

"Wow, glad I brought the magic with me. I do want to point out that NASA Base was infiltrated by Club Fifty-One."

"Oh, I'm sure that wasn't the first time, either. But we didn't know of any prior to your most timely arrival. However, we have a whole section of our population who can merely touch an image and know everything about the person in the image."

"Yes, I know. Christopher and Serene as examples of the strongest."

"Yes. And we have a larger population that doesn't want to feel that they're being watched, more than watched, every moment, especially by their leaders. Our empaths use blocks to keep other's emotions away from them unless it's necessary for them to be open to all the emotions, but knowing they're there tends to keep others' emotions in check."

"Having and using aren't the same thing."

"Human and A-C nature would suggest that someone would use that access inappropriately. I'm sure Christopher would have when he was young, just because those are the kinds of things the young do."

"Thanks for that, Dad," Christopher said.

White chuckled. "When you were younger, son. Now I know you're the picture of restraint. And yes, Missus Martini, along with your husband and everyone else, I realize camera feeds could keep us safer. However, we're focused outward and will remain that way under normal circumstances. Something about free will and all that."

"Huh." Knew when White was trying to tell me to drop it. Perhaps Algar functioned as the security camera feeds as part of his Operations job. Perhaps not. Hard to guess. Memory nudged. "Gladys has expanded talents, doesn't she? She's a memory reader-empath combo, right?"

"Yes," White said.

"And she's been the Head of Security since you all got here?"

"Yes," Gower confirmed.

"That's why she doesn't need the screens. She's reading everyone's emotions and memories if necessary."

"Yes," Jeff said. "So, no screens. Again, we haven't needed them before now. And yes, before you can say it, whine about it, or badger us about it, we'll rectify this lack and make the appropriate changes once we're not in the middle of a major crisis. To get us back on the actual issue of the hour, James and I searched this area already. There weren't any signs of struggle."

"Not good," Chuckie said.

"It gets worse," Reader said. He was sitting in what I figured was the Command Chair, and had a set of headphones on. They were clearly the new "look" for the good guys. "On the positive side, all our people in the Science Center are back under their own mental control. We have a lot of concussions to deal with, however."

"Do we have medical to handle that?" I asked.

"Normally," Tito replied. "But it's all housed here, and everything in the Science Center we didn't bring in should be considered suspect, adrenaline and other regenerative fluids in particular."

"We're on that already," Reader said. "We're transferring all injured to Caliente Base as needed. All equipment and supplies are being searched. So far, no contaminants. But they did far worse. All computer data is confirmed wiped, at Home Base and here."

"How are you communicating then?"

Reader shot me the cover boy grin over his shoulder. "Backup systems. Ours and some from the military, courtesy of your friend Colonel Franklin. We're considering this a terrorist attack on both American Centaurion and the U.S.A., so we have more options than we might have." The grin faded. "However, we have more bad news." He turned back to the command center stuff. "Personnel in the Center have been checked and verified. Happily, most are accounted for."

"Who are we missing?" Jeff asked.

Reader was quiet for a few long seconds. He cleared his throat. "Emily Balducci, Jennifer Barone, Jeremy Barone, Melanie Colangelo, Brian Dwyer, Abigail Gower, Gladys Gower, Michael Gower, Naomi Gower-Reynolds, and Walter Ward."

CHAPTER 41

GOWER, CHUCKIE, SERENE, LORRAINE, and Clau-dia all looked stricken. Couldn't blame them and could definitely relate. Joe and Randy went to their wives and hugged them. Chuckie put one arm around Serene and the other around Gower.

"Why do they want Brian?" Serene asked piteously. "He's not really part of us."

"He's your husband and our friend and he does work with us. And they took him during Operation Confusion, too. So it's the same for Brian as with the others. We all care about them."

"I care about my dad, too," Lorraine said, her voice break-ing. "Is he okay?" Joe hugged her tighter and kissed her head.

"Both Edward Colangelo and Zachary Balducci are on premises and fine," Reader said. Claudia sagged into Randy. "And, before anyone asks, everyone's been checked and ver-ified as human, A-C, or hybrid. The only android was the one impersonating Gladys."

"Why?"

Everyone looked at me. "Why ask why?" Jerry said. "They want to hurt us."

"No, I mean why only one android? Once they had Gladys switched they could have brought in a thousand androids. Why only the one?"

"The one was all they needed," Chuckie said.

"Why only take those specific ten people? All of you who

were here when this started are valuable as hostages, valuable to the rest of us, and loaded with at least as much information as Gladys, and more than most of the others. Turn Alpha and Airborne into androids, control all of Centaurion Division."

"We held out against the mind control," Hughes suggested.

"No way in the world I buy that Naomi and Abigail fell under Ronaldo's control. Powers burned out or not, I don't buy it. And we know Walter held out, at least long enough to warn me."

Reader spun around so fast I thought he'd fly off the chair. "What do you mean?"

"Embassy Team activated because Walter called me, on a non-assigned phone, I might add, to warn me that everyone here was in danger. He was cut off mid-sentence, but he gave me enough for us to roll."

My phone rang before I could say any more. Dug it out of my purse and pulled out one of my earbuds. "William, are you okay?"

"Yes, Ambassador. Embassy is still secure as are all personnel who were here when you left, children and animals included. Are you able to safely get to a video monitor of some kind?"

"Lemme check. James, can we go to the Bat Cave? William says we need to see things that Security doesn't allow us to see."

"You go, I'll stay here," Reader said.

"No," William replied urgently. "Commander Reader needs to go, too."

"Gotcha. All of us. Now. Fast as we can."

"Yes, Ambassador. Please hurry. Will send feed to Imageering Central Command at Dulce."

"Run out, form A-C and human teams as you exit," Jeff said, Commander Voice on full. "Don't worry about holding onto 'your' human, just make sure none are without an A-C. Move out."

Kevin came over to me. He had his phone out. "I've brought your mother up to speed. We have other issues going on in D.C., too, but she agrees this is top priority."

"Good. Your family is safe."

He gave me a relieved smile. "Thanks. Wish everyone else's was, too."

"Go," Jeff said strongly to both of us.

We ran through, Jeff right behind us. He grabbed both of us and kept on running. We reached the third level quickly and headed to Field and Imageering Central Command.

These were two large connected rooms within the Bat Cave. As with so many other things, it always resembled a superhero inner sanctum to me. Lots of big screens, lots of computer terminals, lots of other things I still couldn't identify.

That was the Field side. Imageering was the same, but it was loaded with monitors as well. Normally there was an A-C in front of every one. Today, there was no one. It was unnerving, a testament to how badly we'd been hit.

The next book in the Testament of How Much Things Sucked appeared onscreen. Both Field and Imageering had multiple screens that could be all one image or a variety of images. They each had a single biggie, too. And we had an interesting scene in front of us on the main Imageering screen.

Someone was filming live. It was easy to tell due to the fact that the camera wasn't steady, it was panning around the room, stopping for a few seconds to show us the faces of the people in that room, and it had a convenient timer noting the date and the time, which was right now.

The hostages were all tied up to the walls, similar to how the guys had been in Paris during Operation Confusion. Clearly this was a look Ronaldo enjoyed.

The people were our missing members. Brian and Michael were stripped to the waist. The women were still in the female Armani Standard issue, but their shirtsleeves were ripped off.

They were all conscious, they didn't look mind controlled, in part because they all looked frightened but as if they were trying to hide it, even Gladys, though she also looked furious. None of them were too successful in hiding the fear, possibly because A-Cs were terrible liars and because Brian had spent a lot of time around them.

"William, we're here. Can you patch through to the command area instead of my phone?"

"Yes, but we need to patch through the audio as well as the visual." My phone went dead and William's voice came on over the com. "Screens went live all at the same time, all bases worldwide. Audio going live now."

"I hope I have your attention," a woman's voice purred. It wasn't a voice I recognized and yet it was vaguely familiar. "Gave you a couple of minutes to get everyone clustered around their televisions."

"William, do we have two-way communications, or can they hear us even if we can't respond?" I asked.

"No. It's a broadcast feed. Barring them having installed a return feed in the Science Center somehow, they shouldn't hear any of us, either."

Christopher flipped on the Imageering Commander's screen and put his hands on it. "I can't feel anything," Jeff said. "The emotional blockers are still in place. Should I get outside?"

"No," Reader said. "They'll have blockers with them, I can guarantee it. Christopher, what do you have?"

"Nothing."

"What do you mean, nothing?" Reader asked.

Serene ran over and put her hands onto the screen. "I don't have anything either!"

"They've found a way to block the imageers. That's why they wanted to get in here. They could slag the computers from Home Base, but not install whatever imageering blockers they've created." Had to give it to the League of Evil Geniuses—they were scary smart.

"Makes sense," Jeff agreed. Chuckie nodded. He was staring at the screen intently. Of course, so was everyone else.

"Fine," Reader said, in a tone that said it wasn't. "Christopher, can you just find them?"

The camera panned around the room again and I realized that three people I expected to be there weren't. "Where're Walter and the Barones?"

"What do you mean?" William asked.

"Walter isn't here, and neither are Jennifer and Jeremy. We figured they'd been taken with the others, but I don't see them. William, can you read your screen?" William was the most powerful imageer after Christopher and Serene.

"No, I get nothing. And the Embassy has not been compromised. No imageer at any base can get a reading. No empaths can feel anything. Well, from the screen. We have empaths down already from the stress around them."

Was suddenly glad that the blockers were here, if only because it meant Jeff wouldn't be at more risk, though we'd both have taken the risk and more to get everyone back safely. "Chuckie, could they have sent an imageer blocker in along with the viruses?"

"Maybe, ask Stryker."

"On it," William said. "The computer lab is on with us as well."

"I hope you're all having fun discovering that you can't tell where we are." The woman speaking was either holding the video camera or staying behind the cameraman. "Don't want this show interrupted, after all."

"Christopher," Reader snapped. "What do you have? Can you get a lock on anyone?"

Christopher turned around, shooting Patented Glare #5 at everyone. "No. I can't lock on them." He looked right at me, lost the glare, then looked down. "I . . ."

Why he was ashamed was beyond me, but I didn't want anyone haranguing him to do something he no longer could. "Christopher's Surcenthumain boost is gone, other than that he can still run at Flash levels. Someone find a picture of anyone in the room. Let's try this the old-fashioned way."

Chuckie pulled out his wallet, took out a picture, and handed it to Serene. She could "see" someone if they were in range. Normally she wouldn't need to have a picture if it was someone she knew, but with everyone this stressed it was a good idea to make it as easy as possible.

She touched the picture and shook her head. "My range is still only about fifty miles. They aren't within that radius."

"Well, that tells us something." Had to stay Polly Positive, because things were not looking good in the room with the captives. There were two people in with them, though, because the camera was still panning from the center of the room, but as it went around again, it was clear that the captives had been roughed up, more so than when we'd first seen them. "Christopher, what do you get?"

"Nothing relevant to the situation. We get what the person's done up to the point of the picture. Not what they're doing right now." He handed the picture back to Chuckie. "She was really happy."

Risked a glance. It was a picture from their honeymoon. Started to get extremely angry. Good. Went nearer to the big screen. "Where's Walter? Where are the Barones?"

"No idea," Jeff said.

"Can we track them? And the others? I know that's normally done out of the Science Center, but can anyone else give it a go?"

Heard a lot of cursing. "Kitty, more bad news," Stryker said. "All tracking is offline."

"Bring it up online, Eddy."

"Can't. I mean it's gone. The chips are deactivated."

CHAPTER 42

THAT SAT ON THE AIR for a few long moments. We could hear the sounds of people being hit and trying not to let on that they were being hit.

"That's impossible," Jeff said finally. "They're all internal, and the only way to deactivate them is to remove them."

"Or dissolve them," White said quietly.

"And that's what we think was done," Stryker said. "NASA Base has done the confirmations."

We were all quiet again. More sounds of abuse coming from the room, and as the camera panned again, the team again looked worse for wear. "Well," I said finally, "at least the chips didn't self-destruct."

"Failsafe," White said.

"Yeah, you're big on them, I remember."

"Now that I have your full and undivided attention," the woman in the room with our friends and family said, "I want you to listen to me very carefully. I'm going to do terrible things to one of your friends here until I get what I want."

Something caught my eye, but the camera went out of range. "William, Eddy, someone, are we recording this?"

"Yes, Ambassador."

"Great. Toss the recording up onto our many other screens. I need to see something that needs a freeze frame."

"Kitty, it's Henry. Yuri and I have some vocal confirmation. Female speaker is likely from South Florida."

"You and Omega Red rock, Henry. Okay, that means this

is Raul the Pissed Off and Now Dead Assassin's chick, Annette Dier, who is also an assassin."

"You can't be sure of that," Jeff said.

"Yes, actually, I can. I have my Megalomaniac Girl hat on
and everything."

"This is her area of expertise," Chuckie said curtly. "Let
her work."

"Thanks. William, Eddy, someone rewind on a non-main
screen to right when she was threatening a few seconds ago.
I don't need the audio, just the visual."

Dier went on talking as a couple of the smaller screens in
the room rewound. "We're going to start with the human."
Serene sobbed and Chuckie put his arm around her again.

"Why Brian?" Jeff asked.

"Because he can't regenerate and he has no fast healing.
William, slow down the forward on my special view, will
you?" The frames slowed down. "There! I thought I saw
something."

What I'd seen was Michael Gower. "What's he doing?"
Claudia asked.

"He's working to get his hands free using hyperspeed. The
camera only caught the start, when he was moving at human
speeds."

Couldn't be sure, of course, but it looked like Michael was
going to manage to get his hands free.

"Their feet aren't tied," Chuckie said. "Just their hands.
He gets free, he has a real shot at doing something."

"How can he get out when the others can't?" Adriana
asked.

"He's an astronaut, so he's in incredible shape, he works
with us all the time, and for all I know he and Caroline do
interesting things in the bedroom. But either they didn't tie
him as well as they thought, he knew what he was doing, or
he got lucky, because I think he's going to get free."

There was no way anyone, not even an A-C, could be this
close to getting free in just a couple minutes. Meaning they'd
been wherever they were for a while. Our enemies had had
plenty of time to get anywhere in the world and tons of mind-
controlled A-Cs to help them get there.

"Kitty, we're still unable to trace the feed," Stryker shared.

"It's being bounced all over the world, but we can't get a reading on the origination point."

"They're in the tunnels. Exactly where Mahin thought they were."

"How can you be sure?" Reader asked. "Letting her work, Reynolds, stop shooting me the death glare, just need the confirmation of how she's making these leaps."

"During Operation Destruction video went out of the tunnels with no problem, but no empath or imageer could read through them. They're not sending via one of our cameras, so we can't trace it. And they told Mahin that's where they were going." Heard Tito quietly explaining who Mahin was for those who'd missed the outdoor entertainment.

"The tunnels are worldwide," White said. "We'll have a challenge finding them in time."

Dier moved into camera range. She was blonde. She also had a knife. A very nasty, very sharp-looking knife. Aimed at Brian. Went for the crazy and sent a text to Buchanan and my dad.

"I think we'll start with the smaller things first," Dier purred as she did the Typical Bad Guy Knife Move and ran the flat of the blade against the side of Brian's face. "Fingers. Toes. Eyes. Parts that will ensure you're no longer a man."

Brian blanched. "You're a crazy psycho."

Dier laughed. "You wish. No, I'm a professional."

"Confirmation, that's Annette Dier."

"I agree," Chuckie said.

Dier leaned closer to Brian. "And I'm very good at what I do."

"Leave him alone," Gladys said, with a lot of authority in her tone. "You want to terrorize someone? Try me."

Dier went to Gladys, camera following her. She backhanded Gladys hard across her face. "You'll speak when spoken to, and not before. You're no longer necessary, didn't you realize that earlier?"

She went back to Brian. "Now, where were we? Oh, right, I was about to torture you, slowly, and cut you up, bit by bit."

Serene was sobbing and I was pretty sure she was only upright because Chuckie was holding her up. "Why are they doing this?" she asked. "They haven't even asked us for anything."

The realization of what they were doing dawned on me. "They can't ask us for what they want."

"Why not?" Jeff asked.

"Because they want Patrick. And Jamie."

"How would this get them?" Adriana asked. "None of you would put the children at risk. No one in that room would agree to that trade, not even to save their own lives."

"I agree. However, this set of bad guys has an interesting view. They thought Jamie could time warp to Jeff in Paris. They undoubtedly think Patrick can do the same. And if he can and if he goes, she'll go with him."

"How do you know that?" Jeff asked quietly.

"Because I wouldn't let my friend go alone and neither will she."

"Why take anyone else, then?" Reader asked. "Why not just take Brian?"

"They want ACE. They either want to bring him to them or have Paul bring him to them. Maybe they think they can contain ACE, destroy him, something. Ronaldo spent a lot of time with the Z'porrah, remember. I'm sure he has tricks we know nothing of."

"I could be wrong," Tim said, as Dier ran the side of the knife over Brian some more, "but this seems like a time to ask ACE for help, Kitty, Paul."

Looked at Gower. He looked trapped. Time to come clean. But, as with Christopher, clearly I was the one who was going to have to do it. "ACE can't help us. ACE isn't here. He hasn't been here since the tunnels went back to impenetrable, after Operation Destruction. He's . . . hurt and in trouble, but it's trouble we can't help with. We don't know how to get him back, only that he's still out there somewhere and hasn't really left us. But ACE intervening is not an option."

Dead silence met this announcement. Which meant I didn't have any trouble hearing my phone's text sound alert. Checked it out. "Great. William, Malcolm is going to call you. You need to get a camera feed of what's going on into wherever he is, pronto."

"On it Ambassador, and on with Mister Buchanan right now."

"What's having him and your dad see this going to do?" Jeff asked.

"Other than upset Dad and piss Malcolm off? Nothing. But we have only one shot to figure out where our hostages are. It's a shot in the sandstorm, but when all you've got available is the crazy, then the crazy is the shot worth taking."

CHAPTER 43

COULDN'T WAIT FOR DAD and Buchanan to show Mahin the video and get her to crack. Could be fast. Might be slow. Had to think of something else.

But events in the room with the hostages weren't waiting. "Did you know that there are places where I can cut you and you'll bleed out slowly?" Dier cooed at Brian.

"Isn't that pretty much anywhere?" Brian asked. I was impressed. He sounded insolent.

"Leave him alone you raving bitch," Michael growled.

She turned and was in profile to the camera. Only for a moment, then the camera got behind her again. "William, we need the frames with her face frozen and possibly blown up." These flashed onto some other screens. "Jeff, Chuckie, does she look at all familiar to you? Even a little?"

"Not really," Jeff said.

"Maybe," Chuckie said slowly. "But I don't know why."

Dier was in front of Michael now. "So brave. But don't worry, you'll get your turn."

"Ambassador, Mister Joel Oliver is here. He feels the woman is familiar, too."

"Have Pierre take a look. I'm certain this is the same woman who was casing us all during Operation Sherlock's horrible Dinner Party of Death." But there was something else about her—I felt I'd seen her somewhere else.

"Untie me and let's see how brave you are," Michael said. "You're nothing but a tall woman, about five foot nine, a hundred and forty pounds, brown eyes, hair's obviously dyed, about thirty, and—"

She backhanded him. "Shut up. I told all of you to shut up."

"Why should we?" Gladys asked. "You're going to torture us no matter what. We might as well talk about how the man with the camera isn't the man in charge. My half brother isn't here, because he's too much of a coward to take the risk."

"But the man with the camera's also your brother, Gladys," Melanie said. The camera swung to her. "He's just got no actual talents he's shown, other than being subservient to Ronaldo Al Dejahl."

"He's short for a man, about the crazy knife wielder's height," Emily added. "Dark, swarthy, sounds Middle Eastern. Kind of chubby. Definitely unattractive." A swarthy man's hand slapped Emily across her face.

This put the cameraman closer to her and, because of how they were tied up, to Melanie. It was hard to be sure, but it sounded like Emily kicked or kneed him in the balls. At least the camera dropping to the floor while we heard the sound of male whimpering was indicative.

Heard another kick. "I think I just kicked your helper in the head," Melanie said. "Sorry. Not really at all."

"I love our team. I just have to say. They're awesome."

The rest of the hostages were getting into it, tossing off descriptions, sharing what they could remember of the abduction, and so forth. What was the most interesting was that Dier didn't actually cut anyone. Meaning Ronaldo wanted most of them alive and presumably in one piece.

"Ambassador, a Peregrine is here," William said. "I think he wants to talk to you."

"Seriously?" Tim asked.

"Yes. Put Bruno on." Assumed it was Bruno, anyway. Heard some bird screeches. Yep, Bruno. He screeched, clucked, and warbled. "Got it. You da bird, Bruno."

"Do we want to know?" Jeff asked.

"Bruno says she's who set the bomb in Cliff Goodman's car. She was also in the crowd of reporters. She was the one trying to incite them to riot on us right after the explosion."

Bruno screeched again. "Oh, right. And Bruno says she

was in the Embassy during Jamie's birthday party, but since she was there as press, the Peregrines watched her but didn't attack lest they create a scene we couldn't recover from. She was sent out with the rest of the press by Cliff, so she wasn't inside all that long."

"One minute is too long," Jeff growled. "And how did they actually comprehend she was press and that a problem could be created if they'd merely ripped her to shreds at the time? And why didn't they tell you what was going on?"

More Bruno screeches. "Ah. They listened to how the people were allowed in. And they were clear that I had other, far more vital things to accomplish at that party. Their understanding is based on human and A-C reactions, but is now really the time? I'm sure Bruno can explain all this to you when we're not in the middle of trying to figure out how to stop being impotently kept from the people we want to save."

"Good point," Jeff said. "Anything from Buchanan?"

"No word yet, Congressman."

The camera was up off the floor and we were back to filming the hostages talking smack to their captors. Dier headed toward Brian flashing her knife around. The camera was again focused toward Brian. Abigail and Naomi were to Brian's left, Michael was to his right. From what we'd seen, this meant the door was behind the camera, so basically opposite Brian.

There was a lot of noise in the room—the hostages were all talking, either giving information or trying to distract Dier, so it was hard to make out anything too clearly now. White joined me at my monitor.

Dier put the knife up against Brian's throat. "Shut up or I do this the fast way. Less fun for me. He'll be dead a lot quicker, though." Her voice was icy, and it was pretty clear she meant it.

The room quieted. "That's better," the Swarthy Slapper said. Well, assumed it was him. No one had acted like a new person had entered the room.

"Shut up," Dier said tiredly. "As if they're actually afraid of *you*?"

"You treat me with respect," he snarled. "My brother—"

"Your brother has you signed on as camera crew. If he felt

you were capable, he'd have given you an actual assignment."

"I have an assignment," he muttered.

Dier ignored him. "Pay attention. This is going to be what happens to all of you." She put the knife's tip against Brian's inner arm and cut him. Not too much, not too deeply, but that didn't mean it didn't hurt. Or that he didn't bleed. Brian hissed in pain.

"Get away from him!" Michael shouted. "Leave him alone!"

Dier laughed. "Hardly. And what are you going to do about it anyway?"

Serene was hysterical. It was only a matter of time before we found out if Patrick and Jamie could indeed time warp, only a matter of time before people we loved were maimed or murdered. We had to do something, anything. "William, is Bruno still there?"

"Yes, Ambassador."

"Bruno, I need the Poofs assembled. Maybe they can find and rescue everyone. Fuzzball should be able to find Michael. They need to hurry."

Bruno squawked. "He's disappeared, Ambassador," William confirmed.

"Good." The Poofs normally came through, and they'd been able to access the tunnels when no one else had been. Didn't understand why they'd waited for me to give the order, but the Poofs had their own weird hierarchy and I was just glad they normally did as requested.

There was an odd, muffled, snapping noise. Couldn't be sure, but it sounded like it was coming from outside of the room the hostages were in.

As if she was reading my mind, Dier stepped away from Brian and went out of camera range. Heard a door open, then shut. She was back in range, with something in her hand. What looked like a round ball made of mesh, but it gleamed in an odd way.

The ball wasn't empty. There was a Poof inside it, trembling. I recognized it as Michael's Poof, Fuzzball. "I hope you don't think this is going to save the day in some way,"

Dier said. "We have friends from far away who understand how to capture dangerous animals."

She tossed the ball into the air, pulled a gun from somewhere, and fired. The Poof gave a short, tiny scream. The metal cage landed on the floor. Blood seeped out and Fuzzball didn't move. I felt sick—I'd sent Fuzzball into a trap.

"You murderous bitch!" Michael roared. "You killed my Poof! What did Fuzzball ever do to you? Get away from my friend and my family!" With that, Michael broke free.

He was an A-C and he had hyperspeed. Dier was a trained assassin. It didn't seem like a fair fight.

It wasn't.

Three shots rang out, close together. Rapid-fire technique.

And then the camera pointed at the floor. Michael was lying there, next to Fuzzball, eyes wide and unblinking, blood spreading across his chest from three different entry wounds.

CHAPTER 44

THE HORRIFIED SILENCE was filled with a scream, from Naomi. I assumed many people were screaming, but we could hear Naomi. She was screaming her brother's name.

Dier slapped her. "Shut up. Your brother was an idiot. Brave, but an idiot. As if I haven't been training in how to deal with you people?" She shook her head. "Heroics. That's what you'll all get if you try anything else. You'll get dead."

"I don't care what it'll take," Brian said evenly, though he was pale and shaking. "But there are a lot more of us than there are of you. We'll hunt you down and kill you for this. I'll hunt you with my last breath for murdering my best friend."

Forced myself to look away from the screen. Jeff was holding Paul, who was sobbing silently. Chuckie was clutching Serene and vice versa, White was holding Reader who, like Gower, was crying. Everyone else in the room had looks of shocked, stricken horror on their faces, even Rahmi and Rhee.

Other than Adriana. Her eyes were narrowed, and she came up to me. "What now?" she asked quietly.

"Now? Just what Brian said—that bitch must pay. And the son of a bitch who hired and trained her is going to pay, too. They're all going to pay, because I'm going to kill them all or die trying."

She nodded. "Grandmother would agree. And I agree as well. Count me in."

A crashing sound made everyone look back at the screens, and the cameraman turned toward the door. So we got a jumbled but fairly clear look at Walter, Jennifer, and Jeremy busting in.

The camera dropped to the ground on its side. Apparently that was a requirement of the cosmos.

More shots were fired, but Walter was trained Security, and the Barones were a trained Field team. The fight was over fast. Only this time, the people on the ground were Dier and the cameraman. The Barones tied them up, with a great deal of unnecessary extra violence I wholeheartedly approved of.

Walter got Melanie and Emily untied first and they both started doing CPR on Michael. Because of the way the camera had fallen we could see this, albeit everyone who was watching had to tilt their heads to the left.

"We need to get medical to them," Tito said. "If we can—"

He was interrupted by Emily taking her hands away from Michael's body as she started crying. Melanie joined her in that as Naomi and Abigail threw themselves onto Michael's body, sobbing.

"We're going to stop filming," Gladys said, voice shaking with grief and anger, as she picked the camera up off the ground. "Because I don't want our people witnessing what we're going to do next."

But before the camera could be turned off, more people came into the room. These people were Marines.

An older man I knew very well entered the room. "We'll take it from here," he said gently.

"No," Gladys snapped. "This is our business."

"No, ma'am, it's not. I'm Major General Mortimer Katt of the United States Marines and we now have jurisdiction. Per Angela Katt of the Presidential Terrorism Control Unit."

My phone rang. I answered it. "Missus Chief," Buchanan said, very gently, "Mahin gave us the location. I'm sorry the Marines arrived a . . . little late."

"Yeah. So, is she on our side or just didn't want anyone tortured or killed while she was watching?"

"Your father and I aren't sure yet. Do you want us to keep working her or do you want us to come back to be with you at the Embassy?"

"I don't know, Malcolm. I—you decide, okay? Whatever you think will get us to the brains of the operation the fastest. So I can kill him."

Buchanan cleared his throat. "Ah, can I speak to your husband?"

"No. He's trying to console his cousin over an inconsolable loss. I'm fine, Malcolm."

"No," he said gently. "You're not. Just promise me that you'll call me before you roll any plan, okay? Call me and run it by me first."

"Okay."

"Promise me, Kitty," he said sternly. "No one is emotionally okay right now. You're all willing to do whatever sounds right, and that's dangerous for everyone."

"She killed Michael's Poof like it was a toy target."

"I know."

"Now Caroline won't even have Fuzzball to remember Michael by." The tears were starting. I didn't have time to cry.

Adriana put her arm around my shoulders. "Let me speak with him, please." Handed her the phone. She hugged me. "Cry. Let me handle this side for right now."

While Adriana had a conversation with Buchanan I couldn't even focus on, I watched the screen with tears streaming down my face. For some reason, the camera was still going, now being handled by a Marine. Probably to keep our people from killing Dier and the Swarthy Slapper.

Marines were escorting our people out, two to an A-C, presumably because the A-Cs didn't want to leave Michael's body or Dier alive and the Marines were having to use a gentle form of force.

Brian knelt down next to Michael, picked up the cage that Fuzzball was in, and tried to open it. It required a lot of strength, because I could see his muscles straining. But he got it open finally.

He took the Poof out and gently placed it on Michael's chest. "Make sure this travels with him," he said to the Marines around him. "It was his pet, and it died trying to protect him." He held onto the cage.

"We will do, son," Uncle Mort said. He helped Brian up and gave him a hug—Uncle Mort had known Brian since I was in high school, after all. "Let's get you home to your family, Brian."

"Yes, sir." Brian let Uncle Mort lead him out.

Once all the hostages were out of the room, the Marines brought in a stretcher. Walter looked into the camera, blocking what was happening from us. I knew it was intentional. He looked older than he ever had before. "Chief, I know you're watching. We're going to stay with Michael and ensure he's returned to the American Centaurion Embassy." He looked down, then back up. "I'm sorry we were too late to prevent this."

"It wasn't Walter's fault, or the Marines' fault," I said to no one in particular. "It was my fault. If I hadn't asked the Poofs to get involved, Fuzzball wouldn't have gone, wouldn't have been captured, wouldn't have been killed, and then Michael might not have had enough rage to break free when he did."

Someone took me away from Adriana, who was still quietly discussing strategy and tactics with Buchanan. But the someone wasn't Jeff.

"It's not your fault, Kitty," Christopher said as he hugged me tightly. "You were the only one with ideas. And your ideas worked."

"In the wrong way."

"In the right way. There's no way you could have known our enemies had found a way to trap the Poofs. But the Marines are there, and based on who you were talking to, that's because they were sent by Buchanan or your father."

"Dad. He always calls Uncle Mort when things are dangerous."

"Right, and they could only do that because you had the idea to send the feed to them, so they could get Mahin to break."

"But Michael's dead. And so is Fuzzball. What am I going to tell Caroline?" I started to sob. Christopher put my face into his chest and rocked me.

"You'll tell her the truth. That she was the only woman who made him stop playing the field, that he was a hero, and that he died a hero. He died trying to protect his family and friend and to avenge the senseless murder of his pet. There's no shame in any of that."

"None of it brings him back."

"No. It doesn't." He kissed my head. "And we'll make them pay. But right now, we all need to get home." He sighed. "We're back to where we were when you joined us."

"How do you mean?"

"We're fighting an enemy who knows us, has us at a complete disadvantage, and who we know little to nothing about. And either our enemy or circumstances have set us up so that the things we used to have that gave us the extra edge are gone."

I pulled back a bit and looked at him. "That sounds far more like the Mastermind than Ronaldo Al Dejahl."

"The Mastermind's had plenty of time to regroup. And we need to regroup, too."

"We do," Tim said, as he came over to us. "Christopher, you need to help Jeff. I don't think Paul can really walk right now, he's too upset."

Christopher nodded and handed me off to Tim. Who hugged me. "Christopher's right, it's not your fault."

"Feels like my fault."

"I know. Kitty, we all feel that way. I know this isn't a great time, but I don't want us to forget this."

"Michael's murder? I think I'll remember."

"No, I don't want you or me to forget what I'm going to say right now. The Poofs are guardians, right? When we were in Paris and this same sort of thing was going on, the Poofs were with you. In fact, you told me they knew where we were and were why you and Richard arrived in time."

"Right."

"Okay, so this time, the only Poof that left the Embassy was Michael's, and only because of your direct order. You asked for Poofs, but only one Poof came, the one you'd specifically asked for by name."

"Not making me feel any better or less guilty, Tim."

He shook his head. "That's not my intention or my point. My point is this—why didn't the Poofs leave the Embassy? Or, put another way, what or who were the Poofs keeping out? Or keeping in? And why did it take literally all of them to do so?"

CHAPTER 45

OUR PEOPLE WERE IN CONTROL of Home Base and the Science Center again. The P.T.C.U. was overseeing a complete, inch-by-inch scan and search of both facilities and all equipment. Meaning Kevin had stayed in Dulce. Alpha and Airborne, though, had come back with us to the Embassy.

Everyone else was back in their usual places, though all the hostages, Gladys included, were at the Embassy, too. Michael's body was in one of the rooms in the infirmary, Fuzzball's little body still with him, and all the Gowers, Reader, White, Chuckie, and Caroline were there. The less said about their emotional states the better, but Jeff had had to hug them all and then leave the room under Tito and Nurse Carter's watchful eyes.

Dad and Buchanan were still in Guantanamo and Mom was with Kevin, but she'd called to tell me she was coming by soon and, as with Buchanan, not to roll any plan until she'd heard and approved it. Figured Buchanan had already told her he was worried. He was right to be.

We checked on the kids—they and the pets all seemed anxious, but relieved when we all got home. Tim gave me the "something's up and off" look. Had to agree. But I was too heartsick to figure out what right now. I just hugged Jamie tightly and told her what a good girl she'd been. That she didn't ask why we were all crying was proof to me that she, and the other kids, already knew why, and it wasn't because Denise had told them.

We left the kids with Denise, Len and Kyle still on guard. The rest of us, spouses and the rest of the Embassy staff and any guests like Mr. Joel Oliver included, went upstairs to our apartment. Jeff felt we all needed to be in an environment that didn't seem work-like or threatening. I figured we needed to be near our in-room isolation chamber so that when he collapsed from all the extreme emotions going on around him, it'd be that much quicker for Tito and Nurse Carter to get him safely taken care of.

The sheer number of people in it actually made our living room look like it was an ordinary size. Would have preferred a happier reason for the impromptu gathering, but what I wanted hadn't been happening, so why change things now?

Serene and Brian had their reunion. Once she was feeling semi-normal he handed her the cage that had trapped Fuzzball. "Here's a souvenir I picked up for you from the most horrible trip I've ever taken. The Marines didn't try to take this away from me; not sure if they didn't realize it was alien in nature, wanted us to research it, or were just too distracted with everything else to notice."

"We need to know what that's made of," Jeff said. "I know we're all emotionally drained and the real anguish hasn't hit everyone yet. But we have to keep going."

I'd had Hacker International join us, some because Jennifer and Ravi deserved their reunion, too, and some because I didn't want to look at anyone on a video screen right now. I wanted everyone where I could touch them.

Serene examined the cage, then handed it off to Ravi, who examined it as well. "It's going to take some time, Kitty," Ravi said finally.

"If we don't get answers, the terrorists win."

"The Marines are taking them to Guantanamo," Tim said. "We should know something soon."

"I'd like to know how Walter, Jennifer, and Jeremy arrived in time to save the day." In part because I wanted to talk about something, anything positive.

"We were too late," Walter said quietly. The Barones looked like they agreed.

"No, you weren't," Jeff said. "They were going to torture

and kill everyone in that room. You arrived in time to save the people Michael died trying to protect. That's not failure, that's commendable."

"Jeff's right. And I'd like to know how you all avoided the mind control. The last we knew, you were calling me on a non-Embassy phone and were cut off mid-word."

Walter perked up a little. "Well, I'd held out against the mind control before, but since I'd succumbed eventually, I did some research on how to avoid and overcome brainwashing, mind control, and things like that."

"He flipped a couple flags on our systems while doing it," Stryker said. "So, when we looked into it, we all did the training."

"So, everyone other than the actual media-facing Embassy personnel are trained?" Christopher snapped. "Why leave us out?"

Walter and Stryker exchanged a look. I sighed. "Because they figured we already could, Christopher."

Stryker nodded. "You can't focus on one thing for too long, Kitty. That makes you hard to mentally control."

"So I've heard and keep on hearing. Jeff, Christopher, just assume that everyone thinks you're both awesome and let it go. So, Walter, you held out. How did they not catch you?"

"I pretended to be under the influence. I hung up the phone and did the whole 'yes, master' thing that everyone else was doing."

Jennifer grinned. "Jeremy and I did the same thing. None of us were near each other when this started, though."

"We had to let them separate the teams," Walter went on. "But I followed Al Dejahl. I was able to because he kept a full complement of us nearby, to assign tasks to."

"We were sent to 'guard' the top level," Jeremy said. "When Walter came in with Al Dejahl and the hostages, I knew he was faking."

"How?" Jeff asked. "I couldn't feel anything."

Jeremy, Jennifer, and Walter all shot each other guilty looks. "Well, Jennifer and I have used signs since we were kids to tell each other things so no one else would know. Walter caught on; so the three of us have been sending signals to each other for, ah, months now. So, we just did it again here."

They all still looked guilty, like somehow this was them being bad. "Great initiative," I said quickly. "So then what?"

Got relieved looks and Jeremy continued. "They used a gate to leave, and then we signaled each other, and got out of range of the others so we could make a plan."

"Who was running the gate for them?" Christopher asked.

Jeremy grimaced. "Gladys. She was fully controlled. We're lucky she was, though, because if she hadn't been fully under she might have noticed that we weren't complying like everyone else."

"So her talents weren't really working when she was under control?" Jeff asked.

"As far as we know, no," Walter said. "Once Al Dejahl and the hostages left we decided the three of us weren't enough to fight everyone else, and we didn't have any idea where Alpha or Airborne were. So we decided it was wisest to follow Al Dejahl."

"That was the easy part," Jennifer added. "The gate was calibrated for Home Base, so we waited a few minutes and followed."

"They weren't there, of course," Walter said.

"No, but you figured out where they'd gone."

"It wasn't easy, because they'd taken a floater gate," Jennifer said. "But Walter figured it out. It was pretty amazing."

"I ran gates at Dulce before I was assigned to the Embassy. All the gates at Home Base were calibrated for the Science Center, meaning they hadn't used any of them."

"I get how you'd tell they used a floater, but not how to follow it." Clearly Walter was being underutilized here at the Embassy. Considered giving him over to Alpha. Decided I was going to be selfish and keep him with me.

He looked a little bashful. "There's a way to determine trace patterns and cross-reference against prior transfers and I did it, that's all. It's a good skill, but I'm not the only one who knows how to apply it."

"We'd have never found them without Walter," Jeremy said. "Because Al Dejahl wasn't anywhere close by."

"We figured he wasn't within fifty miles of the Science Center because Serene couldn't find any of the hostages."

"They weren't," Walter confirmed. "They came back here, to Washington. Right outside the Lincoln Memorial."

"How interesting. Al Dejahl really likes his own version of the classics, doesn't he? I assume they weren't in or around the Memorial, though."

"No. The gate let them out in some foliage on the side. We found the tunnel entrance and followed it down. We found some recent tire tracks and followed them," Walter said. "Determining where the floater had been set for took a long time. Too long," he added, looking down.

"Stop blaming yourself," Jeff said gently. "You did more than anyone on Alpha or Airborne could have, and you did it under extreme duress."

"We could have contacted the Dome," Jeremy said, "but we really weren't sure how far the infiltration went and if we'd called and they'd taken the Dome already, any hope we'd have of rescuing anyone would be gone."

"That was, absolutely, the right thing to do," Jeff said firmly. "And I'm saying that as the former Head of Field. The three of you did everything we could have hoped for and more. I realize everyone wants to blame themselves, but the three of you, more than anyone else, are completely blameless of anything other than saving six lives."

Our little Gang of Three looked a little bit perkier than they had before. Jeff was really such a good, natural leader.

He turned to Brian. "Did you see anything?"

Brian shook his head. "We were blindfolded at Home Base. So I have no idea what anything looked like before we were chained up. We definitely went through all at once when we did the next gate transfer, though. And we traveled the last part in what felt like a Jeep, so that corroborates what Walter and the others have said."

"Were they in one of the dead zone rooms?" Jeff asked Walter. Walter and the Barones all shook their head.

"But they were in a room," Christopher said. "We all saw the room on camera."

Jennifer nodded. "They were. It's new, built since the last time we were down there. I'm guessing it was constructed very recently."

"Within the last few days recently," Jeremy added. "Maybe less."

"More good news. So, where were they?" I asked.

"In the same general area where Mister Buchanan's body was found when he was hit with that suspended animation drug," Walter replied. "In the tunnels, underneath Gaultier Enterprises."

CHAPTER 46

LET THAT SIT ON THE AIR for a bit. "It so figures."

"I cannot wait to take over that company and clean house," Amy said. "Literally *and* figuratively."

Was going to say something else when Tim's phone rang. He answered and blanched white. Knew whatever was going on wasn't going to be good.

"I see," Tim said finally. "Do we need to send a team? Okay, keep me posted. Any detail, no matter how small. And . . . send our condolences, please." Tim hung up, took a deep breath, and let it out slowly. "The prisoners have escaped."

My stomach clenched. "Were they already at Guantanamo?" Because if they were, then that meant that Dad and Buchanan were in danger.

"No. Still on their way." My stomach relaxed a little. Tim closed his eyes. "They were in a military jet, because your Uncle Mort didn't want them to risk a gate, in case of tampering."

My stomach reclenched. "Is Uncle Mort . . . ?"

"No." Tim opened his eyes. "He came back with Brian and the other hostages, to protect them. Thank God. Because the jet was attacked in the air. No one knows by what yet, but it didn't appear to be another aircraft. Prisoners were removed. The pilot was good, but it's hard to land a plane safely when there's a huge hole in it. They haven't found all the bodies yet, but all personnel on board are presumed dead."

"Where?" Jeff asked.

"Over the Caribbean Sea. I guess Al Dejahl wanted to save his brother." Tim shrugged. "The copilot was able to share what happened, at least somewhat. The reports aren't clear. It sounds like a Marine went nuts and started shooting before the plane was attacked externally, but with all personnel lost, they'll have to recover the black box, and that could take weeks."

Realized that I had to stop blaming myself for Michael and Fuzzball's deaths, at least for the moment, and really think. This meant I needed to run my mouth. Oh well, surely the gang was used to this by now.

"So it's clear why they did a strike—Dier is a highly trained assassin, and, with Raul and Bernie both dead, the only assassin out there who's likely to work for Al Dejahl for the Personal Vendetta of the Thing reasons."

"How can you feel confident of that?" Jeff asked.

"I have no real confirmation, but since the two best assassins in the business have essentially adopted me as their niece, it seems unlikely that too many of their brethren are going to take hits on me and mine. Not that it can't happen, just seems unlikely."

"I'd agree with the Ambassador's assessment," Raj said. "I've had feelers out since the end of the last operation. If there are hits assigned to our personnel, they haven't made the standard channels."

"I agree as well," Oliver said. "I have informants all over the world, and they all know of my deep interest in Centaurion Division and all its many people. Your 'uncles' seem to have put a moratorium on you and yours. For which we should all be grateful."

"Can't speak for anyone else, but I'm grateful. So, the likelihood is that Dier is by now completely one with the Al Dejahl Cause. A well-trained human like that would be a hard loss to him and his plans, whatever they may be. I can get why she was rescued. But why do it in a big, showy way? Why not simply save them before they were in the air? Unless . . ." Unless we were forgetting something really important. Like the fact that good old Ronaldo had more than the ability to control minds.

"Unless what?" Jeff asked patiently.

"Unless the Swarthy Slapper isn't Al Dejahl's brother." Everyone stared at me. Fortunately, or not, depending on how you looked at it, Chuckie and Reader came in as I said this.

"I just updated our status for Cliff, Vander, and anyone else who demanded it," Chuckie said. He sounded exhausted and he and Reader both looked exhausted. "Did I leave out anything they'll need to know immediately?"

Tim brought them up to speed on the latest suckage, then everyone turned back to me. "Explain what you mean, please, about Al Dejahl siblings," Chuckie said.

"I don't think there is a brother, at least not that was working the camera with the hostages. I think the Swarthy Slapper was Ronaldo Al Dejahl. Where did he go otherwise? Walter and his team didn't see some guy lurking in the tunnel outside the new room underneath Gaultier."

"No, we didn't," Walter confirmed. "And we were expecting an ambush."

"We did see the cages," Jennifer pointed to the one that had trapped Fuzzball. "They were all over the area near the room. But they didn't do anything when we were near them."

"The Marines told us they found no one else in the tunnels," Jeremy added.

"What happened to the rest of the cages?" Serene asked.

Jeremy shook his head. "I don't know. My guess would be that that Marines collected them, but it's only a guess."

"We need to find that out," Reader said to Tim, who nodded and sent a text. "Go back to thinking out loud, Kitty."

"Will do. So, Ronaldo was doing his imageer thing where he changed to look like the Swarthy Slapper. And he's a troubadour, so that means if he wanted them to believe he was the loser half brother, everyone would."

Raj nodded. "It's one of the effects of troubadour talent."

"The theory's possible," Chuckie said. "But why?"

"To keep an eye on Dier when she didn't know he was there. To determine her loyalty and to see what she would or wouldn't do if he wasn't right there to stop her or give her orders."

"Maybe not," Tim said. "She could have been in the know.

He might have thought they'd get more out of the hostages if they thought Al Dejahl wasn't in the room."

"Why not just mind control everyone then?" Brian asked.

"He didn't need to. Gladys is susceptible to his powers. He let her go, so that you'd all 'know' he wasn't around. He could always get her back, right? And, if the Marines hadn't arrived when they did, what Gladys would have done after the camera was turned off was to release the prisoners and probably kill Walter, Jennifer, and Jeremy."

"I don't know," Reader said slowly. "It seems like you're reaching, Kitty."

"It makes sense to me," Tim said.

"I've missed you, Megalomaniac Lad."

"Tim and Kitty voting for it doesn't mean it's the right answer," Christopher said.

"When isn't it?" Jerry asked. The other flyboys nodded. Nice to see Airborne continued to support their leaders, both current and former.

"Seriously," Lorraine agreed.

Claudia nodded. "Honestly, when are they wrong with stuff like this?"

"Do we have time for me to recite the list?" Christopher snapped.

Amy leaned back and gave him a long look. "What happened that you didn't tell me about?"

"Nothing," he muttered.

Amy raised her eyebrow, but she let it go. "I'm with Kitty and Tim. He was pulling the same stunt when I met all of you."

"Yeah," I said slowly. "He was."

Chuckie's head swiveled toward me. "I know that tone of voice. What are you thinking?"

"He's not very creative, is he? I mean, he's using plays from his last two offensives against us. Both of which we know were created by Amy's father and evil stepmother, with Madeleine Cartwright, Esteban Cantu, John Cooper, and the Z'porrah adding in, I'd assume. The scene in that room in the tunnels was like Paris all over again, only with more women than men."

"You know, he recognized me." Brian said slowly. "I realize that's not significant, but it was . . . odd. He said 'nice to see you again,' and then he laughed. I thought he was just being a jerk. But he really seemed to be enjoying himself, and not like, say, Howard Taft was enjoying himself when he wanted to kill all of us. It was like he was having fun, playing around."

"Ronald Regan."

This definitely got the entire room looking at me.

"What does the Great Communicator have to do with this?" Reader asked.

"He was the only President who didn't seem to age while he was in office. I can remember my Aunt Carla saying that he hadn't aged because he was an actor and for an actor there's no better role than being President."

"Does that woman have a view that's not insulting to someone, anyone, somewhere?" Jeff asked.

"Not really. But she has a point. Actors love a role of a lifetime, don't they?"

Raj nodded. "And, as so many like to share all the time, troubadours are pretty much tailor-made for roles in the entertainment industry." Saw the light go on in Raj's eyes. "You don't think he's the one in charge this time, either, do you, Ambassador?"

Now wasn't the time to tell Raj to stop it with the formality, but made a mental note to remind him later. Everyone was stressed out, and in times of stress, we all reverted to what was comfortable or familiar, after all. "No, I don't think he's in charge. Someone else is." Looked at Tim.

Who nodded. "Like you said to Christopher back at the Science Center, this sounds a lot more like the Mastermind."

CHAPTER 47

JEFF GROANED. "We've had enough 'fun' with the Mastermind to last a lifetime."

"He, or she, isn't stopping. And, let's face it, for all we know, Apprentice Tryouts have started up again."

"So, what was the point of taking our people?" Christopher asked as Gower, Naomi, Abigail, Gladys, and White joined us. "You said you thought it was to get Patrick and Jamie."

"And I still do. Tim pointed out that only the Poof I asked for by name went to help." I swallowed. "I shouldn't have sent him, either, because despite what happened, I don't think they ever intended to hurt anyone in the room other than Brian."

"Why are you all here?" Jeff asked the newest arrivals. "You need to be with your parents."

Gower shook his head. "Uncle Alfred and Aunt Lucinda are here now. We don't have time to indulge the grief. We've never been this exposed or vulnerable."

"I don't understand why ACE didn't help us," Abigail said softly. Gower's shoulders slumped.

I really felt for Gower. He'd been through more than enough. Time to be the Resident Bearer of Bad News again. "ACE is gone. In a way. He hasn't been with us since the end of Operation Destruction. We don't know how to get him back. So, right now, ACE can't be in any equation we're working."

"It wouldn't have mattered if we'd still had our talents," Naomi said.

"Don't blame yourselves—"

"I don't," she said before I could finish. "I blame you."

"How is it Kitty's fault?" Tim asked.

"She's the one who had us burn ourselves out during the invasion. If we hadn't, we'd have been able to get away from Al Dejahl and my brother would still be alive."

"Never, *ever* let me hear you complain about that again," Gower said, with full Authority of the Office of the Supreme Pontifex in his tone. "Our jobs are to protect the innocent. That was the best reason to burn out talent that anyone's ever had. You two saved tens of thousands as well as national treasures this country could never reclaim."

"She didn't mean it that way," Abigail said. "It's just . . . we couldn't do anything."

"We could do even less," Jeff said. "None of us like feeling impotent, but that's not a reason to attack each other."

Naomi seemed to ignore what they were saying and, instead, advanced on me, eyes flashing. "You called for Fuzzball, I know you did. You're the only one the Poofs listen to. If you'd stayed the hell out of it—"

"You'd all be dead," White said calmly. "And Naomi, as our Supreme Pontifex said, that's enough."

"No, it's not. Michael's dead and for what? So we can do whatever Kitty says again? And get more of our people killed?"

I knew she was grieving, but Naomi was reminding me a lot of when she'd been a total Bridezilla. It wasn't a good personality style for her. And it was a complete 180-degree change from this morning and how she normally was.

"Mimi, calm down," Chuckie said soothingly. Amy and I both winced in anticipation.

Sure enough, Naomi spun around and turned on him. "You always take her side! You think she never makes mistakes! You act like she walks on water! I'm sick of it! I'm sick of all of this. My brother's dead and all you're all doing is lounging around chatting."

She was getting hysterical. And, while grief and stress did terrible things to people, Naomi wasn't normally a raging bitch. Brian had been blindfolded, and that meant the others probably had, too. The men had been stripped to the waist but all the women had had their shirtsleeves torn off. Why?

I knew in my gut that Michael wasn't supposed to have been killed—he was one of the few adult hybrids out there, he was more valuable to the bad guys alive. But none of the hostages had really had time to compare notes.

Naomi was still freaking out and most of the others didn't seem to know what to do. Tito and Nurse Carter were speaking quietly to Melanie and Emily, so I knew they were coming up with a medical response. However, I wanted this stopped now, and I knew how, and I knew Amy did as well. She and I exchanged a look and she nodded. Fine, she had my back on this one if necessary.

Rahmi and Rhee had noted my little exchange with Amy, and they both nodded to me. Good, if necessary, I'd have Amazonian backup, too. Hoped it wouldn't be necessary.

Went to Naomi, who was now screaming at Gower, White, and Abigail about how they never supported her or loved Michael. This was officially too much, and I stopped worrying about her or anyone else's reaction to what I was going to do. I spun her toward me, and slapped her as hard as I could.

She stared at me. "What the hell?"

I grabbed her arms and yanked them toward me. Sure enough, there was a needle mark and a forming bruise. "You were injected with something during capture, weren't you?"

"Yes!" She was back to screaming. "We were attacked and—"

Slapped her again. "I don't know if they gave it to everyone else or just you. But you were the one screaming before, and you're really off the charts right now. You're not acting at all normally. And since you're not planning a wedding, and only a couple of hours ago you were totally normal, I'm going to just spitball this one and say that you've been given Surcenthumain."

Naomi's eyes were still flashing. She reminded me of how Jeff had looked when he'd been given the huge dose of Surcenthumain during Operation Drug Addict. And yet, she didn't feel any stronger than an average A-C. I could keep hold of her wrists without really trying.

"Kitty, Melanie, and I weren't injected with anything," Emily said.

"I wasn't injected, either," Brian confirmed.

"Or me," Abigail said, showing her arms.

"Why pick Mimi?" Chuckie asked.

"Because she's your wife and whoever's in charge of all this really hates you."

"Remember that comment," Tim said. "I guarantee Kitty's right."

Tito and Nurse Carter came over. "We're going to give you adrenaline," Tito told Naomi. "It counters the drug."

"I don't want it," Naomi said. "I just want my brother back." She started crying. "I just want my brother back."

"Do it, please," Chuckie said. "Mimi, let's go get you feeling better." He put his arm around her and she leaned against him.

"Take her into the guest bedroom," Jeff suggested, as Melanie and Emily came to help and relieve me from holding onto Naomi. Chuckie kept a hold of her, but Melanie and Emily each held one of Naomi's arms.

Gladys was examining herself. "I could have been injected. You don't really . . . remember correctly when you're under mind control."

"Come with us and we'll examine you to be sure," Nurse Carter said. Gladys joined the group heading to our guest bedroom, which, seeing as it was in the Embassy, was the size of a small apartment. So they'd have plenty of room. One tiny one for the win column. Decided to take it.

"Well," Reader said when the door closed, "that was fun. We need to catch everyone up on all we know, but it should probably wait until Reynolds is back with us."

"Kitty, Naomi didn't mean it, not really," Abigail said, as she came over and gave me a hug. "We know it wasn't your fault."

Hugged her back. "Thanks. But it still feels like my fault."

"It does to everyone. I'm not sure if my talents are coming back, or if the grief and guilt is so strong from everyone that

I can feel it without talent, but everyone feels the same as you do. And none of us are to blame."

"She's right," Jeff said, as Abigail and I broke apart.

Chuckie came out of the guest room. "Doctor Hernandez is giving her something so she can sleep." He rubbed the back of his neck. "She's got a drug cocktail inside her right now."

"She'll be okay," Jeff said reassuringly.

"Right now, it doesn't feel like anyone's ever going to be okay ever again," Chuckie said morosely.

Took a deep breath. I was going to lose it and I knew it. "I'll be right back." Squeezed Jeff's hand as he gave me a worried look. "Just need to piddle. You guys catch everyone else up while I go."

Went to our bedroom, closed the door, went into the closet, and closed that door. Like everything else in our apartment, the closet was huge, so there was plenty of room. Sat down near the hamper.

"I miss ACE. You know what I want, Operations Team of One? Elf of the Elves? I want ACE back. Let's have Michael and Fuzzball back, too. Can you do that, or are you really only good for delivering Cokes and clean clothes?"

The hamper was silent, as hampers usually are. I hit it, simply because I wanted to hit something.

"Hey, Mister I'm Immortal, I'm talking to you. Why did you let them kill Michael and Fuzzball? Is that how you get your jollies?"

I didn't expect an answer, so I was kind of shocked when Algar appeared, sitting right on top of the hamper.

CHAPTER 48

GAPED FOR A MOMENT, then found my voice. "I knew that was your portal."

He shrugged. "I have a lot of portals. As you wisely surmised. You're angry, I get it."

"Do you? You know ACE wouldn't have let Michael die, and probably not Fuzzball, either."

Algar nodded. "You're correct. But people, many people, and animals, die every day," he said gently. "Some are, like your friend, murdered. Some die from disease, old age, accidents, violence of one kind or another. It's part of the circle of life."

"Thanks for that, Mufasa."

He rolled his eyes. "Let me explain, again, the differences between me and what you call ACE. ACE sees all the death and knows it can't do anything to stop it, but it *wants* to stop it. I see all the death and know that while I *could* stop it, free will demands that I don't."

Let that sink in. "You've been here a lot more than just the last few decades, haven't you? I don't mean living here on Earth, but you dropped by to visit, check the place out, kick the tires. Or else you'd never have either sent Ronald Yates here or come here yourself."

"True enough."

"So, are you the one Martin Luther threw the ink bottle at?"

Algar smiled. "That's for me to know and you to find out.

Just realize that everyone and everything dies. Planets, solar systems, galaxies, even. Gods can die. Immortals can be destroyed. Death is part of life—death is a *vital* part of life. Without death, there's no room for new life. Without new life, there's no hope for new ideas, new discoveries, new wisdom."

"That's awesome in the abstract, but it really sucks in reality."

"Yes, it does." He sighed. "The thing about free will is that it's pretty much an all or nothing thing. Either you have free will, or you don't. If you don't, if all is preordained, what's the point of existence?"

"Are all Black Hole People philosophers, or are they all just jerks like you?"

He chuckled. "Immortality sounds great until you have it. Immortality practically demands a philosophical outlook, at least over time. And it takes a long time to redeem a single mistake, and many bad things can and will happen in the course of that redemption."

"Christopher says we're back to square one, or worse."

"Perhaps. Of course, he's got his own problems that are shading his outlook. Just like everyone."

"It's my fault Fuzzball and Michael are dead."

Algar's eyes flashed. "Have you listened to a word I've said? Free will means they make their choices and they live, or die, with the consequences of them. Did you influence their deaths? Maybe. But the Poof made the choice to do what you asked, and it could have made the choice not to— there have been plenty of times when the Poofs have ignored your direct orders. Michael was trying to break free anyway. Because that's what hero-types always do, and he fit that mold."

"He wanted to break free to save everyone."

"Which proves the adage: Be careful what you wish for, because you just might get it."

"Are you saying he shouldn't have fought back?"

"I'm saying that he made a *choice*, because he had free will. If that choice had gone the other way, if he and the Poof had won, you wouldn't be sitting here berating me for allowing the Poof to eat your enemies or Michael to have beaten them to death. You'd be doing the happy dance."

"Well, yeah."

"You think the people you consider bad guys don't pray to their gods like you do? You think they don't consider this small victory proof that they're in the right?"

"I know, I know, this is the oldest argument about why wars happen and never stop. Why people we consider terrorists are considered freedom fighters or heroes by others."

"Exactly. Yes, they're doing bad things, but they're following a plan that outlines why, if they do all these bad things, the future will be better. Better for them, to be sure, but still, better." Algar hopped down off the hamper. "You need to pull yourself together. Listen to some tunes, have sex with your husband."

"I don't feel like listening to anything and I doubt anyone feels like doing the deed right now."

"On the contrary. One of the best things about the life forms in this part of the galaxy is that you all still have the primal urge of reproduction going strong—every species in this part of the galaxy is focused, at their cores, on proliferation of their species. Death creates the desire for life. And there's only one natural way to bring life about."

"You just want to turn on your Embassy Porn Channel."

He laughed. "One day, maybe I'll explain to you why that's hilarious, on so many different levels." He patted my shoulder. "But not today."

"Before you disappear, I have to ask—did you hang out with Alpha Four's king, or Richard, or Paul, as much as you're now hanging out with me?"

"The first king of Alpha Four, yes. You're a lot like him. One smart, inquisitive, brave, non-linear-thinking, cute little ape."

"Did you call him a cute little ape, too?"

He grinned. "Nope. You're just lucky that way." Then he snapped his fingers and disappeared.

"I know you're just doing that finger snap to be funny," I said to no one. My iPod was still clipped to my jeans. I put my headphones in and hit play. "Sympathy for the Devil" by the Rolling Stones came on.

Started to laugh, then cried, bawled, and, as Jeff came in to get me, laughed again.

"You okay, baby?" he asked me softly, as he picked me up off the floor.

"As okay as everyone else."

"You want to talk about it?"

"Maybe later. We have a war room meeting to get back to."

"No, we don't. We're bringing spouses and families here, we have enough room between the Embassy and the Zoo."

"Everyone's going to be part of the discussion of next steps?"

"No," Jeff said firmly. "Everyone's going to go to bed and rest. We need to regroup, and we all need to calm down. The grief isn't going to go away quickly, but everyone just going into their own little family groups in a semblance of safety is a start."

"Where're Chuckie and Naomi?"

"In the guest room we permanently assigned to Reynolds before they got married. So they can be alone and we can be alone. I'm going to get Jamie, and we're all going to just relax and try to get some sleep."

"It's not really bedtime."

Jeff kissed my forehead. "I'm saying that today bedtime is right now. By Congressional Decree."

Buried my face in his neck. "Whatever you say."

"I love it when you listen to reason." He chuckled. "Yes."

"Yes what?"

"Yes, most everyone probably does want to have sex. Not at this exact moment, but sooner than anyone would admit to out loud."

"You reading my mind?"

"Yeah. And, especially right now, I appreciate your focus on the priorities."

CHAPTER 49

JEFF GOT JAMIE FROM DAYCARE while I requested dinner from the King of the Elves. Had to give this to Algar—he made great food. Had no idea how he snapped it into existence, and decided not to care.

We had a quiet dinner, spent some time snuggling with Jamie and all the pets, the Poofs in particular, then followed our nightly family routine to the letter. Read stories to Jamie, then her bath time, tucked her in, sang songs. Jeff moved all the Poof Condos into the nursery.

Jamie wasn't in a crib any more. While I'd felt a twin bed was just fine, Jeff hadn't, and Jamie was in a queen. This left plenty of room for the pets, most of whom slept with Jamie these days. Jamie truly insisted that the animals be with her 24/7 as much as possible, and they all seemed good with the arrangement.

In addition to her Poof, Mous-Mous, a variety of other, unattached Poofs, were cuddled next to her. All the Poofs mewed at me, and Harlie and Poofikins both jumped onto my shoulders, purring, and gave me love-rubs, before settling into bed with Jamie as well. So at least they didn't hate me for calling for Fuzzball. One for the win column.

The cats rubbed up against me and Jeff, then went with the Poofs and settled themselves on the bed with Jamie. The dogs normally slept in their doggy beds in our room, but all four of them walked into the nursery, gave us both snuffles, got pets, then sat down and looked at Jeff expectantly. He moved their beds in there, too, and the dogs happily settled in for the night.

This left Bruno and Lola, our Peregrine pair. Lola squawked gently at us and settled herself at the foot of Jamie's bed. Bruno surveyed the scene, squawked a command to his troops, then trotted out.

The animals all seemed quieter and a little huddled, which was to be expected. They'd lost one of their own, too. Wanted to apologize but really didn't know how.

Jamie gave me an extra hug. "It'll be okay, Mommy."

Didn't really know what to say to this, so I hugged her back and kissed her head. "Yes, it will. Mommy and Daddy will make sure of it." Hoped that covered any little girl worries the day and my guilty worrying had created, but wasn't willing to bet the farm on it. However, did my best to focus on how much I loved Jamie and the rest of our family, whether on four legs or two, and hoped it would do the trick.

Once we were out and Jamie's door was closed tightly, Bruno squawked at me. After some head bobs, intricate clawing motions, wing flaps, and more squawks, he waited for his scritchy-scratch, which I gave him right between his wings where the Peregrines liked it best, and he trotted off.

"What did he and the other animals have to say?" Jeff asked, managing not to sound freaked out, which was awesome personal growth on his part.

"Um, whatever's going on, they agree that Jamie is the focus. All the animals are sleeping with one eye open."

"All?"

"All. Bruno's going to be on patrol in our apartment, and Walter's Peregrines are sleeping with Brian, Serene, and Patrick, along with a variety of extra Poofs, because they agree that Patrick is a target as well."

"Is that all they said?" Jeff asked gently.

Heaved a sigh. "No. They insist that Fuzzball and Michael being murdered wasn't my fault."

Jeff hugged me. "They're right. Let's get into bed and try to get some sleep. We all need it."

"How are you doing? I've been worried about you all day."

He nuzzled my hair. "I'm fine. Just need some sleep like everyone else."

Didn't believe him but decided not to argue. If Tito hadn't demanded Jeff go into isolation, then maybe all Jeff really did need was sleep. "Are your blocks up?" I asked as we got undressed and into our standard A-C issue nightclothes, consisting of white T-shirts and blue pajama bottoms.

"Yes. They need to be."

"I know this is the worst for the empaths, isn't it? You especially."

"In a way. However, it's never as bad for us as it is for those closest to the deceased."

"In this case, that means it's just as bad for you, or worse."

"Not worse. I'm not happy, and I'll be the first to admit that part of me still doesn't believe what happened is real. But, baby, you need to remember—every Field agent is trained to expect death. Of people they know, their partner, even themselves. Michael was an astronaut—he was trained to expect things to go wrong, too."

"You've said that before, and I still say that while you can be trained and be told, and even expect it, it's still a shock when death shows up and kicks you in the gut. And most people really don't believe they're ever going to die, let alone like . . . what happened today."

Jeff pulled me into bed. "I know. And I agree. That's why everyone needs to just be together with their families tonight."

"Where's Caroline?" I hadn't seen her since we'd left her and the rest of the Gowers with Michael's body. My old friend Guilt dropped in to mention that I was undoubtedly winning the Worst Friend in the World Award.

"She's with Abigail. Aunt Ericka and Uncle Stanley are in the guest room next to them, so two down from Naomi and Chuck. James and Paul are on the other side. They're all together, and my mother and father are there, too. And everyone understands that we're leaving them alone until they're ready for us."

"I should have gone down and spent time with them."

"Why?" Jeff sat up in bed and looked at me. "So you can tell them, again, that you think what happened is all your fault? So they can tell you, again, it's not? So that you can say, again, that you're sorry?"

"Yeah, I guess. I mean, it's what you're supposed to do. And I didn't. Not enough. And you're supposed to be there to comfort your friends and I didn't even know what room Caroline was in until just now."

"While you were supposedly going to the bathroom but were actually crying in the closet, Uncle Richard told us that the family just wanted to be together. No one blames you, and they said that, too."

"Naomi does." Which made the whole thing hurt all the more.

"Naomi's under the influence of a drug. Which you discovered so it could be countered, I might add. No one in control of their own mind blames you, baby. If I'd had any way to call in a strike team and tell them where to go, I would have. You activated the only things that had a shot of finding our people. You didn't know Walter and his team were on the way, any more than we were advised that the Marines were deployed."

"But my order is the reason two of our own are dead."

Jeff made the exasperation sound. "Are you listening to me? At all? I can't tell. I realize you want to wallow in guilt for some reason, but it's misplaced. Leaders make calls, run plays, try different tactics and strategies. And sometimes what they try works, and sometimes it doesn't."

"I'm listening. I just—what we tried worked, but the wrong way."

Jeff stroked my face. "I know. But, we're in a war, baby. It's covert, but it's still a war. And in wars, we lose people. Did I want to see my cousin murdered in front of me? No, of course not. Did we do everything we could to prevent it? Yes, we did. The outcome is one of the worst we could have ended up with, but death is a part of life. We can complain about it, but we can't change that."

Algar had certainly said the same. Decided I was exhausted and just wanted to sleep. Jeff realized, because he lay back down next to me, pulled me close to him, and kissed my forehead. "Go to sleep, baby. Let's put this day from hell into the past."

"O-kay," I said, with a yawn between syllables. Focused

on the hair on Jeff's chest, how nice it felt when my face was snuggled in between his awesome pecs, and drifted off.

Was rudely awakened by someone tapping my shoulder.

"Missus Martini, how nice to see you again."

Looked around. Lucky me. There I was, back in front of my friends, The Congressional Grand Inquisition.

CHAPTER 50

PERFECT. Because the day just hadn't been "fun" enough already.

"Why are we here?" I asked.

The congressmen looked at each other and shrugged. The Senator in Charge turned back to me. "We're here to pass judgment on your latest failures."

"Oh. Good. Look, per everyone, I need the sleep."

"Per us, you need to explain why things went haywire today," one of the Committee said.

"Just lucky, I guess."

"Let's put her in prison and get on with it," one of the other Committee members said. "I want to convict someone, and she's conveniently here."

"I want a lawyer."

"I'll represent the accused." Turned to see Michael standing there. He didn't look like he'd been shot. Heard a mewling sound and Fuzzball jumped up onto Michael's shoulder. "My associate will give the opening arguments."

The Poof started mewing. Hopped up and down. Lots of tiny growls. Went large and toothy for a bit, still jumping up and down, though the growling was a lot louder. It finished up, went small, and jumped back on Michael's shoulder.

"I see," the Senator in Charge said. He turned to me. "What do you have to add to the learned council's comments?"

"Ahhhh . . ." I had no idea what the Poof had been saying. At all. It was just so much cuteness from what, if I looked at it out of the corner of my eyes, was a somewhat insubstantial version of Fuzzball. Michael looked somewhat insubstantial, too.

"I say we sentence her now," one of the other Committee members said. "I have a golf game to get back to."

"No, my client is more important than your golf game," Michael said. The Committee and all the rest of Congress, all of whom were, once again, in attendance, grumbled but finally they waved at Michael to continue. "My client will make her statement now."

Turned to him. "Are you a ghost? Or just a figment of my imagination?"

He flashed me his typical "you so hot, babe" smile, the one he gave to any woman between the ages of 18 and 98. "I'm whatever you want me to be."

Chose to not take this as a come-on line, seeing as Michael was both engaged to Caroline and also dead. Though he looked alive right now. Very, vibrantly alive. Turned my head and looked at him again out of the corner of my eye. He looked insubstantial again.

Turned back. He looked alive again. Worked for me. "I want you to be alive and unharmed and all of yesterday to have been a really bad dream."

Michael shook his head. "Doesn't work that way. You need to explain what happened yesterday. In a bottom line way."

"We want to know who's responsible for what happened," the lead senator said.

"I am. I was the acting Head of Field."

"Can we just send her to the chair?" one of the others on the Committee asked. "She wants to take the blame for what the terrorists did, after all. Having a scapegoat is wonderful. Gives us something to focus the people on, instead of the bigger picture, or what's really going on."

"No," Michael said. "We find the other side's scapegoat, that's great. But that only avenges us for who pulled the trigger, not who gave the order."

"I gave the order."

Michael gave me the "really?" look. "So, you told the assassin to kidnap, torture, and kill us?"

"Well, no, of course not."

"You gave the order to overtake Home Base and the Science Center?"

"No."

"You called in me and Brian, along with other non-Security personnel, so we'd be easier to capture?"

"No, Gladys did that."

"Did you tell her to?"

"No, Ronaldo Al Dejahl did."

Michael nodded. "The Defense rests."

"We do?"

Fuzzball jumped up and down on Michael's shoulder. "Ah," he said, "good point. My colleague would like to ask if anyone believes that Ronaldo Al Dejahl is in charge."

"He took his own sweet time showing up on the scene," the Senator in Charge said. "Seems to me he's a convenient face for the new Al Dejahl terrorist group."

"Not as if his father ever acknowledged him, after all," the Committee member who wanted to send me to the chair said. "It seems to me that he was found after his father was killed."

"By someone who was told where to look," the Committee member who wanted to play golf added. "Despite his claims to the contrary."

The others all nodded.

"Wow, you're all buying in to the idea that the Mastermind is behind all of this?"

Everyone in the room looked at me. "There is another," the Senator in Charge said.

"Right, right, another Jedi out there. Or another Sith. You mean the Apprentice."

"Someone won the job," Michael said. "Or else this wouldn't have happened." Fuzzball mewed again. "Oh, right. Kitty, try to remember that you're not responsible for what anyone else does."

"Right, everyone chooses their own path. I don't remember being this hung up on *Star Wars* as a kid, but I guess I was."

"What makes you say that?" Michael asked.

"Well, this is my dream, right? So all of this is coming from my subconscious."

Congress faded away, until there was just me, Michael,

and Fuzzball standing in a gray, formless mass. Michael smiled again. "Is it?"

"Isn't it? If it's not my subconscious, if I'm not asleep, or whatever, then what is it, whatever 'it' is?"

Michael shrugged. "It's whatever it needs to be."

"Okay, then, is death really only the beginning?"

He laughed. "I don't really know yet." He looked around. "I think it might be. We'll find out." He patted Fuzzball. "And we're not going alone."

"That's good. I guess."

"It is."

Fuzzball mewed, purred, and rubbed against Michael.

"See? Fuzzball agrees."

"Okay. Um, are you . . . with ACE by any chance?"

"Not yet."

"Will you be?"

"That will depend on a lot of things."

"Like what?"

He gave me a funny look. "If everyone lets us go."

With that Fuzzball jumped onto my shoulder, gave me a nuzzle, and jumped back to Michael's shoulder. Michael kissed my forehead. Then they both faded away into the gray nothingness.

Looked around. I was very alone. Wasn't a fan. "If this is my dream, I want to wake up now."

Nothing happened.

"If this isn't my dream, I still want to wake up now."

Nada.

"I got the message. I swear! Stop wallowing in guilt, find and stop the Apprentice, get that much closer to the Mastermind. Right?"

Still alone in the gray mass.

"Um, if ACE is out there, we'd like him to be able to come home, please. I've met the guy who's his sorta replacement, and ACE is now even more sorely missed."

Could have sworn I heard someone chuckling. It so freaking figured.

"Algar, I know that's you."

"Who are you talking to?" Jeff asked sleepily.

I blinked and I wasn't in the gray nothingness anymore. I was in bed next to Jeff. "Ah . . . what did I say?"

"You said 'I know it's you.' Were you talking to me or someone else?"

"I have no idea any more. It was just a weird dream. I'm sorry I woke you up."

"Mmm," Jeff said, as he pulled me closer to him. "That's okay, baby. I have the perfect way for you to make it up to me."

CHAPTER 51

JEFF REACHED OUT AND BACK and hit something. Music came on. Hall and Oates' "One on One," to be exact.

"You're all prepared," I said with a laugh.

"Yeah," Jeff said as he nuzzled my hair. "New mix. I'd been saving it, but I think now's the right time to roll it out."

I opened my mouth to say that I was good with it, but his mouth covered mine before I could speak. Jeff kissed me, slowly at first, but soon with a lot more intensity. Chose to show that I'd listened to everyone and kissed him right back.

Jeff was the best kisser in, I figured, the galaxy. His tongue had more moves than most men's entire bodies. While his tongue twined with mine and proved it was still Galaxy Class, his fingers slid under my T-shirt and traced my skin.

Pre-Jamie we'd taken a long time with foreplay. Post-Jamie we'd learned to get to the gusto as fast as possible. Clearly Jeff was going for a retro approach tonight, and potentially a kissing record, because instead of getting our nightclothes off, he let his fingertips wander all over my stomach, coming close to, but not quite touching my breasts.

As the music changed to "Sexy Girl" by Glenn Frey, he slowly ended our kiss, but only to move his mouth to my main erogenous zone, better known as my neck. He bit my neck gently and, as my hips bucked, he finally shoved my T-shirt up over my breasts.

"He must have written this song about you, baby," Jeff

growled as he trailed his teeth down my neck to my breasts.
I'd have commented, but I was too busy moaning.

Happily, the Embassy was the most soundproofed place
we'd ever lived, so I'd gotten over worrying about waking
Jamie up. Which was good, because Jeff's mouth and hands
were busy toying, licking, and sucking on my breasts, and I
was already at my cat-in-heat stage of yowling.

Shakira's "Hips Don't Lie" came on and my hips were
certainly not lying about wanting Jeff to keep on with what
he was doing, potentially forever.

From day one, Jeff had been able to bring me to orgasm at
second base. He was clearly determined to do so again, and,
as he sucked both nipples then rubbed them gently between
his fingers while he bit my neck again, my body obliged. You
know, just to show I was a good wife and all that.

As I came down from the climax, he pulled his shirt off,
then mine, tossing the T-shirts to the floor. Then he was back
to my breasts, presumably because he'd ignored them for
approximately five seconds and realized this was a terrible
error that needed to be instantly rectified.

Jeff was now sideways to me, and I reached out to stroke
his chest. I loved the way the hair on his chest felt, especially
over his awesome pecs and amazing abs. And, you know,
since my hand was going down anyway, figured I should follow the Happy Trail and just continue on down.

As I slid my hand under his pajama pants, Jeff made the
growl that sounded more like a purr. Poison's "Sexual Thing"
came on, and I started stroking to the beat. Jeff chuckled,
purred even louder, then shifted again, tongue trailing down
my stomach. While his tongue traced my navel, he pulled my
pajama bottoms off.

He shifted a little more, and I used the new position to get
his pajama bottoms, if not off, then at least down and out of
my way. As his tongue delved inside me, I gasped. Then figured that, you know, since he was right there and my mouth
was open, might as well do the old Two Can Play That Game.

Jeff really growled against me as he started licking and
sucking with more intensity. I matched him as the music
went to "Get Down, Make Love" from Queen. We were in
time together and with the song.

As I wrapped my legs around his head and his body shuddered, we climaxed together, and with most human men, that would have been it. Great and satisfying, but it. However, aliens in general and Jeff in particular had increased stamina and regeneration.

As our bodies calmed a bit, Jeff flipped us over and around, so I was on top of him and we were head to head again. He had the, happily redundant, "jungle cat about to eat me" look on his face—eyelids half-lowered, half-smile, all sexy. I loved that look. I ground against him and was rewarded with proof that he was ready to go again.

He slid into me as Oingo Boingo's "Wild Sex (In the Working Class)" came on. Jeff had put some serious thought into this mix, proving yet again that he truly deserved the title of Sexual God.

He thrust into me and moved me up into a sitting position. While his hands squeezed my breasts I rocked my hips back and forth and he continued to buck his hips, driving himself deeper into me. We were like this through the entire song, and through half of the next, "Sex Is Not the Enemy" by Garbage.

We went faster and faster, and another orgasm hit me. As I wailed along with Shirley Manson and my body shook, Jeff flipped us again, so that he was on top of me. He flipped my legs up, put his arms behind my knees and his hands at the sides of my hips, and started thrusting again, as my body rocked with the aftereffects of my latest climax.

"Violent Love" from Oingo Boingo came on, and Jeff ratcheted us up to frenzy. I grabbed his pecs as we slammed into each other, each thrust going deeper and faster.

It didn't take too long at this pace for me to get worked right back up to the edge of climax, and I could tell he was ready to go over the edge, too.

"Harder," I managed to whisper.

He gave a half-laugh, half-growl, and slammed into me even harder than before. I cried out and so did he, as I went over and took him with me. He groaned as he exploded inside me and I clutched at his chest, the orgasm too intense for me to make any sound.

He let my legs slide down slowly as he lowered himself

gently onto me and kissed me again, deeply and passionately. I wrapped my legs around his lower body and my arms around his neck. We kissed like this until both our bodies stilled.

As "Accident Sex" by Vendetta Red came on, Jeff slowly rolled us onto our sides. He wrapped one leg around mine and pulled me closer as he pulled the sheet, which was somehow still on the bed, up and over us.

My head was pillowed on his arm, my face nestled back in between his pecs, while I let how wonderful making love with him was and how much I loved him wash over me.

He kissed my head. "I love you, Kitty."

"I love you, too, Jeff."

He smiled against my forehead. "I know. I can feel it." He hugged me. "It's the best feeling in the world. Now, let's do what the song says, baby, and go to sleep."

"Whatever you say, as long as it's preceded by what we just did."

He chuckled. "I say that we do this again in the morning, to make sure we start the day off right."

"That's one campaign promise I'm going to make you keep, Congressman."

"Finally, a perk of being in office."

CHAPTER 52

BECAUSE JAMIE DID US A SOLID and slept in, we did indeed start the day out right. Fortunately we chose not to get too fancy, because we only had time for a couple of orgasms before the baby monitor shared that Jamie and all the pets were up and ready to get on with their day.

Was glad we'd taken the time to do the deed, though, because once we were up, dressed, breakfasted, had dropped Jamie and the pets off at daycare, and joined the others, the happy glow was quickly replaced with the reality that the prior day had been all too real.

Most of those in the Embassy and Zoo were still reeling from what had happened. White, however, insisted that we needed to continue to function and get at least the necessary work done. Hard to argue with the guy who'd been dealing with things like this for decades, so we agreed.

This was the day we normally did the weekly Embassy briefing, so we had the main Embassy staff who were up to it convene in the conference room. There hadn't been a conference room when we'd moved in, but Pierre had finally had it with us constantly doing big meetings in the ballroom, and had had a couple of the salons on the second floor combined into a nice, spacious conference room.

In addition to me, Jeff, and White, we had Raj, Doreen, Irving, Amy, Christopher, Pierre, Kevin, who was finally back from Dulce, and Stryker, representing Hacker International. No one felt it was appropriate to ask any of the Gowers to attend, though Chuckie insisted that since the rest of the Gowers were with Naomi, he should be involved in the meeting.

Tim and Serene came to represent Alpha & Airborne; Brian was staying with Patrick and the rest of the kids at the daycare center. Len and Kyle were being relieved of child care protection duty by the Barones, so they were with us, along with Buchanan, Adriana, and Mister Joel Oliver.

Rahmi and Rhee asked if I wanted them to stand honor guard over Michael's body, or if it would be better for them to guard Jamie. I hadn't forgotten Tim's point about the animals either keeping things in or out, so I figured we couldn't have too many trained people guarding the kids, and some-one watching out for Brian wouldn't be a bad idea, either.

Plus it would give the princesses more to do, and while they were much improved in how they dealt and reacted to Earth things in general and men in specific from when they'd first been sent to us, they'd probably get more out of spending time with Denise, Brian, and the kids. So had them join the Barones on Daycare Center Guard Duty.

"How bad is it in terms of Imageering?" Jeff asked once everyone was assembled.

Serene shook her head. "It's bad. All video is corrupted. And I do mean all. Including archival footage. We can't read anything."

"What about film?" Chuckie asked.

"We can still read film images. But most of our work re-volves around live video. Why?"

"Film is a chemical process, but video stores magneti-cally. There's more to it, but whatever they hit us with, it must do something to affect the magnetization of video."

"Mahin's like Storm. Maybe they've got a Magneto in the Yates Band of Half Siblings from Hell."

Chuckie nodded. "Anything's possible."

"How would they have sent the virus through everything, though?" Christopher asked. "Serene's not just talking about our archives. We can't read anything, anywhere."

"YatesCorp is a huge media conglomerate," I reminded him. "They have access to the airwaves; they practically con-trol them."

"The hack was good enough that I'd believe whoever did it could also have infected all existing media," Stryker said.

"The bigger question is, can we combat it?" Jeff asked. "Or are our imageers rendered as impotent as our empaths?"

"We don't know yet," Serene said. "We're still in too much disarray."

"Speaking of Mahin, where is she and what's being done about her?" I asked Buchanan.

"She's still in Guantanamo. She helped us, but neither your father nor I can be sure she's changed sides. We *are* sure she didn't expect any of the hostages to be hurt, let alone murdered."

"Well, that's something, I guess." This also brought up a question. "You know, I get why they took Brian, and all the Gowers. But what I don't understand is why they grabbed Melanie and Emily. They aren't hybrids, and they aren't that close to either Alfred or Richard's bloodlines. And they aren't in positions of real power, not like Gladys, for example. Or their daughters. Speaking of whom, where *are* Lorraine and Claudia?"

"Verifying that everything's back in order at the Science Center," Tim said. "They'll be joining us soon, I'm sure." He grinned at Kevin. "We trust you, but it always pays to have another couple sets of eyes on things."

"No argument," Kevin said with a laugh. "But I think Kitty has a good point about the specific hostages chosen."

"Before we delve into that, we have another pressing issue that's also political in nature," Raj said. "The President wants to do a full-on hero's funeral."

Every A-C either grimaced or looked appalled. Realized I'd never seen an A-C funeral. Wasn't thrilled that I was going to be seeing one far sooner than later. "What's wrong with that? It's a sign of respect."

"For humans," Jeff said. "For us, it's pretty much against our religion."

"Really?"

White nodded. "We believe that once the soul has left the body, there are a few days set aside, if feasible, for the family to visit and come to grips with the reality. Then we cremate the body and scatter the ashes."

"The President expects a coffin," Raj said. "And a full,

military-style, twenty-one-gun salute type of ceremony. In part because Michael was an astronaut, and therefore an American hero, and in part because he died defending people against a terrorist attack and is, therefore, a worldwide hero."

"How much press is there on this?"

Raj handed me the morning's newspapers. Every one of them had Michael's death as a front-page headline, the *World Weekly News* among them. The pictures chosen were all different, though most of them showed him geared up as an astronaut. The *World Weekly News'* picture, however, showed him and Brian from when we were all in Paris during Operation Confusion, when we'd had them take the credit for saving innocent people from terrorists.

Jeff glared at Oliver. "Glad you didn't miss a chance to report on this."

Oliver shook his head. "Some things are required. It *is* my job."

"If he doesn't write the story, then everyone questions validity," Chuckie added. "He's known to be your confidant."

"I did run the piece by the Embassy Public Relations Minister." This was Raj's official title.

"Did anyone else clear their stories with you?" Jeff asked Raj.

"Yes, the *Stars and Stripes*. Otherwise, no."

Jeff ran his hand through his hair. "So we have two out of nine. I suppose those are good odds for us."

"None of the stories say anything detrimental to our reputations," Raj said. "They're all focused on showing Michael to be a hero. Most of them are speculating on the risk of more terrorist activity, though."

"Which is, let's be honest, quite likely," Oliver said.

"Very likely," Stryker agreed. "And not just the Al Dejahl organization. This kind of thing can easily become a game of one-upmanship between the different terrorist factions."

"Does it get better?" Jeff asked.

"It does," Amy said. "The Gaultier Board is trying to use this as a reason I'm not fit to take over in any capacity."

"Why, because one of your family by marriage was murdered by terrorists?" Didn't even try to keep the shock out of my voice.

Amy nodded. "Ansom Somerall, Janelle Gardiner, and Quinton Cross graced me with a surprise conference call this morning at seven. Too bad for them that I was up already. They expressed their fake condolences, then shared that my ties to terrorist targets clearly puts Gaultier Enterprises at risk, and for the good of the company, its employees, and shareholders, I should stop trying to gain any kind of control."

"What did you say to that?" Doreen asked.

"I said that I'd be more than willing to share with any number of the reporters calling to get a story that because my cousin-by-marriage, who is being touted as a true American hero, was brutally murdered, Gaultier Enterprises feels that they now no longer want anything to do with American Centaurion. Then I said I'd be forced to ask those same reporters if they thought Gaultier's Board had made that decision because they were racist, xenophobic, in bed with the terrorists themselves, or potentially all three."

"Oh, so you told them to go screw themselves in business-speak. That's my girl."

"That's what that actually meant?" Jeff asked.

"Yes," Amy said with a laugh. "They backed down, and in fact are now trying to offer any assistance they can to 'catch those parties responsible for this atrocity.'"

Stryker nodded. "They released a statement to several online news outlets within five minutes of Amy's phone call ending. They also made calls to a variety of other numbers we're still tracing."

"You've tapped Gaultier's phones?" This was news to me.

"Henry's been working on a phone trace program that, once it makes contact with either the cell phone or the landline the call originated from, can then lock on to any other calls made from that cell or line. So yes, but only this morning. And he's still working out the kinks. However, I can say for sure that at least three of the calls they made were to overseas, two were to the C.I.A., and one was to the F.B.I. We don't have exact office or personnel matches yet, so don't demand them, Chuck. And, as I said, we're still working on the others."

"What countries?" Chuckie asked.

"France, Paraguay, and Russia."

"Figures. Do we think we have more supersoldiers, more androids, more Yates progeny, or all three? Show of hands?"

"How was that program not wiped out yesterday?" Christopher asked, shooting Patented Glare #3 at me while also ignoring my question.

"Henry does his initial work on paper," Stryker replied. "So he had all his notes."

"Still that's pretty complex, even for you guys, to get back up and running in less than a day," Tim said.

Stryker shook his head. "*We* were wiped out. Our friends who aren't attached to Centaurion weren't. We called in some favors. We were trying to use Henry's program to vector where the video feed was coming from, since it was the best option we had at hand."

Refrained from asking who they'd called in favors from—between the five of them they had a huge circle of friends, acquaintances, fans, and frenemies. Chose to also not ask if they'd been careful with what they'd shared with whom—yesterday all anyone had been focused on was trying to rescue our people. If some of us messed up security, we'd deal with it along the way.

"That's a lot of calls made early in the day immediately after Ames threatened them. To me, that says she did more than tell them to screw off—I think she hit a nerve."

"I doubt it's a worry that they'll be shown to be racist or xenophobic," Doreen said.

Len nodded. "From what I've seen of Gaultier, they cover most of the 'good steward of the planet and a lover of all people' hype."

"I agree. Besides, those worries would mean a call to their advertising, marketing, and PR agencies, not heavy hitter government agencies. Did they call Homeland Security?"

"Not as far as we know yet," Stryker said. "Why?"

"To cover that they were worried about a terrorist connection or attack, I'd think they'd have contacted Homeland Security as well as the C.I.A. and F.B.I. If only to be able to say they did."

"We're still getting back up to speed, so maybe they did and Henry just hasn't traced that back yet." Stryker sighed.

"The bigger issue from the technology side of the house is the information we've lost. Yuri still insists we were hit by Chernobog."

Adriana sat up. "Chernobog the Ultimate?"

"You know him?" I asked her.

"He's a myth," Stryker said.

Adriana shook her head. "No. Chernobog is real. Very real."

Oliver, Len, Kyle, and I all exchanged a glance. "Don't tell me," I said, "let me guess. Olga not only knows Chernobog, but they're cronies and go way back."

Adriana's eyes flashed. "She knows Chernobog, yes, and from way back. But friends? No. They're not friends—they're bitter enemies."

CHAPTER 53

STRYKER STARED AT ADRIANA. "There's no way. The Chernobog myth started in the eighties."

Adriana shrugged. "Grandmother was certainly alive and quite . . . active, at that time."

"Olga's former KGB, Eddy. Get with the program. Does she know Chernobog on sight or merely by reputation?"

"You'll have to ask her," Adriana said. She stood up, pulled her phone out, and stepped away to have a fast conversation in Romanian. She hung up and nodded. "If Len and Kyle will assist me, Grandmother would like to join us."

"We can go there," I offered. Olga was wheelchair-bound due to multiple sclerosis. Saw no reason to put her out.

"No, she said that under the circumstances, she would prefer to come here."

"I'll go along as well," White said. He and the boys followed Adriana out.

"We'll never hear the end of it from Yuri," Stryker muttered.

"Whatever. I'm just happy that Chernobog is real. Because a real person can be found, reasoned with, threatened, and, above all, stopped."

Tito, Melanie, and Emily joined us before anyone in the room could tell me I was wrong. Melanie looked like Raquel Welch when she'd been starring in movies mostly naked and Emily resembled a young Sophia Loren. It wasn't hard to see where Lorraine and Claudia got their Dazzler good looks.

Both women looked no worse for their hostage ordeal, though like everyone else, they did look a little more tired than normal. But, they and Tito looked worried.

"What's wrong?" Jeff asked before I could.

"You mean besides the fact that the only research we have left is what's on Tito's laptop?" Melanie asked.

"Meaning if there's a new strain of Surcenthumain out there, we don't know how to counter it any more?" Emily added. "Other than that and all the other fun from yesterday, Tito's got another question we can't answer."

"I've been thinking about yesterday's attacks," Tito said. "Kevin, I was wondering—was any other agency hit or affected by the computer virus that wiped us out, do you know?"

Kevin shook his head. "Didn't have time to think about asking."

"I asked," Buchanan said, shocking me not at all. "The only agency reporting any issues was the C.I.A.'s Extra-Terrestrial Division."

"My division," Chuckie said with a groan. "Nice. What did we lose?"

"Your systems back up differently from Centaurion's, so you lost less. Plus, some of your data was sent over to Homeland Security and the F.B.I., so you've probably lost less than it'll first appear. Damage was still being verified this morning. Angela is aware and investigating, and before you ask, we didn't tell you until just now because you needed to focus on your wife and her family yesterday." Buchanan turned back to Tito. "That was a good question. Why are you asking it?"

"It dawned on me last night, after we all went to bed, that there had to be a reason they stole and wiped out our data."

"Tito asked us, but we didn't hear anything while we were captives that seems relevant," Emily said.

"They did it to cripple us," Christopher suggested.

"There are easier ways to do that than computer hacking," Tito said.

"To learn what we know," Irving suggested.

Tito nodded. "I agree with that. However, why wipe us out? They could have hacked us and gotten the information without our knowing it."

"Two days ago I'd have told you that was impossible," Stryker said. "And, yeah, if we accept that Chernobog is real, then that means it's possible that everything we've ever been told he's done is real. And if he could do what he did yesterday, then he absolutely could have hacked our systems without us knowing."

"So why let us know?" Irving asked. "To panic or distract us?"

"To prevent us from being able to rescue our people at Home Base and the Science Center?" Christopher suggested.

Tim shook his head. "No. That makes no sense."

"Why not?" Amy asked.

Considered Tim's statement. "We only lost one person, and they only installed one android."

"We were lucky," Jeff said. "Because we almost didn't save anyone."

"That's inaccurate," Raj countered. "While the loss is still painful, to only lose one person during this kind of takeover is more than an acceptable loss ratio. And before anyone starts yelling at me, I'm no happier than anyone else that Michael lost his life because of these terrorists. However, Kitty's correct—why take over two entire facilities to only install one android, which is already destroyed, and only kill one person?"

"We know they installed whatever they've created that can block the imageers while they were there," I said. "Could that have been the only reason they took over the facilities?"

"No," Irving said. "Think about it. Whoever hacked us hacked every single A-C facility. If they could do that remotely, they could certainly install whatever's affecting the imageers remotely as well."

Stryker straightened up. "Did they do everything remotely? Or even anything remotely? Proximity equals access."

"As Henry proved when we hacked Gaultier," Amy agreed.

Tim and I looked at each other. "Revenge," Tim said.

"Yeah. We took their stuff, they go one further and not only take, but wipe out, all of ours."

"Okay," Jeff said slowly. "I can see that. And it would

prevent us from using their information against them. But that means you two are saying that Gaultier was involved with what happened yesterday."

"Why not? We were pretty sure that Gaultier had someone vying for the Apprentice job, potentially more than one." My vote was every one of the Land Sharks. Maybe they were an Apprentice Collective. "What if whoever over there won the job?"

"Or if new trials are going on," Raj said.

"Any one of the three trying to block me could be the Apprentice," Amy agreed. "I wouldn't be surprised if all three were going for the job, in that sense. They work together, but they're not tight. I'd call them rivals, at best."

"Titan and YatesCorp have to be considered," Buchanan said. "The room the hostages were in could have been put under Gaultier to throw suspicion onto them."

"That's also the part of the tunnels no cameras catch," Stryker said. "So the possibility of coincidence is there."

"The room was gone by the time we went back to examine it," Buchanan added. "And by 'we' I mean the P.T.C.U. and by 'gone' I mean gone without a trace, Poof Traps as well."

"We were chained up in a room," Melanie said dryly. "Believe me, there were walls and a door."

"Plywood and chicken wire go up fast and come down faster," Buchanan said. "But if I hadn't seen Walter's team and the Marines on video while it was happening, I'd have said the entire thing was faked."

"Just like the moon landing," Stryker said.

"Not now, Eddy. Real conspiracies are afoot, let's focus on those." Forged on while Stryker grumbled to himself. "We need to figure out who hired Chernobog. We find out who's signing the Ultimate Hacker Checks, we find out who's really in charge."

"Chernobog might not be doing it for money," Stryker said. "If we assume some of the myths are real, then he's worked just for the fun of it as often as he's done it for a paycheck."

"She," Olga said, as Len wheeled her into the room. "Chernobog is a woman, though she allows the world to think of her as male."

"How *Yentl* of her."

Olga gave a short laugh. "Yes, in that sense. Part of the reason Chernobog is so . . . vicious . . . in her attacks is because she was tired of constantly being doubted because she was a woman."

"I'm sure you and my mom went through similar discrimination, and yet you're not trying to take out the computer systems of the entire free world."

"Chernobog is not . . . stable." Olga looked at Stryker. "I'm sad to say that every myth about Chernobog is real."

"Can we protect against her?" Stryker asked. "Because two days ago I'd have said yes, but yesterday we were hacked like we were preschoolers."

Olga nodded. "Yes, but it will take more help." She turned to me. "Your friends the Israelis would be of much assistance with this."

"They have good hackers?" Potentially they did. I had no idea; it wasn't something I'd ever chatted about with our Mossad friends who were attached to the Israeli Embassy. We were usually talking to them about assassins and interstellar invasions and things of that kind of fun nature. Of course, hackers and their ilk fell under Chuckie and Stryker's bailiwick as far as I was concerned.

Olga barked another short laugh. "Yes, but not as good as those working for you. No, the Israelis have something much, much better and, to Chernobog, far more valuable." She smiled. "They have Chernobog's son."

CHAPTER 54

I'S HARD TO MAKE a room full of people silent, but Olga was a pro at it.

I liked to play Stump the Room, too, though, so I had a comeback question. "Do you happen to know who her son's father might have been?"

Olga looked surprised. Managed not to jump up and try to high five anyone, though it took effort. For all I knew, she was just being encouraging so that I'd continue to ask intelligent questions versus the kindergarten-level ones I usually managed.

"No one knows for sure, other than Chernobog, at least presumably." Olga's lips twitched. "She was not an . . . attractive woman in our youth and I doubt she's improved with age."

Ronald Yates hadn't been all that selective. Or rather, I knew he'd been willing to spread the "love" around a lot, and having a kid with the world's best hacker would seem like a total Mephistopheles move as well.

"Christopher, can you still rev up enough imageering juice to draw a picture on the air?"

This earned me Patented Glare #5. "Yes. Why?"

"Kitty wants us to describe the cameraman to you so you can draw him," Melanie said.

"So that we can see if he's anyone someone recognizes," Emily added.

"Yeah, and be glad Lorraine and Claudia aren't here yet,

because they'd have said the same, only they'd have both added a big 'duh.' My impression of Ronaldo Al Dejahl is that he imitates real people. I don't know that he has the ability or desire to make up a 'new' person. The idea might never have occurred to him."

"Probably not," Christopher said. "It's not like shape-shifting. It's creating a three-dimensional drawing and then superimposing it over and around you."

"Okay, then we need the Swarthy Slapper 'drawn.'"

Christopher heaved a sigh, but he got up and the three of them went to the part of the room where Pierre had installed a nice motorized projector screen. Melanie lowered it and they got Christopher working on his version of shadow puppets.

"Why?" Jeff asked. "Who do you think he is, or Al Dejahl was pretending to be?"

"Well, some will depend on whether or not he looks like anyone we or Olga know. Olga, what's Chernobog's real name, and what's her son's name?"

"Her real name was erased before I ever knew her, and she never stayed with one code name too long, other then Chernobog, which she only uses for computer-related work. Her son goes by many names. The Israelis know him as Russell Kozlow."

Tim was busy texting. "Oren, Jakob, and Leah are checking into him for us. The three of them say that they don't know who he is."

Olga nodded. "They are young, and Kozlow was imprisoned at least fifteen years ago." She was being vague, so either she wasn't sure, or there was a reason she hadn't given us a firm date of imprisonment.

"For what, exactly? I'm assuming terrorist activity of some kind, but the specific kind could be quite relevant to our current interests. And, while I know your first, second, third, *and* fourth instincts are to make us all work for it, after the day in Hell we had yesterday, we're all just flat out begging you to make it easy on us and simply share the intel without the usual fun and games."

Olga laughed softly. "As you wish. Yes, terrorist activity. Cyber crimes, mostly. Much of it focused on American business interests."

"YatesCorp, specifically?"

Olga smiled. "See? You didn't need to beg for the information. Some focused on Titan and Gaultier as well, though."

"Gotcha. Nice to know the main Businesses O' Evil all got some cyber terrorist love. Okay, so what are the odds that Kozlow is yet another Yates kid running around?"

"With the way our luck runs?" Tim asked with a short laugh. "High."

"Ready, Kitty," Melanie called.

"It's hard for me to hold this image," Christopher said through gritted teeth. "So you'd better look fast."

Most of the room pulled out their cell phones and snapped pictures of the man Christopher had superimposed on the wall.

"Or you could all take pictures because they last longer," Emily said with a laugh.

"Keep it up as long as you can anyway, Christopher," I said.

"Said the Actress to the Bishop," Amy added.

The humans in the room all snickered. The A-Cs all looked blank. Cultural differences continued to keep things interesting.

The man was just as Emily had described him—a little shorter than Christopher, swarthy, kind of chubby, definitely not a looker. He'd sounded Middle Eastern but accents could be faked. He definitely had a "browned by the sun" look, though.

"I don't see enough of a resemblance to how I remember Chernobog to be sure," Olga said regretfully.

"I don't see family in there, either," White added, as the image flickered and then disappeared.

"Christopher, can you make the skin tone lighter?" I handed him my phone.

He fiddled with the screen for a bit while I watched over his shoulder. "Anything else?"

"Make him thinner. Not skinny, stocky, maybe, but take off the chub."

"Making your perfect man?" Christopher asked, sarcasm knob heading toward eleven.

"No, I married my perfect man."

"Thanks, baby. What are you doing, though?"

"Ronaldo is more used to doing the image overlay than Christopher is. And while I don't credit him with a lot of creativity on his own, if he's imitating a real person, and that person comes from an espionage background, he might have had Ronaldo make some specific changes."

Christopher finished. "Ignoring the dig at my abilities, changing skin tone wouldn't be difficult, especially if you had someone with the right tone nearby to imitate. Same with the extra weight—you'd start with the original, then alter from there, and again, it's easier to do if you have a model to copy."

"Which they do, because a goodly number of their recruits are from the Middle East and I'm sure there are at least a few of them who aren't lean, mean, fighting machines. So, Richard, Olga, take a look now."

Stryker took the phone from me and hooked it up to the fancy projector Pierre had also installed. The picture flashed up nice and large onto the screen. The man no longer looked Middle Eastern but Slavic.

"I can see Chernobog in him now," Olga said finally, after studying the image for a good couple of minutes. "Frankly, more than I would expect."

"Human genetics are dominant for external."

"I'm not sure if I see any familial resemblance to the rest of us though," White said.

"Well, whoever his father is, that's Russell Kozlow," Tim said, as he handed his phone to Stryker. A new picture went up onto the screen, next to the one Christopher had created. They were clearly the same person. "Got that from Leah, and, here's the fun news that's not going to surprise anyone— Kozlow somehow broke out of Mossad's most secure prison two days ago. His escape was helped by, wait for it, a huge sandstorm."

"Well, it's just one big reunion of Ronnie's Kids, isn't it?"

"Let's make it bigger," White said. He stepped aside and made a quick call.

"There's no real similarity in body structures," Stryker said. "I mean, if we go by the people in this room who all have the Yates gene in them, I don't see consistency, and none of you look like Kozlow."

Jeff motioned to the others and he, Christopher, and Serene all went and stood by the screen. White finished his call and joined them. As he did so, Gladys and Jeff's mother, Lucinda, came in the room. They said their hellos as they joined the others in our own special lineup.

"It's likely to be the eyes. Christopher has his dad's eyes, nose, and mouth." He did, though his eye color—green flecked with blue—was like his late mother's. "Look at everyone else's eyes, do they all have a similar shape?"

"Somewhat. I see similarities in the mouths, too," Chuckie agreed. "But not from Martini."

"Jeff favors his father." At least in looks and most of his personality. I'd discovered his jealous streak came from Lucinda, though.

There was general agreement that Jeff had a similar body structure to White's but otherwise he was a clear Royal Family Descendant versus a Yates Looker. Worked for me. Jeff left the lineup.

"Christopher and Serene have Richard's nose," Melanie said. "And I think Kozlow does, too. But I don't know if that's enough to go on."

"Kozlow's mouth is like Gladys and Lucinda's," Emily added. "Without a genetic sample to compare to, I think that's the best we're going to get right now. But we've rolled with less."

"Every operation Kitty's in charge of," Christopher muttered.

Chose to ignore him. "So, why was Kozlow attacking YatesCorp? If there's a clause for the proof of the Yates Gene, why not just show up, have the blood test, and take your Seat of Power?"

"The gene's harder to identify and even harder to confirm," Tito said. "Possibly because of his combining with the Mephistopheles superbeing, Yates' DNA appears to have been altered. My research is still inconclusive, but if I had to postulate a theory, it would be that without enough of a known genetic sample to compare to, no one would be able to say they were Ronald Yates' relatives."

And suddenly everything that was going on made sense.

CHAPTER 55

I OPENED MY MOUTH and then shut it again. I wanted to
share what I'd figured out, but I realized I couldn't. Because Gladys was in the room, and we pretty much had proof
that, with the slightest effort on Ronaldo's part, she was
likely to tell the bad guys everything they wanted to know.
For all I knew she was reading me right now and would be
relaying what I was thinking to our enemies shortly.

Could tell Jeff, Chuckie, Buchanan, and Tim all noted me
gaping like a fish. Thankfully none of them asked what was
going on.

"Let's get back to the most pressing issue," Jeff said
smoothly, presumably because he had for sure read my mind
and/or emotions. "We need to determine what we're going to
do about the funeral the President's requesting."

"You know," Chuckie said, "I don't think any humans
have a right to add in on this one—this is a very personal
discussion that all of you need to agree upon. I need to contact Vander and Cliff anyway, so Kitty, Buchanan, why don't
you two come with me and we'll leave your husband to manage whatever the official American Centaurion decision is for
Michael's funeral."

"Reynolds, you okay if the other humans come along?"
Tim asked. "Your discussion undoubtedly affects Alpha
Team."

"Sure. Martini, can we use your office?"

"Sure, Chuck, go ahead."

I was impressed. Gave Jeff a quick kiss. "You rock," I said softly. Nodded to Len and Kyle who wheeled Olga out behind Chuckie. The rest of the humans trailed out behind us.

"We could also have this meeting at our embassy," Olga said as we waited for the elevator. "Or over at your Zoo facility."

Assumed Olga had made the same leaps I had and that she wasn't sure of Gladys' range. Neither was I. Gladys ran the entire Science Center, after all.

"I think the Zoo might be best," Buchanan said. Considered the distances. Yep, the Zoo was farther away than the Romanian Embassy, hence the most likely reason why Buchanan was voting that way. "We're on the right floor to just walk over anyway."

As he said this the elevator opened and Lorraine and Claudia stepped out. "Awesome, you two are here. Come with us. But first, Tito, please go with the girls and get your laptop. Don't pass go, don't check in on the conference room, just grab your laptop and any backups you have, and bring them and Nurse Carter back with you."

To everyone's credit, no one asked why, though Stryker really looked like he wanted to. The girls just shrugged and stepped back into the elevator, Tito joining them. Assumed at least half of those with me had connected the same dots I had, and I was pretty sure everyone was clear that whatever we were going to talk about needed to be done in a secure location.

"You want the rest of the guys meeting us?" Stryker asked.

"Yeah, that's a good idea. Have them meet us on the second floor."

While Stryker sent a text, Kevin and Irving exchanged a glance. "You want Pierre, too, Kitty?" Irving asked.

"Not yet." Mostly because I had to figure that Pierre would be the one human the A-Cs would expect to be instantly available if they needed something, and I didn't want to arouse more suspicion than we might have already.

"Do you want Denise to weigh in on any of this?" Kevin asked. "She might have a different perspective."

Denise liked Gladys a lot, and knew her far better than I

did, and I knew Kevin knew this. However, some things took precedence, Jamie being Number One. "No, but only because she's on kidlet duty, and that goes the same for Brian."

The girls and Tito returned, Nurse Carter in tow. "Let's move," Chuckie said.

"While we go," Buchanan said as we all headed for the bridge that connected the Embassy to the Zoo building down the block, "yesterday's events caused this to move down in importance, but we still need to get Field teams into every embassy in your neighborhood, as well as into the residences of any openly pro-alien politicians."

Was about to ask if he was sure this was necessary when we reached the bridge. It was made of steel and reinforced bulletproof glass, so we could see outside while walking across and stay safe at the same time. Which was currently a very good thing, because there was quite a crowd in our street.

"What's going on?" Claudia asked.

"That wasn't there when we got Olga," Len said.

"Looks like a protest," Tim said, squinting. "And, if I'm reading that right, they're protesting . . . us."

A-Cs had better vision than humans, so Lorraine, Claudia, and I all looked more closely. Sure enough, there were signs saying things like "Alien Go Home," "Aliens are NOT Americans," "If You Weren't Born Here, Leave," "One Dead Alien is a Good Start," and other pleasant things. Many of the signs were familiar from yesterday morning.

There were also people passing out pamphlets, and a table with what looked like a petition or two being signed was set up in front of the Irish Embassy. "Looks like Club Fifty-One is out in force."

"Not just them," Lorraine said, her voice tight. "Those horrible people who protest at military and other funerals are there, too."

"Oh, fantastic. The least Christian Christians in the world and the most xenophobic morons together at last. Two bad tastes that taste even worse together. But, I have to figure that's a love match made in hell, right there." Wondered if they'd done their hook up yesterday, after chasing us. Probably.

"Undoubtedly," Buchanan said.

"Com on!"

"Yes, Chief?"

"Walter, you're back on the job so fast?"

"Yes, Chief, though William's still here with me."

"Good. William, please stick around. Bring the wife and kids over if you'd like, but do it via a gate. Shields need to be up on the entire Embassy complex."

"William suggested I keep shields active, Chief. Shields have not been off since he first turned them on yesterday."

"You two rock. We have a situation outside that could quickly turn into a riot. I'm certain people will try to get in. We need to let friends in and keep enemies out. Good luck with figuring out which are which."

"On it, Chief. Do you want the com to remain open?"

"No, but please advise Jeff of what's going on. He's still with some of the others in the conference room."

"I don't know that Field teams are the right answer," Chuckie said once Walter had turned off the com. "I think we might need the National Guard."

"We need to discuss this at the Zoo," Olga reminded us.

We started across the bridge, meaning we were now easily seen from the street. This clearly made the crowd's day. They turned their random focus onto us. Happily, the thick glass and metal and other materials made the bridge pretty sound-proofed, so we couldn't hear what they were yelling. I could guess, though. I'd heard most of it already.

We could, however, see them surging at us, which wasn't fun to experience. They weren't all that coordinated, but there were a lot of them. Wanted to pull my Glock out of my purse, but since bulletproof glass worked both ways, con-trolled my fight impulse, though it took effort.

Someone tossed something at the bridge, and that, of course, meant that others followed suit. Good to know this was one of their signature moves.

Happily, the shields were indeed on and working quite well. Whatever was being thrown was tossed right back. Tried not to feel vindictive joy when signs, rotten fruit, and other nasty things bounced back onto the crowd. Failed.

We reached the Zoo and were able to at least not look at

the scene outside. The Zoo's first floor was where the Alpha Four animals were on display on random days and times for our protection, the fourth and fifth were housing and the Computer Lab. The third floor was where we now hosted gala events where sometimes our guests didn't die.

But the second floor was mostly a huge kitchen, a row of bathrooms, one of which housed a gate, a couple of elevators, and open space. It made for a good For Your Ears Only meeting room, because there was almost nothing anyone could hide in or behind.

The rest of Hacker International were waiting for us, looking worried. "Did you look outside?" Ravi asked.

"We walked over from the Embassy, what do you think?" Stryker replied.

Showing that Dazzlers were always on top of things, Lorraine and Claudia did a fast check of the floor and stairwells while Hacker International bickered amongst themselves about who was on top of looking at the mob outside and who wasn't.

"We're alone," Claudia said when they returned, a few seconds later.

The one thing this floor didn't have was chairs. Oh well. Olga's chair traveled with her, and everyone else could follow my lead and sit their butts down on Mr. Clean Floor. Most of them did—we looked like the most formal bunch of Fireside Friends ever—though Buchanan remained standing, and because he did, Len and Kyle did as well.

"Great. Okay, I know what's going on and I know why, at least, most of it. But first, to explain why we're here and everyone else is in the conference room, you know how I've been saying off and on that we have a mole?"

Everyone nodded. "Going to steal your thunder," Chuckie said. "It's Gladys, isn't it?"

"Yes, and before you all start protesting, I don't think she's been a willing mole."

"No," Tito agreed. "However, she's given in to Al Dejahl's mind control at least twice that we know of. Who's to say it hasn't been more often?"

"I'd think she'd have told someone if that were the case, Richard maybe," Lorraine said.

"Not if she doesn't remember it. She said that things are fuzzy when she's under mind control and she can't remember everything."

"How long have you known about Ronaldo Al Dejahl?" Olga asked.

"Since Jamie was born. But he was a French businessman and philanthropist well before then. And he had to have been protected in some way, because Mom never made the connection to him and the Al Dejahl terrorist group until then."

"While I'm sure he's been protected," Buchanan said, "your mother checked him out years ago. But Al Dejahl and its derivatives are common names in a small, very rural part of Europe and also in a few remote regions in the Middle East, and he had legitimate lineage to those areas. Ronaldo wasn't shown to be anything but a successful businessman until Baby Chief's birth."

"So, where does this leave us?" Adriana asked.

"Besides exposed and under attack both from the mob outside and from our other enemies? It leaves us with this—I know, exactly, what the bad guys are after." Pointed to Tito's laptop. "From now on, Tito, that laptop, its backups, Melanie, Emily, and Magdalena are considered second only to Jamie and the rest of the kids in terms of protection needs."

Nurse Carter looked confused. "Why? And why am I on that list?"

"Because what our enemies are searching so desperately for is the one thing they couldn't have found when they stole and wiped our data yesterday—the research on the Yates Gene."

CHAPTER 56

IT WAS A GOOD THING I wasn't hoping for gasps of surprise or horror, because I didn't get many, though Nurse Carter came through in a big way. Of course, she was the only one who wasn't an active member of Alpha Team, who wasn't determined to never let me know I'd surprised them, and who hadn't been in the conference room with us.

"Why are you sure?" Chuckie asked. "I can tell you're sure, and I'm inclined to agree, but I want to know your thinking first."

"Because they took Melanie and Emily hostage. And there was no reason. They didn't take Walter or the Barones, who are actively working in the Embassy. They didn't try to lure Alfred and Lucinda or any of the rest of Jeff's family into the trap. They had freaking Alpha and Airborne captive, and they *left* them. So they wanted Melanie and Emily, specifically, and there's only one reason in the world why they'd be more appealing as hostages than anyone else I've named, and it's because they're the only ones who work with Tito on the Yates Gene project and also assist at all hybrid births."

"Makes sense to me," Tim said. "But do you think Gladys, or any of the other A-Cs, have figured out the connection you just made?"

"Jeff has because he can read me so easily and he went out of his way to help us get out of the room."

"Christopher hasn't," Amy said. "And not because I think my husband's stupid or unobservant. But he's been distracted and moody like I've never seen, for the past few weeks, really, and I honestly think he was paying more attention to the inside of his own head than anything else going on."

Chose not to share why I knew Amy was probably accurate. "Raj and Richard, maybe. Lucinda probably not. Gladys? Let's just hope not."

"Doreen might have," Irving said. "But if she did, she won't say anything."

"Yeah, she's our best untrained liar, well, her and Richard. And Raj." Okay, we had some A-Cs really coming along in terms of lying. Good for us, I hoped. "Speaking of which, we need to contact our trained liar. How soon can we get in touch with Camilla?"

Chuckie shook his head. "There's almost nothing you can say that will make it worthwhile to risk her cover."

"We need to get into Gaultier and get our data back, while also wiping our theirs."

"Not sure escalation's the right answer, Kitty," Tim said.

"Not sure allowing them access to all our work on superbeing genetics is the right answer, either," Lorraine countered. "They could figure out what Tito has, or at least what the missing links are, with all the work we've done over the decades."

"Gladys is in there with our moms," Claudia said, worry clear. "They know what we know and what Tito knows."

"I don't think Gladys will do anything while she's in the Embassy," Irving said.

"Really? Like she wouldn't in the Science Center? I think that she won't do anything because our enemies currently think they've won, and that's the only reason."

"We won't have long before Chernobog drills down and discovers that what they want they don't have," Omega Red added. "Hours, not days."

"There's decades' worth of data, and Chernobog isn't an A-C. We may have days. But I'm with Yuri—whether it's days or it's hours, we won't have as much time as we'd like."

"If we want into Gaultier, we'll need to have Camilla's help," Amy said. "There's no way they're going to leave things unprotected long enough for us to find what we need, hyperspeed or no hyperspeed."

"Don't suppose we can do like Al Dejahl and pull an older move of our own, like just flipping their fire alarm to clear out the building," Tim said with a laugh.

"Oh, Megalomaniac Lad, there are times when I just don't know how I function without you by my side on a regular basis. That's it."

"There's no way a fire alarm will clear out everyone we need," Amy said. "Gaultier's equipment is state-of-the-art. And I wouldn't leave my special, evil brews and ill-gotten data unprotected, fire or no fire."

"There's more than one way to clear out a building. And when push comes to shove, we can use an effective weapon—public opinion. Besides, we don't need everyone out, just the people who can give orders."

"You mind explaining that?" Chuckie asked. "Because while we followed you on everything else, I guarantee none of us know what you're talking about right now."

"So few ever do, Chuckie. So few ever do. Hang on." Sent Jeff a text. Happily, or un-, depending on whose viewpoint you went with, the A-Cs had decided that they needed to support the President's wishes, or else it would look like the protestors had won. Good, that played into my plan.

Verified one other thing, and got another happy reply, and the additional news that Gladys and Lucinda were heading back to join the rest of the Gowers and their closer relatives and share the group's decision, meaning that the rest of our gang was on their way over to join us.

Seeing as they were all A-Cs, they were with us by the time I finished reading Jeff's text.

Brought them quickly up to speed. Interestingly, only Christopher was shocked by the revelations. Amy was right—he was really distracted. He'd admitted why to pretty much everyone here, other than his wife, and I was fairly sure she was the last person he wanted to tell. But we'd deal with Christopher's issues later.

"Kitty has a plan, but, as always, we don't know what it is," Chuckie said when we were done with the catching up.

"Blah, blah, blah. Just wanted the rest of the team over here so I didn't have to say it twice. But first, a couple of questions. Am I right in thinking that no one has actually ever seen an A-C funeral because you really don't do them anything like humans do and no one outside of Centaurion Division would have had cause to attend?"

"That's right," White said. "We've attended human funerals, of course, but only our personnel have ever attended one of ours."

"Super. We need to use the funeral. I realize that's totally disrespectful, but I worked with Michael plenty of times, and I can guarantee that he'd be okay with it if it meant we caught the people who killed him and Fuzzball."

"I agree," Jeff said. "At least, about Michael. I have no idea what your plan is, other than that you're really excited about it and you expect me not to be."

"Right, because you're not going to be in on the action. None of the men are."

"Why *not*?" Chuckie asked.

I shrugged. "Because men in this country don't wear veils."

CHAPTER 57

"YOU MIND EXPLAINING THAT?" Jeff asked.

"I get it," Tim said. "But I think you're expecting too much out of Gaultier."

Shook my head. "No, and here's why. They pissed Amy off, right? She already threatened to go to the press. So, we're going to the press. MJO, am I right in feeling confident that you could write an article that would practically require the Gaultier Enterprises Board and other top dogs to ensure they were at Michael's funeral?"

Oliver nodded slowly. "I'd suggest including Titan and YatesCorp in that goal as well. I can focus in such a way as to insinuate that non-attendance means anti-alien sentiments, along with non-support of the President."

"But what if they don't care?" Amy asked. "There's a freaking mob outside, and we have politicians who hate us. They may use it as an excuse *not* to come."

"Well, as to that, I think we'll make our 'friends' outside work for us, not against us."

"Only Tim and Amy seem clear on your idea, baby. I'm not clear, and looking at Chuck's expression, he's not either. If *he* can't follow you, no one else can."

"Okay, here's my plan. We not only agree to the President's wishes, we go one better. We go overboard. We bring out all our top people, with the clear expectation, since we're honoring a war hero, that everyone else will be showing up. A few calls made on our behalf by my good friends Lillian

Culver and Guy Gadoire and we have plenty of important people who realize this is a be seen or never expect a favor from American Centaurion again event."

"I'm sort of stuck on the veils," Jeff said.

"No one's going to expect us to do anything during Michael's funeral. Everyone should be attending, right? And that means we need to be visible. However, funeral attire includes veils for women. So, we make it a new 'rule' that all women have to be heavily veiled, so that no one can see their faces. Gloves on the hands. Sensible shoes. And all that."

Raj smiled. "I can find the body doubles. They'll need to be able to imitate mannerisms. We have plenty of troubadour women, all bored, because the science and mathematics sides don't feel it's an impressive skill, either." Oh look, Raj had a sarcasm knob just like the rest of us.

"We're about to make your brothers and sisters in acting talent feel very needed and vital to the cause, Raj."

"Good. We can delay the funeral about a week, maybe a little more. Preparations have to be made, and we can claim cultural needs to create what will seem like a natural delay versus an invented one."

"Like sitting shiva."

"Right. In fact, we can use the Jewish traditions as examples, with specific details changed to our advantage."

"Instead of rending the outer garment, make it like a burka and make us even harder to identify, type of thing."

"Exactly, though more tailored. We can't stall too long, but it should be enough time for my troubadours to be able to imitate their assigned doubles well enough to make it through the event itself."

"Here's what I don't like, if I'm following your so-called plan correctly," Chuckie said. "The only people who will be disguised are the American Centaurion women. Meaning those same women will be the ones doing the guerrilla raid."

"Yes, that's exactly what the plan is. Look, we need to get in and find out what the hell Gaultier is up to and retrieve our stolen data, right? And that means we need to get our hackers inside so we can all sing the Proximity Equals Access Song. But none of them are trained in fieldwork, so they have to go in as part of a team."

"Got that right," Stryker muttered. The rest of Hacker International nodded their agreement with their leader's assessment of their lack of B&E skills.

"I don't want to send in our Field teams, in no small part because they aren't able to avoid the Al Dejahl Mind Control Trick and apparently all of us are. And if we get caught, we need someone who can talk their way out of things and think on their feet."

"I know where this is going," Jeff said, "and you're right, I officially don't like it."

Ignored him and forged on. "So that means we need to have a team of experienced operatives. The only people who can be so covered up no one could tell if they were the real people or impersonators are the women. So, we're going in with the hackers."

"The funeral can be made to be very long," White said. "So that should give you time, but even so, it might not be enough time. The facility is quite large."

"And there are those hidden levels we couldn't find," Amy added. "Where you just know they're hiding all the evil stuff."

"And our data, I'm sure. And God knows what else, but I'm willing to bet that it's the new drug that Vander's worried about. So we'll be helping our new friend at the F.B.I., too."

"You're okay with this plan?" Jeff asked White.

Who shrugged. "We have limited options, Jeffrey, and we do need to find out what's going on over there. Besides, Kathy's right as always."

"Thanks, Rick honey."

"I hate it when you two do that," Jeff muttered.

"Who are you planning to take with you?" Chuckie asked.

"Lorraine and Claudia." Who high-fived each other. I loved my girls. "And Serene, complete with your bomb arsenal."

She bounced up to high-five Lorraine and Claudia. "I've been playing around with more miniaturization in my spare time. You'll love what I've got for us!"

"I'm sure, as long as you're not throwing the bombs at me."

"I'm on the team too," Adriana said. Who then got high-

fives from both Lorraine and Claudia and a hug from Serene.
We were all fired up about being the All Girl Power team. I'd
have to play Good Charlotte's "Riot Girl" when we rolled.

"And me," Buchanan added. So much for All Girl Power.
However, on the good side, Jeff and Chuckie both noticeably
relaxed. "No one would expect me to be at the funeral, and
most of your enemies still seem unaware that I exist, which
is how we want it. You two," he pointed to Len and Kyle,
"obviously 'guarding' whoever's pretending to be Missus
Chief will mean that most observers buy the ruse."

"Children are not allowed at funerals," White said. "A new
rule that I'm sure our current Pontifex will be glad to enforce."

"Good one, Mister White. Meaning that we won't need to
worry about any of the kids blowing their moms' covers. And
Kevin, that means Denise stays in the Embassy, hopefully
where it's safe."

"Who else is on your team?" Chuckie asked.

"Me," Amy said indignantly.

"Nope. Ames, you need to be at the funeral. You're the
only one who will have enough pull with the Gaultier bigwigs to keep them at the event. Especially since we think one
of them is the current Apprentice, we need to keep them
where all of you can see them. And Caroline will need you,
because there's no way she's going to be a part of the guerrilla team."

"Why not?" Caroline asked as she, Naomi, and Abigail all
joined us.

"What are you guys doing here?"

"Whatever they gave me brought my powers back,"
Naomi said. "Just a little, but I could feel all of you over here.
I realized we were needed." She looked right at me. "Blaming the wrong people for Michael's death doesn't bring him
back. But making the people who killed him pay in ways
they don't want to will at least avenge him."

"So Sis and I are in," Abigail added.

"Okay." This earned a lot of angry looks from the menfolk. "Look, dudes, it's all great that you want to tell me that
we delicate little flowers need to stay close to home and safe.
Only no one was safe *at* their home yesterday. And we can
use the A-C powers, even if they're just the standard ones."

"And no one would believe we wouldn't be at our brother's funeral," Abigail said. "Meaning that we're great choices to go undercover."

"So I'm going, too," Caroline said. She was still wearing both her engagement ring and the Unity Necklace Michael had given her. My heart hurt looking at them.

"No," I said as gently as I could. "You need to be at the funeral. Both because of who Michael was to you, and because you need to be seen."

"No one would believe that Kitty wouldn't be there with you," Chuckie said slowly. "In that sense, you become the perfect cover."

Caroline took a deep breath and let it out slowly. "You're right, Chuck. And Kitty, I know you're right, too. I won't have any trouble being dramatic if you'll need me to."

"Probably will. You and Amy are going to have to work on how you'll signal each other." Swallowed hard. "I'm sorry I won't be there, Caro."

She managed a sad little smile. "I wish none of us had to be." Her expression hardened. "But we do, so, let's make sure that it's worth it and get these bastards where they live."

CHAPTER 58

GOT UP AND GAVE Caroline a big hug. "That's my girl. And I'm still sorry . . . for everything, up to and including the fact that I won't be there with you."

She hugged me back. "It's okay. None of this was your fault. You're going to be doing what needs to be done. Just . . ." She hugged me tighter. "Don't let them get one of my best friends right after they've taken my fiancé, okay?"

Swallowed the latest lump in my throat. "I'll do my best, I promise."

Naomi grabbed me next. "I'm so sorry," she said quietly as we hugged each other.

"It's okay. Really."

We separated and I sat back down next to Jeff and my purse, while Caroline and the Gower Girls settled in next to Chuckie in our ever-widening Campfire Circle.

"What about me?" Doreen asked once everyone other than Buchanan, Len, and Kyle were once again on their butts.

"You, I'm of two minds about. You've proven you can handle the fieldwork along with the rest of us. But you're also one of the only Embassy A-Cs who can believably lie. And you know everyone, and that means you'll know people Amy and Caro don't."

She nodded. "I'd like to go with your team, but I think you're right, I'll probably be of more use at the funeral itself."

"Okay," Jeff said with a sigh. "I give up. You're all going

in, fine. But explain how you're planning to use our friends the protestors to ensure that the various corporate heads we want at the funeral actually will attend."

"If I may?" Oliver asked.

"Go for it, MJO."

"While freedom of speech is our country's watchword, the majority of people in this country don't agree with the so-called religious who are busy protesting that Michael deserved to die because he was an alien and his older brother is openly gay. They're a small, hideous, quite vocal group, but the operative word is 'small.' Most corporations—and certainly huge ones like Gaultier, Titan, and YatesCorp—aren't going to give in to these people's demands. It does their businesses more good to oppose them."

"That's true," Amy said. "And, as Len said earlier, Gaultier prides itself on being a very open company. At least in its PR."

"Reality's always different than the marketing hype, Ames. I think it's to our advantage that the Religious Asshats Du Jour are creating a love connection with Club Fifty-One. Sure there are plenty of people out there who may agree with the Club Fifty-One nuts, but a lot of them will not want to be associated with the Religious Asshats. And vice versa."

"So their collective power gets diluted," Oliver agreed. "Then, all it takes is some well placed media commentary, and you can get a firestorm of support going. Which is what my part of this operation will entail."

"Exactly. They either attend Michael's funeral, or all these corporate heads and politicians are flat out saying to the world that they support Club Fifty-One and the Religious Asshats. Most of them won't be willing to risk that."

Chuckie nodded. "In this case, I think you're correct. While there's still plenty of anti-alien activity going on, even someone like Langston Whitmore wouldn't be able to avoid the fallout he'd get from non-attendance."

"Yeah, let's make sure someone's keeping an eye on our beloved Secretary of Transportation, because he's also high on my list of potential Apprentices."

"The P.T.C.U. will be out in force, as will other protective government agencies," Buchanan said. "They'll be watching everyone. This funeral will have the potential to be the site of another attack."

"In which case, our men will hustle the women to safety and then kick some butt. At least, that would be my plan. Jeff?"

"I'm sure we can handle it," Christopher answered for him, sarcasm knob already at eleven and heading for twelve, "should Michael's funeral devolve into chaos like everything else we do."

"I have to ask this," Kyle said, looking and sounding embarrassed. "I don't understand how all of you are so calm about this plan."

"Funerals don't mean the same things to us that they do to humans," Jeff said, clearly happy with the subject change. "Michael's soul has left his body. There's no great glory in honoring his corpse."

"Funerals do more than that," Kyle said. "They honor the person's life."

"They do," White agreed. "But we'll have made our peace with Michael's death well before the official funeral. So, for us, using the funeral as a way to get our team inside Gaultier and able to hopefully retrieve our stolen data is a more palatable reason to have the funeral than the ones we have to give lip service to."

"But that lip service *must* be given to Gladys. I'm not sure how her talents work, but we have to do everything we can to keep her believing that we're all actually there, at the funeral, not doing a guerrilla raid."

"How?" Amy asked. "I'm surprised she didn't realize we were all up to something earlier."

White shook his head. "Her talents don't work like Jeffrey's, even though she's an empath. Her dream reading talent is dominant, meaning she reads most emotions when she's asleep. Because of that, she learned young to go in and out of sleep without issue. I believe the term is 'cat naps,' but basically she sleeps in short bursts throughout the day and night."

Well, that explained a lot about why the A-C Security team worked in the way they did. "That must be how they're getting her, via her dreams."

"Perhaps," White acknowledged. "But we don't know for sure."

"If Sis and I were back to normal, we could combat, counter, or protect her," Abigail said regretfully. Naomi nodded.

"But you're not, meaning Paul's likely the only one who can."

"Not without ACE's help," Naomi said. "Paul's a dream reader, not a manipulator. ACE could help him, but I don't think he could do it on his own."

Had an overwhelming urge to look at my iPod. Went with it and dug it out while the others discussed ways to circumvent Gladys' powers. Didn't bother to put my earbuds in, just turned it on and looked at the song. "I'm Not Sleepin'" by Big Bad Voodoo Daddy. And, just in case I wasn't clear, the next song was "I'm Not Sleeping" by the Counting Crows. Clearly Algar thought I was a little slow.

Or else, he was suggesting that more than Gladys not sleep. Sleep deprivation wasn't a good plan for most people, be they human, A-C, or hybrid. So had to contemplate what he was going for here.

Thought about the songs' lyrics. The Big Bad Voodoo Daddy one was about not sleeping to avoid dealing with problems and memories of the past. But the Counting Crows song was about being haunted by someone.

Algar might be referring to Michael having visited me in my sleep, but I still wasn't sure if that had been real or my subconscious, though it had felt more real. Had a feeling I was going to need to really listen to both songs, potentially more than a few times.

Of course, Algar could simply be telling me he wasn't sleeping on the job, but per what he'd told me he also wasn't "on" the job, either. Unless I wanted a Coke or a snack. Huh.

"I'm getting something to drink," I said quietly to Jeff. "You want anything?"

"Not that the Operations Team can deliver."

Had my doubts about that, but trotted off into the kitchen area. There were several huge refrigerators housed here. Chose the one farthest from the group and looked at it. "A Cherry Coke and a little help, please and thank you."

Then I opened the door.

CHAPTER 59

ALGAR WAS SITTING CROSS-LEGGED in the fridge, holding a frosty Cherry Coke, a straw, and an ironic expression.

"Wow, that's some service." Took the soda and the straw.

He rolled his eyes but didn't say anything. Resisted the urge to be overly sarcastic, hard as it was. "I don't think anyone can hear us. I realize you want to tell me something. I have no clue as to what that is, though."

He gave me a look that could only be described as derisive and snapped his fingers.

Took a quick look around. Everyone seemed frozen. "Oh. So, I guess that was a summoning hint, wasn't it?"

"You think?"

"Wow, trying to remember why it's an honor that, out of all the naked apes out there, you've picked me as your new favorite."

"Trying to remember why myself."

"Okay, as fun as this bantering is, why did you summon me, oh Master of the Cupboard?"

"I like your plan."

Waited. That appeared to be it.

"Um, thanks. I think. I'm finding it hard to believe you wanted to see me to give me an 'atta girl' in person, especially since you don't really strike me as the 'atta girl' type."

"Your enemies are planning, too, of course."

"Ah, now there's the Algar I've recently come to know

and pretend to love. So, the bad guys aren't sleeping, either. I figured, and I promise you, everyone else over there on the floor has figured as well. It's just that we, unlike you, aren't privy to what's going on elsewhere."

"Really?" He stared at me.

"Really. I get that you're trying to give me a clue here. The happy news is that I've got no ego attached to saying these three little words: I don't know. I don't know what you're trying to make me realize, other than that Gladys needs to be kept from sleeping, God alone knows how we're going to do that."

"I'm sure Gladys would agree with you."

"Awesome. No-Doze for Gladys, please and thank you."

This earned me a dirty look. "Just because someone agrees with you doesn't mean they're right."

"Good to know. I'll ponder that."

Algar heaved a sigh. "The First King of Alpha Four wasn't this willfully dim."

"And yet you like me better. We can both contemplate all that says about both of us later. But, you know, before you go, I do have a question that's been bugging me since I moved into the Embassy."

"Yes, there's a hidden gate and it would be the best thing in the world if you found it, sooner as opposed to later."

"Wow. That was, honestly, rather impressive. Any shot of you giving me a clue to its whereabouts, since everyone's been over the entire facility with many fine-toothed combs and all we've found is a pamphlet saying Kitty's A Paranoid?"

"No one's looked correctly."

"Really? That's your answer? Obviously no one's looked in the correct place, since we haven't found it."

"I didn't say that. I said that no one's looked *correctly*." With that he handed me a box, snapped his fingers and disappeared.

Resisted the urge to say either "goodbye" or "good riddance" but it took effort. Closed the fridge door and looked at the box in my hand. It wasn't No-Doze. It was a box of Unisom.

Stared at the box as I walked slowly back to the group. "I

have a question." Didn't wait for the go-ahead; I'd already interrupted the conversation. "Has anyone actually discussed her powers and how they work with Gladys?"

"I have," White said. "Somewhat at least. And of course Paul has."

"Of course, because he's got a similar talent. Jeff, Naomi, Abigail?"

"No," Jeff said. "But that was because of Aunt Terry."

"Right, the glowing cube she programmed that we now know was a Z'porrah construct." Realized Algar worked in sneaky and, once you saw the pattern, not all that mysterious ways. But they were effective ways. One day I might even admit that to the little jerk's face, too.

I needed to ask the Poofs if they'd let me have a cube, or, better yet, tell me if there was one they hadn't confiscated. But didn't say so out loud because I didn't want to derail this line of thought by having everyone tell me I was crazy to still think there was a hidden gate hanging around.

Forged on with the other line of reasoning Algar clearly wanted me on. I'd figure out why the being who'd spent a lot of time protesting that he wasn't picking sides was clearly helping one side quite a lot. Had some suspicions, but Algar's long game wasn't of prime concern at the moment.

"Mimi, Abby? What about you two?"

"Well, no one knew about our powers until just a few years ago," Naomi said. "But yes, after that, Aunt Gladys worked with me a little."

"Uh huh. She does most of her work while she's asleep, right?"

"Right. Which is why we want to keep her awake for, I guess, over a week."

"Actually, we want her snoozing."

"What the hell changed your mind on that in the less than a minute it took for you to get a Coke and come back?" Chuckie asked.

Could feel myself not being allowed to articulate the real source of my inspiration. Which was okay because I didn't want to try to explain Algar to anyone—I was sure I'd get a migraine if I even tried. Besides, the source wasn't as important as the actual idea.

"We think Ronaldo's reaching Gladys through her dreams. But doors go both ways. Meaning perhaps she can reach him through his dreams as well."

"Why would we want her to reach Al Dejahl?" Christopher asked. "To give away even more of what we're doing? So we can all be killed? One wasn't enough?"

"What is *wrong* with you?" Amy asked him. "Why are you acting like Kitty's your enemy?"

"I'm not," he mumbled.

I was still looking at the Unisom box while working through how I wanted to phrase what I thought we needed Gladys to do. So I didn't pay a lot of attention to my mouth. "He's just lashing out at the only safe person he can, Ames. It's tough for men when they're having what they perceive as performance issues."

Played that back as the last word left my mouth and winced. Decided to look up from the box, in case I had to run really fast.

Christopher wasn't glaring at me. His expression was more like betrayed shock. "Thanks a lot," he said finally.

"Oh for God's sake," Amy said. "Is this about your extra powers disappearing? That's ancient news. I figured it out weeks ago, and we all heard the confirmation from Kitty when you were at Dulce yesterday. And really, who cares? So you're slightly less amazing than you were before. I didn't marry you because you'd shot up with Surcenthumain, you know."

"But . . ." Christopher started. "I . . ."

Amy rolled her eyes. "So all the extra angst and brooding was because of that? I don't know whether to be relieved or seriously angry. I thought you were unhappy being married to me."

"No!" Christopher now looked panicked. "I love being married to you."

"You haven't acted like it recently."

Decided to just go for it. "He also feels like he's been shunted aside and has no real role any more. Jeff's a congressman, you're trying to run a huge conglomerate, even his dad kicks more butt than Christopher does. His position would be important if we didn't have an ambassador on site.

But we do, and it's me, not him. Kevin's the Defense Attaché. And we have a troubadour in a much more important face position than Christopher has, which is pretty much the textbook definition of rubbing salt in the wound. There's more to it, of course, but that's the gist."

Everyone, not just Christopher, gaped at me. "Really?" Amy asked finally.

"Yeah. And no, Christopher didn't tell me. I'm just not as totally dim and unobservant as my nearest and dearest apparently think I am, and I can figure out when I'm the focus of someone's impotent railing, and then I can also figure out why." Looked at Chuckie. "I did have a really good teacher that way." Chuckie grinned.

"Gosh, glad that's all straightened out," Jeff said quickly, as Christopher looked worried and upset and Amy looked pissed and confused. "You two please fight and make up once we're sure of what Kitty's talking about."

"I need your help, you know," Amy said to Christopher in a low voice.

"Not now," Chuckie said, with a lot of authority. "Later, and in private, and that's an order. Right now you can both have me as the mutual focus of hatred, I'm used to it. So, Kitty, why are you suddenly the pitchwoman for Unisom?"

"Oh, this, right. I think maybe we're looking at the situation the wrong way, or at least some of it. We have a great offensive plan for later, but we have nothing but defense planned until then. But we know what our enemy doesn't, which is that they don't have what they really want, and we know who our enemy is and they don't necessarily know that we do. That means we have the advantage. I think we need to press it."

"It's risky," Buchanan said.

"Not if we all actually believe that Gladys is on our side and doesn't like being used by our enemies. If we have anyone who thinks otherwise, now is truly the time to share those concerns."

The room was quiet for a few long moments, then one hand raised.

CHAPTER 60

"I HAVE EXPERIENCE with long-term moles," Olga said as she put her hand down. "And you need to prove to me, right now, that this woman is not exactly that."

"I don't believe they can." Gladys stepped out of the bathroom with the gate in it. Okay, so I should have had the bathroom doors propped open. My bad.

"Are you saying you're a traitor?" Olga asked her calmly. Buchanan, Len, Kyle, Chuckie, and Adriana all shifted in how they were sitting or standing. Just a bit, but all five of them were ready to attack or defend.

"No," Gladys said. She shot an amused look toward Buchanan. "You're good, my boy, but you're not good enough to take me."

"Don't give me a reason to find out," Buchanan said calmly.

Gladys snorted. "Oh, noted." She looked back to Olga. "I have no idea how I've been controlled, but based on everything that happened, it's obvious I have been. There's only one way for an android copy of me to have gotten into the Science Center, and I'd have had to have allowed it through."

"So, what do we do with you?" Olga asked.

It was interesting in that these two women were pretty much ignoring everyone else in the room. Had the feeling they felt that, should it come to it, they could easily dispatch all of us without trying too hard. Had a feeling they were right.

"I think we hear the rest of what Kitty has to say." My mother sauntered out of the gate bathroom. She was dressed in her P.T.C.U. gear—black pants, shirt, bulletproof vest, P.T.C.U. baseball cap, and lots of snazzy guns. All holstered. Hoped that was a good sign and not an indication that Mom was too trusting. "And Gladys, trust me—I *can* take you. Without trying hard."

"Mom? How did you get here? I mean, aside from the obvious 'took a gate' answer." Good lord, we weren't having a For Your Ears Only Meeting. We were having a Clandestine Kegger. Clearly I should have asked Pierre to cater something on the casual side. Probably wasn't too late.

Mom and Gladys both gave me the "duh" look. "Walter told us where you were," Mom said. "When we asked. Without coercion."

"You didn't tell him the meeting was private?" Jeff asked me.

"No, because we were trying to be stealthy. And all that."

"Only my girl. So, Aunt Gladys, Angela, welcome to the party. Olga was just pointing out that we have no way of proving Gladys is or isn't a long-term mole. We'd love your input." Jeff shot them both his Charming the In-Laws Smile.

"Why are you all sitting on the floor like the biggest bunch of Scouts in the known world?" Mom asked.

"Good grief! We were trying to have a super secret club meeting, what do you think? Mom, focus. How do we prove that Gladys isn't evil?"

Mom heaved a sigh. "Really? I mean *really*? You're asking this, all of you?" All heads in the room nodded. "Charles, Malcolm, even you two?"

Chuckie nodded. "Consider us clueless."

"Truly." Mom rolled her eyes. "Olga, are you honestly questioning?"

Olga laughed softly. "Oh, no. I'm very aware of what will prove Gladys is not willingly working for the enemy. However, they do need to be taught. American schools don't seem to focus on logical thought and deductive reasoning. And, no offense meant, A-C schools appear to be even worse."

"True enough." Mom shook her head. "It's a very simple answer. I hope you're all listening closely. Ready?" All heads nodded again, even Gladys'. So there was that. "Fine. Kitty, you're alive."

"Beg pardon?"

"Oh," Chuckie said. "Yeah, okay."

Buchanan chuckled. "Good point. That's why you're the boss."

"Mind clarifying that, Secret Agent Man or Men?"

"I will." Buchanan turned to me. "You're the number one target on your enemies' hit lists, and you have been since you first joined Centaurion Division. Sure, Mister Former Chief and the Minister of Sulky Looks were watching over you, but there are so many different ways to kill someone and make it look like an accident that I could list them from now until the funeral and not be done."

"Gladys moved you away from the Science Center," Mom added while I tried to control the Inner Hyena over Buchanan's nickname for Christopher, with only limited success. "I know Richard was influential in that decision, but I also know he didn't make that decision alone."

"True enough," White said. "For the record, only Madame Olga raised the issue of Gladys' trustworthiness."

"Richard, I realize you're my older brother, but sometimes you're just too decent and trusting. Of *course* you should be determining if I'm your enemy or not. I allowed our enemies in and they murdered Michael in cold blood. You should be running me through every test you have."

"No need," White said. "Since Angela's point is well taken. I'd add that Jamie is under your guard quite frequently and is still safely with us."

"Super. So, we're all on the same team. In keeping with our campout traditions, we'll sing "Kumbaya" and make s'mores later. However, I do actually have something I want Gladys doing between now and Michael's funeral."

"And that is?" Gladys asked me.

Tossed her the box of Unisom. "I want you spying for our side. We're pretty sure your half brother's controlling you through your dreams. So, you know how he does it, even if you're not consciously aware of it."

"I'm not sure I can discover that in the timeframe we need."

"Chuckie, you're up. I know the C.I.A.'s done studies on this stuff, and not just because of *The Men Who Stare At Goats*. So, you get to oversee Gladys' dream indoctrination. Naomi, you'll need to help him with that. It's a fun couples project."

"What are we looking for?" Naomi asked. "Dreams don't work like waking thought, even dreams you control."

"Ronald Yates clearly was spreading the love around in every corner of the world. That means there's any number of Yates half siblings running around. You're looking for them, for signs that indicate what Ronaldo is planning, for signs of who he's taking his directions from. We should be so lucky that you discover who the Master or Apprentice is. Look for them, too, but I have to figure you'll find out the plan before you'll get a real clue to their identities."

"We'll need Paul's help," Naomi said.

Waited for him to appear. Shockingly, he didn't. Wondered why not. "Everyone else is here—so where are Paul and James, anyway?"

"Dealing with the riot that's at your front door," Mom said. "That's why I'm here in the first place. Pierre contacted me. Apparently he's the only person in this entire Embassy complex who felt that a riot in the streets in front of your Embassy wasn't good for public safety or relations." Yeah, Mom's sarcasm knob went well past eleven.

"It came up fast," Kyle said. "When we went to get Olga there was no one on the street."

Len nodded. "When we walked from the Embassy to the Zoo, it was only about fifteen or twenty minutes later, and the mob was already formed."

"I think people going in and out of the Embassy was the trigger," Buchanan said. "Based on what I've been dealing with the past few days, at any rate. You all going in and out was proof that there were people in here to threaten and terrorize."

"We'll deal with them," Mom said. "Just deciding if we want to call in the National Guard or not."

"What are Paul and James actually doing, do you know?"

"They're talking with Colonel Franklin and your Uncle Mort to determine if they want to have a show of military force of some kind, use Field agents, or both."

"We could send out the Amazons," Jeff said. "They'd love to knock some heads, I'm sure."

Thought fast. "No, we don't want to go for fighting back if we can help it. I think I have another solution."

CHAPTER 61

"I HATE THIS PLAN," Jeff said, as he and I stood at the front door. "I might hate it even more than when you had us use the alligators to rescue people at the Space Center."

"It's the easiest way, will ensure that no one's hurt, and will get rid of the Loser Brigade out front without any real effort or a lot of time."

Rahmi and Rhee were with us. They were both almost vibrating with the excitement of getting to do something, even though they'd been told it was a non-fighting something.

The com turned on. "We're ready, Chief," Walter shared.

"Okay, girls, it's show time. Remember that we'll want to run back into the Embassy in case anything goes wrong. Inside, retreating, *not* going forward to attack."

The princesses looked at the pictures Jeff and I were holding, and shapeshifted.

"We are clear on our required roles," Rahmi said. "We are to smile and wave and then go back inside when you tell us to."

"I love the sparkles," Rhee added.

"Good. You two look great, just like the pictures. Walter, let's activate Mission: Get Off My Lawn."

With that, Jeff opened the door and we four stepped out.

The gasp from the crowd was audible. Because of my enhanced vision, I could see the huge floater gate that spanned the length of our facility. But no one on the street could.

The four of us waved to the crowd, which, true to expectations, surged toward us. Even the people at the tables with the petitions got up and came a'running.

As the first people hit the floater gate, they disappeared. But it was a big crowd, and we had people shoving in the back to get close enough to see if who they thought was standing with us were indeed two people thought long dead.

Proving that the human Curiosity Gene was much stronger than the human Common Sense Gene, in a matter of seconds, there was no one on the street. Trotted inside. "Okay, Walter, turn off the gate."

"Off, Chief."

The four of us used hyperspeed to grab the tables, chairs, and other paraphernalia left outside. We were back inside in under ten seconds and there was no trace of the mob left anywhere. Gave myself a virtual pat on the back.

"What do we do with all this crap?" Jeff asked.

"Keep the paperwork, we'll want to look at it to see what they're trying to do. Just leave the tables and chairs here. I'll have the Operations Team get rid of them."

Raj and Reader joined us in the foyer. "All protestors arrived safely and are accounted for," Raj said.

"They're also all under arrest," Reader added with a grin. "Colonel Franklin said to tell you that he took pictures of their expressions, because he knew you'd appreciate them."

"He rocks. Okay girls, you can change back now."

Reader laughed. "Ronald Regan and Elvis. The reports on this should be great."

"Yep. How to ensure your enemies sound like lunatic crackpots without really trying."

"What if someone took pictures?" Jeff asked. "Imageering can't alter them right now."

"Colonel Franklin has confiscated all phones and cameras," Raj said. "Since the protestors are being treated as terrorists."

"Hey, not my fault those people managed to sneak onto Andrews Air Force Base *en masse* and threaten the U.S. Government."

Reader put his arm around my shoulders as we headed off to get back to the real business of the day. "Girlfriend, I have to say it—I just love watching you work."

CHAPTER 62

THE NEXT WEEK was spent getting ready for Michael's funeral and our side's answer to Operation Infiltration.

We'd used the excuse of religious necessities to explain why no one, Jeff in particular, was going to work until after the funeral. It seemed to work, in part because Oliver was fanning the media flames as promised, and much news coverage was being focused on how devastating this loss was to American Centaurion.

There were, of course, the opposing views, but thanks to the success of Mission: Get Off My Lawn, the opposition looked like the biggest bunch of dangerous wingnuts around, which helped Oliver's efforts. Didn't let it go to my head—one mission firmly in the win column did not an entire successful Operation make.

At Buchanan's repeated insistence, Reader had assigned Field teams into the neighboring embassies and regular residences in our area. All these agents had supposedly passed their Anti-Mind Control Training. A handful of the embassies and regular folks refused to be occupied, so we and our friends in the D.C.P.D.'s K-9 division were watching them for signs of danger to the residents or anti-alien activity from said residents. The rest seemed relieved to have the extra protection, because no one had missed the excitement of the Mob O' Losers.

Pierre had our personal fashion designer, Akiko, working on creating the appropriate "funeral attire" for all the female

A-Cs of importance. This included women not involved in the actual operation, so Akiko was busy and had to get A-C assistance to have a hope of completing everything in time for the event, to the point of having her design studio and factory temporarily moved into the second floor of the Zoo.

Raj indeed had the Troubadour Connection. There were a lot of troubadours out there—more than I'd ever heard about—and they seemed almost pathetically eager to get to do some actual work. It was interesting, how shoved to the side these particular A-Cs were. Clearly Christopher's views about troubadours were the dominant ones for the A-Cs of Earth. Wondered how much that had to do with the fact that King Adolphus of Alpha Four had been a troubadour.

In addition to the Dazzlers who were on Imitation Duty, we had some male troubadours who were going to add in, to cover effective confusion if needed and give us some more people to pretend to be Embassy staff.

Spent much time with my assigned imitator, Francine, who was from Euro Base. She was good and pretty much "got me" right away. She was even able to imitate my voice.

All the troubadours were practicing sounding like their assigned double, and most were really good at it. The gal imitating Serene, Nadine, was having the most trouble, but even she was pretty good after a few days of immersion.

Immersion had been hard on everyone, though, because it meant our assigned troubadours were eating, working, and hanging out with us. Jeff drew the line at sleeping with us, but other than that, each woman on Team Infiltration had a shadow.

Jamie and the other kids had really gotten into the whole "extra mommies and aunties" idea. I wasn't sure if they understood what we were doing or not—though if forced I'd have voted for the idea that they did—but they were having a ball with it. Double the attention, double the fun seemed to be the kids' motto. Part of me was tempted to have the kids go along to the funeral, but protective wisdom said they'd be much safer in the Embassy, so I didn't suggest it.

"I really walk like that?" I asked Reader as Francine and Jeff strolled up and down in front of us in the ballroom, which was where our little team of me, Jeff, Francine, and

Reader, who was our assigned "verifier," were practicing this afternoon. We had a trial run scheduled for early evening, and every team was prepping because we only had a couple of days before the funeral and no one wanted to be on the team that fooled no one.

"Yeah, girlfriend, you do."

"I accepted three years ago that I look like a cheetah on drugs when I'm running, but I had no idea my butt swayed that much when I was walking."

"I think it's sexy, baby," Jeff said with a grin. "When you do it," he added quickly, losing the grin in the process. "Right now, it's just uncomfortable and awkward."

"Thank you so very much," Francine said, as she shot me a long-suffering look. "I'm going to be heavily veiled and we aren't going to be expected to kiss during the event, so you can stop treating me as if I'm the mistress you don't want to have."

"I *don't* want a mistress," Jeff said. "I also don't think this plan is going to work in reality."

"If it doesn't, it'll be because of you and the other men, Jeff," Reader said. "Because I'm with Kitty—I think it'll fool enough people for long enough, and we only need just long enough."

Speaking of long enough, the real downside of immersion for me was that I hadn't been able to search for the hidden gate in the Embassy, because Francine would have expected to come with me, and I had no legitimate way of getting rid of her.

Inspiration struck, however. "You know, why don't I leave the room for a while? Maybe Jeff will chill out a bit if I'm not here, watching him 'cheat' on me with my permission."

This earned me a dirty look from my husband. "Sure, go ahead, desert me," he said, sarcasm knob only at about three on the scale. "Just don't be gone too long."

"Yeah, I might throw myself on your husband in a fit of mad passion," Francine added. Her sarcasm knob had hit eleven on Day One, right after Jeff had acted like she had a disease for over an hour. Her knob was, by my calculation, currently turned to twenty and heading for twenty-five.

"You'd need to watch us have sex to do it just right,

though," I said as I headed out the door. My last view was of Jeff's horrified, embarrassed expression and Francine and Reader laughing their heads off.

Had no good idea of where to go, so I headed up to our apartment. Jamie was at daycare and everyone else was off doing their prep for the event, so I was definitely alone.

Double-checked the whole apartment just in case, though. Then I went to the farthest room from the front door, which was one of the many large bedrooms we used for absolutely nothing.

Wasn't sure why I wanted to be so far away, but I did and decided not question it. Either there was a reason or there wasn't. Either way, I'd find out soon enough.

Cleared my throat. "Poofs and Peregrines, please assemble."

Instantly had a lot of furred and feathered company. All twenty-four Peregrines and more Poofs than I could count were in the room with me. This was the first time in ages that I'd seen all the Alpha Four animals together outside of the daycare center. Hoped this meant that the kids were currently safe.

"Kitty would like a word."

Bird heads bobbed, Poofs purred.

"Super. First off, show of paws and wings for who's staying at the Embassy when we go to Michael and Fuzzball's funeral."

All female Peregrine wings and many Poof paws went up.

"Super. Who's going with Jeff and the others to the funeral?"

More Poof paws—all Poofs attached to funeral attendees, plus a few extras—and about half of the male Peregrine wings. There were a variety of Peregrine squawks and Poof mews.

"Great. And yes, Kitty understands that you'll be in stealth mode. Kitty also understands that she shouldn't worry about her Poofs and Peregrines because you're all rough, tough fighting machines. I know I can count on all of you to protect everyone who needs protecting. And now, who's going into Gaultier with Kitty?"

No paws or wings went up.

"Really? Kitty finds this hard to believe."

Bruno raised his wing, Harlie and Poofikins raised their paws.

"Just the three of you? What are the rest of your teams going to be doing?"

Bruno squawked and bobbed his head. Harlie mewed and jumped up and down.

"Huh. Not sure that I like that plan. What if there are Poof Traps at Titan or YatesCorp? What about Peregrine traps? We don't know, and without someone with opposable thumbs along, that could be bad news."

More squawking, head bobbing, mewing, and bouncing up and down.

"Don't care. We've already lost Fuzzball. Kitty doesn't want to lose any more Poofies or start in with losing Peregrines."

They seemed touched by my concern but unconvinced otherwise. Okay, time to try a different approach.

"So, I might be okay with it, if I knew I could get to you all without a problem."

Heads all tilted at me. It was a cuteness overload. Forced myself to soldier on without snuggling and skritchy-scratching each and every one of them.

"If Kitty could know where the hidden gate in the Embassy is, that would mean Kitty could get to you quickly."

Got hit with a lot of totally innocent looks. It was like a sea of Animal Innocence in front of me. So, they all knew exactly what I was talking about. Contemplated why they hadn't told anyone where this gate was. Figured my guess about it being a Z'porrah cube was probably right.

"Kitty promises not to tell anyone where the cube is hidden, or that you're all using it as your animal gateway. But I think I need to be able to use it, too." Decided to go for it. "Or else Kitty needs a cube of her own."

The animals went into a huddle. Sure, it was a big, fluffy huddle, but a huddle nonetheless, complete with the Peregrines spreading their wings to essentially surround the Poofs. Off and on heads bobbed up or turned toward me. Clearly this was quite the big deal.

While the animals discussed whether or not they could or

should tell me about what I was now thinking of as the Cube Gate, I considered where in the world it could actually be.

It couldn't be something the Poofs or Peregrines kept on their persons. Sure, the Poofs were capable of ingesting and regurgitating things—they'd done that to get all the Z'porrah cubes at the end of Operation Invasion, after all. However, they were clearly using them, and potentially had been since they'd come to Earth.

One thing I hadn't asked was how the Poofs got around on Alpha Four. They had hyperspeed and so did the Peregrines. But whether or not Poofs could be there one minute and across Alpha Four's globe the next I'd never asked about.

For all I knew, no one here actually had the answer. The likelihood that Alfred had needed Harlie to zap across the world when he was young and on the home planet seemed slim. Before Jeff and I had gotten engaged, there had only been two Poofs left on Alpha Four, Harlie and Tenley, who was attached to Alexander's mother, Victoria.

Since the Poofs were androgynous and only mated when a Royal Wedding was imminent, six Poofs had been created by Harlie and Tenley the moment Jeff gave me his family's Unity Necklace. And those six, Fuzzball among them, had come to Earth with Harlie and the Alpha Centauri Planetary Council. One of them had gone back to Alpha Four with Alexander, of course, but that had still left us with six original Earth Poofs.

The Poof Population Explosion had happened here on Earth. So perhaps much of what our Poofs did they could do because the Z'porrah had riddled the interior of our planet with their amazing, glowing, power cubes.

That they'd shared the itel with the Peregrines was obvious, and presumably done because I'd told them all to get along and work together and they had.

However, my feeling about the hidden gate in the Embassy was that the former Diplomatic Corps, or at least one of them, had been using it. We knew Clarence Valentino had found the cube Terry had presumably snatched from Ronald Yates and left for Jeff and Christopher. And not to speak ill of the dead, but Clarence wasn't an Idea Man. He was muscle.

So, he'd probably given that cube to the people he worked most closely with, the former heads of the Diplomatic Corps and Doreen's late parents, Robert and Barbara Coleman. The Poofs had eaten them, with relish, during Operation Confusion. But when we'd taken over the Embassy it was as empty as a new home. Everything was gone.

We'd assumed the Diplomatic Corps had sent all their crap to Alpha Four, where they'd planned to hide out and take over, but King Alexander and Councilor Leonidas had never found said crap. So either LaRue and Ronaldo had taken it with them into the far reaches of space—always possible—or the former Diplomatic Corps' stuff was still hidden somewhere. Potentially with the Cube Gate. Or inside it.

I wanted access to that gate and not just because it would be nice to be right. I wanted access because Algar had told me it was vital, and I knew he hadn't said that merely to be dramatic.

Contemplated what I could say. And realized I could say what I both wanted and needed to.

"Kitty knows about Algar."

Had to say this—results were immediate.

CHAPTER 63

HAPPILY, FOR ONCE, they were the results I was hoping for.

All the animals turned to me, looks of shocked relief on their faces. Harlie mewed questioningly at me.

"He said I remind him of the first King of Alpha Four. And, yes, I know that Richard and Paul know about him. We can't talk about him, though, he prevents it. I think he's allowing me to talk about him with all of you because you don't really talk to anyone else like you talk to Kitty, and Algar wants me to find that Cube Gate."

Bruno did his head bob thing and scratched gently at the carpet.

"I'm not sure why he wants me to find the hidden gate, but if I have to guess, it's because Algar wants Kitty to use the gate to get in and out of Gaultier safely. Or something along those lines."

Lola, Bruno's mate, and Poofikins started squawking and mewing. Was pretty sure they were telling Bruno and Harlie that I should be told where the hidden gate was.

I'd gotten really good at understanding what the animals were saying, or at least what they were trying to get across to me. However, that only worked when they actually *wanted* me to know what they were saying. When they didn't, as now, it was much more guesswork than certain knowledge on my part.

The animals finally reached agreement. The Peregrines

cooed at me in a lovely manner, then they disappeared. The
Poofs all purred at me, which was also a lovely sound, then
they took off, too. Bruno, Harlie, and Poofikins were all who
remained.

Bruno flapped his wings at me, while doing the head bob
thing.

"Okay." Put my purse over my head. "Ready."

Harlie and Poofikins jumped onto my shoulders. Bruno
trotted out of this room and I followed.

He headed for the nursery, which made me more than a
little worried. But we went through it and into the isolation
chamber that was attached to the master bedroom.

It was really more of an isolation bedroom, complete with
a king-size bed, two regular beds, and all the tubes and needles you could ask for. But considering that Jeff needed isolation regularly, it was nice to have it so close and safe. Jamie
and I also needed isolation sometimes, and I was a lot less
panicky with this room than the regular isolation chambers.

Everything in this room was very white. For whatever reason, white seemed to be the operative color of choice for an
isolation bedroom. The isolation chambers weren't this
monochromatic, but Jeff never complained about this color
scheme, or lack thereof, so I hadn't worried about it.

The Colemans hadn't had any A-C talents, but Terry had,
and I knew this suite had been hers before she'd been infected by the Yates/Mephistopheles in-control superbeing
and died. In fact, the memory she'd programmed Jeff to im-
plant in me had shown her and the boys lying in the king bed
in this isolation chamber. I just hadn't realized that until we'd
moved in here and I'd spent some time in this room with Jeff.

One of the many things I hadn't paid much attention to
until this very moment was the fact that the big bed was attached to the wall. I'd figured this was because it was an
extra-large hospital bed and the isolation equipment was
fragile.

However, Bruno jumped onto this bed and stared at the
headboard. Oh, goody, a test. Nice to know even the animal
kingdom wanted me to keep the skills sharp.

Looked at the headboard. It looked like a headboard. It
appeared to be made of wood, painted white, shocker, with

some inlaid wooden squares also painted white. There were five of these, all about five inches square, in a line across the headboard. A sixth, slightly larger, square was in the middle of the headboard, near the top. Not the most exciting of designs, but great if you were really into geometric shapes and straight angles.

Bruno looked at me over his shoulder, then turned back to the study of the headboard. Clearly I was slow to react.

Dawned on me that the squares in the headboard could be one side of a cube. The square up top in particular, since closer inspection showed that it wasn't quite like the others.

"Huh. Algar said we'd been looking incorrectly. Everyone was searching for an actual gate, not a cube that's hidden in plain sight. How does it work?"

Bruno flapped his wings on the bed. I took the hint and climbed up, Poofs still on my shoulders. I was on my knees in front of the main square. Bruno came over and squawked. Took the hint and picked him up. He was heavier than my cats but thankfully lighter than our smallest dog, Duchess.

Harlie mewed at me in an urgent manner.

"Okay. Does it matter if you're all thinking of different places than me?"

Bruno cooed.

"Good to know. Touch is key, got it. You're sure it won't drop us onto, or worse, into someone or something?"

Got reassuring purrs and coos, along with some extra cautionary advice.

"And you're positive we can get back?"

Mews and purrs confirmed that the Poofs and Peregrines had their Ways and I was good as long as I was with them or Bruno.

"Gotcha. Kitty's ready for the wild ride. I hope."

With that I reached out and touched the top square.

And again, results were immediate.

CHAPTER 64

I'D THOUGHT OF THE LAIR, where Jeff and I had lived during the first part of my tenure with Centaurion Division. And in the Lair I was. Unlike a gate transfer, there was no nausea. Cube travel was definitely the way to go.

We were in the living room, in front of the TV, facing the couch, which was exactly what I'd seen in my mind.

There was a glittery square right in front of me. Reached for it and therefore touched it, and was right back on the bed in the isolation chamber. "Wow."

Touched the cube again and was right back in the Lair. "Cool." Now that I was here, contemplated wandering around. However, there was a lot going on, and besides, someone was going to notice that I was here, instead of in the Embassy, and I didn't want to explain the Cube Gate to random people at this precise time. Did wonder what Algar was up to, but now probably wasn't the time to try to visit him. So I touched the floating square.

Only, this time, I'd been thinking about Algar. And that's where I ended up. "Whoops."

I was in the weird reclamation area again, right on the tank platform I'd been on before. The room looked even bigger than when I'd been here before, but I was too shocked to really examine too much. Algar looked surprised, so there was that.

Harlie and Poofikins purred loudly, jumped off my shoulders and onto Algar's, and rubbed up against him like he was their long-lost bestie. Wasn't so shocked that this was lost on me.

Algar recovered faster than me. "Well, I see you've found the gate and figured out how to use it."

"Um, sort of." Saw a pile of glittery things in the far corner of the room.

"Good. Carry on." With that, he snapped his fingers and Bruno and I were back in the isolation room at the Embassy.

Put Bruno down on the bed. "Care to explain all that to me?"

Bruno shot me the "I'm An Innocent Birdie" look. Gave him my Death Glare in return. I won. Bruno flapped his wings, cooed, squawked, and did some serious head bobbing that could have qualified him for any major urban hip-hop competition.

"Ah." Cleared my throat. "Harlie, Poofikins, come to Kitty." The Poofs appeared, both still purring happily. I sat down cross-legged on the bed. "I think it's time we played the Guess Where I'm From game."

The Poofs gave Bruno their own versions of the Death Glare. Bruno glared right back. Picked him up and put him in my lap. "Beings from this universe gotta stick together, kids."

The Poofs looked sad, so I picked them up, too, and gave them a cuddle. "Kitty still loves her Poofies, you know that." Received happy purrs. Put the Poofs on Bruno's back, so I could look at them. "Okay, I expect some animal honesty. First off, while Bruno really is an Alpha Four animal, it appears that my Poofies are not, at least in terms of ancestry."

The Poofs mewed. They sounded apologetic.

"Oh, I get it. Until Kitty knew about Algar, Kitty couldn't know who brought the Poofies to this universe. But that's where you're from, isn't it, the Black Hole Universe?"

The Poofs acknowledged that this was so.

Which explained a whole lot, especially things like how they went large and toothy and then back to small, how they got all over the place, probably how they'd found the Z'por-rah's power cubes, let alone ingested and regurgitated them without issue, and potentially more.

"Algar brought you with him when he left home, like Mom and Dad brought the cats and dogs here, right? Because you take your pets with you if you're moving far, far away."

Received more Poof purrs for confirmation.

I could see the rest of it. Algar had gotten himself in trouble, and he'd wandered the universe, being sure to keep ahead of the other Black Hole People who were searching for him. He found an out of the way place to hang out. And because he'd liked the first King of Alpha Four, he'd given him his Poofs as pets and protectors, so Algar could concentrate on taking out the trash and being sure he wasn't discovered. And it gave the Poofs someone to belong to, just in case Algar was caught.

"You're sort of helping with the whole free will issue, right?"

This question earned a lot of Poof mewling and jumping up and down in response.

"Ah, gotcha. Noninvolvement unless it's vital to the overall long-term plan." Patted them. "But sometimes you ignore the long-term plan, don't you?"

The Poofs mewed and purred. They attached to us, like we attached to them, and therefore, as animals will, they protected those they loved.

"That pile of glittery things I saw in Algar's personal water reclamation plant, those are the Z'porrah power cubes, aren't they? And Algar lets you take them if you feel you need to, because you get to have free will, just like everyone else, right?"

Poof purrs confirmed that I was right on. Bruno clucked to show that he still felt I was the coolest, smartest chick on the planet.

Resisted the urge to agree with them, because I hadn't really been sure until now. But now I was certain—Algar was trying to fix his big mistake. In a very long-term way, but if you're immortal, what's a few thousand years, let alone a few decades?

This explained why the Poofs had almost died out on Alpha Four—their real owner had left them. Algar really was a jerk, because it was clear the Poofs still loved him, even though he'd left them alone on Alpha Four for decades. Maybe he'd done it for one of his free will reasons, but it still sucked.

Harlie mewed at me.

"Huh? Yeah, I do think he's kind of a jerk."

Harlie mewed in a very serious fashion.

"Really? So when Jeff gave me the Unity Necklace it triggered more than just Alpha Four's impressive light show? Interesting. And, well, I guess if you guys didn't object to the plan I'm okay with it."

The Poofs were okay with being left because they'd been waiting, and been content to wait, for the next part of the long-term plan to roll slowly into action. Stopped trying to figure out how immortal or close-to-it beings thought and just chose to focus on the good fact that the Poofs had attached to us, versus the bad guys. Which Algar had obviously intended.

They lived a long time; White and Alfred had confirmed that. For all I knew, Harlie and Tenley were the original Poofs Algar had brought with him to our universe. "Fuzzball's dead, though."

This earned a lot of Poofy growls, which, because the Poofs were small, were adorable instead of scary.

"Yeah, Kitty really hates the Z'porrah, too. They're very sore losers. How did they make the Poof Traps?"

The Poofs mewed in distress. Interesting. They didn't know. This wasn't good, but there were a lot of weird things out there in this universe, including a lot of other universes, apparently, so I probably didn't need to know how the Z'porrah had created their Poof Traps. I only needed to know how to protect the Poofs from and destroy them.

Because I wasn't letting our enemies kill any more of my Poofs, Black Hole Universe animals or not. In my heart and my mind, they were *my* Poofs, all of them, even if they were attached to someone else. Maybe Algar felt the same way. Wasn't sure I wanted to ask him, though, in case I didn't like his answer.

Algar had said immortals could be destroyed. But I'd seen Fuzzball with Michael in my dream, and Michael had pretty much insinuated they were together in the afterlife, if that's what it was.

Decided I needed to get off this train of thought and onto one that would help me more with the next phase of my short-term plan.

"So you don't actually need or use this gate."

Bruno cawed. The Poofs didn't use it, but the Peregrines did. The Peregrines had hyperspeed and, per Bruno, they could use their beaks and claws to open doors. So they'd found the Cube Gate and the Poofs had shared how and why to use it, because after I'd told them all to work together they'd agreed this was the right thing to do.

Algar was absolutely stacking the deck in favor of how he wanted things to turn out. But he wasn't doing too much, because as he'd told me, too much would turn on the Bat Signal and the other Black Hole People would know where he was. But if we all thought of the Poofs as pets, and they and the Peregrines didn't do too much for us, then the signal wouldn't go off and Algar's plan remained on track.

Wanted to test out the Cube Gate a little more and ask a lot more questions of the Poofs, but I was interrupted by a knock at our front door.

Moved the animals off my lap and rolled off the bed. The four of us trotted out, me closing the isolation room, nursery, and bedroom doors firmly, just in case.

Opened the front door to see Gladys standing there. "Hi, you're awake."

"I am. May I come in?"

"Sure." She entered and headed for our living room. I followed. Noted that the Poofs had disappeared and Bruno had either joined them or gone to stealth mode. "Um, don't take this the wrong way, but are you the real Gladys or a new android version?"

She snorted. "I'm the real one. Trust me, all facilities, the Embassy in particular, are on continuous scans right now." She heaved a sigh. "Look, I'm here because I think I figured out where my half brother's hiding out."

"That's great. But why are you telling me this in private, instead of, you know, calling everyone in for the big briefing so we can plan the raid or takedown or whatever?"

Gladys sat down on the loveseat. "When your daughter was born, and Ronaldo had us under his mind control, you and Richard fought him, and you were losing. But Jeffrey arrived in time."

"Yeah, Jeff really kicked Ronnie's butt." Got all misty

thinking about it. Jeff had been in Major Protective Mode, which I always found incredibly sexy.

"Right. Jeffrey was about to kill Ronaldo—but he wanted Richard's order to do so. Richard stepped down as Pontifex because he couldn't bring himself to actually give the order to kill Ronaldo, and he also could no longer deal with the idea of turning the other cheek."

"Right, I remember. Paul was able to give that order, because that's kind of what the Pontifex needs to do, right? Be the better person?"

"That's right. So, let me ask you a question. Do you, in your heart, believe that Paul would be able to give that same order now?"

Didn't have to think too hard on this one. "I'd like to say yes. Because I think Paul is that good a person."

"I do, too. But here's my dilemma—I don't want to discover he's not. I don't want our people to discover that our Pontifex is unable to do the right thing all the time. There's no one else trained or even close to ready—Paul couldn't step down to avoid the decision. And the decision, whether he makes the right one or the wrong one, would eat at him. For the rest of his life."

"Okay, I see the problem. Why are you discussing it with me and only me?"

"Because, when it comes right down to it, you're your mother's daughter."

Thought about this, about the specific event Gladys was talking about. Mom had point-blank asked me why Jeff didn't just kill Ronaldo and be done with it. And, frankly, Mom had been right, because Ronaldo had escaped, and he'd helped bring an alien invasion down on Earth. He'd tried to destroy our world, my world. And he'd tried to steal my baby girl while doing so.

"Don't tell me, let me guess. You want us to do a commando raid and finish the job Jeff started."

Gladys smiled. "I'd prefer to think of it as a fun, girl's bonding excursion."

"Gladys, I believe this could be the beginning of a beautiful friendship."

CHAPTER 65

"YOU WANT ANYONE besides the two of us?" I asked as I ensured I had everything I could possibly need in my purse, which included a variety of Poofs On Board. Harlie gave me a little purr. Great, the Poofs were all for the raid.

Squinted. Bruno was in stealth mode but I could just make him out next to my right foot. He looked up at me and winked. Excellent, Bruno was in as well.

"I'd love to grab your mother and Adriana. But your mother might need a warrant and you need Adriana for the funeral raid, so we can't risk her getting hurt."

"What about the princesses?"

"I prefer to fight with people for whom battle isn't the highest honor, just something that has to get done. They're learning, but they're too green to trust with this."

"Works for me. So, where's Ronaldo at?"

She sighed. "That's the one problem. I saw where he was, but it was in a dream so it's fragmented. However, I know you've found a way to leave and return without using the Embassy's gate."

"How?"

"Walter and William noted that you disappeared, reappeared, disappeared, and reappeared again. Because it was quick and they could determine that you were here, they decided it was equipment failure due to the hack. Of course, the Science Center advised me that you were there, and then not there, and then there again, and so on. So I assume you've found that hidden gate you've had everyone looking for for the past year and a half and were testing it out."

"Wow. You're good. Yeah, I have." Gave it a shot. "I've also met—" Dang, couldn't say the name. But I could try something else. "The A-C Elf." Ha! Take that, Algar. Chose not to wonder whether he'd allowed me to say this or not.

Gladys seemed impressed. "Good for you. I was told by . . . someone in my dream . . . that this gate works differently from the others."

"It does. I think it works based on thoughts. I'm pretty sure it's a Z'porrah power cube." So Algar had given Gladys the suggestion to come see me. It wasn't a surprise that he visited her in her dreams, after all. Passive noninvolvement my ass.

Of course, there was always the chance that Gladys had been turned again and was working for the bad guys. Bruno nudged up against me, I looked down, and he turned visible, looked straight at Gladys, looked back at me, cooed, and went invisible again.

"What was that all about?" Gladys asked.

"You just got the Peregrine Stamp of Approval."

"Good to know. Let's get going before Jeffrey notices that you're revved up and excited and comes to find out why."

Headed us to the isolation room and crawled up onto the big bed.

"Seriously?" Gladys asked as she clambered up with me.

"Don't complain to me, I think the Colemans are responsible for this location."

"Figures."

"Okay, hold my hand and think of the place where you saw Ronaldo. Then touch the square. Supposedly we can't land in something solid or on top of someone or some such. I haven't tested enough to know for sure."

"You only live once, kiddo."

"Kiddo? Really?"

She laughed. "It's better than what I used to call you." With that she took firm hold of my hand, and put her other onto the Cube Gate.

We were instantly in a dark room. Looked around. I didn't see anyone. "Where are we?" I whispered.

"No idea," she whispered back. "But this is what I saw in my dream, the dark room before the room where he is."

There was some light near the floor, but father away. Light coming in from under a door. We crept toward it. Looked back and around. "I don't see the return square."

Gladys put her hand over my mouth and I shut up. Heard what she had—voices.

So, Ronaldo wasn't alone. Well, there were two of us. The voices weren't raised so it was hard to make them out. But I had a feeling there were more than two people in the next room. No worries, Gladys and I were both capable of kicking major butt.

We reached the door and listened harder. No keyhole and the door was shut, both of which were really inconsiderate of the cosmos.

My eyes were adjusting to the dark and I could make out some of the things around us. Most of said things were boxes. The room appeared to have no windows and just the one door we were standing by. Could make out a stamp on the side of a box on the floor that the light was hitting—GB: NAS.

Contemplated what these letters could stand for as the voices died down and Gladys slowly turned the door handle. Maybe whoever was in the room hadn't noticed the handle turning. Or else they'd noticed, were really good, and were lying in wait for us. Gave it fifty-fifty odds either way.

Door opened a crack to discover that, for once, the odds were on our side. Well, sort of. The door didn't open up to another room—it opened up to a hallway.

From what little we could see, it was a long hallway, with what looked like many doors, and a T-intersection at the far end from us.

As we looked, people came walking by, speaking to each other. These people were in Navy and Marine uniforms. They went past without looking at our door, which was a relief.

My brain decided to mention that it had a really good idea what NAS stood for—Naval Air Station. And that meant, by both process of elimination and the total way our luck worked, that GB most likely stood for Guantanamo Bay.

Nudged Gladys. "We're in Guantanamo," I whispered in her ear. "I don't think that's good."

"If we're here, it's because my half brother is here."

"Good point. Just saying, I think we could be really screwed if we're caught."

"Better caught by the Navy than caught by our enemies."

Found the light switch, closed the door, and turned the light on. Sure enough, we were in a storage room that confirmed we were in Guantanamo—lots of boxes stacked all over the place, clipboards hanging on the walls near different stacks, a couple of plain tables holding stuff. Of course the sign that said "Supply Room #30, Naval Air Station: Guantanamo Bay" was also a clue.

There was an emergency exit map on one wall. Wished Chuckie was here—he'd have memorized it in two seconds. For me, it just looked like a lot of red lines on a rat maze. All I got was that we were "here" and our ability to get out "there" was going to be dependent upon making a lot of twists and turns. Awesome.

Gladys turned off the lights. "What the hell is wrong with you?"

"I wanted to be sure we weren't sitting on top of bombs or Ronaldo." Felt around in my purse for my Glock, patted the Poofs, found the Glock, flipped off the safety, put it on top of the Poofs. Figured it wasn't wise to have it in my hand, but I wanted it close by and ready.

She made a quiet sound of disgust and slowly opened the door another crack. We waited. Didn't hear anyone. "Let's go," Gladys said as she grabbed a nearby clipboard and opened the door. "Walk with purpose, don't look furtive, and if we run into anyone, let me do the talking."

"Check. Will do my best not to blow our total lack of cover."

We stepped out as Gladys shot me a look that said she was regretting who she'd chosen for this commando raid and shut the door behind us. We were at the end of this hallway right by steps that led up to another level. There weren't any here going down, so either we were on the lowest level, or the down staircase was elsewhere.

Gladys headed for the other end of the hall. Decided not to ask why. When you have no freaking idea where to go, one way's as good as another.

Every door in this hallway indicated it was storage, which seemed odd. Then again, I wasn't clear on how the military stored things. Maybe they were really anal about not mixing up the paper products with the bullets. Gladys used hyperspeed and checked every door, though. "All clear, just supplies."

Reached the T-intersection without running into anyone. "Which way now?" I asked softly.

"No idea." She stared right and left. "I think . . . this all looks vaguely familiar, more to the right than to the left. So, we'll try the right and if that leads nowhere, we'll come back."

"Why aren't we using hyperspeed?"

"Why use up the energy for nothing when we might need it later?"

Refrained from mentioning that all the Field agents I'd ever worked with used up the energy in part to avoid surveillance cameras and in other part to hurry the hell up. "Okay. I guess." I saw no cameras about, but I still had to figure that time was going to be of the essence.

Gladys sighed. "We're apparently in Cuba. In case we literally have to swim for U.S. soil, I'd rather have all my hyperspeed available, wouldn't you?"

"Good point. Hate where your head's at, but still, good point. We're in a Naval base, though, so that means there should be a gate here somewhere."

"Right, and if and when we find it, we can rejoice. We have little access to this facility—NASA Base is close enough and the American government likes to feel as if it's got the upper hand in some areas. This is one of those areas. Now, can we go?"

"I'm not stopping us." Looked around. Didn't see the sparkling square. Figured that meant it was still in Supply Room #30. Hoped I'd remember how to get back there in case we didn't find the gates on the base.

Which hopes were quickly dashed as we found the stairs going down. Naturally Gladys wanted to go lower—maybe it was some weird A-C thing, where they had burrowing creatures in their ancient DNA. But they sure had no issues being underground.

So down we went, into a much darker hallway system with a lot of twists and turns. I was officially lost within five minutes. However, I had a really good guess as to where we were heading, because we weren't walking by storage rooms any more—we were walking by a lot of metal doors that had tiny windows with bars in them.

As we approached yet another intersection I was about to ask if Gladys had a clue as to where we were going when I heard voices.

We flattened against the near wall.

"Do you want out or not?" The voice was familiar—Ronaldo Al Dejahl was indeed in the house.

CHAPTER 66

CONTEMPLATED ASKING GLADYS if she'd seen that we'd be in the bowels of Guantanamo when we found Ronaldo but I knew she'd had no idea. Algar enjoyed his little jokes, after all. Prick.

"You've made me a murderer." This voice I also recognized—it was Mahin.

"Things happen," Ronaldo replied.

"You told me no one would get hurt, that we were just going to find and rescue the rest of our family. But I watched *you* murder one of those people."

"Oh, please." So, Annette Dier was here, too. Good. I'd be really happy to break her neck. "Casualties of war. Look, we don't have long. Either you're coming with us or you'll get to stay here and rot, or worse."

"We're your family now," Ronaldo said. "You're your father's daughter."

"My father, the man who raised me, wasn't a killer. He was a decent man. He thought war was wrong."

"And he's dead because of war, so what does that prove?" Ronaldo asked.

"It proves she's a liability," Dier said. Heard a gun cock. "The hell with her so-called talent. We have orders—she comes or she dies. Period."

Wasn't sure what to do here, even as I grabbed my Glock out of my purse. But what Gladys did wouldn't have been in my playbook, constant accusations of recklessness or no. She ran around the corner without looking to see what, exactly, was around said corner.

She ran at hyperspeed, so there was that. Which I guess was so that she could hit into Ronaldo that much harder.

I followed her, in part because it wasn't like I was going to stay undetected for long and in other part because I didn't want to give Dier time to recover and shoot the gun I figured she had out and cocked.

As I rounded the corner and could see clearly, I was surprised to see a cell door standing open, though Mahin wasn't in the hallway. I wasn't at all surprised to see that Ronaldo and Dier weren't alone, Mahin still in her cell or no.

There were two other men with them. One was Kozlow; the other was someone I hadn't seen before. He was younger and appeared to be having a really fun vacation—he looked eager and excited and very one with Ronaldo and his Cause.

He also didn't look like any of the people here so much as he resembled a younger, male version of Serene. Which might mean he was a full-blooded A-C, or it just might mean that Ronald Yates had sort of had a type when he was being choosy.

All of them were dressed alike, in khaki pants, T-shirts, and hooded sweat jackets. They looked like an odd group of Marines getting ready for a workout. Clearly they'd planned ahead.

Gladys knocked the gun out of Dier's hand with the clipboard as she slammed into Ronaldo. Those two hit against the wall while Dier's gun flew into the air.

Unfortunately, while Dier wasn't able to catch the gun, Kozlow did. Decided I didn't care and shot at the three of them.

The young kid knocked Dier out of the way, so I missed him and her. Winged Kozlow, though, so there was that. Of course, didn't hit him enough to stop him from firing right back at me. I flipped into a forward roll, so the bullets missed me. And it was bullets plural—Kozlow fired wildly and emptied the clip. Had the feeling he expected more people coming behind me. You know, like would have been smart. Lucky for whoever would have been there to take bullets, Gladys and I hadn't been smart.

I was up and had my gun aimed before the three of them recovered. Which would have been great if Gladys and Ronaldo were still fighting. Only they weren't.

"Tell you what," Ronaldo said pleasantly, as he wiped some blood off of his lip. "I'll be nice and leave you here, with the sister of mine who isn't good for anything, while I take my other sister, who's really my favorite, along with us."

"What are you talking about?" Had a feeling I knew, but keeping the bad guys talking was one of my specialties and I saw no reason to hold that move back.

"Some people are easier to control than others, that's what I'm talking about. You were a fool to bring her with you to try to take me. She can't say no to her little brother."

He turned Gladys around, keeping his hands on her upper arms. She looked right at me. "Sorry, kiddo," she said as she tossed the clipboard down at my feet. "I could kill her for you, little brother."

Gladys was small and Ronaldo was tall. My gun was out and ready and I was in a good position, so I could shoot him in the head. However, I wasn't certain that he wouldn't find a way to throw Gladys up in front of the bullet. He was holding her in such a way I was pretty sure that was his plan, and he definitely had the strength and hyperspeed to do it. Plus I was fairly sure he'd love it if I killed Gladys by accident; it was his kind of thing.

"No, that would upset Mahin," Ronaldo said with a nasty little laugh. "We have someone much better now, and they're going to have some fun explaining why this one's down here trying to break Mahin out while the base is exploding."

"I really think we should kill her," Dier said.

"Well, I don't think we'll have time for you to reload before she shoots you," Ronaldo replied. "Russell needs some weapons training. Now, get moving."

"Who's the kid?" I asked. "Yet another illegitimate son of Ronald Yates?"

"As if legitimacy mattered?" Ronaldo asked.

"Sure it matters. It matters a lot. That's why you're trying to gather up all your half siblings, so that you can claim a seat on the YatesCorp board. Of course, if your father had really wanted you to be able to claim that seat, he'd have written your name clearly on the paperwork."

Ronaldo's eyes flashed. "He wanted all of us able to take our rightful places."

"Hardly. If he knew about you, then why not just list your names on the document? Why force you to have to prove his paternity? Especially since you can't."

Ronaldo opened his mouth, but it was Dier who actually spoke. "Stop being an idiot. We leave, right now, or I kill her, right now." There was something in her tone—she sounded like the one in charge.

Ronaldo reacted like she was as well. He shut up and nodded.

"Um, hate to ask, but how do you think you're going to get past me?" I got a variety of "duh" looks from all five of them, and then they ran off down a hall I hadn't realized was there. "Oh. That's how."

Trotted closer to Mahin's cell and looked in. She was against the back wall, looking scared. "What are you going to do to me?" she asked.

"Just ask a question or two. What are they up to?"

"I believe they're going to blow this base up."

"Fantastic. Why'd you have your change of heart?"

She shrugged. "Your father . . . he reminded me of my father. He asked me if I was doing what I believed was right, or just what sounded right." She swallowed hard. "And then I watched them kill . . ." She looked down. "You'd said they were my relatives, too."

"They are. All the A-Cs are related back there. Like the Jews are."

"Your father told me. He said . . ." She looked back up. "He said they'd still forgive me and let me be a part of their family. But I don't see how."

"You didn't kill anyone. You tried, sure, but you didn't succeed. And you actually protected all of us when the plane and tank exploded. And you told Malcolm and my dad where Ronaldo and Dier were."

"You knew it was him? I didn't know it was him."

"Yeah, we figured it out. Looking like someone else is

part of his talent. Look, I either have to run after them or we have to run after them. You pick."

She stared at me. "You'd trust me?"

"I'm stupid that way, yeah. Like to live on the edge, sort of thing. Frankly, I don't know if they were putting on a show for our benefit and knew Gladys and I were there or not, but I need to go back her up."

"But, she's back under his control."

"Maybe." I didn't think so, though. She'd called me kiddo, and I had a feeling she'd done that on purpose. "So, why are you still standing in your cell?"

"I'm not sure that you won't shoot me if I move."

Heaved a sigh and put my left hand out toward her. "Come with me if you want to live."

"You'll kill me if I don't go?"

"Wow, really? They didn't show *The Terminator* wherever you grew up? No wonder you feel like you had a sad childhood."

She stepped forward and tentatively reached out her hand. I grabbed her, turned, and ran off the way Gladys and the others had gone.

CHAPTER 67

NATURALLY THE CORRIDOR WAS DARK and also naturally it was long. "Any guess as to where they're going?"

"I'm not sure, but I believe they've planted the bombs underground, so the base will collapse into the sea."

"Nice. I really hate these people. So, any chance you can use your talents and blow the bombs up or away or something?"

"My power doesn't work like that. I can move earth, things like dirt and sand. But I don't control wind."

"You made a freaking dust storm when you tried to kill me and my team before."

"Yes, there was so much sand, dust, and dirt, I could control it to make it dance. The dance, the movement of the sand or dirt, makes the wind, not the other way around."

"That's what you call it? Dirt dancing? Well, in a way I guess it was like a mosh pit with sand instead of people slamming about. So, you're not really Storm, you're more like an earthbender."

"Excuse me?"

"Seriously? *Avatar: The Last Airbender*? You've never seen it? The movie was awful, I grant you, but the animated series rocked."

"Aren't you a little old for cartoons?"

"Oh, my God, animation is more than cartoons, but just as a tip, I still read comics. I used to read them because they were fun and cool and interesting. Now I read them because, frankly, they work really well as a guide for how to survive my life."

"I honestly don't understand half of what you're saying."

"Few do, Mahin. Few ever do." We reached a dead end. "Well, either there's a hidden door—which I would never, ever count out as a possibility—or we've missed whatever turn they took. Or, you know, we're trapped with the bombs and are about to die. I give it even odds, any way you want to call it."

"Why did they want to leave you with me?" Mahin asked slowly. "They didn't seem to care that you were there . . ."

"Crap. They planted a bomb in or around your cell."

No sooner were these words out of my mouth than the sound of an explosion reached us. It was a big explosion, and even though the corridor was long, it wasn't long enough. Flames and debris billowed toward us.

Contemplated options. They seemed slim. Was about to try to send Jeff an emotional goodbye message, when Mahin put up her hands. The billowing continued, but it rolled back onto itself, then back down the corridor, until it died down.

"So, you can stop flames? Not that I'm complaining."

"No. There was a lot of dust, dirt and debris. I can control that."

"Huh." Looked around as the emergency sirens went off. "You realize, then, that everything around us is, essentially, dirt, dust, and debris that's all put together."

She sighed. "Yes, I know that. I can't move it, though. I've tried. But it's too . . . heavy for me to move it when it's in a more solid form."

Decided now wasn't the time to work on Mahin's talents. Now was the time to get the heck out of here, find the other bombs, and stop the bad guys.

Of course, now was also the time to discover exactly where in the Guantanamo complex we were. We were underground and, as I noted something starting to swirl toward us, under the water line.

"Um, how are you with liquids?"

"Useless." She put her hands up and out and a wall of dirt went up between us and the water that was definitely starting to flood this area. "I can hold it off for a little while, but not too long."

"Okay, hold it as long as you can, I'll be right back." Ran down the corridor and looked around carefully. There were no doors here. There was no way Ronaldo and company had teleported out of this area. There was no gate. Meaning there was a hidden door somewhere, because there was no way they'd have set off a bomb in this area until they were safely away from it.

"Hurry!" Mahin called. She sounded strained. "I can't hold it much longer."

Considered all the options, which were slim and getting slimmer. Had no clue what to do. Decided going for the crazy was probably in my best interests. Dropped my Glock into my purse, pulled out my iPod, and hit play.

Van Halen's "Jump" was the current song of choice. "Thanks. You're really earning the milk and pennies in shoes or whatever today." Dumped the iPod back into my purse.

Looked at the ceiling as I headed back to Mahin. Just before I reached her I saw what looked like a rectangular outline that wasn't the same as the rest of the ceiling. I jumped up. Couldn't reach it. Squatted down and did my best frog jump. Still missed.

"What are you doing?" Mahin asked.

"I think there's a trick door above us."

"Why would a military base have something like that?"

"No freaking idea. Maybe it's part of someone's old escape plan. We can figure out how it got here once we get through it."

Ran down the corridor back to Mahin's dirt wall. Water was starting to seep through it. Turned and ran as fast as I could. Jumped at the last minute and was rewarded by being able to slam my hands against the rectangle. It moved.

I landed and spun around. "Screw the dirt wall. Make a hand stirrup and give me a boost."

Mahin stared at me for a long moment. Then she nodded and dropped her hands into the classic stirrup boost. I stepped onto her hands, and she grunted but was able to get me up.

Slammed my hands against the trapdoor and this time I was able to move it. Grabbed the lip. "Shove hard!" She did, and I was able to pull myself up. Didn't stop to take in my surroundings, just lay on my stomach, held onto the edge, and put my hand down. "Jump and grab my hand, wrist to wrist!"

She had the A-C ability to jump, which was good, because the water was pouring in. Mahin and I managed to get a good hold on each other's arms at the wrist, and then the fun of trying to pull her up began.

I wasn't losing her, but the water made her heavier and it was causing her some issues. Also, if I couldn't get her up and into this room with me in time to slam the trapdoor shut, we were both going to drown, just on different levels.

Felt something brush by me, and Mahin felt a lot lighter. I tugged, and she flew up with me. Literally. She looked as though something had her clothes held in its talons. She was in, and I slammed the trapdoor down. "Good job, Bruno."

Looked around. We were in a dark room with what looked like a lot of boxes in it. Pulled my phone out and used it as a flashlight. Had a lot of missed texts and calls. Decided now wasn't the time to check them out. Checked out the room instead.

Sadly, we weren't in Supply Room #30. On the other hand, we weren't drowned or blown up, so chose to see this as one for the win column. Found the light switch and turned it on. Nothing. So they'd taken out the power, at least to this area.

"Any guess as to where they are or we are?"

Mahin shook her head. "I've never been here before. In case you weren't sure." Oh good, Mahin had a sarcasm knob.

"Help me shove these boxes onto that door. Hopefully it'll keep the water out."

Tried to figure out my next move as we did this. Didn't have a lot of ideas other than "get the bad guys and save the base." Didn't feel this was my most sophisticated plan ever.

Remembered I had help with me it was about damn time to use. Opened up my purse only to see that there were no Poofs in it. "Really? Bruno, my bird, I hope you're still around, because the Poofs have done a runner." Either to avoid the water or, more likely, to follow Gladys. However, the bad guys had Poof Traps and I had no Poofs on Board. Both were not things that made me happy.

Bruno squawked. He wasn't going derelict in his duties, thank you very much.

"Excellent. Get us out of here, preferably before the next bombs explode."

Bruno went visible and Mahin jumped. "Where did that come from?"

"That is Bruno, and he's been with us the whole time. I think. He's what helped pull you up out of the water."

"Oh. Thank you."

Bruno looked at her, cocked his head, studied her some more, then went over and nudged against her. Mahin looked surprised, but she bent down and petted him. "I can't tell by the light from your phone—is he a peacock?"

"Peregrine. It's an Alpha Four bird."

"Alpha Four?"

"Wow, they didn't tell you squat, did they? I'll fill you in later. Right now, we need to find the rest of the bombs and hopefully defuse them."

"What if we can't?"

I shrugged. "Then we do the next best thing and you use your earthbending powers to engulf, control, and contain the blasts."

Mahin nodded. "I can do that."

Bruno screeched and headed to the door. Used my phone's light to follow him, then once I was at the door, dropped my phone back into my purse. Decided I'd spent long enough without music, and besides, why make it hard for Algar to give me musical clues? Clipped my iPod to my jeans and put my earbuds in. "Zoot Suit Riot" from the Cherry Poppin' Daddies came on my personal airwaves. That boded.

"Let's go. Be ready for a lot of chaos."

Opened the door and Bruno trotted out. Grabbed Mahin's hand and headed out after my big bird.

CHAPTER 68

I **WOULD HAVE LOVED** to have discovered that Bruno knew where the hell we were and how to get out. What I discovered was that he was better at mazes than I was, but not prescient.

So, we made several wrong turns, backtracked a few times, but did manage to be close but not too close when the next bomb went off on the level we were on now. Mahin did her thing, explosion wasn't stopped but was contained, and Bruno took off again, with us in hot pursuit.

"He's trying to find the bombs?" Mahin asked as we ran up a new set of stairs.

"I have no idea. If we find another one, then the answer is yes."

"Why explode something on each level?" she asked as we crested the stairs and Bruno screamed at us.

Didn't bother to answer, just grabbed her hand again, scooped Bruno up in my free arm, and ran at the fastest hyperspeed I could manage, which, considering I was revved up on a combination of anger and panic, was pretty damn fast. Which was a good thing. Because I'd understood Bruno's scream, and it interpreted to, "We need to run away like bats out of hell."

He hadn't been exaggerating. The explosion was huge, and it knocked us down. We rolled over and Mahin got her hands up just in time, the flames were engulfed and the debris settled down. But the stairs we'd just come up were no more.

"For the record, your talents are really cool, especially when people are trying to blow us up. They're cutting off access. But why?"

"Maybe someone or something is down there they want, or don't want anyone to get."

"You and I would be the only things I can think of."

"I'd want to get rid of us. They were supposed to kill me if I didn't go with them and we both know they want to kill you."

"Good points. Bruno, where to now?"

He took off, and we took off after him, as the music changed to Pink's "Runaway," as if we needed telling. Fortunately, the next set of stairs were easy to find, in part because there were a lot of people in uniform running down them, toward us. Ah perhaps my musical clue was for them more than for me and Mahin.

"Explosions are contained," I barked out in the most authoritative tone I could manage. "All of you, get back up to ground level!"

"Do it! Evacuate!" a deep voice bellowed. It was a voice of authority, and all the military personnel stopped, spun around, and headed back up. It was also a voice I happened to know well.

My Uncle Mort was there, giving me a look I could only think of as "I knew it" crossed with "why me?" He was an older, tougher, far more imposing version of my father. And he was one of the most comforting things I could have seen right about now. If my Uncle Mort was here, I wasn't going to the brig, and we had a shot at winning or at least coming out even.

"What are you doing here, Katherine?" Uh oh. Uncle Mort only called me Katherine when I was in trouble. Then again, I was in the middle of an exploding Guantanamo—of course I was in trouble. On the plus side, there's no way Ronaldo would know that. "Besides listening to music at an inappropriate time, which is no surprise to me, of course." Yep, it was the real Uncle Mort.

"Hey, I have it low enough that I can hear everything clearly, including the explosions, unfortunately. And, um, as for what we're doing, ah, well, breaking Mahin out of prison before she was murdered by our enemies, trying to at least

contain the explosions because we've been too late to stop
them, and running for our lives. That about covers it, right?"
I asked her.

"Right. Oh, and Gladys is under Ronaldo's control again."

"Right, forgot that. Uncle Mort, we need to get to ground
level. Bawl me out once we know if the bombs are done going boom and we've caught and hopefully killed all the bad
guys. Which may not actually include Gladys."

He shook his head. "We have people down there."

Thought about it—we hadn't passed anyone. At all. And
we'd been all over the place. Maybe Bruno hadn't been
lost—maybe Bruno had been confirming that the Poofs had
found everyone they'd gone to rescue. "No, I don't think you
do. Where would a very intelligent animal put the people
who were down here?"

Had to say this for Uncle Mort—nothing, absolutely nothing, fazed him, including questions like this. He'd seen a lot
in his years with the Corps and he'd known me all my life.
On, as Hacker International called it, the Kitty Weird Scale,
this question was likely only a three or four. He'd heard far
weirder from me over the course of my lifetime. "Probably
in one of the empty hangars. There's one close by."

"Then let's go there."

"What if you're wrong?"

"Then at least we don't blow up or drown." Decided not
to let Uncle Mort argue any more or possibly win this battle
of wills. Put Bruno down. "Let's go, big guy." Grabbed Uncle Mort's hand, Bruno took off at Bird Hyperspeed, and we
followed.

Only one more flight of stairs, and, therefore, only one
more bomb that went off right after we went past it. Mahin
was getting really good at Explosion Containment by now.
We stopped, Uncle Mort gagged from the hyperspeed while
Mahin got things under control, and we took off again.

"They wanted to trap personnel," I said as we exited into
daylight. "That's why that last bomb went off so late."

"Seems logical. Does your father know you're here?" Uncle Mort asked.

"Um, what do you think?"

"I think I want to officially request whatever it is your

human agents are taking to help them not toss their cookies after running at hyperspeed."

"You got it, I'll have Tito send you your own private stash."

We reached the hangar and ran inside. There were a lot of people there. Many were in uniform, and they were all standing with weapons drawn, surrounding a variety of those not in uniform who were sitting in reasonably neat rows.

The nearest uniform saluted as soon as Uncle Mort stopped gagging. "All prisoners and personnel from Major Containment present and accounted for, sir."

Looked around. "Where are the Poofs?"

"Ah, if you mean the fluffy creatures who turned gigantic and picked us up in their mouths before we could activate weapons, took us here, and gave us the nonverbal but extremely clear suggestions to stay put, ma'am, they left once we were all in the hangar and military were surrounding the prisoners."

"Good job. Uncle Mort, where would you go if you needed to get about six people off the base quickly?"

"Plane or car, meaning anywhere on the base," Uncle Mort answered promptly. "I'm more concerned with there being other explosives we haven't found yet."

A thought occurred. Two thoughts, really. The first thought was that there was more than one reason to blow things up. And the second thought was that the best reason to blow things up aside from creating mayhem and destruction was as a really effective distraction. B.o.B.'s "Bombs Away" came onto my iPod. Apparently Algar wanted me to consider that our enemies were probably going for a twofer. "Where's your main computer center?"

"Nowhere close to prisoner containment." Uncle Mort's expression said he'd made the same leap I had, without the benefit of musical clues. Well, he was older and more experienced. "Who, exactly, is on this base without authorization? Aside from you, I mean."

"The same people who were screwing things up over at the Science Center last week." Mahin and I gave Uncle Mort a quick description of the five we knew about. "I don't know that Gladys is really mind controlled or not," I finished up.

"Unless you can be sure, we have to treat her like a hostile," Uncle Mort said.

"Jeff might be able to tell, if he were here and they weren't using an emotional blocker or enhancer." Cleared my throat. "So, um, never mind."

"Well, I can't speak to whatever empathic doodads your enemies are running with, but I can say that the rest of the troops have arrived." Uncle Mort nodded his head behind me.

Spun around to see a shimmering, and then Jeff, Christopher, White, Chuckie, Reader, Tim, and the flyboys stepped through the floater gate. Sure enough, the cavalry was here.

"No Field agents?"

Reader shook his head. "The only ones indoctrinated against mind control so far are assigned to protect your neighborhood." He flashed the cover boy grin. "You'll have to make do with us, girlfriend."

"I'll manage."

Jeff looked around. "I'm not even going to ask. Why is she with you?" He pointed to Mahin.

"She's on our side now. Bruno approved."

Jeff studied her for a few long moments. "Okay. Who are we after?"

"Gladys, who may or may not be under the mind control, Ronaldo, Dier, Kozlow, who's been shot but sadly only winged, and a kid who looks like he could be Serene's younger brother."

Reader grimaced. "It's a big area to cover without an A-C."

Christopher shot Patented Glare #1 at him. "I'll manage. Alone. Without a problem."

"The main containment area's been blow up in certain areas," I told him. "It's unlikely they're there, but possible. I'd check everywhere else first, though, and I'd suggest starting with all the vehicles, because they're probably going to do their thing and then split."

"Don't go alone," Jeff said.

"We'll go with him," Hughes said, indicating himself and Walker. "We've taken our Hyperspeed Dramamine and we're good with the high supersonic speeds. We'll be fine."

"And that way Christopher won't get to kick butt all by

himself and will have to share the fun, and the glory, with me and Matt," Walker added with a grin.

"Yeah, it'll be a party," Christopher said. But he grabbed Hughes and Walker and they all took off.

"Where are we headed?" Jeff asked me. "Since Christopher and his flyboys are off to check the entire base."

"Just because he's fast doesn't mean they'll find who we're looking for. If our Gang of Four Plus One have done their bad deeds, they'll be looking to escape. We, however, are going to the main computer center. Because the bad deeds Ronaldo and his gang are perpetrating are either going to turn out to be hacking into the military's system, launching missiles, or both."

"Both," Uncle Mort said. "They're not here for grins and giggles."

"I can agree with that. So, if we're right, and Ronaldo and his merry gang are going for or have already hit the computers, that means they either had a linkup to Chernobog or Chernobog is here. If she's here, would she be on the base?"

"Unlikely," Uncle Mort said. "However, she could easily be in Cuba. In fact, it would make a lot of sense. They'd certainly be happy to house an enemy of ours."

"Where's the base commander?" Jeff asked. "I know you're not officially in charge here, Mort."

"In the same building as the computer center. At least, hopefully." Uncle Mort sounded grim. Couldn't blame him. I wasn't confident we weren't going to find a lot of dead bodies littered all over the base. They'd already killed some Marines when they broke Dier and Ronaldo out of the air—why stop there?

I was ready to run to the computer center, but my feet didn't choose to move. Because something was wrong with all of this. The problem was that I didn't know what. My memory really wanted me to remember something, too.

My music changed to "Who's That Creepin'" by Big Bad Voodoo Daddy. Apparently Algar was a fan of this band. Went with it. The song was about someone breaking into the singer's house. My memory deigned to share that the bad guys had been dressed like Marines.

"I think we need to split into two teams. Most of you need

to go with Uncle Mort. Mahin and I need to check out something else."

Jeff snorted. "I'm going with you. Period."

"No, you need to go with Uncle Mort. He has to have someone who can protect him. But," I said quickly, before anyone else could complain, "we'll take Richard, okay?"

Jeff nodded. "James and Tim are the ones in charge, so they'll be going with Mort. Jerry, Joe, and Randy can go along for muscle. It's up to Chuck and Uncle Richard if they're going with them or us, but I meant it, baby, I'm coming with you."

"I'm going with you as well," Chuckie said. He was giving me a look that said he knew that I was up to something. He was as hard to fool as Jeff sometimes.

"I wouldn't miss working with my partner for anything," White added solemnly.

"Who goes with whom isn't as important as us all actually going," Uncle Mort said. "I've managed most of my career without an A-C to drag me along, Kitty. We'll be fine. We've wasted enough time. Let's move out. *Now*."

CHAPTER 69

UNCLE MORT'S TEAM trotted off at a military run that I knew they could all keep up for miles. "I still wish you'd gone with him," I said to Jeff as we went to the door. "No A-C in that group could be a problem."

"Why did you want to get rid of us, Missus Martini?" White asked. "What are you and Mahin up to?"

Mahin shook her head. "I have no idea. I also don't know why we're stopping here instead of going somewhere."

"I want to think." Actually, I wanted to be sure we were far enough away from the other people in this hangar that they couldn't hear our conversation.

"I agree with Richard," Chuckie said. "I know that innocent look you're trying to keep on your face, Kitty."

"I know, sorry, I just don't want anything to happen to my uncle."

"He'll be protected," Jeff said. "Now, take off your iPod and tell us what's going on."

Wanted to argue, but the music stopped, mid-song. Okay, Algar apparently wasn't going to be sharing any more right now anyway. Pulled my earbuds out and tossed them and the iPod into my purse.

"Something's wrong, and I mean above what we all know about. Ronaldo and Dier were 'rescued' a few days ago, right? Before they reached Guantanamo. And yet they're here. Why go through a huge in-air rescue, and kill all those Marines, only to end up in Guantanamo anyway?"

"Because they aren't prisoners this way," Jeff said.

"Ronaldo used his mind control on the Marines, it's obvious from the reports Tim got."

"I agree," Chuckie said. "And so do Cliff and Vander. And yes, I've shared intel with them in part because I have to and in part because we need their help."

"Okay, let me know if they offered any good insights. Otherwise, I'll keep going." Chuckie nodded and I continued to think, or, as everyone else liked to call it, run my mouth. "Ronaldo can't control us, and he can't control Mahin, because she wouldn't go with him earlier and he wanted her to. But he can't fly, and Dier certainly can't. So, how did they get out of the air alive?"

"No reports indicate another aircraft in the vicinity," Chuckie said. "And believe me, we've been looking for one."

"Okay. So, who rescued them?"

"I think it was the boy, Darryl," Mahin said.

"What's his full name?" Chuckie asked.

"Darryl Lowe. I believe, anyway. I haven't seen his talents, but from what they said before Kitty and Gladys arrived, I believe he can do with the air what I do with the earth. I'm not certain, though."

"Fabulous. We have an airbender, too. Does it get any better?"

"I actually know what you mean, because you made me watch that whole series," Jeff said. "More than once. And I suppose it's possible. But what of it, baby? Or, more to the point, we told your uncle we were splitting up, and yet we haven't gone anywhere."

Turned around and looked at all the people still in the hangar with us. "No, we're still here." Cleared my throat and spoke very softly. "Poofs assemble." Nothing. "Poofies, Kitty needs you." No bundles of cuteness appeared. "Mahin, I have a question. When you were left to try to stop us out there in the desert, what were your orders? I mean if you weren't able to kill us?"

"I was to go with you as a prisoner of war. They said they would rescue me. Which, they did try to do. Though I honestly expected them to arrive much sooner."

"Uh huh. Mister White, we're really predictable, aren't

we? Especially if you have access to Gladys, who knows our entire playbook."

"Yes, Missus Martini. They assumed we'd take Mahin to the Embassy. I believe we guessed that before."

"We did, but they didn't really count on Malcolm, and no one would have guessed Dad would be along. And they made the difference, in more than just where Mahin got taken."

"Yes," Mahin agreed. "I wouldn't have been open to listening to you if I hadn't spent time with your father."

Pulled out my phone and sent a text.

"What are you doing?" Jeff asked.

"Telling Christopher, James, and Tim to figure the base commander's under Ronaldo's influence or actually is Ronaldo. They escaped so we'd *know* they escaped and assume they were anywhere but here. They killed people because they could and also because those were the only Marines who would know what Dier looked like in person. Put her into a uniform, and she looks like a regular servicewoman. She's good at that kind of blending in."

"You think they've infiltrated this entire Naval station?" Mahin asked. "Then why did they leave me in captivity for days?"

"To see if you'd go with them or not when they showed up. You didn't go where they expected you to, so they adapted. And that's not a Ronaldo move. That's a Mastermind move. And Dier sounded like she was in charge, and she was working with Clarence's team during Operation Sherlock, and he was absolutely not hanging with Ronaldo at that time. Clarence was working with the Mastermind."

"So why are we standing here?" Jeff asked.

"In part because I want to know if the people here are under mind control or not. And in other part because I'm trying to figure out how they captured the Poofs." And I was betting it was all the Poofs. I'd had more Poofs than just Harlie and Poofikins in my purse when we'd come, but there were a lot of people in front of us, and my gut said Harlie had called in the Poof Cavalry, especially since no Poofs at all had come when I'd called.

"You think the Poofs are captured?" Chuckie asked. "Why?"

"Because they aren't here. They did their jobs—they

saved everyone from being blown up or buried alive. And what are the odds that whoever's calling the plays knew they'd do that?"

"I'd say good, Missus Martini." White was looking around. Assumed he was doing what I was and trying to spot which of the Gang of Four Plus One might be hiding in plain sight.

"Uncle Mort felt this hangar was the obvious place to take all those people who needed saving, and sure enough, here they all are."

"I don't see Gladys," Jeff said in a low voice.

"She's likely to be with Ronaldo or the Poofs, depending." On whether or not she was fooling Ronaldo.

Looked around. No one in this hangar was acting like an automaton. They were all watching us with varying degrees of suspicion or interest, prisoners included, which likely meant they were in control of their own minds. After all, Uncle Mort hadn't told them to leave or do anything else, and where else would they take all these prisoners anyway?

But the person I'd choose to leave here hiding in plain sight would be the one who knew how to blend in the best and who was also the most ruthless killer.

Sending an A-C to tackle Dier would be the smart choice. Only she'd proved that she knew how to shoot and kill someone moving at hyperspeed, and I'd be damned if I was going to watch either my husband or White get shot in front of me. Besides, while the Poofs were powerful, they were still animals. Animals who loved me and protected me, and who needed my protection in return.

Of course, first I had to figure out which one she was, without letting her know I'd figured out which one she was. Which, considering how many people were in here, was harder than it sounded. Everyone had something on their heads, all the women had their hair up or back, and the prisoners were even better covered.

"Remember," Chuckie said quietly, "we need to capture these people alive to have a hope of finding the Mastermind, let alone foiling whatever their end game is."

"James just texted me," Jeff said. "He thinks the base commander's been under mind control. They were about to send missiles into the Science Center, but your uncle stopped it. The squatters are countering."

"Tell them Chernobog's in Cuba somewhere. Maybe they can find her signal somehow." I wasn't looking at Jeff. I was looking at the prisoners. Most of the prisoners were doing what the military personnel were doing—watching the weird people who were hanging around the doorway.

One wasn't. He was pointedly looking down at his lap. And he was sitting near to a female in military garb. And they were both at the far end from the door.

"Okay, let's get out of here. We'll meet up with the others at the computer center."

We stepped outside. "What are you planning?" Chuckie asked. "And trust me, we all know you're planning something."

"Yeah, I am. Mahin, lots of dirt around here."

"Yes, there is."

"Awesome. On my signal, make a dirt wall and put it around all of you."

"What?" Jeff asked. "What in the hell—"

"Now!" I ran, and got on the other side as the wall went up. Knew I didn't have long, but hopefully I'd be faster than Jeff or the others.

Ran back into hangar and headed right for the two people I'd spotted. Aimed for the woman and hit into her before anyone saw me.

It was Dier for sure, which was nice, because I slammed her back and down and started beating the crap out of her. She was fighting back, but I'd knocked the weapon out of her hands and was definitely stronger than she was.

I probably would have won, too, because I was angry and I'd had the element of surprise. But I'd neglected to remember a couple of key facts.

One of which was that while Mahin had to have dirt and dust around to do her thing, Darryl would pretty much always have air handy.

And, of course, no one else with a gun actually realized that the Navy Ensign I was beating up was a bad guy.

So, when I was flung high up into the air, every gun in the hangar was no longer focused on the prisoners, but was, instead, pointed directly at me. Always the way.

CHAPTER 70

"LEAVE HER ALONE!" The voice wasn't Jeff's or Chuckie's—it was Mahin's.

Dirt flew into everyone's eyes, military and prisoners alike. Which was great in some ways and not in others.

In terms of great, it meant that no one could see to shoot at me, and they were all trained well enough that they didn't just randomly fire at each other.

It wasn't so great in that being somewhat blinded meant Darryl also lost concentration. At least I assumed that's why I was no longer being held up in the air via his snazzy air-bending moves and was, instead, plummeting straight for the concrete far below as if Gravity was pissed that I'd once again thought I was too good for it and truly wanted to teach me a lesson this time.

"Gotcha!" Jeff said, right before he caught me. Then he said, "Oof!" But I was incredibly happy to not have my legs shattered, so chose not to complain.

"You rock the awesome catching as always."

"I've had so much practice since I met you, it's instinctive at this point." He hugged me tightly, hearts pounding. "We're going to have a really big fight about the stunt you just pulled, but not right now."

I hugged him back. "I couldn't risk her shooting you."

"Speaking of shooting," Jeff said, as the military personnel began to recover and once again had their weapons at the ready. All pointed at us, of course.

"Hands up," Dier said as she got to her feet. "Shoot them if they so much as move." She looked happily vindictive.

"How can we put our hands up if you're going to shoot us if we move? Just asking and all."

Someone knocked every gun out of every hand before anyone had a time to answer the conundrum I'd posed. Nice to know Christopher was back. Nicer still that his timing was impeccable.

He'd clearly taken in the scene properly, because he'd dropped Hughes and Walker off right by Dier, and they proceeded to hit the vindictive look off her face. I was quite pleased that they'd decided the "no hitting girls" rule didn't apply to psychopathic assassins.

Darryl was on his hands and knees and started to crawl away. "The kid near her on the ground is an airbender!" Hughes kicked Darryl in the head. Darryl went down. "Nice work!" Hey, I believed in positive reinforcement.

Some of the other prisoners made a half-hearted attempt to run away, but Christopher used the first one to really go for it as a human baseball bat, and the rest decided sitting right back down was the better part of valor. The guy who'd been used as the bat looked like he'd recover. Soon enough.

In a matter of a minute we were back in seeming control of the situation. Chuckie took the opportunity to wave his impressive C.I.A. badge around and the military personnel seemed much happier. Chuckie and my mom had the best badges—no one ever reacted in the same way to anything I tossed around.

Chuckie got Dier and Darryl into handcuffs. "What do we do to keep him from using his talents against us?" Chuckie asked Mahin.

"I have to use my hands to focus the power. But I don't know what he does or doesn't need to do."

"Keep him knocked out," Chuckie said to Hughes and Walker, who were now on Prisoner Containment Duty. "Who do you answer to?" he asked Dier.

She glared at him, but didn't speak.

"Can you read her?" Chuckie asked Jeff.

"No, so she's got a blocker on her somewhere or it's on the base, because I'm not getting anyone, Kitty included. Which is how you fooled me," he added softly.

"I'll let you punish me for being a bad girl later. But I need you to put me down right now."

He obliged. "I'll hold you to that, baby."

"Good." I went to Dier and punched her right in the face. Was pretty sure I broke her nose. "You murdered my friend." Punched her again. "And you weren't supposed to, were you?" Punched her in the stomach, just to mix it up. "So talk, or I'll just punch you until you can't do anything but be a human target."

"You don't get how this all works, do you?" she asked me. "Hit me all you want. You won't get anything out of me."

"Yeah? Where are my Poofs?"

Dier smirked. "Saying goodbye."

Grabbed the nearest person in uniform, whose uniform declared him Lt. Pierce. "Where are the trash compactors, or the fiery furnaces, or whatever it is you guys use to get rid of garbage?"

"I found them already," Christopher said, as he grabbed me and we took off. Unfortunately for Lt. Pierce, I was still holding onto him. Oh well. Maybe we'd need him.

Christopher was, of course, using the super fast Flash Level hyperspeed. Figured the nausea would be worth it if we were able to find and save the Poofs.

We reached a building that proclaimed itself to be waste management and went inside, where Christopher stopped. Pierce hit the ground on hands and knees, retching. I managed to merely gag while standing up. "Where would those diabolical fiends put my Poofs?"

"Incinerator," Pierce gagged out.

Took a look around. There were a lot of incinerators. "Crap. You take one side, I'll take the other."

Christopher and I zipped through the facility. No Poofs. Tried not to panic. Ran back to Pierce. "Where else could they be?"

He shook his head and I lost it and started shaking him. "My uncle is Major General Mortimer Katt. My husband is Congressman Jeffrey Martini. And I'm the Ambassador for American Centaurion. But if my pets have been murdered on American soil I will declare war and I will start by actually letting the bad guys blow this base to kingdom come!"

Pierce managed to shove me off of him, helped by Christopher, who was literally holding me back. "I'm trying to help you, ma'am," Pierce gasped out. "If you think someone's trying to dispose of live animals, this wouldn't be the most likely place."

"They're evil people and they want the animals to suffer before they die."

"Ah. Then this would be the place. But if they're not in the furnaces yet, then they might be up there." He pointed up to a conveyor belt that had big metal baskets hanging from it.

"It so figures. Lieutenant, how do we turn this conveyor belt off?"

"I don't know. I don't work this job."

"I can read," Christopher said as he took off.

I could read too, and I didn't see anything that said Off Button for the conveyor. I did see something sparkling up above, though. The Poof cages had been weirdly shiny. "They're up there for sure."

Wondered if I could run fast enough to run up the walls. Maybe. But that would just put me in the basket with the Poofs or worse, and I had just enough self-control to realize that would only make things more terrible.

Heard a squawk, then Bruno arrived, followed by Jeff and Mahin. Bruno flew up and started screaming. He was hovering over a basket that looked ready to tip. "We need to get up there!" I shouted desperately.

A dust devil formed. It wasn't huge but it looked solid. Small, but solid. It dawned on me that Mahin needed more dirt.

Ran outside and dug into the ground with my hands, ran back and tossed the dirt into the room. The dust devil got bigger. The conveyor belt stopped, but based on where it was when the belt came to a halt, the bin Bruno was near was rocking. A lot. In that way that indicated momentum was going to ensure it rocked farther and faster, versus slowed down.

Jeff followed me outside. He had some scrap metal in his hands, which he used like a shovel. He dug; I threw the dirt into the room. We were both moving at the fastest hyperspeed we could. Wasn't sure if it would be enough.

Bruno had something in his claws and he managed to get down to the ground with it. It was a Poof in a Poof Trap alright. Bruno looked wilted. "Stay here, Bruno. The heat's too much for you." Meaning it was incredibly hot, because Alpha Four was a very warm planet.

The Poof Trap was hard to open, but I'd seen Brian do it, so I did what he had and was able to rip it apart. The Poof was an unattached one. "Can you save the other Poofies?"

It mewed piteously. No, it couldn't. The substance the Traps were made of was something the Poofs couldn't work with or around.

Resisted the urge to curse. Especially when I looked up to see the bin tip over.

CHAPTER 71

THE POOF TRAPS poured out as I clutched the one Poof to me. I was too horrified to scream. At least out loud. I was screaming in my head, though.

But there were no horrible little answering screams from my trapped pets. The Poofs poured into the dust devil. And they didn't pour right out again.

Mahin was sweating, and she didn't look like she could hold the dust devil too much longer. Tried to think of what to tell her.

"Relax," Christopher said, sounding like he did when he and I worked on my control. "You've got it. Channel up from your feet, they're touching the source of your power."

Mahin nodded. "Have to move them. But . . . it's hard . . ."

"No, you don't have to move anything but the dirt, and you control it. You just have to move the dirt," he said, sounding calm and unworried. "They'll go with the dirt. Just bring the dirt back to you, where it all belongs. You control the dirt."

"Yes, but . . ."

"Breathe. In and out. Relax and just let it all flow. You've done this a million times. Right now it's just another time, that's all."

Mahin took a deep breath and let it out slowly. The dirt looked more solid. It sailed away from the incinerator, swirled down and around, and settled in a pile in front of Mahin.

There were a lot of Poofs in traps, covered with dirt. Jeff

and Christopher started digging them out and opening up the traps. I got up and hugged Mahin. Then I burst into tears. Felt stupid, but I couldn't help it.

She hugged me back. "Did we get all of them?"

The Poof I was holding mewed. "Yes, all that were here." Took a deep breath and got it together. "They have my Poof, Poofikins, and the Head Poof, Harlie." To do something nefarious with them, I was sure. Probably starting with telling us these were the last Poofs around. Hadn't thought it was possible for me to hate these people more than I already did, but found out it was.

"You can understand what it says?" she asked, as we separated and the unattached Poof jumped onto Mahin's shoulder and rubbed against her neck. She giggled. "That tickles. They're little fluff balls, aren't they?"

The Poof purred and looked at me with a very satisfied expression. "Ah, Mahin? This one's yours."

"Oh, you don't have to give me one," she said a little regretfully. "I owed you this. At least this."

"Not going to debate that at the present time. However, the way it works for the Poofs is if you name it, you're attached to it, and it to you. Meet your Poof, Fluffball."

The Poof purred even louder. "Really?" Mahin asked. "It thinks that's its name? It thinks it's mine?"

"That is now its name and it is now yours."

"Yeah," Jeff said, as he got the last Poof Trap opened. "Welcome to the family."

Mahin looked like she was going to follow my lead and burst into tears. "I don't know what to say." Her voice broke. "I've been alone since my parents died."

"I know." Jeff put his arm around her shoulders. "I read you before. Look, the bird approved you, the Poofs approved you, and you've done nothing but help us since you found out you'd aligned with the wrong side. People make mistakes. You didn't pull the trigger, the assassin did, and you helped us capture her, twice. Stop beating yourself up."

I jerked. "You can feel her emotions?"

"Yeah. And yeah, I know that means that the emotional blocker was on Dier, not just randomly on the base. Have no idea what *that* means, however."

"It means if we strip search that bitch we can find another blocker or enhancer that Serene and her team can take apart. The kid probably has one on him, too."

"Tim just sent me a text," Christopher said. "They haven't found Al Dejahl, Kozlow, or Gladys anywhere in the building where the computer center is. Our computer team has what might be a lead on Chernobog, though."

Considered our options, and our quarries' options. "You know, I shot Kozlow. I only winged him, but, faster healing or not, he'd want medical attention. Would the base infirmary be in the same building as the computer center?"

"No," Pierce said. "It's nearby, though."

"Great," Jeff said, as he took firm hold of my hand and Christopher gathered up all the empty Poof Traps into a ratty-looking duffel bag he'd scrounged up. "We're going back to the hangar and we can determine who's going where after that."

"Who are you and what have you done with my husband?"

This got a laugh out of Christopher but Jeff just looked confused. "What do you mean?"

"When did being a politician start being your go-to move? You were Head of Field, and we're in a Field situation, and they have our Poofs. You can go to the hangar, but I'm going to see if I can find Kozlow."

Christopher slung the sack of Poof Traps on his back. "I'm with Kitty on this one, Jeff. In part because I have no desire to stop being in a Field situation until Gladys is back and the people who murdered Michael are all in prison or dead."

"What Christopher said. To the tenth power."

Jeff stared at us for a long moment. "Good points. You," he pointed to Lt. Pierce. "Take us to the infirmary."

"Ah, could we go at a normal speed?" Pierce asked. "I don't know that I have anything left to throw up."

"Everyone's so picky."

"No," Christopher said as he finished sending a text and grabbed Pierce. "But if you're nice about it, I might go sort of slowly."

"But I wouldn't count on it," I added. "All Poofs with me,

please and thank you." My purse felt heavier. Scooped Bruno up with my free arm. "Let's roll."

"You sound so street when you say that," Jeff said.

We headed for the infirmary but before we got there Mahin jerked at us and stopped running. "Look!" We all stopped, while Pierce started gagging.

Mahin pointed down one of the main, paved roads. There were three people on it, running toward the west, meaning toward the Cuban side. One of them was quite short, and one had what looked like a bandage on his upper arm.

"That's them, I hit Kozlow in the arm. Lieutenant, when you get your stomach back under control, get to the hangar and let our people know that we have the fugitives in sight and are pursuing."

Put Bruno down. He still seemed wilted from the heat—wondered if whatever the Poof Traps were made of affected the Peregrines negatively too, because I wouldn't have expected any being from Alpha Four to have issues with heat. Cold yes, but not heat. Gave him a pat. "Make sure he gets to everyone safely and wait for orders, you need to recover."

Bruno squawked and bobbed his head. He'd get Mr. Weak Stomach to safety and remain on guard. We left Pierce happily puking under Bruno's watchful eye, and took off on our new course.

Could still see our targets in the distance, and we were gaining on them. "Why are they running at regular speeds?"

"They're not," Christopher said. "Good to see all the training's starting to pay off—you're seeing human and hyperspeed without trying or realizing you're switching back and forth."

"Oh. Go me. You're a good coach."

"Yes, you are," Mahin agreed.

"Helps to have good students," Christopher said.

"The love on the base is making me as sick as that lieutenant we left," Jeff said. "Where the hell are they going? And why? If it were me, I'd be trying to get to a gate."

"James locked them down," Christopher said. "No one can get through without his authorization right now."

"They may or may not know that. But my bet is they're heading for the Cuban side, because Chernobog's there, somewhere." Was about to ask Christopher if he was able to go to Flash levels when both the why and the where of what our quarries were going to was answered.

A low-flying "Little Bird" helicopter—the kind that looked like sleek, black bubbles holding some serious firepower while also being incredibly maneuverable—came over the horizon. It didn't take genius to realize that Ronaldo and what was left of his gang were headed for it.

It also didn't take genius to figure out where all the weapons this particular chopper had—and it had a lot—were aimed. They were aimed at us.

CHAPTER 72

"WE CAN'T LET THEM get into that chopper!"

"We also can't let it shoot its missiles," Jeff said. "It has Stingers and Hellfires on it. With those they can blow up the base and kill everyone here."

"I'm more concerned with the guns," Christopher said. "Since those can kill all of us without blowing us up."

So much of what was going on was explained. Pity none of us were going to have time to let Chuckie and Reader know that all the disparate crap was connected, at least not until Guantanamo was under attack.

We were a good two miles away from where we'd been, near a grouping of tan buildings clearly designed to blend in with the ground when viewed from above, surrounded by chain link fencing with barbed wire wrapped all around it. There were guard shacks at each corner, outside the fencing.

There was a lot of dirt around—Mahin wouldn't need to worry about having her version of ammunition. There was a decent amount of foliage a little ways away. Close enough that you could see it from this area but far enough to be too far if you were locked up inside and guards were in the shacks.

Unfortunately, the foliage was much closer to the people we were chasing than to us, and there was no way we would want to get into what looked like a detention compound because that would make us even better targets than we already were.

"Scatter!" Jeff shouted, as he dragged me down and away

from a spray of the bullets Christopher was correct to be worried about.

Christopher dropped the bag of Poof Traps as he grabbed Mahin and pulled her the opposite way. As bullets ripped through the duffel, the traps rolled onto the ground. I didn't remember any of us closing them, but closed they were, all round balls of weird, shiny, mesh, like alien whiffle balls.

"All Poofs, spread out and go to Chuckie and James and Richard and the rest of our team! Protect them and the rest of the good people. And protect yourselves, too!" My purse felt lighter, which was good.

"Stop being the crazy Poof lady and keep moving," Jeff said, as he pulled me to my feet and zipped us around in a serpentine pattern.

"How can they see us to shoot? We're moving at hyper-speed." Looked up at the helicopter—there was more than one person in it. "One of them has to be an A-C or a hybrid."

"This detail helps us how?" Jeff asked as we just barely kept ahead of the bullets, which sprayed into the dirt.

Mahin had her hands out and a dirt devil quickly formed. Fortunately Christopher tackled her right before the bullets ripped into her. The dirt devil collapsed back onto the ground.

Looked back at the chopper in time to see them aiming in such a way that they'd hit both me and Jeff. Pulled out of Jeff's grasp and shoved him away. The bullets just missed him.

I tumbled backward so they missed me, too. I landed on the Poof Traps. Always the way. Mahin was trying to get a dirt tornado going, meaning that she was the recipient of most of the chopper's firepower. It was clear that she needed to be able to concentrate to get said tornado going, and unsurprisingly, the people she'd recently been aligned with knew this. Christopher was spending his time pulling her to safety, meaning neither one of them was effective and both were targets.

Grabbed one of the Poof Traps and threw it as hard as I could at the helicopter, mostly out of frustrated rage but also because, well, you never knew what might work.

To my complete surprise, not only did the trap hit the helicopter, but it dinged it. An idea formed, but I couldn't do it myself. "Mahin, Christopher! We need fastballs, and we need them now!"

Christopher ran over, grabbed a couple of the traps, and threw them with impressive accuracy and speed. The helicopter was definitely being affected. We both tossed a couple more, then had to scatter again, as they fired at us again.

Mahin joined us as we regrouped and Christopher sent several into the chopper, one of which cracked its windshield. The pilot had been coming closer to us, but pulled up now to get out of range.

"How long do you need to get a dirt tornado going?"

"Longer than they're giving me," she said as we threw a couple of traps and then had to run. "Once I really get it going I can hold it as long as I'm conscious, but getting enough dirt going to really create enough mass takes—" Whatever she was going to say was cut short by both of us having to leap in opposite directions to avoid bullets.

"They're covered with dirt," I said as we regrouped and I tossed her a couple traps. "See if you can work with them."

"But . . ." She looked uncertain. "I don't know what these are made of, but I don't think I can move them."

"And you'll never know unless you try," Christopher snapped. "Stop making excuses for what you can't do and focus on what you can. You control the earth. So, control it. Focus on the dirt." He threw another trap and hit again, though the chopper was getting out of range, at least for us to hit it. It wasn't so far away that whatever it was shooting at us wasn't going to hurt or kill.

"He has a point. And while necessity is indeed the mother of invention, I've always found panic to be the father of ability. And it's good to honor both father *and* mother."

Speaking of honoring my mother, I had a gun on me, and it was high damn time to use it. Dug it out of my purse as I ran in the serpentine pattern we were currently all so fond of because it was keeping us alive.

Jeff hadn't joined us at the pitching range—he'd chosen to go after the people we were still trying to catch. They in turn were emboldened by having their snazzy escape vehicle here and shooting at us, so they'd turned and were attacking him. The only positive on this was that the helicopter wasn't shooting at Jeff because he was embroiled with the three of them.

Only, it wasn't really three of them.

I'd seen Android Gladys fight. The real Gladys either had none of the moves her android had, or else she was so damn good that she looked like she was attacking Jeff while actually hitting Kozlow and Ronaldo. I voted for the latter.

The good thing was that Jeff seemed to be doing well in this fight so far, and the others didn't appear to have caught on that Gladys was hitting them instead of Jeff yet. The bad thing was that my gun was useless—there was no way I could be sure I wouldn't shoot Jeff.

The helicopter wasn't close enough that I thought my shots would have a good enough effect and I didn't have an unlimited number of clips with me. Better to conserve the bullets for when they wouldn't be wasted for sure. For once remembered to set the safety, shoved the gun into the back of my pants, and contemplated my options while I did a rolling leap to get away from another burst of bullets.

Christopher was running out of Poof Traps to throw, which was bad because whoever was in the chopper had figured that out and was shooting both to hit and keep Christopher back from where the traps had landed.

"Mahin," I shouted, "if you can't use your powers to toss them, use your powers to bring them back."

Didn't stop to wait to see if she could manage it. Decided instead to gather some up and toss them from another angle. They were fairly easy to spot, because of how they caught the sunlight. They weren't easy to get to, though, because of bullets and the wind being created by the helicopter blades. The only saving grace was that I was in jeans instead of a ripped dress. Otherwise, this was causing me some nostalgia for the end of Operation Drug Addict.

The chopper's pilot had noted we were pretty much out of our impromptu ammo, and he started lowering toward us again. This created a hell of a lot of wind and therefore even more dirt and dust were flying up.

"Get down!" Mahin shouted. She wasn't up to Jeff's bellowing ability, but she wasn't bad. She was also creating a dust devil, thanks to the assist the chopper was providing.

This version of dirt tornado sparkled here and there—Mahin had figured out how to move the Poof Traps, and they were swirling up and around within the tornado.

CHAPTER 73

CHRISTOPHER WAS BEHIND MAHIN. I could tell he was ready to grab her to get her out of the way of bullets.

But bullets weren't coming at us right now, because the pilot was having trouble with the dirt, and when the Poof Traps hit into it, they continued to cause the chopper problems.

I was under the chopper and contemplated if getting out of the way would be a smart idea. Entertained the notion of jumping up and trying to climb into the cockpit. But before I could either run away or give jumping a shot, someone ran past me and did it first.

Had to give it to Ronaldo, he had the A-C jumping ability. He grabbed a hold of one of the chopper's skids and hung on. He was just low enough for me to reach, and there was no way I was letting him get away. Jumped up and grabbed his legs.

This meant two people were hanging off of one skid while a tornado of dirt filled with alien-made Poof Traps was hitting the chopper. Of course, this meant the dirt and traps were hitting me and Ronaldo, too. Missed having my parachute outfit on but otherwise chose not to care. He had something of mine and I wasn't letting him get away with them.

"Let go, you lunatic!" he shouted at me. "You'll bring this down on top of us."

"Where are my Poofs you giant prick?" Clawed at his pants pockets, but didn't feel anything. Couldn't safely reach his sweat jacket, though. Decided it was time to start climbing up his body.

Ronaldo didn't care for this at all, at least if I took his cursing at me to be a clue. His thrashing about was also an issue, so while I was inching up, it wasn't anything like climbing up a rope.

Just as I reached his waist, and therefore could grab at the pockets of his sweat jacket, I took a Poof Trap to the back that timed out with Ronaldo flailing his legs just right and I lost my grip. Didn't have too far to fall, but someone broke my landing anyway.

However the someone wasn't Jeff. It was Gladys.

We scrambled to our feet and Gladys dragged me off a ways, so we weren't under the chopper any more. It was wobbling but didn't have my weight pulling it down any more, and the pilot seemed to be getting the chopper under control. He was trying to get higher up into the air, but the dirt storm was still working and he had to focus more on actually staying in the air as opposed to getting to a better position.

"Get everyone out of here," Gladys shouted. "I'll handle my little brother."

"I can shoot him. He has my Poofs. Let me rephrase. I can, and will, shoot him."

She waved my Glock at me. "Not any more, kiddo. Jeffrey has Kozlow, and he's who you'll need the most." She looked at Mahin. "One saved for one lost. Not the trade I would have chosen, but still, worthwhile in its own right."

"I won't kill him. I know we need to take Ronaldo alive. He has answers. We need the people in the chopper, too. I just want to, um, hurt them a lot. And I want my Poofs back."

Gladys shook her head. "This ends now. The safety of the many outweighs the need for information of the few." She shoved her cell phone into my purse. "There's something in there I'd like you to see later on."

"Gladys, what—?"

She smiled at me. "You've been a pain in the ass from day one, but you were also just what we needed. Keep on recruiting, you're almost as good at that as you are in finding trouble. I'm glad I got to work an op with you, kiddo. So stay out of this so I don't have to shoot you in the leg. I have unfinished business."

"What are you going to do?"

"I'm going to get that asshole out of my head, and everyone else's heads, too. Permanently."

With that she turned and ran and, despite her size, jumped up and caught Ronaldo's feet.

Unlike me, she seemed to have no issues climbing up Ronaldo's body. She was on his back, legs wrapped around his waist, one arm around his neck, in a short period of time. Her gun hand was free. She put the gun to Ronaldo's head.

He reached into his pocket and tossed something on the ground. Two somethings. Two Poof Traps.

Ran and got them. Harlie and Poofikins were inside. I got out of the way of the chopper, then ripped the traps open. The Poofs jumped into my arms. They were both trembling.

Told to stay on the ground or not, Ronaldo was going to pay. Looked back up at the chopper. It was a lot higher in the air than it had been. And Gladys was now standing on top of Ronaldo, balanced on him and the skid. She grabbed the person who'd been shooting at us and flung him out of the chopper, grabbing his gun as he went down. I was hella impressed.

Ran over to the guy who'd just had his own fight with Gravity. He was definitely an A-C or a hybrid, because he was getting to his feet. Couldn't have that. Sent a roundhouse kick into the side of his head.

He spun and went down, but he got up again. Definitely an A-C, that kick had been one of my best.

Poofikins growled and went Jeff-sized. The guy I was fighting screamed like a little girl, turned, and ran. Poofikins caught him, easily. In its giant jaws filled with lots of giant teeth.

Apparently my Poof wasn't into the idea of eating this guy, though. Instead. Poofikins and its prisoner bounded over to where Jeff was. Poofikins spat the latest prisoner out of its mouth, then stood on top of him and Kozlow both, growling. Jeff patted it.

Looked up again. Gladys was in the cockpit and she hauled Ronaldo inside. Had a moment's worry—what if she'd been under the mind control after all? Heard Mahin scream and turned to see her Poof go large and toothy. Fluffball grabbed her gently in its mouth and raced over to Jeff, who was, as I looked around and actually thought about it, the farthest away from the chopper. Toby, Christopher's Poof, did the same with him.

Harlie went large and in charge. "Hang on, Harlie, I don't need to be carried yet." I ran over to the others, because it was clear the Poofs wanted us together.

Shockingly, the surprise of her Poof going giant-sized and seeming to want to eat her had thrown off Mahin's earth-bending groove, and the dirt tornado collapsed. The helicopter rose up higher and adjusted itself, wobbling a bit, but not so much that it wasn't going to be able to send a missile into our little group.

And that was definitely the intention, because the chopper turned so it was pointing weapons at us again. While Christopher explained Poof Protocol to Mahin, the three Poofs that weren't on Prisoner Detainment Duty surrounded us. Didn't think this was necessarily the right plan. "Is it maybe time to run away?"

As I said this we saw blood splatter hit the inside of the helicopter's windshield along with a lot of bullet holes. The chopper started to spin out of control. Heard more gunfire and saw flames. Gladys must have hit the fuel tanks, on purpose presumably.

Waited for Gladys to jump out or try to control the chopper, too fast A-C reflexes or not. But she didn't do either.

Could see her in the chopper's open doorway—she had Ronaldo in a headlock. She looked at me and smiled. Then she shot him in the head. Twice. She dropped his body onto the floor and, because of the way the chopper was spinning, it slid out of view. The flames were getting larger.

"Come on!" I screamed. "Jump out!" Tried to get out of the Poof Huddle, but they wouldn't let me. They were protecting us, but also keeping us away. Realized Gladys must have given them a request before she'd rescued Harlie and Poofikins.

"Get down," Jeff bellowed. "It's going to crash!" He pulled me down, and Christopher did the same with Mahin.

But I got out of Jeff's hold and back up again. The second to last thing I saw was Gladys saluting me with my Glock. Then the helicopter crashed into the nearby buildings and exploded.

CHAPTER 74

I DIDN'T HAVE TIME to react before Mahin had shoved Christopher off of her and was standing next to me, palms up and out. Just as she'd done in the desert, a dirt wall formed between us and the explosion. And as before, it fell onto the explosion, smothering the flames.

I tried to run but Jeff had his arm firmly around my waist. "She could still be alive." I said desperately. I knew she wasn't, though. Because the last thing I'd seen before the crash had been Gladys pointing the Glock at her own head. But I still wanted to believe she hadn't pulled the trigger and was merely trapped in the wreckage, alive and okay.

"I can't feel her," Jeff said, voice choked.

"They're wearing emotional blockers or whatever. I mean, can you feel the rest of us?"

"No," Jeff admitted. He hugged me. "Not even you."

"So that's probably a good thing."

"I'll search," Christopher said. "I'm best equipped."

Decided not to ask him how he was better equipped than the rest of us to do this, because he looked as stricken as Jeff sounded. "We'll all go," Jeff said. "Just in case."

"I can't guarantee that nothing more will explode," Mahin said. "I know the flames are out but . . ."

Before we could decide how foolhardy we wanted to be, the rest of our team arrived, let by White. Could see regular military personnel coming in the distance.

"Let the military search," I told Christopher. "That way, we can't be accused of anything."

"But—" He looked ready to go anyway.

"Trust me. Please."

"Bomb units are on the way," Chuckie said. "Kitty's right—it would be better to allow human military to handle the rest."

Mahin was crying softly. Jeff reached out and pulled her to us. "It'll be okay," he said. He remained a terrible liar. The Poofs went small and jumped into pockets or my purse, depending.

"What happened?" White asked softly, as he pulled Christopher into his arms.

"Gladys . . . Gladys wasn't mind controlled. She's killed Ronaldo." Managed not to add "and herself," but White's expression said that he knew. "She was in the crash."

"I'm so sorry," Mahin sobbed. "If I hadn't listened to them, none of this would have happened."

White took her from Jeff and hugged her. "We make mistakes. It's part of what makes us who we all are. And part of who you are is my younger sister, just as Gladys was."

"They'd have done it anyway," Jeff said. "It's what our enemies do. But by leaving them you weaken them and strengthen us."

Wanted to follow that line of reasoning, but now wasn't the time. Made a mental note that I needed to return to that point. Later.

Uncle Mort was on site now, and he had the bomb unit delving into the wreckage. They had dogs, which was sort of a surprise, but at least I knew if someone was still somehow alive the dogs would sniff them out.

I went to my uncle. "There should be three, possibly four, bodies. One of them will be a small woman who's an A-C. If we can get her body back, that would be . . . good."

Uncle Mort hugged me. "Gladys?"

"Yeah."

"She was a brave woman."

"She was. Uncle Mort . . . I think . . . I think she wanted to die. Why? She was a fighter, more like Mom and you than Dad or Richard. Why would she just . . . give up?"

He was quiet for a few moments, as he patted my back and stroked my hair, just like he'd done when I was a teenager and had had to call him to get me out of trouble when I couldn't reach my parents. "My guess is because she knew, ultimately, who was responsible for what's happened. And she didn't want to live with that knowledge."

"But she has a husband and a family."

"Yes. And she'd know for the rest of her life that because she was susceptible to your enemy that she'd caused the deaths of many people, including those she loved. Never forget, Kitty—those who share the information with the enemy are as guilty as those who pull the triggers. Guiltier in many ways. There's a reason we consider high treason to be a heinous crime."

"But she didn't betray us on purpose."

"No, I presume she did not. How would that make her feel better?"

"She killed Ronaldo before the crash. I saw her do it, and I could tell he was dead. So why . . . go down with the ship?"

He sighed. "If you can be controlled by one, who's to say you can't be controlled by another? You're talking about the woman who held every military secret Centaurion Division has ever had. And she was read as easily as you or I would read a children's book. That kind of security breach can destroy an entire country, or more. Would she want to know she was responsible for destroying her people? How could she prevent being controlled the next time? How could she be sure she wasn't being controlled every moment of her life? When your decisions are not your own, when your mind is not your own, there is no such thing as free will, and you cease to really exist as anything but a shell, even if you live for a hundred years."

"There's isolation." But as I said it, I realized it wasn't a life. Jeff went into isolation to be regenerated, not to spend the rest of his life there.

"You can still be found, even on the remotest part of the planet, or out in a universe that you now know is teeming with life. No, I understand her decision. Is it the choice I would have made? I'm thankful that I can't say, but I *can* say that I hope I'm never put in the position Gladys was in. And I hope you never are, either."

One of the bomb unit came over. "Sir, the dogs aren't finding any signs of life."

"I'll let you handle this." Gave Uncle Mort another hug, then headed back to Jeff and the others.

White reached out and pulled me to him. "She's dead for certain?"

"Yes. Richard, I'm so sorry."

He kissed the top of my head. "I as well. I regret not getting to say goodbye."

Remembered Gladys had given me her phone. "Hang on." Dug into my purse and got her cell out. Turned it on. "She said there was something she wanted me to see." Scrolled through and found it in videos. The "Hey, Kiddo" title was something of a clue.

I hit play. Gladys' face filled the screen.

"Recording this before I leave to go get you and head us over to Guantanamo. I'm pretty sure that my dream was being controlled by my younger brother, but what he doesn't know is that I've figured out how to tell it's him."

Jeff and Christopher joined us.

Gladys grimaced. "But it's a hell of a lot of work. I have to pay attention twenty-four-seven, and that means my life from now on will be watching for mind control, and that's an all-consuming task. Meaning that unless he's dead, I'll never be free. I don't know what all he's gotten from me, but I do know that it's more than we want him or our enemies having. So I'm going to take steps."

The rest of our team was huddled around the phone now. I ensured the volume was at full.

"I'm going to kill Ronaldo. I know, once we've got him and you're thinking clearly, you'll tell me he needs to stay alive so that he can be questioned. But I also know he's never had an original thought in his head, no one who knows him would trust him with real information, and the only place he'll lead you is astray. You have others who know more and are of far more value. Catch, contain, and don't lose them."

Her expression went to sad anger. "My favorite nephew is dead, because of me. I never had children, and of all of the kids out there, Michael was most like the son I'd always wanted. Without being in the Yates bloodline, he still had the good parts of my father in him somehow, without the bad. I know everyone else wanted to blame themselves, you especially, for his murder. But the buck stops here, kiddo. Any other deaths that happen because of my being mind controlled are all on me, too. Your mother will understand."

She looked at something, then back at the camera. "I've said goodbye to my husband, though he probably doesn't know it. He's a lover, not a fighter, and Richard and Stanley will help get him through this, just as he'll help them. Tell Richard I was prepared and he'll find whatever's needed to transition my role to someone else. And also, please tell Richard, and anyone else, that we say goodbye every day, and that I know they loved me and I want them to know that I loved them right back."

Gladys sighed. "If my plan works, this is the last thing you'll hear from me. I know you and the others are all going to question my choices, but there are worse things than dying, and I'm staring some of those things in the face right now.

"I'll leave you with this—I agree that there's a Mastermind. And I know Ronaldo was working for whoever that is. Remember that the Mastermind is your ultimate goal, but don't forget that wars are won one battle at a time. And no matter how it might seem right now, kiddo, this battle isn't actually over."

Gladys grinned. "So, stop sniveling about my death and go do what you do best—fight for right, protect my people, and kick bad guy ass."

CHAPTER 75

WE WERE BACK AT THE EMBASSY. It was hard to tell Gower that he'd now lost his aunt as well as his brother. It was harder to tell everyone else.

White managed it, of course, because he'd been managing horrible things like this since well before the A-Cs had been exiled to Earth. Once the news was out, White had sequestered himself and Gower, doing Pontifex stuff, which I presumed meant White was prepping Gower for how to hold it together during Michael's funeral which was now the day after tomorrow.

Chuckie had Dier, Darryl the Airbender, Kozlow, and the guy Gladys had tossed out of the chopper in custody. They were in the containment center under the Pentagon, and, despite complaints from the F.B.I., Homeland Security, and the rest of the C.I.A., only Mom or Chuckie, and whoever they chose to bring along, were allowed access.

The prisoners were in Magneto Level cells, but so far, no one had gotten anything much out of them. Jeff and Christopher were due to go over with Mom, Chuckie, and a Polaroid camera to see what they could get. But first we had to make sense of what had happened at Guantanamo.

Uncle Mort had insisted on this because he wanted to be sure Mom had all the pertinent details and he wanted to hear anything he'd missed as well. I'd backed him up on doing this right away, because there were things I wanted to be sure we considered before I headed a commando raid into Gaultier.

Mom had agreed with both of us. Jeff had insisted that he wanted all Embassy staff, Alpha, and Airborne, other than White and Gower, in attendance as well. Jeff, Christopher, Mahin and I were all filthy, though, and the rest of the team wasn't looking too much better. So everyone was given an hour to get bathed and changed, Mahin and Uncle Mort were assigned rooms, and everyone cleaned up.

Dad was at the Embassy staying with Jamie, who was happy to see us, but not as happy as we were to see her. We didn't have as long a family reunion as either Jeff or I would have liked, but it was a better reunion than the Gowers were getting to have. Forced myself not to think about that while we were with Jamie, difficult though it was.

An hour later, give or take, we were all packed into the conference room like a group of well-dressed sardines, Hacker International attending via video conferencing.

Like me and all the other women, Mahin was now in the Standard Female Armani Fatigues of black slim skirt and white oxford, Fluffball on her shoulder. The clothes and Poof looked natural on her. She was actually kind of huddling next to me, which was understandable, even though no one had accused her of anything, not even via their expressions, not even Naomi or Abigail.

Pierre had provided a lovely drinks and snacks arrangement, which was great since it was well past dinnertime and many of us hadn't eaten for hours before that. I did my best not to shovel the fruit, veggies, dip, cheese, and chocolate into my mouth, but it took effort.

Food and drinks at everyone's place, we rolled into our recap. I covered why I'd gone with Gladys, Jeff covered why he and the others had come after us, Uncle Mort and Reader shared what they'd found at the computer center, and Chuckie finished up with what they'd done with the various prisoners, the ones we cared about and the others. We played Gladys' farewell message for everyone.

"Mort and I had the prisoners searched, of course," Chuckie said, probably to break the sad silence in the room after the video finished up. He slid four small disks onto the table. "The four we have in maximum lockup all had these on them. The prisoners who were in Guantanamo originally didn't."

"At least it wasn't in them." Got the usual WTF looks. Heaved a sigh. "These are small. I'm amazed our enemies aren't installing them inside their operatives like how we all used to be tagged for the American Centaurion Herd Protection Program."

Chuckie's eyes narrowed. "That's a good point. We've lost all the data on these, of course, but I wonder if there's something toxic to humans or A-Cs, or both, in the metal."

"Not that we've found yet," Serene said. "But then again, they've been almost impossible to examine past the shell."

"That would make sense," Jeff said. "Because I'm with Kitty—why not at least put them under the skin if they're harmless? We'd have a harder time finding them, not to mention there's less risk of loss."

"Maybe they think we'll figure out how to destroy them, like they destroyed our chips," Christopher said. "And theirs explode when you try to open them."

"Good point. But they could make them with a non-explosive shell if they wanted to. Unless there's a really good reason to have them remain outside of a body, and again, toxicity would be my guess, because it's not like the bad guys ever seem to care about losing minions."

"I wasn't given one of those," Mahin said. "I've never even seen one before, and I didn't know there were things that could affect empaths until you mentioned it. If I understand everything that's been going on correctly, I should have had one, shouldn't I?"

"Yeah," Jeff said. "You were on the front lines and I've been able to read you pretty clearly."

Something was bothering me. Something small. But as with Algar or the Poofs or Jamie, small didn't necessarily mean unimportant. Remembered that Jeff had said something about Mahin joining us and so had Gladys, and both had struck me as vital to explore. "You know, I wonder . . . why were we there and are we all here?"

Got a replay of all the WTF looks. Heaved a sigh but soldiered on. "By there I mean those of us who were at Guantanamo, and by here, I mean all of us, right here, as we are at this very moment." Looked around. "None of you seem remotely shocked that Mahin's got a Poof on her shoulder, or that we're acting like she's part of the team. She's still feeling unsure of whether or not she fits in, but none of you seem even a little surprised."

Tim shrugged. "We're not. It's what you do, why you got moved to Head of Recruitment."

"Yeah," Jerry said with a grin. "You find the talent, you do something that makes the talent realize you're great and worthy of following, you recruit the talent, the talent says you're da girl and sticks around. Sometimes the talent even marries in," he added, with a wink for Joe and Randy. Lorraine and Claudia both chuckled.

"And she's family," Naomi said softly. Serene nodded.

"Right. So I have to go back to something that occurred to me when we were fighting Mahin the first time, in the desert. It seemed like her side hadn't told her the truth—she thought they were all somewhere in the tunnel system, when they'd never even gone into it."

"Some of them went into it," Abigail pointed out.

"After they used gates to get out and across the country. Mahin thought they'd gone in at the Science Center."

"Yes, they told me they were taking everyone underground and going to use special vehicles to get back to D.C. If I survived and won, I was to meet them at the coordinates I gave Mister Buchanan."

"Not quite," Buchanan said. "The location where she was to rendezvous was across the street from the Gaultier Research facility. I just took the logical step of figuring our enemies would be in the tunnels underneath versus actually out in the open."

"How were you supposed to get across the country on your own?" Claudia asked.

"They told me how to work a gate. I was to go back to Area Fifty-One and either take a gate or commandeer a vehicle." Mahin gave a weak smile. "It wasn't a good plan, now that I share it aloud."

"They used her," Reader pointed out. "So? They do that all the time."

"But why? Why lie to her? Why give her the coordinates but not the truth of the rest? Did they expect us to kill her? Naomi's right, she's family, but so was Ronaldo and it wasn't like we were inviting him over for Arrival Day Dinner. And we didn't know Mahin existed until this action. So why didn't she get an emotional blocker or enhancer? Why wasn't she told anything much? It's as if they never figured she'd stick with them, like they knew she'd move over to the side of right somewhere along the way."

Everyone looked at Mahin. She leaned a little closer to me. "I didn't know any of you existed until the invasion, either. And I never suspected I was one of you, in that sense, until Ronaldo found me. I just thought I was different. My mother never told me who my . . . real father was. So how would anyone know what I would or wouldn't do?"

"Research," Chuckie answered. "They've known where you, and probably the others they've found, were. Potentially for years. And they studied all of you and extrapolated likely reactions. Well in advance of this action."

"My guess, by the way, is that Ronald Yates kept a Little Black Book of all his sexual conquests, either because he was just that kind of man, or because he wanted to be sure to be able to find his offspring easily."

"Then why wait until now to find them?" Claudia asked.

"And before you say they wanted to wait until he was dead," Lorraine added, "he's been dead for over three years now."

"And Serene was identified and used by our enemies within six months of his death. Ronaldo was activated around that time, too, if we pay attention to the timelines of how various Operations played out. So, my bet is that Leventhal Reid, who we all agree was the first Apprentice, had that Little Black Book and used it once Yates was dead."

"Does that mean the current Mastermind has it now?" Doreen asked.

"Give you three guesses and the first two don't count. My bet would be that the Apprentices were charged with legwork in finding the Yates Offspring. Our current Mastermind was better at this than Reid, or else Reid was more motivated to ID these people once he became the Mastermind. But that would mean they likely have detailed information on every one of the Yates Offspring they've managed to find."

"They got what they needed from me the most before I

was captured," Mahin said slowly. "I helped break Russell out of Israel, and my skills were truly what allowed them to get him. And I was convinced you were all dangerous and evil when I attacked you in the desert."

"And you really almost killed us," Christopher said.

"I note that you're sitting here, alive and well. Thanks to my skills that you constantly want to run down, Mister I Can't Actually Fly A Plane Myself But Love to Backseat Drive One."

"If she'd killed any of us she would never have been allowed in," Jeff said before Christopher had a chance to come back with anything other than Patented Glare #3. "So if that had worked, then they'd have had Mahin with them forever, because she wouldn't have had any options."

"Which is why they gave her the coordinates," Tim said. "So she could get back to them and they could retrieve her if she was successful."

"So they win either way," Chuckie said.

"Right. Especially since there was no way they were getting Chernobog's cooperation without Russell freed and in a position to collect on the YatesCorp prize."

Everyone gave me shocked looks other than Mom, Buchanan, and Chuckie, who all nodded. "Based on the intel Olga gave us," Chuckie said, "that's absolutely accurate. Chernobog hasn't been this active and obvious in at least a decade."

"That's an interesting point I don't want us to forget, but I want to get back to the whole Mahin issue. I realize our thinking just confirms that the Mastermind is back, bigger than ever, but I think what they did and didn't do with Mahin is hugely key. Because if they were always figuring that the odds were that they'd lose Mahin to us, what else were and are they already banking on?"

"Everything you did from the point you and Gladys got to Guantanamo," Christopher suggested.

"Maybe," Reader said. "But I have a question we didn't have time to ask before now. Mort, why was Mahin held at the Air Station, instead of over at the Detention Camp? And why were all these other prisoners there at all?"

"They were scheduled for release," Uncle Mort said. "Politically, we're being cooperative and moved them over to the Air Base, where it's more pleasant and better for photo ops. Realistically, they're all likely to be terrorists, but we do have to play nicey-nice for the politicians. No offense," he added to Jeff.

"None taken," Jeff said. "What country are they associated with?"

Chuckie's eyes narrowed. "You think they were or are part of the overall plan?"

"I think it's possible," Jeff said.

"Me too. Because Mahin was at the Air Base the whole time, right?"

Uncle Mort nodded. "Yes, but that was so it would be less unpleasant for your father and Mister Buchanan to question her. And to answer Jeff's question, the rest of the prisoners there are from a variety of countries. Most are considered low-level threats. I could get you a full roster if you need it, Angela, Charles."

"Yes, we'll want that." Chuckie rubbed the back of his neck. "The complexity just keeps adding in, doesn't it?"

"The Mastermind knows us," I pointed out. "And that means Mahin would have been put at the Air Base regardless, because someone from Centaurion Division or the P.T.C.U. would have been questioning her."

"But they left me there for days," Mahin said. "And no one contacted me before today."

"Uncle Mort, when did the release orders for those prisoners come down?"

"Within this week." He looked grim. "You think they're connected to all this business, don't you, just like Jeff and Charles do?"

"I do. The Mastermind has pull." Pull I was sure wasn't going to be traceable back *to* the Mastermind, of course, but I was getting used to that by now. Besides, all it took was finding the end of one thread in the tangle to unravel it. As long as we could find a thread, let alone an end to it.

"What would be the point?" Randy asked. "They didn't do anything."

"They utilized manpower," Joe replied. "That might have been reason enough."

Hughes and Walker both nodded. "And there was nowhere to put them, since the detention area was blown up," Hughes said.

"If we hadn't come back when we did, they might have done something as well," Walker added. "They tried, Christopher just stopped them in a way that ensured they didn't want to try again."

Thought about what Hughes had just said and where Ronaldo and the others had been running. "Uncle Mort, why were you at Guantanamo?"

"We had a high level terrorist in captivity." He nodded toward Mahin. "I was on site to ensure things remained . . . calm."

"Who knew you were there?"

"Only your mother. Top Brass wasn't advised. Neither was the base commander." He grinned. "In these kinds of cases, I use a gate to come and go. Much easier that way."

"So it's very likely that the Mastermind didn't know you'd be at Guantanamo. Which makes a lot of sense. So, let me ask this—let's say that you hadn't been there. The base commander was mind controlled, but that was only one part of the plan. Where would someone like, say, Lieutenant Pierce have ultimately taken the prisoners?"

"There would have been no prisoners left alive if not for your Poofs," Uncle Mort pointed out.

"Yeah, but I was always supposed to be there—remember, Gladys said she thought Ronaldo had sent her the dream to 'come' to him. So the expectation was always to catch me and the Poofs. And I'm sure the related expectation was that Jeff and some others would come after us. You were the wrinkle in their plans, not me or the others. So, Uncle Wrinkle, tell me where they'd have taken those prisoners, because I have a guess and I'd like to know if I'm right."

Jeff and Christopher both sat up straight. But Mahin spoke first. "They'd have been taken to those old buildings, where the helicopter crashed, right?"

Uncle Mort nodded. "I don't know why you children ask questions when you already know the answers."

"Because we like to keep you oldsters on your toes. So, the idea would have been to have a riot far away from the main area, or even to have a prison break where they all got to head right into Cuba and be likely welcomed with open arms. This would follow right after Guantanamo bombed our Science Center. I'd say that a war between the U.S. and American Centaurion, let alone however many other countries, would seem likely."

"It would take the Pontifex being in agreement with Alpha Team and the Diplomatic Corps for that to truly happen," Reader said.

Looked at Naomi and Abigail. "Paul has a breaking point, and I'd have to guess that seeing his brother murdered and then having most of his people blown up by the United States military would send him well damn past that point."

Naomi nodded. "Hell yes. I'm sure he's close right now, but that? That would send him and the rest of us over the edge. If there were any of us left that is."

"Yeah," Abigail agreed. "Jeff and Christopher, you know what you'd do."

Jeff nodded. "It's all too easy to see. Even if we believed the attack was an accident, that's a direct act of war."

"We'd be looking to move," Christopher said. "We'd want to pull the rest of our people out of U.S. territories, go somewhere we felt was safer. Maybe leave the planet, if we could. We have options now that we didn't have before, ACE or no ACE."

"Where are those prisoners now?" Mom asked.

"Had to send them back to the Detention Camp," Uncle Mort said. "And now I'm glad of that. Kitty, do you really think the goal is war? And why war with American Centaurion?"

Chuckie's phone rang. He looked at it and groaned. "Horn's calling. I'm sure he wants to know where we are on finding the new superdrug."

Stared at him. "Oh. My God. I know what the hell is going on, all of it. And why."

CHAPTER 76

"DO I TAKE VANDER'S CALL OR NOT?" Chuckie asked.

"Take it and tell him you're in a meeting, making progress, and that you'll call him back. And hurry. I'm saving this until you're done."

This earned me a dirty look, but Chuckie got up and walked out of the room as he answered. "Vander, it's been so long since we talked. What, half a day?"

"You're really going to make us wait until he's back in the room?" Christopher asked.

"Yep." Took the opportunity to eat some more and get my thoughts into a semblance of order. "Len, Kyle, we need Adriana. Can you guys see if she's free?"

"Mister Joel Oliver's at the Romanian Embassy," Len said. "Olga asked him to stay. You want him, too?"

"Could my saying no actually keep him away? Besides, he's always good for insights. And of course if Olga wants to come over and see if any of us have caught up or caught on, she's always welcome."

Len and Kyle trotted out. Without calling or texting anyone. Had a feeling Adriana, Oliver, and Olga were already all on standby and just waiting for their official invitation.

Uncle Mort got up. "I'm going to send in an order to keep all those prisoners at Guantanamo. Some politicians won't like it, and I'll be sure we note which ones. I'll be back when Charles is."

"While we wait for you to actually tell us what you think is going on, Kitty," Stryker said from Hacker Headquarters, "you want what we got on Chernobog?"

"Yes. She's in Cuba, near Guantanamo, maybe actually physically on the American side, and absolutely using their computer systems."

All five Hackers had clearly been taking glaring lessons from Christopher, because I was getting a full pantheon of glares from them, even Omega Red.

"Way to steal a guy's moment," Stryker grumbled.

"Part of my charm. Why pick Guantanamo unless someone they needed to work with was there? There are plenty of bases around the world, hell, they were *at* Home Base originally, so that one had to be chosen for more reasons than Mahin being taken there."

"Fine, still don't see how you made the leap that Chernobog's on the American side," Stryker said.

"That's because you're convinced I'm a moron and I rarely waste time trying to convince you otherwise. As for the rest, they had too easy a time getting onto the base and running around it. Hyperspeed's great, but that's an active base loaded with personnel—someone was going to spot a bunch of civilians they didn't know and ask questions. Meaning our gang was staying somewhere close to the Air Station but not necessarily right on the base. However, being on the American side means access to all that great equipment and energy, and, let's face it—Chernobog's an old woman by now. Why would she choose to rough it if she doesn't have to?"

"She wouldn't," Olga said as Len and Kyle returned, confirming my suspicion that Team Romania had been waiting at their front door. Well, better to have allies who were eager, right?

Chuckie and Uncle Mort came back. "All taken care of," Uncle Mort said as they seated themselves.

"Vander wants more than platitudes, Kitty," Chuckie said. "So I want to know what you figured out, and I want to know now."

"Dude, was only waiting for your Secret Agent Ears to return to the War Room. And that's what this is all about. Not so much the war, but what Gaultier, Titan, and YatesCorp gain by us being at war."

"Titan makes weapons, so I can see that one," Uncle Mort said. "But I hope you have more than just good guessing."

"*Et tu*, Uncle Wrinkle? *Et tu*? Of course I have more. We were more than halfway there earlier, when we were discussing what we'd have done if the Guantanamo attack had worked out how the Mastermind wanted. We'd be in chaos and running scared. We'd be looking for a new safe haven. It's amazing how your morals shift when you think the country you swore allegiance to has betrayed you in the worst way possible."

"You think we'd join with our enemies?" Jeff sounded appalled. It was always endearing when the reality of how basically *decent* the majority of A-Cs were waved at me. The humans in the room were all nodding their heads in agreement with me. The A-Cs looked shocked and uncomfortable.

Mahin, however, had been raised as a human. "Kitty's right. Enemies of the United States would be lining up to give you all a new home base."

"You tip the balance of power. You always have. But there's more. If they'd succeeded in destroying the Science Center, we'd have lost, what, half of your people? And most of your women. Jeff, you've said this to me before—having a choice of interspecies marriage is one thing. Having no choice in the matter is another. So we'd be very open to options. And, you know, you, Serene, and Christopher are all okay, right? And Jamie and Patrick are advanced but not freaks, right?"

"I know where you're going with this," Jeff said. "You think we'd okay giving the new version of Surcenthumain to our people."

"Well, you'd have to. Because regular humans would already be taking it, and that would mean they were catching up to the A-Cs. Junkies and criminals and experimental teenagers and casual drug users would all be super powered. Then, once they didn't all drop dead, soldiers would be taking the drug."

"Soldiers on all sides, by the way," Tito said. "The drug replicates and continues to expand powers."

"And it's addictive," Christopher added. "Very addictive. You want more because of how it makes you feel, and then you want more because of how it changes you."

"I'm betting the new stuff is even more addictive. So self-defense and preservation would say that the A-Cs would need to bulk up in turn, so to speak."

"You're talking about an arms race but with drugs, versus weapons," Chuckie said.

"I point to Exhibits A, B, and C." I indicated Serene, Jeff, and Christopher. "What Christopher, in particular, could do after he shot up Surcenthumain for a while was nothing short of amazing. Imagine what we could do if everyone had the new strain running through their veins."

The room was quiet for a few long moments. Amy broke the silence. "So, short of burning Gaultier to the ground, how do we expose what they're doing?"

"I don't think we can expose anything, Ames. Gaultier's got too many ties to too many different yet important places. Same with YatesCorp. Hell, Titan was proven to be building freaking supersoldiers that they sent against the President of the United States and all of Congress, and yet there they are, back in business, and everyone's acting like they just had a little run of bad management."

"Then what are we going to do?" Naomi asked.

"We're going to go very Old Testament on their butts." This earned a lot of blank looks, though Mom put her head in her hand and Uncle Mort grinned.

"Mind explaining that?" Jeff asked.

"An eye for an eye, a tooth for a tooth. We're going to find their drugs and destroy them, along with the formulas and all their data. Sorry, Ames, but we're going to run your father's company out of business."

"Fine with me," Amy said. "I can always rebuild it, this time without secret levels of evil and aligning with every maniac in the world."

"What does YatesCorp gain out of all of this?" Mom asked. "Their connection isn't clear, and you can't convince me that Amos Tobin wants to add on anyone else to their Board, let alone a bunch of unknown Yates relatives."

"He doesn't, I'm very sure. There's a possibility he's willing to add on a whole bunch of yes-men and -women to gain a stronger power base. There's also a possibility that he's not involved and the Yates Gene Project is being driven by Gaultier or Titan or both, so that they can gain more control of YatesCorp. There are other possibilities, too."

"Here's one," Tito said. "The Yates Gene is corrupted, because of his combining with the Mephistopheles parasite, meaning the only pure samples of his DNA come from Richard, Gladys, or Lucinda."

"Assume they have a sample from Gladys. If they wanted it, they'd have gotten it from her using mind control."

Tito nodded. "So, based on what we know they've created— androids and supersoldiers and copies of every male of influence in Centaurion Division—my bet for their next steps would be cloning. The bait given to the genetic samples may be to get a seat on the YatesCorp Board. But the goal of those behind the plan may be to clone another Ronald Yates."

"Or another Mephistopheles," Tim suggested.

"Tito Hernandez, put on your cape and join Team Megalomania and stand right there next to Megalomaniac Lad. Because those sound like winner ideas to me. So to speak. So, we pretty much need to ensure we wipe every piece of data Gaultier has, except possibly the information on their baby wipes."

"I wouldn't trust those, either," Reader said.

"Kitty, that sounds like a great plan," Stryker said. "But you're forgetting one thing. Chernobog is working for the other side. That means they'll have protections in place that, frankly, we probably can't hack."

Looked at Olga. "But we have the best leverage in the world. And I'm not afraid to play hardball. Olga, what's the best way for us to contact Chernobog in a private manner she'll respond to?"

"I can provide an old KGB code that will absolutely gain her attention."

"Boo-yah, you rock. Mahin, what's Russell's power? Does he have any?"

She shook her head. "I don't know. I didn't see any example of talent or power from him. But everyone acted as though he was very important."

"He is and was. He was the key to getting the world's best hacker on their side."

"What are you planning to do with him?" Jeff asked.

"Honestly? Something I'll only discuss with Mom, Chuckie, Kevin, Malcolm, Olga, and Uncle Mort."

Jeff stared at me. "And why is that?"

"Because you'll be too busy with Tito, working to finalize the identification process of the Yates Gene."

CHAPTER 77

"IT'S GOING TO TAKE MORE THAN A DAY, Kitty," Tito said.

"I know. But you guys need to get started. And we need to prep for our commando raid, and the rest of you need to prep for the funeral. So, off you go."

"I'm not letting you do whatever without me," Jeff said firmly.

Mom rolled her eyes. "Let me make this easier for you, Jeff. I know exactly what to do with the prisoner we have, and I don't need anyone other than Olga and Mort."

"Works for me." It did. I was sure that Mom wasn't going to be against doing terrible things to Kozlow if it was needed, and after all that had happened, most of it due to Chernobog working with our enemies, I was more than happy to have her bring out the Zippo lighters and trained rats. However, Jeff was never pro this kind of thing. "You want to take some Poofs with you?" Hey, the Poofs were with me on the Tough Interrogation side of the house.

Mom snorted. "Thank you, but no. I'm good."

"The best," Kevin said loyally. Buchanan and Chuckie nodded. All the rest of the men in the room nodded and added in Mom-based atta girls as well.

Uncle Mort laughed. "You have your boys trained well, Angela."

"I learned how to keep the troops in line from you, Mort."

"The love in the room is awesome. Mom, can we scatter?"

"Everyone but you, kitten, yes. My team, I expect you back in ten." Jeff opened his mouth, to protest, most likely, but Mom put up her hand. "I need my daughter for five minutes, Jeff. You can handle the separation."

Jeff closed his mouth and gave me a quick kiss on the cheek. "I can't feel anyone because Chuck brought those blockers. So promise me you'll let me know before you run off again."

"I promise."

"If only I believed you." Jeff kissed my cheek again, then he ushered out any stragglers and closed the door after Uncle Mort wheeled Olga out, accompanied by Adriana. The room went from packed to almost empty in a matter of moments.

Mom turned off the video conference. "We'll get what we can out of Kozlow and Chernobog, but that can take time. You're rolling a huge con and an infiltration at the same time, and I can guarantee something's going to go wrong. So, what's the backup plan?"

"I plan to not need a backup plan."

Mom shook her head. "You're going into a part of Gaultier that your hacker team, Amy, and three A-Cs couldn't find. How are you even planning to get in?"

"I found the secret gate that's in the Embassy." Brought Mom up to speed on the gate and my plan. "So, I know Amy has the blueprints of the Gaultier building that we lifted because she had Stryker print them out. Based on how Gladys got us to Guantanamo, I think I can just have a room that's on one of the secret levels in my mind and get us there."

"But you aren't sure, and you weren't able to test this gate in a real situation fully," Mom said when I finished. "You got *to* Guantanamo using it, but you didn't get *out* using it. And you were in far less danger in Cuba than you will be going into Gaultier. So, what's the backup?"

"Call for a floater gate."

"And what if that doesn't work?"

Considered this. "Blast our way out?"

She sighed. "It's a time honored way to fail, I'll give you that."

"Thanks for the confidence boost, Mom. It worked for Han, Luke, and Chewie."

"They ended up in the garbage, I'd like you to recall. Which is fitting because I think you're going to have company at Gaultier far sooner than you're expecting you will."

"But we have that super speed and all that. It works really well for sneaking about."

"Yes, but even if we ignore the fact that there will inevitably be security personnel and measures you're not prepared for, fast or not, somewhere along the line someone's going to figure out Francine is not you. The moment that's discovered, there will be nothing Amy can do to keep anyone from Gaultier at Michael's funeral. And it *will* be discovered."

"Everyone's been practicing, and our body doubles are fooling our own husbands."

"That's nice. Has anyone considered the fact that there will be people in attendance who know you well but who are not part of the real inner circle? People like Nathalie Brewer and Vance Beaumont? Both of whom are going to expect to be comforting you. Both of whom know you well enough to blow Francine's cover without trying or meaning to. And neither of whom are trustworthy enough to allow in on this plan."

Hadn't thought of this particular wrinkle. Damn. Knew why Mom was in the position she was—if I was the President I'd want her covering my butt, too. "Ah, boo-yah denied. No, you got me on this one, Mom. But they're trustworthy. Nathalie probably more than Vance, but still."

"Kitten, no they're not. Any more than your friends at the Bahraini and Israeli Embassies can be told. People talk. They tell a 'secret' to the wrong person. You have too many people who know about this raid already. Commando raids only work when *only* a handful know when and where a small team is going. You have a small commando team, but a huge distraction team, and someone somewhere is going to blow your cover."

"So, what do you suggest?"

Mom gave me a long, appraising look. "Do you want the recommendation from your mother or from the head of the P.T.C.U.?"

Interesting question. "I'd like to hear both."

"Fine. As your mother, go to bed, call off the raid, call off the subterfuge, handle Gaultier another way, go to Michael's funeral and regroup."

"Okay, what's the head of the P.T.C.U.'s suggestion?"

"Slip everyone's husband a mickey and go tonight."

Let that sit on the air for a few moments. "So, that's why you had Chuckie bring the emotional blockers he found on the prisoners into the Embassy."

Mom smiled. "I have no idea why Eddy and the others think you're an idiot."

"Protective coloration."

"Yes, Charles has explained that theory to me."

"Speaking of which and whom, I think I'd prefer if you demanded that the men all help you with prisoner interrogation. Chuckie, Jeff, and Christopher are already expecting to go to that with you anyway. You can have the flyboys along for added muscle, which would get Joe and Randy out of the way. Maybe tell Brian you want him with you to add the pathos and rage of the best friend spin to the fun, in case it's needed."

"Drugging them is easier."

"But it's so Bad Guy Move. I'd rather try it the Good Guy Way. At least for this."

"If you insist. However, if you're going to do the raid, either tonight or during the funeral, then I strongly suggest you leave Naomi and Abigail Gower at the Embassy."

"Why?"

"Naomi was already given the new drug, meaning it's working on her. She said herself that some of her power is back, even though it's just a small amount. If you're actually successful, you're going to find that drug. Evander Horn is hoping you'll find all of it, and if you do, that's going to mean more drugs in one place than I honestly believe you can imagine. An entire candy store filled with free sweets is a hard thing for a sugar addict to avoid."

"Abigail didn't get shot up."

"She's got her sister's example, though. They're close. It wouldn't be hard to believe Naomi could convince Abigail to try the drug, too."

"I don't think she would, Mom. Naomi was given one dose and it was flushed out of her almost immediately. Could she really become addicted that quickly?"

"Ask Christopher how fast he was addicted. To a less virulent form of this drug, I might add."

The door opened and, speak of the devil, Naomi came in. Awkward.

"You're right, Angela, my powers are back somewhat. And the emotional blocker doesn't work on me. I know why you're worried, and I understand that. But I want you to know that I would never do something to harm my sister, let alone anyone else I love."

"No addict believes they're harming anyone," Mom said calmly. "That doesn't mean they aren't, just that they don't see it. Usually until it's too late."

Naomi shook her head. "I'm not addicted. And I've seen the ground we have to cover—Kitty needs our help. They murdered my brother and gave my aunt the feeling she needed to die to protect us. I want this stopped before more lives are lost and families irreparably damaged."

"Then stay here and run interference with the husbands," Mom suggested.

"No. Kitty needs us, so we're going. Period. And you're not my mother, so don't think that you can tell me what to do. Like Kitty, I was raised to think for myself and to do what I know is right. And I know this is right."

Mom didn't look convinced. But all she did was shrug. "Believe me, Naomi, I'd love to be proven wrong about this. So, you remember that I'm expecting you to come back and show me that I was wrong. Because I don't want to have to say 'I told you so.' I'll say it if I have to, but I'm not looking forward to it."

Naomi grinned. "I look forward to proving you wrong, Angela."

"Great, we're all good to go, then. Mom, any suggestions for how I get the word to my team, three of whom are, like me, mothers of small children, that they're going out tonight without their family's knowledge *without* triggering suspicion in either Jeff or Chuckie? And don't say 'send them a text' because that will just mean it's the one night everyone's husband reads their texts for whatever reason."

"So, you're set on doing the raid?"

"Did you seriously think I wouldn't be?"

She smiled. "No. I know you. I'll take the men with me in an hour or so. That will give you time to grab your team. Have the children brought over to your apartment. Your father will enjoy watching the boys and Jamie enjoys bossing them around."

"Really? I've never seen her do that."

"She does," Naomi confirmed. "She's definitely her mother's daughter."

Mom laughed. "True enough."

"I feel the love."

"Speaking of which, if any of them don't sound enthusiastic about going, leave them and have them cover for you here. They need to be at least as determined to go as Naomi is or you don't want them along."

"What about the Princesses?" We were going into battle. There was no way Rahmi and Rhee wouldn't be enthusiastic beyond belief.

"They're doing a ritual to honor Gladys," Naomi said. "And Rhee told me the higher ranking the warrior the longer it takes, so for Gladys it's going to take hours."

Unless of course they were doing a religious ritual for a fallen female warrior, and then, maybe not. "Ah. Then I don't know if we want to interrupt them."

"No, we don't," Mom said. "And it would be wise to have them watching Mahin, just in case. I'll use my 'warrior status' and leave them instructions for when they're done, but I agree with Naomi—this is not the time to interrupt them, chances for glorious victory or the honor of noble defeat or not." Mom's sarcasm knob went well past eleven.

"Works for me. How are you going to explain why Malcolm isn't with you and the other men?"

"Simple. I'm going to tell your still jealous but hiding it so much better husband that I was furious that Malcolm had let you go to Cuba without him, and he's assigned to literally sleep outside your door."

"Mom, that's mean. Jeff's upset enough."

"True. But I already told Malcolm he was to stay in the Embassy for at least the next week, so I'll share that with Jeff. If you're here, so is Malcolm. I know he's clear about that."

"I don't have my Glock any more."

Mom sighed. "I'll make sure I leave one for you in your room."

"You rock, Mom, thanks."

Mom stood up, so presumably this meeting was over. Naomi was already standing so I joined the club. Mom gave me one of her breath-stopping bear hugs. "Be careful, kitten," she said quietly. "For every successful capture of Osama Bin Laden there's an Iran Hostage Crisis. And many times, which place in history you end up in is determined by the blink of an eye, a split second decision, or whether or not a small piece of equipment does or doesn't work."

Hugged her back. "I'll do my best, Mom, I promise."

She kissed my head. "I know you will, Kitty. That's why I'm letting you go. And I'm your backup plan. If you can't get out, you find a way to let me know. And I'll get you out."

"You got it, Mom."

"Great. Now, you two go lie to your husbands. Naomi, it'll be a little more challenging for you, but, trust me, men are easy to fool. Just focus them on food, sports, or sex, and you'll be fine."

Naomi and I exchanged a glance. "I know which one I'm voting for," she said.

"And with my mom's permission and everything. Boo-yah reinstated."

CHAPTER 78

WE DECIDED THAT NAOMI would tell her sister what was going on, and then Abigail would play Post Office and tell the other girls what was going on. We included Amy in this, since we needed the blueprints and, if we were going tonight, she could go along if she was properly thrilled and enthusiastic up to Mom's standards.

Mom would advise Buchanan, who would be assigned to alert Adriana. In this way, the two of us with the husbands most likely to catch on would be essentially clear and free and out of it, and Naomi wouldn't have to try to lie to Chuckie about what was going on, because she could truthfully say she just wanted to talk to her sister to ensure they had couple time.

Finding Jeff wasn't difficult—he was lurking down the hall from the conference room. "What did your mother need to say to you?" Showing that he wasn't an idiot, either, he sounded worried and suspicious.

"Girl stuff." Nudged up against him. "Along the lines of us maybe doing something to take our minds off of all the bad stuff that's been happening."

Jeff brightened up. "I have the best mother-in-law in the world."

"True enough. I think Mom's planning on doing prisoner interrogation soon, and that means taking you with her."

Jeff's eyes drooped a little and he got the "jungle cat about to eat me" look on his face. "Then we'd better take care of our much more important business right away."

Excellent. The finding and the convincing were handled and I could at least look forward to some happy times in the very near future. However, where to go to do the deed was a problem. Dad and Jamie were upstairs, meaning that if we went upstairs, sex was going to be the last thing we were having.

Sure, I was the Chief of Mission, but us "taking a guest room" in either the Embassy or the Zoo was going to raise some questions, and I just didn't feel like essentially broadcasting that we were going to go have sex to the entire complex. Same with sneaking into any rooms in the complex—if we did, the odds went up to 100% that someone would walk in on us.

The basement and tunnels were out. Not only were there cameras in the tunnels, doing it in the basement wasn't sexy so much as nerve-wracking, because a part of me didn't trust that something horrible wasn't going to come up from the tunnels and attack.

Leaving the Embassy complex was out for a variety of reasons. And on and on.

As I saw it, this left us only two options. "So, do we go for the location that keeps on giving and lock down one of the elevators, or do we sneak down to the garage and do it in the back of one of the limos?"

Jeff considered. "I don't want to have to use hyperspeed." He grinned. "I'm not against it, but I don't want to be limited."

"Oooh, I like where your head's at. Garage it is."

Jeff took my hand and we zipped to the stairs leading down to the underground garage. For a race of people who couldn't handle human machinery like cars and planes because their reflexes were actually *too* good, the A-Cs sure had a lot of nice cars and planes. It was one of the many perks of being a part of American Centaurion, and none of the humans ever complained.

My Lexus IS 300 was here now. I rarely if ever got to drive it, but I wanted it at hand in case I had the time. I loved that car. However, its backseat was not made for sexy times, at least not with a guy as big as Jeff.

We picked a limo without a baby seat in it, Jeff got in the

back, and I plugged in my iPod. Put on Jewel's *0304* album. It was actually her more rocking album, at least for Jewel, meaning not rocking to anyone but Jewel fans. But I liked it, and it was great background music for doing the deed since at least half the songs on it were about being in and making love.

"Mmmm, I'm glad you put on the skirt when you changed," Jeff purred, as I joined him in the backseat and "Run 2 U" came on. He was already lying back and had his jacket and tie off. He pulled me over so I was straddling him then shoved the skirt up slowly, running his fingers over my thighs as he did so.

This caused me to grind against him, just to get comfortable and all. It was very comfortable, especially since I could tell he was definitely ready to go.

His hands slid up my body, then he slowly and sexily unbuttoned my shirt while I moved in time with the music and resisted the strong urge to beg him to go faster. Once my shirt was finally open, he ran his fingertips over my exposed skin. By now I was ready to go, and his touch sent tingles through my body.

I contemplated doing the same with him, but patience was rarely my watchword, especially when it came to seeing Jeff naked. I ripped his shirt open. He grinned as I ran my hands over his chest, letting my fingers run through the hair, over his pecs, and down his abdomen.

Jeff gave a low growl, slid my shirt to my mid-back, then used it to pull me to him. He kissed me deeply, one hand behind my head, the other stroking the small of my back. Our tongues twined as I rubbed my chest against his.

As "Leave the Lights On" came on, Jeff moved me back to a sitting position and, using a well-practiced move, flicked my bra open with his thumb. "Now," he purred, "that's better. I like to see the sexiest girl in the galaxy up close."

He began to toy with my breasts while I kneaded his chest in return. When we were like this it was a competition—see who could hold out the longest.

I usually "lost" because, frankly, whenever I looked at Jeff's bare chest, I wanted to get my mouth on it as fast as possible, and tonight was no exception. Besides, I never considered my face against Jeff's chest to be losing in any sense of the word.

He chuckled as I nuzzled between his impressive pecs. "You held out a whole five seconds, baby. Could be a new world record."

"Mmmm." My mouth and tongue were busy and didn't feel the need to chat.

Jeff's fingers slid over my back and then toyed with my neck. This caused me to grind against him. Which caused him to pull me up to ravage my mouth again. I was good with that.

Once this kiss ended, Jeff held my hips so that I was balanced, but not on him. Then his lips, teeth and tongue went to work on my neck. I wasn't in a position to do too much, other than moan and shove my hips against his hands. Grabbed the door to keep my upper body lifted.

This caused my breasts to brush against Jeff's chest, which was beyond arousing. For both of us, because he shifted me again and took one breast into his mouth, then the other, back and forth, until I was at my go-to move—wailing like a cat in heat.

As was normal, I was mostly incoherent by this time. Jeff had gotten really good at figuring out what my various wails and moans meant, so even though there were emotional blockers in the Embassy, he wasn't missing a beat for what to do to ensure that he continued to be able to be called Mr. 2nd Base.

As his tongue slid in between my breasts, I went over the edge. As always, this was Jeff's signal to step up his game.

Hyperspeed and A-C strength were good for many things. Getting out of pants and underwear were only two of them. Jeff lifted me up with one hand, slid my panties off with the other, and put me back down, all in about two seconds. I used that time to unzip his pants. Hey, I was doing my part.

Once he had me straddling him again, I did my best to get to my favorite body part. I mean, I was a fan of all of Jeff's parts, but, you know, a girl had her preferences. As "2 Become 1" came on, I succeeded. Jeff's jungle cat look was matched with a smooth jungle cat move as he slid into me.

My head fell back as we started to truly bump and grind.

Jeff rocked his hips and I rocked mine as well, riding him while my legs squeezed against his sides and my hands clutched at his abs and chest.

We were like this for quite a while, our bodies moving faster and faster, heading toward frenzy. As "Doin' Fine" came on, so did I. Loudly. As I began to quiet a bit, Jeff bucked and I fell forward. His hands caught my breasts and he lowered them to his face so that he could tease them both at the same time. Meanwhile, I was holding onto the side of the car again, some to keep myself from just collapsing on him, and some because the position my body was in was a good one for building up to another orgasm.

While Jeff sucked, stroked, squeezed, and nibbled at my breasts, he continued to thrust into me. I let him build me back up, then, breath somewhat caught, I matched his rhythm again.

This was great for a while, but this really was a good spot for me, and I started going faster and faster. As my movements became more and more frantic, he sucked harder on my breasts and growled against my already hypersensitive skin.

Sure enough, this flipped me over again. Happily we were in the garage and the limos were pretty soundproofed, too, because otherwise someone was going to come down to see how mating cats had gotten in here.

"Sweet Temptation" came on as Jeff gently sat me upright again, hands still on and massaging my breasts. "Stretch for me, baby," he purred. I did, hands up on the inner roof of the car, back arched. Jeff's purring increased. "God, I love it when you do that."

Decided to see if he loved something else, and while he was thrusting, I moved like I was twirling a hula-hoop. It was a small, circular, intense movement. Felt great to me, and, based on Jeff's gasps and stronger thrusts, it felt great to him, too.

Kept time to the song, which was a mid-tempo number. Jeff was getting more and more out of control, and I enjoyed being in a position to both cause it and see it. The song changed to "Yes U Can," which was a faster song. I sped up accordingly.

Jeff's hands went to my hips and he clutched at me. "Kitty . . ." he panted, "God . . . so good . . . I can't . . ."

"Oh, yes you can," I said in my own purr. He wasn't the only one who was close to the edge, and I clenched around him.

He shouted and erupted in me, which triggered another climax for me. Our bodies shook in time together as we both rode the wave of pleasure and satisfaction.

Finally we both relaxed and Jeff gently pulled me back down to him and kissed me. "I love you, Kitty," he murmured as he ended our kiss. "And you can do that move again any time you want."

"I love you, too, Jeff. And how about right away, only this time at hyperspeed? Christopher says I should practice all the time, after all."

"God, I love how you think."

CHAPTER 79

MY PHONE BEEPED. I was snuggled on top of Jeff, my head pillowed on his chest, after several more rounds of fabulous sex. Much as a part of me just wanted to stay like this and pretend nothing else in the world mattered, I knew duty was calling. Or, in this case, texting.

Sat up and stretched. Jeff gave me a lazy, satisfied smile. "Well, I feel ready to face the night."

"Mmm, me too."

After a few more long, lingering kisses, we got our clothes buttoned back up and such, then I checked my phone. Sure enough, it was a text from Mom saying she wanted to get people pulled together to go do prisoner interrogation.

Jeff took me upstairs so he could say good night to Jamie and Dad. This was fine with me—my team was going to be leaving from here anyway.

"Who's going over with you?" Dad asked.

"Me, Christopher, James, Chuck, Kevin, the flyboys. Apparently Angela wants them along for extra muscle. Brian's going, too."

"That's a lot of people," Dad said, making me wonder if Mom had filled him in on what we were doing or not. Remembered my father's ability to lie was, for the most part, not much better than the A-C's ability, and figured she hadn't.

"Mom wants to do the old Impressive Show of Force thing, and I think Bri's along to bring the pathos if it looks like it might work."

"I have a simple rule," Jeff said. "I don't argue with my mother-in-law unless I think it's a true life-or-death situation."

"It's always nice to know my daughter married a smart man."

Jeff grinned, hugged Dad, kissed and cuddled Jamie, then really kissed me. "You be good, baby," he murmured. "I'll be home as soon as possible."

"Good."

There was a knock at our door. We opened it to find Christopher and Amy there. "You ready?" Christopher asked Jeff.

"Yep. See you girls later." They zipped off.

Amy came in and shut the door. She picked up Jamie and chatted with Dad while we waited. Sure enough, about five minutes later Mom sent me a text. The menfolk were off-site and Chuckie had given the emotional blockers or enhancers to Serene.

Mom reminded me that they were going to a place where their cell phones wouldn't work, but she insinuated that Buchanan would be able to reach her if need be. Hoped both that she was right and that we wouldn't need to reach her.

"Okay, let's call the rest of the team," I said to Amy.

"I'll go get the blueprints." She handed Jamie to me and trotted out.

"Do I want to know?" Dad asked.

"You up for babysitting more than Jamie? And having the kids do a sleepover in the playroom?"

"Sure, kitten. As long as you tell me what's going on."

"I'll tell you once the other kids are here." Hopefully having her friends over would distract Jamie enough that she wouldn't be aware of what I and the others were doing.

Dad looked at Jamie then back at me. "That's fine."

Gave Dad a peck on the cheek, then trotted into my bedroom to get changed. Black pants, a long-sleeved black T-shirt that had Aerosmith's logo in a slightly different shade of black, comfortable black boots that looked like they were for hiking and other outdoor sports, and a black bandana were waiting for me. Clearly Algar planned ahead, or else he did his own silk-screening, because the T-shirt wasn't one that I owned. Well, I owned it now, but I hadn't purchased it.

"Like the shirt, thank you. And I hope this means you

approve of what we're doing." I started to get undressed but stopped. Looked around and checked carefully—if Algar was watching, he wasn't being obvious about it. Good.

Finished getting changed—despite having never seen these boots before and their looking brand-new, they were already broken-in and comfortable. "You do great work, I have to admit. Boots are super, thanks. And I note they have the quiet yet rugged soles, so thanks for thinking ahead."

Dumped my other clothes into the hamper. "I'd ask you why you let Gladys die, but I already know your answer. And while I still hate it, having heard your speech from my uncle, I get it. I still think it sucks, mind you, but I get it."

Took a deep breath and let it out. "I just hope you feel bad that she's gone, that's all. Well, not all, but all I can say right now." Wanted to thank him for helping, as much as he had, without making it so clear that I knew that he'd stop helping. Cleared my throat. "Oh, and thanks for the support. Clean clothes matter."

Contemplated another thing that needed to be handled. The Poofs and Peregrines had been planning their own raids during Michael's funeral. "Harlie, Poofikins, Bruno," I said in a low voice. They appeared. "Kitty's going to go into Gaultier tonight. I don't want my Poofs or Peregrines on this mission."

Harlie and Poofikins mewed their disapproval, while Bruno gave me a betrayed look.

"Kitty wants her Poofies and Peregrines safe. You'll be our backup plan, okay? Kitty will call for you if she needs you." Hey, Mom had wanted me to have a backup plan, and for all I knew we'd have a better shot of reaching the animals.

They grumbled a bit, but finally agreed to stay at home and on call. Gave them pets and pats and they disappeared.

Made sure my new Glock was in my purse, then trotted out as the rest of the girls, and kids, arrived. We were all dressed similarly, though each girl had the logo of her band of choice, in black, just like I did.

We all got a raised eyebrow from Dad, but he didn't say anything until Serene had the kids in the playroom, all watching *101 Dalmatians*, the animated version, which was a Daycare Favorite.

Once Serene gave us the thumbs up and confirmed that kidlet sleepover equipment was in place courtesy of the Operations team, I figured it was safe to share, so caught Dad up on the new, revised plan.

He nodded slowly once I was done. "I understand why your mother wants you to go tonight if you're going. After what happened in Guantanamo, no one would expect you to do anything other than go to bed and regroup. But are you girls sure this is the right thing to do? Especially since your husbands have no idea of what's going on?"

"There's plenty of times you don't know what Angela's doing, Sol," Amy said as she spread the blueprint copies out on our dining room table. "That doesn't mean she shouldn't be doing it."

To Dad's great credit he didn't make comparisons between our skill levels and Mom's. "True enough. Let me know if you need any help. I'm going to keep an eye on the kids." Dad gave me a kiss and went to the playroom.

Another knock at the door revealed Buchanan and Adriana. It was clear Buchanan had been dressed by Algar, because he, too, had a band logo T-shirt—Buchanan apparently favored Motörhead. I approved. Meaning Adriana was odd girl out. Went to my closet. "Really? Adriana doesn't get a shirt?" A shirt appeared. "Thank you, King of the Elves." Trotted out and handed it to her. "We have a theme."

She laughed. "Nightwish! I love them."

"I guessed." I guessed because it was the band on the shirt, but why spoil the illusion that I'd been this prescient?

"Is this everyone?" Buchanan asked.

Did a fast headcount—me, Amy, Naomi, Abigail, Claudia, Lorraine, Serene, Adriana, and Buchanan. "Yep, we're all here."

While Adriana changed shirts, we went over the blueprints one more time. Happily, the version Amy had had compiled by Hacker International from all the various sources, so we possessed what we felt was the most accurate representation of what Gaultier Research really looked like structurally. It looked very large, especially the three hidden, lower levels.

"I think we need to assume that the three lower levels are

close to the tunnels," Buchanan said as Adriana rejoined us. "Especially since we haven't found an entrance from the public Gaultier facility."

There was something about how he'd said the word "we." "Malcolm, have you talked to Camilla about this?"

He smiled. "Who?"

"Oh, fine. I still think Chuckie's being a jerk not letting us coordinate with her on this."

"He's being smart," Buchanan said dryly. "You should be used to that by now."

"Yeah, we are," Amy said. "So, whatever, we'll handle it, since Kitty has a special way to get us over there. Anyway, per Big George, this room seems innocuous and should be a good place to enter and exit." She pointed to a small room roughly in the middle of the lowest hidden level.

"Why do they want us starting at the bottom?" Abigail asked.

"Makes sense. The most hidden level that's closest to the tunnels. I'd bet the worst stuff's down there, so might as well get us closer to it."

Amy nodded. "That was the thinking, yes. Check your phones—Stryker should have sent a copy of these blueprints to all of you."

"You told them what we were doing?" Buchanan asked. He didn't sound thrilled.

"No. They were supposed to be going with you on this raid, if you were going during the funeral, remember? Since Abigail told me Angela wanted a small team and she also didn't mention telling the computer lab team about tonight's raid, I told them Kitty wanted these for the official raid and that we were all going to be getting used to figuring out how to use them right tonight. I'm not a total moron."

"Malcolm's job is to ask those questions, Ames. But good cover story."

"That's what I told Walter, too, and Jennifer and Jeremy," Amy said.

"Good, so if anyone's looking for us, they'll assume we're together and working." Our own people were the least of our worries, of course.

"How are we getting in if we can't find the actual door?" Claudia asked. Speaking of those other worries.

Explained how the special gate worked, and where it was. Many doubts were raised about us actually getting where we wanted to go. "If Gladys could follow a dream and have it work, I can follow a blueprint and have it work."

"And what if you're wrong?" Buchanan asked calmly.

"Supposedly I can't end up in a wall or inside another person, so I can test it if you want."

"No. You're not going over there without me, and we have no idea what we will or won't trip going in, so it's either you and me, only, or it's all of us, but we're not going to play around. Once we go, we *go*."

"Fine. In the same vein, we can study this all night long, or we can get moving. Mom wanted me to make sure that no one's going merely for the thrill, or because they think they'll be considered less worthy or anything. If even a part of you thinks this is a bad idea, you'll do us more good staying here."

There were a few moments of silence. Naomi's hand went up, then Abigail's, and Amy's.

"I brought extra bombs for everyone," Serene said, sounding disappointed. "I mean, I'm sure it won't be a problem if they don't divide up evenly now that three of you aren't going."

"Wait, what?" Amy asked. "I thought we were raising our hands to show we were in! That's why I put my hand up."

"Me too," Abigail said.

"Three," Naomi said. "I already said I was going, no ifs, ands, or buts. Thought I was being the tough girl leading the way and showing my solidarity with our leader."

We girls all burst into laughter, Buchanan looked like he thought he was now chaperoning a Senior Girl Scout Troop, and Serene happily handed out her Bomb Party Favors.

"I also have twenty-petabyte flash drives for each of us, so that should we find the data, we can download the data," Amy said, as she handed her Geek Party Favors out.

"Can we download that data without one of the hackers?" There had been a good reason to want them along, after all.

Lorraine and Claudia nodded. "Sure," Lorraine said. "How hard could it be?"

"We work with computers all the time," Claudia added.

"We can always call Stryker," Amy said. "It's not like they ever seem to sleep."

Buchanan shook his head. "Well, we're a finely oiled machine already, Missus Chief. I'm betting we get caught within three minutes of arriving."

"Oh, Malcolm, you disappoint me. I expect to be caught within one minute and then talk my way out of it. Like always."

CHAPTER 80

THE FOUR MOTHERS said good night to our children, who were all pretty much ready to go to sleep and were just waiting for their kisses.

"Where are you going, Mommy?" Jamie asked drowsily.

"Girls' night out."

"Can I go?" she asked with a yawn.

"Not this time, it's for big girls only. But one day you'll be big enough to go with Mommy, and that will be fun." Wondered if Mom had ever had conversations like this with me, and figured she probably had. Lots of them. Kissed Jamie one last time, hugged Dad, and went to the isolation bedroom.

The entire team agreed that the placement for the hidden gate was both ingenious and really awkward. However, we presumed that touch would continue to work its magic and pull everyone else along, since it had for me and Gladys.

Most of the team were wearing black backpacks. I wasn't. Instead, I hooked my purse over my neck. Why change what had been working all this time?

Buchanan insisted on being the person holding my hand, and Adriana insisted on bringing up the rear. Let everyone else link up however they wanted because, really, I hoped it wouldn't matter.

We all did one last equipment check, then I looked at the blueprints—which we'd brought to the isolation room and put onto the bed—one last time. Got the image of Gaultier Research in my mind, then the specific room. "Link up."

"Ready," Adriana said.

"Then hold tight and do not let go for anything." With that, I put my hand onto the gate.

As before, the trip was immediate and pleasant. The room wasn't completely dark—there were a couple of red lights on opposite sides. Happily, all of us were here.

"It's hot in here," Abigail said in a low voice. "Is that what we were expecting?"

"This looks like a control room of some kind," Adriana replied in kind. "For power grids or similar. It might control power to the whole facility, or at least the underground portion."

The room did indeed resemble this—there were grids with muted dots of light, lots of levers and switches, and things that seemed very Power Company.

Looked around for the sparkly square and saw it right next to me. "Okay, everyone, see this?" I whispered as I pointed to it. "That's what you need to touch to get back."

They all looked at me blankly. Claudia waved her hand where I was pointing, and her hand went through the square. "There's nothing there, Kitty."

Why I couldn't spot the square when Gladys and I had been in Guantanamo seemed obvious now. "Crap. It's there. But I guess I'm the only one who can see it, and since Claudia actually touched it and nothing happened, that must mean I'm the only one who can activate it."

"Fantastic," Lorraine said. "So, we stick together."

"We have limited time," Buchanan said. "We could have less than five minutes. I realize hyperspeed makes many things easier, but we're not just looking to see what's here, we're searching to see what's going on. Computer downloads will not go as fast as you want, either."

"Malcolm's right, and the plan's always been to split up." Resisted the urge to curse. "Okay, we all know what room this is, we just make sure we're back here and, um together."

"We could all go back and come in separately," Serene suggested.

Before I could say that was a great idea Buchanan put his hand up. "Quiet." He was listening intently and I did the same. Sure enough, there were voices in the distance, coming nearer.

Amy was walking around the room, examining it. "There are two doors, that's what the lights are over."

Buchanan gave her a look that said he was already regretting this wasn't a solo mission.

The voices were getting closer, though I couldn't make out what they were saying, and they sounded like they were near the door opposite from the one Amy was at. She opened hers slowly and carefully.

As she did, the opposite door started to open. A-Cs grabbed humans and—instead of grabbing me and us all jumping back to the Embassy—ran through Amy's door. I could go back to the Embassy or follow my team. I followed, figuring that, for once, I honestly knew how Jeff, Christopher, Chuckie, and the rest of the guys felt when I did stuff like this.

Buchanan got the door shut behind me what sounded like just in time. He motioned for us to keep moving, and we did.

This room wasn't all that interesting because it appeared to be mostly huge pipes and similar. A-Cs have better vision, including night vision, than humans, so only the humans had penlight flashlights. But, other than being higher than normal, probably double the height of a floor on a regular building, this room didn't look like much.

Checked my phone—the blueprint confirmed we were in an L-shaped room. Realized that the blueprints weren't going to help us all that much. Worried for a second that we had only one way out, back the way we'd come in, but there was another door at the other end of the L.

Found a different, better reason to worry—my phone shared that it had no bars and no access to any network. Meaning not only could we not call out for help, but we couldn't call each other.

Sent Buchanan a text. "Really, Missus Chief? I'm right here." He looked at his phone. "Oh." We passed along the information that, from now on, all we had a hope for was in-system texting and that might only work if we were in close proximity.

"The generators in here are huge," Serene said as we walked along and around pipes and such.

"They look large enough to power a city," Claudia agreed.

"Which explains why there's no power drain anyone's noticed because of this facility," Lorraine added.

Ensuring that our luck remained consistent, when we reached the door at the far side of this room it was locked. Showing why Buchanan didn't need any of us along, he picked it in less than a minute.

We exited onto a short corridor. There was nothing to our left but wall, so we went right. Within a few feet we had a choice to turn right or zigzag left. Since we could hear voices to the left, but not clearly enough to understand what they were saying, we went right again.

We were in some sort of weird cubicle farm. There were partitions, and desks, but no barriers between workspaces, and no organized rows either. Sadly, no computer terminals, either.

Each workplace also had a locked metal cabinet attached to the floor. Buchanan picked the first one, then, seeing as there was indeed stuff inside, showed Naomi and Abigail how to pick the next ones. Being Dazzlers, they learned quickly. Adriana already knew how to pick locks, of course.

There were at least a hundred locked cabinets. Buchanan had the Gower girls and Adriana start unlocking while Claudia, Lorraine, and Serene handled the heavy lifting in terms of searching, since they were higher-level scientists than the Gower girls, and certainly a lot higher than the rest of us.

Amy and I were the slow learners of the group in terms of lock picking and searching, but before it became an issue, Buchanan put us on guard duty.

So, zigging and zagging, getting turned around, and backtracking, we managed to search every workspace. Because most of the team was using hyperspeed and Buchanan and Adriana were really efficient, this didn't take as long as it could have. But Buchanan was correct—it took a lot longer than a normal hyperspeed search.

"Most of this stuff has to do with facility maintenance," Lorraine said as we finished the last cabinet.

"There's something else down here," Abigail said. "Beyond what we've seen. The blueprints make it look like the 'outer' walls we're hitting are the real outside, but these rooms aren't coordinating correctly to the blueprints."

"They're not even, either," Serene said. "There isn't as much space in here as there should be."

Managed not to ask how they figured this. I was already hopelessly lost and unsure that I could find our return room without help. I wasn't focused on comparing where each wall sat. Though experience said that I should be.

Adriana nudged me. "I'm back. I found a door I believe we can use to get to the other levels."

She'd left? I hadn't noticed. I was really sucking as Commando Leader. Then again, I expected my team to use initiative, so I wasn't unobservant and unaware so much as a hands-off manager who allowed her personnel to use their own resourcefulness to solve challenges. Yeah, I could still cough up the marketing-speak when I needed to.

"Before we do, where are the people we've heard talking?"

Lorraine and Claudia looked at each other, nodded, and zipped off. They were back quickly. Presumed this was because they'd memorized the maze we were in already.

"There's no one down here but us right now," Claudia said.

"I didn't see or hear anyone when I went to recon the elevators," Adriana added.

"So that means Abby and Serene are right—there are other rooms on this level we haven't found entrances to yet."

"How do you figure?" Amy asked, while thumbing through what looked like the Gaultier version of the Briefing Books of Boredom that Lorraine had put down after her last cubicle search.

"We know people are down here. They went into our entry room, and they were in that area because we heard them. And now they're not here and they didn't stumble on us rifling through their secret stuff. So, they're elsewhere, on this level."

Adriana nodded. "There appears to be only one way to get to the elevator from here and I saw no one in that area, or even close to it."

"We need to find out what's hidden within the hidden level."

"We need to lock everything back up first," Naomi said.

"We haven't found what we came for, or anything useful

yet," Amy pointed out. "The information I've seen just looked like gibberish."

Buchanan stiffened. "Show me."

She handed him the big binder. "The words make sense, and yet they don't."

"There was nothing suspicious in any of that," Lorraine said. "At all."

"That's what I mean," Amy said.

"I agree with Ames. There's no reason something completely mundane should be locked in a cabinet, let alone in a cabinet in a secret level in the bowels of the earth."

Buchanan opened it, took one look, and closed the book. "It's in code. Your father could break this, I'm sure. Are they all the same?"

The A-Cs grabbed two books each and started comparing. Considered helping. Didn't feel confident enough in the skills to be able to guarantee I wouldn't rip the pages, so I refrained.

Didn't matter, they were done quickly. "No," Lorraine said. "They're all different."

"Then there's no choice," Buchanan said, voice clipped. "We need to copy all of them."

Naomi asked the question on everyone's mind. "Why?"

Buchanan heaved a sigh. It was clear he was, again, asking himself how he'd gotten assigned to the Girl Scout Troop. "They're very aware of how easy it is to be hacked—they just did it to you, remember? Anything that's written and coded and down *here* is of the highest-level importance. And that means we need to copy all this data and get it deciphered, as soon as possible."

"We don't have enough time, let alone have a copier machine handy," Amy pointed out.

"No copying equipment that I saw anywhere," Adriana said. The others all nodded.

Considered the dilemma. "Actually, I have a better idea."

CHAPTER 81

EVERYONE LOOKED AT ME EXPECTANTLY, which was nice. "We're just going to take them."

Got a lot of the "you so crazy" looks. "Wouldn't that be, I don't know, the exact opposite of being a covert team?" Naomi asked, clearly once again speaking for everyone.

Heaved a sigh and forged on. "If we cared that they knew we'd been here, then, yes, we'd need to copy these and leave no trace. But, point of fact, we *don't* care. Let them know we've retaliated. Let them panic, and, above all, let them freaking recreate the work they don't have on computer because they're going Old School for this one to avoid having their data found, stolen, or corrupted."

"If we didn't care, why did we bother to pick all these locks?" Buchanan asked, sarcasm knob definitely heading for eleven.

"Ahhh, well, we want to lock them back up. Confuse our enemies a little longer. Sort of thing."

"I have a different question," Adriana said, nicely saving me from my admittedly lame answer. "How are we going to get a hundred and ten binders of this size out of this facility?" She'd counted? She was Olga's granddaughter—of course she'd counted. "We aren't sure that we can get back into the room we came in through, in part because people may be in it. So how do we get out, let alone with all this data?"

I was about to admit that I had absolutely no idea when I heard a soft mewing. Looked into my purse—sure enough, despite my direct order to the contrary, I had Poofs on Board. Sent a silent thank you to Algar and gave myself a "duh" just to be fair. "Poofs assemble."

In moments there was a blanket of adorable fluffy cuteness at my feet. Resisted the urge to snuggle all of them—we had work to do. Decided saying I'd told them to stay home would be both stupid and pointless. "Poofies, can you help Kitty? We need these big binders to get safely home to the Embassy and to my dad. Can you help us do that?"

Harlie purred at me, mewled with authority to the other Poofs, and the Poofs went large, each one gulped a binder, then they went small and disappeared.

"I don't want to leave that way," Amy said. "If we have a choice, I mean."

"Look, I think we're okay now. Everyone has their own Poof, right?" Buchanan and Adriana cleared their throats. "Well, almost everyone and you two are on my mini team. So, for the rest of you, if you're in trouble once we separate, you call your Poof and ask for help getting out of here."

Naomi shook her head. "Kitty, they listen to you." Chose not to mention that, no, they didn't all the time, like tonight. "But when it's us they listen to us like . . . like . . ."

"Like cats or dogs do," Abigail finished. "If they feel like understanding, they do it. If not, not."

"They listen to Richard."

"Because he's with you when they do so and they want to," Naomi said patiently. "But, look, it doesn't matter. It's worth a shot, right? You mentioned separating. Who's going where?"

"You, Abby, and Amy can go to the floor above, Lorraine, Claudia, and Serene go to the one two levels up."

"What if we need locks picked?" Lorraine asked. "No one showed us how to do it."

Buchanan gave us all the brave smile of a Scout Master being forced to teach his troop something they weren't ready for just so they could get one more stupid badge. But he did it. First, he showed everyone how to relock something with the lock picks. Then, after Naomi, Abigail, and Adriana went off to lock up and Amy and I, Klutzy and Klutzier, were put back onto guard duty, he showed the others how to pick locks and lock them right back up again.

This task completed and everyone other than me and Amy sporting their Lock Picking Badge, we followed Adriana through the maze to a long corridor that ended at a steel door.

"Do we need to pick this lock?" I asked.

Buchanan gave me a look that said he feared that I'd taken a blow to the head that he'd missed somehow. He pointed to the flashing box on the wall near the door. "It needs a keycard."

"Do we have such a beast?"

"I do." He pulled a keycard out of his backpack. "Here's the thing—once I put this in it will short out this keycard lock and any others attached to it electronically. Once I pull it out, they'll all go back to normal."

"Wow, the government has some cool toys."

"It's Israeli," Buchanan said. "And it's still experimental."

"Sorry, Mossad has some cool toys." Didn't have to ask how he'd gotten it. Mom was former Mossad and still top of their Most Successful Graduate list. It didn't surprise me to discover they sent their prototypes to her for her to test out and give the thumbs up or thumbs down sign. For all I knew, Mom sent them requests for toys she'd like them to create.

"I'm stuck on the word 'experimental,'" Amy said. "Does that mean you don't know if it works or not?"

"Oh, it works, I've tested it already. The issue isn't whether or not it works. The issues are these. First, we don't know how many locks this will or won't affect—if they're all on the same grid, then it'll probably hit all of them. If they're not, we're limited to this one card. Second, if it works on more than one lock, then anyone trying to use a keycard-protected door will know that something's wrong, because their keycards won't work but the doors will open anyway."

"Where's the experiment in all that?" Naomi asked.

Buchanan shrugged. "We also don't know how long it will work."

"Wow, that adds a special level of excitement to all of this, doesn't it?"

"It lasted an hour when I tested it. I wasn't able to test any longer."

Chose not to ask why, because Buchanan's reason undoubtedly related to national, international, or galactic security. Maybe all three.

"Fine," Amy said. "So what do you propose we do? I thought we were going to split up. We can't do that safely if you only have one card."

"Sure we can." Got everyone's attention again, go me. "First off, this card works just like a regular badge scanner. If we just put it in and take it out, we can go in and out and no one's the wiser. These things blip all the time. Malcolm goes up with everyone while Adriana and I examine the rest of this floor, at least what we can find of it. He lets everyone in, comes back to us, and we move on with this floor. You guys send him a text when you're done, he goes to get you, and we regroup."

"What if we can't get through via text?" Claudia asked.

"Is it a perfect plan? No. And that's what I like about it. Lots of room for initiative and on-the-fly alterations."

"Lots of room to fail," Lorraine said. She shrugged. "On the other hand, it's as well-thought-out as any plan you've ever had, and considering your success rate is still the envy of the rest of Centaurion Division, I say we go for it."

I was the envy of Centaurion Division? Decided now wasn't the time to get the details, but it was still a nice ego boost. Chose not to ask if I was the envy because my plans were bad but we survived anyway. Figured I didn't need any confidence de-boosting.

"Good." Buchanan looked quietly pleased, and it dawned on me that he'd been testing us. Again. No wonder Mom and Olga both loved him.

He inserted the card, we opened the door, he pulled out the card, we all went through the door. Just like any other door in one of the Fortune 500 companies.

The door let us out into an elevator lobby. That's all that was here, a bank of elevators, floor, and walls. The walls, even the ceiling, were all murals that looked hand painted, the floor was Italian marble or I wasn't the Chief of Mission, and the chrome detailing on the elevators gleamed. Whoever had designed this section really wanted to show they had Taste and Refinement.

"This looks just like LaRue," Amy said dismissively. "So now we know who had at least a hand in whatever's going on down here."

"I'd figure she and your father started whatever, and the current crop are just keeping it going, Ames. But it proves we have secret rooms to find."

"Why so?" Naomi asked.

"Because this is a showcase entrance, but where we just came from is not overwhelmingly impressive. It didn't suck, but it also didn't say 'Top Dawgs Hang Here.' So there's something else down here that the Gaultier bigwigs take their special tour groups to see, and it's not what we've seen so far."

It was a good thing we'd chosen the Take the Special Keycard With Us route, because the elevators, of course, needed a keycard to run. However, Buchanan didn't want us using them anyway. "Nothing says 'someone unauthorized is in the building' like an elevator running when it's not supposed to." He looked around. "What facility doesn't mark its stairwells?"

"You mean other than every A-C base worldwide? Those who either don't have one or want to keep it hidden."

Adriana checked the wall opposite the door we'd used. "There's something here . . ." She pushed against it. Nothing. She shoved against the other side of what she felt was the door. Nothing.

Had an odd thought and went with it. Went to the wall where Adriana had pushed the first time. Pushed hard but quickly, more like a fast slam. The wall opened a little. "Or, someone who really wanted to show off how clever they were."

"How did you know?" she asked me as we opened what was absolutely a door.

"It works just like those cabinets that close magnetically. I don't think they're trying to hide this area so much as be arty."

"Yeah, again, that's a LaRue move," Amy agreed. She snorted. "Especially when we see what's in here."

What was in here were seven unisex bathrooms along the left-hand side and the stairwell at the far right corner. This room was done up just like the lobby, but the bathroom doors were more clearly marked. However, they opened in the same way as the door to the elevator lobby did—by pressing hard and fast.

Looked at Buchanan. "You thinking what I'm thinking?"

CHAPTER 82

"IF YOU'RE THINKING that we now can get upstairs without the elevators, Missus Chief, then, yes. If you're thinking something else, then no."

"Wow, Malcolm, I'm shocked. These are bathrooms."

Everyone gave me polite looks. "Do you need to go, Kitty?" Serene asked without a trace of sarcasm.

Resisted the urge to roll my eyes. "No. Bathrooms. What lives in bathrooms?"

"Bacteria," Lorraine answered promptly.

"And other things you don't want to know about," Claudia added.

"Oh, come on, you guys! Gates. Gates live in bathrooms, and Ronald Yates along with the freaking former Diplomatic Corps were best buds forever with Amy's dad and so forth. No wonder no one could find the entrance from the main research facility to this one. It's because no one was looking for a gate."

Abigail and Naomi hypersped through all seven rooms. "No gate," Naomi said when they finished "We looked for the mark, because I have to figure any gate they'd have here is cloaked, but there's nothing."

Knew exactly how Buchanan was feeling about all of our covert ops skills. "It's likely to be a cube, like in the bedroom. Look, I'll search for it while Malcolm helps you guys get going and start searching the other levels."

"I'll stay with Kitty," Adriana said before Buchanan could express the worry clearly written on his face.

"Faster you go, faster you're back," I pointed out.

He nodded. "I haven't found any hidden cameras yet, and they haven't triggered any of my trackers, but that doesn't mean there aren't hidden cameras, just that we haven't found or been caught by them yet."

"Yeah, no one's come to kill us. Yet."

"Be careful and don't leave this area without me, Missus Chief, no matter what you find, unless it's the choice between leaving and being captured, hurt, or killed."

"I promise, Malcolm."

He didn't look like he believed me, and the rest of the girls didn't, either. But they all went to the stairwell, Buchanan checked whatever he was checking, felt all was well, and the seven of them zipped off.

"Where do you want to start searching?" Adriana asked. "And, is it an American thing to have the walls so . . . brightly and garishly colored everywhere, including in the bathroom stalls themselves?"

"No, it's called protective coloration or hiding in plain sight. If everything's sparkly and garish, then the cube gate won't stand out as odd. As for where we start, I think we want to try the end." Because most people didn't go to the farthest point to use the facilities. When you had to go, you grabbed the nearest stall.

Went to the stall farthest from the elevators and therefore nearest to the stairs and started hunting.

These were the nice kinds of individual bathrooms that had a sink and toilet and table all in one room, versus a bank of stalls, very similar to what we had on the second floor of the Zoo. However the décor wasn't the same at all.

While the Zoo was done up in a Tasteful Rich Person Motif, Adriana wasn't kidding—the walls were a riot of color. This was I'm So Much Artier Than You to the max. However, I was sure much of this was being done on purpose, and not only to impress. "You try opening the hidden doors that may or may not be here and I'll see if I can find the cube gate."

We were at this for several minutes. It was amazingly hard to spot something that was likely to be a glittering geometric shape within a mural of glittering geometric shapes. The tiles that made up the bathroom were all little squares, just like the little squares that made up the power cubes. Had to hand it to LaRue, who was the likely designer—the woman was good. Sneaky, sneaky good.

"I can't find anything that seems to be a hidden door," Adriana said. Then she stiffened, went to the door, and opened it a crack. "Someone's coming," she whispered urgently. "And I think they're coming to this stall."

"It so figures." Hadn't found a thing hiding in plain sight here, and we had nowhere to go if someone opened the door. Locking it would just give us a couple of seconds and whoever was trying to get in here a clear sign that intruders were about.

Adriana pulled a gun from somewhere. Not that I thought anyone working here was going to fall on the Side of Right, but killing someone who just wanted to relieve themselves seemed really wrong. Plus sounds in bathrooms echoed and we really didn't want the entire facility alerted to our presence if we could help it.

Looked around frantically and, as I did, I noted that the tiles on the floor were the same small squares as everything else. And no one in their right mind wanted to put their hands on a bathroom floor, no matter how clean it looked.

Thought fast. It wouldn't be likely to be under the sink or right by the toilet, because those areas got cleaned the most and you wouldn't want to risk that the janitor was thinking of, say, how much he'd prefer to be on Hawaii's sandy beaches right when he wiped up around the hidden cube.

But it would still have to be easily accessible. The table in this room wasn't square, it was round, and, if I looked at it clinically, totally out of place.

Hyperspeed was good for many things and right now I was never happier that I had it available to me.

Grabbed Adriana, squatted down, pulled my phone out and randomly looked at a section of the top level while I honestly thought about how where I really wanted to be was with Buchanan, dumped my phone back into my purse, and slammed my hand onto the floor under the table just as the door started to open.

Half a moment later we were in a dark corridor. "Gah!" Buchanan jumped.

Amy, who was next to him, gave a little shriek. "What the hell?"

"Wow," I said as Adriana and I straightened up. "I didn't think you were a jumpy dude, Malcolm. Ames, breathe, it's just us."

"Normally I'm not jumpy, but when two women who are three floors away appear out of nowhere at my feet, it tends to throw me."

"What Malcolm said," Amy added.

"Good to know. But what do you mean by three floors?"

"The number of stairs between this floor and the one technically below it are double what they were to get from the bottom level to the next. But we found no entrance."

"And the blueprints don't show a fourth floor," Amy added. "So, how did you two find us?"

"Well, I think I was looking at the right section of the floor you were on. But I was also thinking of Malcolm, so maybe you can think of a person and the cube gates will work the same way. Which is, hopefully, good news." I was also hoping that, if this was the case, our enemies didn't know about it, because if they did, I had no idea how I'd ever keep Jamie safe.

Shoved that worry away for the moment while we brought Amy and Buchanan up to date on what had transpired. "So, what have you guys been up to?" I asked when we were done.

He opened his mouth, but Naomi and Abigail appeared out of nowhere. They'd only used hyperspeed, though, not a power cube, so Buchanan and Amy didn't freak out.

"It's the same all over," Naomi said. "Hey Kitty, Adriana."

"See? They're calm about our appearance."

"Yeah, nothing you do surprises me or Sis. But you all need to look at this, because it's . . . weird," Abigail said, as she grabbed Adriana. Naomi took Amy. They all zipped off. Decided I was obviously expected to keep up my end of the hyperspeed thing, took a hold of Buchanan, and we ran off after them.

This floor wasn't a maze—it was one big rectangle, at least the corridor was, and it went around the entire floor. The Gower girls zipped us around it all, presumably to ensure we'd seen all they had.

Other than the elevator banks, the outer side of the corridor was just wall, without artwork, done up in the usual industrially approved color of Boring Taupe. The elevator area was nothing like the one on the lowest level—these elevators just let you out, with no fanfare.

The inner side of the corridor had wall to about waist height, and the rest was smoked glass, or it was doors opening into the rooms. Smoked glass or not, these rooms were all lit by what I recognized as A-C style nightlights, and that meant we could see into them.

The rooms were normal sized, but the walls opposite the ones we were looking through were also mostly glass. They looked out onto a larger set of rooms. There were six of these larger rooms in the middle. Their walls divided them up so that, if you were in these interior rooms, you could see out toward the corridor but not to either side or behind. But it was what was in the rooms that was, as Abigail had said, weird.

Every room on this floor was completely empty.

No chairs, no desks, no cubicles, no electronics, no phones, no products, nothing on the walls, and no people. It was like looking at an abandoned warehouse. An abandoned, well-lit warehouse.

While the corridor and the rooms right off of it were lit only by low floor nightlight-style lighting, the six big interior rooms were lit like they were about to host the World Racquetball Championships. Come to think of it, they looked more like racquetball courts than anything else. However, there were no lines painted anywhere, so it seemed unlikely that Gaultier Enterprises had decided that what they really wanted for the top of their Secret Levels of Evil was a snazzy racquetball setup that didn't allow anyone watching to sit.

"Have you gone into any of these rooms?" I asked.

"Not yet," Naomi admitted. "We just got up here, really."

"Why? What was on the second floor?"

"The medical stuff," Amy said.

"Or, as we put it, where the contraband is being created and stored," Buchanan added.

I resisted the impulse to say that I was glad Buchanan hadn't left Naomi down there, but logic would have indicated that Lorraine, Claudia, and Serene do that level anyway. Plus

I was sure Mom had briefed him on her concerns regarding Naomi.

"The floor's set up just like this one," Naomi said. "Only every room is filled with laboratory equipment. And the middle rooms are filled with what we're pretty sure are drugs." She shook her head. "Your mother was right, Kitty. It's more drugs than I think any of us could have conceived of."

"What are the girls doing there?"

"They're getting in and grabbing a sample from each interior room," Buchanan replied. "And gathering what they can out of the anterior rooms as well."

"Are there people in there?"

"Yes," Amy said. "A skeleton crew. They looked like doctors or scientists, maybe lab techs. But they seem to all be humans because they didn't see anyone moving at hyperspeed."

Decided not to express worry. The girls were all on Alpha Team—they could handle whatever it was they needed to do, and they were dealing with what we'd expected to find, so, really, not a problem. Chose to focus on the current weird which might indicate a problem. "Then why is this level completely empty?"

"No idea," Buchanan said. "Unless the latest Gaultier drugs involve invisibility, there's no one and nothing to actually investigate."

"I wouldn't put anything past them. I note there are no bathrooms on this floor. Same on the other one?"

"Yes," Amy confirmed. "We checked."

"Was the elevator area the same as this floor? Boring and nondescript?"

"Yes," Abigail said. "We checked that, too. Why?"

"Because I'm trying to figure out why this building is set up this way. The elevator area makes a ton of sense if you're bringing people down to be all awed and impressed. But since the power cube gate is in the bathroom, that means it's likely that everyone's entering on the lowest level."

"They wouldn't need to," Naomi said. "The power cube goes where you want to go, right? So, if there's one in the normal Gaultier Research building, and I know you think there is, then it doesn't have to connect to the one in the bathroom you just found."

"Mimi, let me mention that I can state without reservation that Chuckie loves you for your mind as well as your looks and personality. Excellent point. So, you bring your tour group in here, or on the other floor, and then you take the elevator down for the Big Reveal."

"I'm worried about what that could be," Naomi said. "Because, honestly, after what we saw on the middle level, I can't imagine what they'd be showing off as more impressive."

"Sadly, I'm sure we're going to find out. But we're still back to the question of why this level is completely empty. Unless . . ." Studied the glass in front of us a little more. I could see our reflections. But I realized what was wrong—I could only see our reflections in the near glass. There was no corresponding reflection in the glass on the other side of the room.

"Stay here." Trotted around and confirmed it was the same all the way—I couldn't see a reflection of me anywhere other than right in front of me. And, when I was perpendicular to where I knew everyone else was, couldn't see them *or* the elevators.

Rejoined the team. "What a sneaky bunch we're dealing with. We need to get into these rooms, but carefully. There's honestly no telling what's inside. The glass is actually painted in some way or has some kind of movie being played against it, something—so what we're seeing is what they want us to see. Nothing."

"Be ready to run," Buchanan said, as he put his hand toward the handle. Abigail and Naomi took Amy and Adriana's hands. I took his free hand in mine.

Buchanan took the handle in his hand and turned it.

CHAPTER 83

"LOCKED." Buchanan let go of my hand, pulled out his lock picking set, knelt down, and got to work.

"Well, that was anticlimactic."

"Still be ready to run," he said. "We could have alerted someone that we're here." Kept my hand hovering over his shoulder. The lock clicked and Buchanan stood up quickly, took my hand, and blocked me and the others as he slowly opened the door.

He stopped, then opened the door a little wider. "Everyone speak very softly or not at all," he said over his shoulder. "And move quietly." Then he stepped inside and the rest of us followed.

It was easy to see why Buchanan wanted us quiet—we weren't in a room. We were on a large metal catwalk that went around the perimeter. Below us was the explanation for why there were extra stairs but no entrance to the "floor" below.

It was a fully automated assembly line. Lots of impressive, gleaming machinery, conveyors, vats, and more, all being run by robotics. It looked like everyone's vision of The Factory of the Future. There were two staircases down—one near us and one on the opposite side.

My phone buzzed in my hand. Lorraine wanted to know where we were. Told her, and they joined us. We all looked for a while, then Buchanan had us back out. He closed but didn't lock the door.

"Well," Claudia said, "that answers the one question we had."

"Which was where were they making the actual drug?" Lorraine explained.

"There are liquid and powder forms," Serene added. "And while the liquid forms are being created in the labs down below, they weren't making enough to explain the amount of the finished product we found."

"We did find pipes and tubing going up here," Claudia said. "This factory must take the raw serum from the science labs, duplicate the liquid form, dilute it for consumption, take some of it and reduce it to powder form, then package and feed the final products into the interior rooms below."

"I have a question. Do we know who Doctor Feelgood actually is?"

There was a distinct pause. "Ahhh, I don't follow you, Kitty," Serene said politely.

"So few ever do. I want to know if we know who created the newer version of the drug, who's behind it all. Is this all based on stuff Amy's dad created originally? Or on what someone else created originally? If so, who's making the new stuff? One person or a collective? Who has the formulas? Who comes up with the ideas for how to make the new versions? Because we need to not only get all of their data and notes, we need to stop them from creating the next level of this stuff, whatever it's going to be."

"Could be anyone out of Somerall, Gardiner, or Cross," Amy said. "They'd be my top picks."

"Maybe, but maybe not. They're the people running things at Gaultier now, yes. But that doesn't mean they're scientists, and even if they are, it doesn't mean they're scientists with the skills to create Surcenthumain and its scary derivatives. It takes a skilled scientist to create a drug that works, especially a superdrug like this."

"Do we want to go down and examine everything?" Abigail asked.

"No. Not yet." This was the start of the tour. We still needed to know what was at the end.

"Can I be sick now then?" Amy asked. "I'd be proud, if this was creating things like cancer cures or something. But this is creating nothing but death."

"Do we know that for sure?" Naomi asked.

"Well, we haven't tested any of the samples yet," Lorraine admitted. "But, who does this kind of work in this kind of facility if what they're doing is for the greater good?"

"Why didn't this show up on the blueprints?" Adriana asked.

"There were, what, five or six sets of blueprints?" I asked. Amy nodded. "They didn't want this to be discovered by anyone. The schematics sort of match up, but not that well. I think the blueprints were there for them to have as a sort of guide, but whoever built this either did it without a final blueprint or they destroyed the final. My bet is on destroyed, by the way."

"I'm sure my father didn't do this on his own," Amy said.

"No, I'm sure Antony Marling, Madeleine Cartwright, and Ronald Yates, at the very least, all added in. This seems very 'them.' And that begs another interesting question."

"What's that?" Adriana asked.

"What's under all of their various buildings and the rest of the Gaultier buildings throughout the world? More hidden, underground facilities? This one has to have been built using some kind of cloaked material or cloaking device, since no one's ever found it."

"How much cloaked material could there be?" Buchanan asked.

"No idea, but if it's the same stuff that the tunnels are made out of, then it's Z'porrah created, and God alone knows how much they gave to our friends in the Evil Genius Society."

"We don't know that no one's found it," Buchanan added. "Just no one on our side."

"Good point, Malcolm. Depressing, but good."

"What do we do?" Abigail asked.

"It seems obvious to me."

Everyone looked at me. "Doesn't seem obvious to us," Naomi shared.

I sighed. "We find out what the hell they're doing down on the lowest level, and then we burn this place to ash."

"That's easier said than done," Serene said. "They have an impressive sprinkler system in place, as well as some other sophisticated equipment to prevent accidents, protect against natural disasters, and so forth."

"How can you tell that from just looking around?"

She handed me a manual. "I found it in one of the labs. It's listing all their emergency procedures."

"You read it already?"

"We all did," Claudia said. "Hyperspeed."

"Right, right." Still wasn't good at reading with hyperspeed. Christopher was a lot more focused on training me on the active side of things. He seemed to feel that this was both more important and more likely for me to actually use.

Flipped the pages. Something near the end caught my eye. "Huh. 'Foremost should be the protection of the Omega Level and all personnel within it. In case of a full facility shutdown, enact Evacuation Omega and ensure all data and subjects are preserved.' That's interesting."

"Did they list twenty-three other evacuation procedures?" Amy asked.

"Why?" Abigail asked back.

"Because omega is the last letter of the Greek alphabet," Amy said. "And since there aren't twenty-four floors, I don't know why you'd go from Evacuation Alpha to Evacuation Omega unless there were a lot of evacuation options."

"Oh, there were only a few evacuation plans, not twenty-four." Serene said. "And none of the others were named for the Greek alphabet. But omega means lots of other things, not just the end. It's used in a wide variety of sciences."

Turned the manual over and looked at the title. *Emergency Plans, Gaultier Center for the Advancement of Humankind.* The type was superimposed on top of a large omega symbol.

Managed not to ask why none of my Dazzlers on Duty had questioned the title, especially after Tito had shared what he thought the bad guys were really after. I also managed to remind myself that, to them, this title probably didn't bode as it did for me. I was the Gregor Mendel fangirl, after all. The YatesCorp clause that would give anyone who could prove they were genetically a Yates offspring a seat on the Yates-Corp Board made much more diabolical sense now, too. But maybe Tito was wrong.

"Um, I've got a very bad feeling about this. Girls, if we were talking genetics, what could omega indicate?"

"Like Serene said, many things," Lorraine replied. "In molecular biology the symbol's used as shorthand to signify a genetic construct introduced by a two-point crossover."

"I dread to ask. What's a two-point crossover?" I had a really, really good guess, but I also wanted to be really, really sure.

"A two-point crossover just means that you select two points on parent organism strings," Claudia said. "Everything between the two points is swapped between the parent organisms, creating two child organisms."

Fantastic. I wasn't wrong. That was indeed my guess, or pretty much. And, double rainbow fantastic, Tito wasn't wrong, either. "Oh. My God."

"Kitty, what are you thinking?" Naomi asked. "You look like you're going to be sick."

"Because I probably am. We need to get downstairs and find whatever's hidden below."

"Tell us what you think is going on first," Buchanan said in a tone of voice that was pretty much brooking no argument. Of course, I heard that tone from Jeff, Chuckie, Christopher, and all the others frequently, too. I was good at ignoring that tone.

Reached into his back pants pocket. Sure enough, the keycard was there. Grabbed it, then his hand, and headed for the stairs. All at hyperspeed. I was impressed with how well hysterical panic ensured that I was able to control the hyperspeed. Almost as well as if I was enraged. That was good. Wasn't sure I could get rage going, but hysterical panic was currently a given and terror loomed on the horizon.

Reached the stairs and continued down at hyperspeed. The others were behind us. "I'll tell you on the way. Basically, I think that we're going to look back on the idea of Gaultier's Zombie Army with great fondness for a simpler time."

CHAPTER 84

WE REACHED THE BOTTOM in no time; I used the keycard and got us all through the bottom stairwell door. Didn't stop to worry about the bathrooms. If someone was in them, they were likely to be the least of our worries.

Went through the elevator lobby door, inserted the keycard, shoved Buchanan through the door, motioned the others along, took the keycard out, got through the door, grabbed Buchanan, and kept on going. "One of you lead us to the section we couldn't go to before. We don't have time for me to lead us around like Moses in the desert."

Lorraine and Claudia took the lead and we were back in the maze section. We zipped through and came to a stop before a set of double doors that led into a room with "Restricted: Omega Level Only" on it.

Used the keycard, shoved Buchanan and everyone else through, shut the door quietly behind us. Once we were in and the door was closed I stopped, mostly because it was dark and we undoubtedly needed to move forward carefully.

Buchanan opened his mouth, probably to ask me what the hell was going on, but I beat him to it. "There's a reason they want the Yates Gene, and the work we've done on it," I said in a low voice. "And it's exactly what Tito said earlier—the clause in the YatesCorp stuff is a lure, the way they get the owners of Yates genetics to show up and freely give them a sample. But what I think they're doing down here is cloning."

"Why do they want Tito's research then?" Serene asked.

Her innocence never failed to astound, impress, and sometimes amuse me.

"So they can clone our kids, Serene. And whoever else they want, like Jeff and Christopher, who were out-of-the-regular-womb powerful."

"Oh." Serene looked ill. "I liked it better when I thought it was all about money."

"Yeah, me too."

"Cloning technology exists already," Lorraine said slowly.

"Yeah, it does. On Beta Twelve, for instance. But I doubt they're trying to make another Dolly the Sheep and I also doubt they had access to whatever process the Free Women are using. We already thought about what it would mean if someone brought back Yates or Mephistopheles. Now think of what you could do if you could do that, and mix in a little Patrick and Jamie for good measure."

Everyone looked slightly ill. Glad to see I'd kept the mood light. "Let's not think of that," Naomi said. "Let's go figure out if Kitty and Tito are right and stop whatever it is, whether they're right or not."

"Don't be offended," Claudia said, "but I'm hoping for not."

Everyone agreed that we were all hoping I was wrong and Tito was Mr. Imagination. But my gut told me Tito didn't come up with outlandish ideas—he was a smart guy who paid attention and my gut felt his guess was the right one.

My gut wasn't sure who all we'd find cloned, but that we'd find someone we didn't want seemed too likely to be ignored. Vacillated between wondering if it was going to be Yates, Mephistopheles, or the combo, and decided I'd just have to enjoy the excitement of discovery.

We crept down a short, dark corridor and came out into a dark room. Dark was really the watchword for this area. Which was a typical Bad Guy Ambiance Theme. The room was large. At least, it felt large. It was hard to see to be sure because it was also filled with a lot of giant metal boxes.

While the small room we'd entered the facility through originally had been warm, and the other rooms and levels had been comfortable temperatures, this area was hella cold. Took a closer look at the nearest metal box. "We're in the mainframe center."

"It's huge," Serene said as we trotted along at the slow hyperspeed, going in and out of what was a really big maze of all right angles and lines. "I've never seen one this big. I've never seen mainframes this big. Ours aren't this big, at any base, not even the Science Center."

"That bodes."

"All of this bodes," Amy said. "It's not like this is any worse than anything else."

"Yet." Hey, I *knew* how our luck ran.

It was like we were walking through the Egyptian Temple of Amun from *Death on the Nile*—huge monoliths on every side, too big to see around, with who knew what lurking at the top or around every corner.

"This place is creepy," Claudia said. The others murmured their agreement, other than Buchanan, who stoically kept his worries to himself, like a good Scout Leader should. Wondered if he'd tell us the campfire story of Bunny, the Idiot Girl Who Ignored Her Scout Master's Instructions and Was Eaten By a Giant Metal Box later on. Or maybe he'd go for the Hook Hand guy. The Jersey Devil. Superbeings. Wait, those were real. Time to stop this line of thought—I was starting to freak myself out. No wonder Mom had never really pushed for the idea of me going off to summer camp.

In this cheery frame of mind we made it to the far wall, which led us to a wide corridor that ran along the back but which, thankfully, had no giant mainframes in it and did have the nightlights going, making it markedly less creepy. It's the little things you treasure.

Naturally this corridor ended at a closed door. Buchanan listened at said door, as did Adriana. Then the A-Cs. Amy and I just looked at each other. As with hyperspeed reading, I hadn't yet caught up to the advanced A-C hearing, so decided I'd let the others tell me what they heard.

"Nothing," Buchanan said, after he listened another time. "That doesn't mean no one or nothing's there, just could be that they're either making no noise, or this section is soundproofed."

He put his hand out. Resisted the urge to slap it. Instead, I gave him back his keycard. He took it from me with a look

I could only consider snide. "Thanks so much." Yep, his sarcasm knob was right there at eleven.

Keycard in, Buchanan opened the door. Which let us into a much narrower but similarly lit hallway. There was a bluish glow at the far end, as if there was a large TV on in the room this hallway led into. We all went through the door. Buchanan retrieved the card, then closed the door quietly behind us.

Adriana grabbed my wrist. "Did you hear that?" she whispered. I shook my head. "A door opened and closed, then opened again, but farther away."

Heard a loud click. "Door's locked," Serene whispered. Buchanan tried the keycard. The door didn't open.

Buchanan shoved in front of us, presumably to take the bullets. Well, that was nice and noble and all that, but I'd pretty much had it with seeing people I cared about die in front of me. I zipped around him, so I reached the end of the corridor first.

And stopped dead.

What was in front of me and spread out to my left looked like a scene out of *Coma*, *Alien Resurrection*, or Wolverine's origin stories. There were glass tanks along the walls, one right next to the other, bubbling gently with some kind of fluid, all with bodies inside of them. The bodies were floating, all with facemasks on and lots of tubes and such going into them. I was pretty sure they were all alive in some way.

Metal bars crisscrossed the ceiling, strong cables hanging from them, in sets of four. Each set of cables held what looked like a space-aged stretcher up off the ground. And every stretcher had a body in it. They all had tubes and such running into the ground. Again, had the distinct impression they were all alive.

The lights were blue. Couldn't tell if they were light bulbs or tubes or something else, but the glow was enough to see decently.

To my immediate left was a wall with an opened door. Regular yellow light washed out from the doorway. It looked jarring against the blue, which was rather soothing. Or would have been if I wasn't revved up on stress.

There was a teenaged kid standing in the doorway. "Who are you?" he asked.

"Ah . . ." I stepped back and shoved whoever was behind me back as well. "Stay back," I said in the lowest voice I could. "He's only seen me."

"Come out here," the kid demanded.

I stepped back into view. "Hi."

The area we were in was separated from the hanging body beds by only open space. The kid didn't look at the bodies—clearly he was used to them.

"Who is it?" A different voice, a girl's, came from whatever room the open door led to.

"I don't know . . ." The kid stepped closer to me. "Oh." He smiled, and there was something very familiar about his smile, but I couldn't place my finger on what. "I know you. Katherine, right?"

"Ah, right." Almost no one called me Katherine. Even White was down to using my full first name only when we were doing something legitimately formal or if he was trying to make a parental-type point.

"You were supposed to be coming the day after tomorrow. You're early."

Score another one for Mom. "We like to mix it up, keep the bad guys guessing."

"Yes, you're good at that, aren't you, Katherine? But you don't go by that name, not really, do you?"

He flipped a switch on the wall near him and the blue lights were overpowered by white fluorescent. The kid's smile widened. "I know what you like to be called."

My stomach clenched. I recognized his smile now. And his eyes. I really recognized his eyes. They were kind of slitted and they glittered. He was slender and had a reptilian look to him.

I was terrified of snakes. And there was one person in my life who, more than anyone else, had reminded me of a snake. Not at all coincidentally, it was the same person who'd terrified me more than any other in my life.

"Here, kitty, kitty." His voice dripped sarcasm and menace. I recognized that, too.

Managed to get the name out. "Leventhal Reid."

His grin went wider. "In the flesh."

CHAPTER 85

"HOW ARE YOU HERE? I saw you die. And it wasn't over a decade ago."

A girl who looked a little younger than the kid in front of me stepped out. She looked vaguely familiar, too. "I checked, she's not alone." She gave me an icy look. And, as with Reid, I recognized this expression.

"LaRue? What the hell? I saw you die, too." A year or so ago.

"Maybe you did." She shrugged. "Maybe you didn't."

"You were shot through the head by Esteban Cantu. I watched you die." Knew I had to be giving off supernova levels of stress and terror right now. Wondered if it would be enough to let Jeff know where I was, but then realized it wouldn't be—this entire facility had to be blocked, otherwise someone would have found it by now.

"We've overcome death," LaRue said with a superior smirk.

"Apparently. How?"

"Oh, let's meet your friends first," LaRue said.

"Come out, come out, wherever you are," Reid called in a singsong voice.

"I'm alone."

They both laughed. "We have sensors, you idiot," LaRue said. Yeah, it was definitely her. Someone or something had locked the door behind us, so had to figure they weren't bluffing.

The rest of my team stepped out of the corridor and fanned out next to and behind me. Reid's eyes lit on Serene, LaRue's on Amy. Then both of them looked at Naomi and Abigail. The expressions on their faces were exactly the same—spiders looking at juicy flies.

"Who's the guy?" Reid asked. "I was expecting your knight in shining armor."

"He's a friend." Interesting. Somehow Buchanan had remained off everyone's radar. What a pity he was going to be on it now.

"Why are we hanging back?" Adriana asked quietly. "They're unarmed."

"Heard that," LaRue said.

I blinked, and somehow Reid had Adriana and was twisting her arm behind her back. Her expression said that he was hurting her. His expression said that he knew he was and was enjoying that he was causing her pain. If I'd needed confirmation that somehow this was really Leventhal Reid, I now had it.

"Let her go," I said as evenly as I could. "You've made your point. You're clones, but you've had that extra special A-C something added in."

"Why shouldn't we just have fun with her?" Reid asked.

"How about because the rest of us will kick your asses?" Naomi asked.

"You can try," LaRue said. "We'd like that."

"Okay," Abigail said.

"No!" Buchanan and I shouted in unison.

Unfortunately, we both shouted slower than the A-Cs moved. Buchanan was able to grab Amy, but the rest of the girls all went for it.

Reid threw Adriana toward the open space between him and the hanging body beds. Lorraine and Claudia both went to catch her. Which they did, but they were staggered back a bit.

In the meantime, LaRue grabbed both Gower girls and tossed them toward Lorraine, Claudia, and Adriana. Serene happened to be between the Gowers and the others, so she got bowled over as they all crashed into each other.

This was done at hyperspeed, so took only a moment. And

in less than that clear walls that had a bluish glow went up around the girls.

"There are booby traps," Buchanan the Scout Master said to the troop that had just earned their Being Taken Hostage Badges. "By the way."

"We guessed," Claudia said. "A little late, but . . ."

"Don't touch the sides," Buchanan said quickly, right as Abigail's hand was heading for one of the "walls." "They look electrical."

"Lasers, actually," LaRue said. "Feel *free* to touch them." The girls carefully moved into the center of the box they were in.

Reid snickered. "This area is really well protected. Father doesn't like us to have uninvited guests."

Father? "Ronald Yates is alive, too? Or do you consider Mephistopheles to be your daddy?"

They both laughed, nasty teenaged laughs. It was like being back in high school. "No," Reid said. "Father doesn't think we need to bring him back, in either form. I think he's right. At first I didn't agree, but I see the wisdom now."

"So, is Father Herbert Gaultier? Antony Marling? Madeleine Cartwright with a sex change?"

More nasty teenaged snickering. "You'll never guess," LaRue said. "So don't hurt yourself trying."

"Who's Doctor Feelgood, then?"

Unsurprisingly, they knew exactly what I meant. What I was saying always seemed super clear to the bad guys, go me. I could tell they got this reference because they looked at each other, smirked, then looked back at me. "Wouldn't you like to know?" Reid asked.

We were moving into my normal definition of DEFCON Worse, meaning we were going to have to get the girls back the old-fashioned way—via my running my mouth. No worries, these two seemed open to talking.

"Yeah, I would. So, who?" They both shrugged and didn't speak. Okay, had to keep them going. "How old are you two? I mean, seriously, you look fourteen and LaRue looks twelve."

"Well, that depends on how you count," Reid said.

"How do you count?"

"Differently," LaRue said.

Okay, so this line of questioning wasn't keeping them going, either. Time to go back to Yates—they seemed to enjoy talking about him. So many of the Megalomaniac League did. "So, Yates was the original Mastermind and you, well, the original you, was his first Apprentice, right?" I asked Reid.

He nodded. "He lasted a long time. Would have lasted longer but for you."

"Yeah, I hear that a lot. So then you took over as the Mastermind and found your Apprentice, right? Or did you always have him picked out?"

"You don't think it was me?" LaRue asked with a smirk.

"Honestly? No. Not saying you weren't smart enough, but I'm willing to bet that whoever Leventhal's Apprentice was is who you're calling Father now."

They both looked mildly impressed. "You're not nearly as stupid as you look, are you?" LaRue asked.

Had no idea how to respond to that in a way that wouldn't get one or all of the girls hurt, so I didn't. Forged on with my Go-To Plan #1: Keeping the Bad Guys Monologuing. "So, your Apprentice is now the Mastermind. But he's got a new Apprentice, and that's not either one of you."

Reid shrugged. "I wasn't supposed to die so early. And again we have you to thank for that." His eyes narrowed and he looked even more reptilian.

Time to continue running my mouth. "So, does the new Apprentice actually know about this facility and the two of you?"

"Which one of them is it?" Amy asked, before Reid or LaRue could reply. Figured I couldn't kick her where they wouldn't see so just had to let it go.

"Who?" LaRue asked.

"Ansom Somerall, Janelle Gardiner, or Quinton Cross. Which one of them is the new Apprentice?" Amy sounded furious, not that I could blame her.

LaRue and Reid both giggled. "All of them," LaRue said.

"None of them," Reid countered.

"What about Langston Whitmore, Thomas Kendrick, or Amos Tobin?" My question earned more giggles, but I'd kind of expected that.

I was far more used to hanging with the Crazed Evil Genius Brigade than Amy was, and even though we were currently spending time with the Megalomaniac Club's Junior Auxiliary League, I was pretty sure I knew what they meant.

"Each one of them currently thinks they're the real Apprentice. And maybe more aspiring evil loons do as well. But none of them actually know about this facility . . . or either one of you. And none of them are actually the real Apprentice. Esteban Cantu was, but he failed, in part because he did kill you, LaRue. So the Apprentice job's been reserved, permanently."

Both Reid and LaRue looked impressed and worried. "You're just guessing," Reid said. He sounded a tiny bit nervous.

"No, it makes sense," Lorraine said. "There are two schools of cloning. One is normal growth—the clone is created as an embryo and is born and grows at a normal species rate."

"The other is a forced gestation that speeds up the clone's growth to maturity," Claudia continued. "The clone grows from embryo to maturity at an accelerated rate, but then when maturity is reached, the aging process carries on normally."

"The issue with forced gestation is that the clones can be unstable, especially mentally," Lorraine added. "Though, from what we know of the two of you, it'll be hard to tell if you're crazier in these versions than you were in your original forms."

"They're not the same," Serene said. "They have A-C DNA in them now."

"How do they have all of their memories?"

"I'd guess indoctrination," Serene said. "Maybe using a form of imageering talent to distill and save all the information received from the most recent image. Probably both." LaRue and Reid looked slightly uncomfortable again, so I figured Serene had called these right.

"Great, and thanks for the scientific confirmation, girls. What's interesting to me though is that Leventhal, correct me if I'm wrong, but when I first met you, or your original, or whatever the hell you clones call the first version of you, he was really anti-alien. In a scary, One Ring To Rule Them All kind of way."

"So what changed?" Adriana asked. "Because you're definitely stronger than a normal teenaged boy should be."

"Father saw the wisdom of us being reborn as hybrids," Reid said. He smiled and looked incredibly proud. "He's brilliant, you know. Smarter than Yates ever was. Smarter than either one of us, even."

"Speak for yourself," LaRue said. "But yeah, he's so smart that *you'll* never figure out who he is," she said to me, as she smirked again. "He's hiding in plain sight and you just can't see him. Not that you'll have too long to worry about it."

"So, Leventhal, right now you're Son, right? And then, when the current Mastermind gets old," or I killed him, but figured that wasn't the right thing to say at this exact moment, "you'll take over as Father, make a new Son out of his DNA?"

"Impressive," Reid said.

"Where does LaRue fit in? Is she Daughter, Mother, Cray-Cray Girlfriend, or what?"

"I'm whatever I want to be." LaRue shrugged. "When you're the idea person who can back it up with action, you get to be whatever you want."

"Interesting." Very interesting. Madeleine Cartwright had been the brains behind Titan and Antony Marling. Chernobog was a woman. The women were the ones coming up with the intricacies, the ones making the plans actually *work*. Something to ponder when we were searching for the most likely New Ideas Apprentice. Meanwhile, I moved Janelle Gardiner up to my #1 Real Apprentice Suspects slot. But that information also told me what I needed to know right now. "And thanks for the confirmation."

They both looked at me. "What do you mean?" LaRue asked, sounding confused for the first time.

"You're our Doctor Feelgood."

CHAPTER 86

"WHAT ARE YOU TALKING ABOUT?" LaRue definitely sounded nervous.

"You're who's come up with the first version of Surcenthumain and all the other versions, too. You were probably assigned to find and turn Herbert Gaultier to the cause, right? I mean, he wasn't always Doctor Mengele."

"No, he wasn't," Amy said quietly. "But I think Chuck called it right—by the time we were all in high school, he'd started to change."

"He found a better option." LaRue smirked.

Heard the sound of a lot of footsteps before Amy or I could think up a suitably cutting comeback. Buchanan, Amy, and I turned to see a variety of people toting guns come around the corner. It so figured that I wasn't even surprised.

"What the hell took you so long?" Reid snapped. "We called for you at least ten minutes ago."

"Sir, we were dealing with explosions in the main laboratory."

Risked a glance over at Serene. Who was looking her usual Innocence on the Hoof self. She caught my eye and winked.

She *had* read the maintenance and security manual, hadn't she? And "difficult" wasn't the same as "impossible." There was so much more to her than most of us ever saw. Wondered how much of it Brian saw.

But big guns being waved in my face tended to drag me back into the moment and right now was no exception.

"What the hell did you do?" LaRue growled. "Turn around and answer me!"

Did as requested and shrugged. "That's for us to know and you to find out. See? I can do it, too. So, what do you plan to do with all of us? People do know we're here." Well, Mom knew but she was busy. Dad knew, too, though, and when we didn't get back, he'd tell Mom and Jeff, and someone would figure out how to come after us. Right?

Chuckie would figure it out, for sure. So, great, no worries. And then, of course, he and Jeff and the others would come into a trap because by that time the Crazed Super Twins would have alerted whoever else they had on their speed dial that the facility was under attack. Presuming that hadn't already happened, which was a big presumption, really.

Time to work our way out of this before the cavalry arrived.

"Well, as for what we're going to do to you," Reid said, "I'm going with torture. But that's just me. LaRue might have other plans." Nice to see that they'd ensured this Reid was exactly like the old Reid, only probably more so.

She rolled her eyes at him. "You are *so* weird. Amy I think we'll want to save, so that we can make another one that will be a lot easier to handle. Oh, but don't worry—it won't upset your late father. He never really loved you, or your pathetic mother."

It was a good thing Buchanan was still holding onto Amy, because she tried to lunge at LaRue. Who smirked. She was big on smirking. This was really like being back in high school, only the "cool kids" were scary sociopaths with a lot more power than I had. Wait, come to think of it, this was exactly like high school. All we were missing was Chuckie getting beaten up, and if we didn't get out of this before too long, I had a horrible feeling that was going to happen also.

"Is Amy's dad actually around?"

LaRue did the teenaged giggle thing. "No, we didn't need him. Cloning is expensive. We only use it for vital personnel."

"There are a lot of bodies around here."

Reid smiled. "Yeah. There are actually more ways to clone than the two your small minds came up with."

"Well, isn't that extra special? So, what, you have these bodies around as spares?" Just like Gaultier had had in the Secret Lab of Hot Zombies.

"Shut up," LaRue snarled at Reid.

"What happens to the grunts?" Buchanan asked. "Do you use them for parts after they're dead, or before?"

"We'll kill the guy," Reid said quickly, apparently doing his best to get them back onto the List of Upcoming Horrors track and to keep said grunts from thinking about Buchanan's very appropriate question. "He's just a human. The others we can use."

"True, but no matter what you're going to want, we have to keep your girlfriend alive." LaRue nodded toward me. "We'll need to use her to get the data Ronaldo and his team couldn't actually find." She shot me another evil little smirk. "They all trust you, after all."

"How fast do you possibly think you can create a clone from any of us?"

They both looked at the bodies on the hanging beds and in the tanks, then back at me. "Fast," LaRue said.

"It won't be as good as we are," Reid said. "But it'll do the trick. We don't need it long-term. Just long enough to get our data and the other things we really want."

"Your children," LaRue confirmed.

Heard a growl from the cage. Realized it was coming from Serene—she looked almost as crazy and ready to kill as when we'd first met her. Abigail hugged her, possibly to keep Serene from throwing herself at the cage to get to LaRue. Claudia and Lorraine just looked furious. Adriana looked as though she was trying to determine how to short their cage out. I couldn't see Naomi; she was behind Claudia and Lorraine.

On the plus side, I was now enraged. Still had no idea of what to do, but at least I'd be able to do it at full hyperspeed.

"You're not killing or using anyone else," Naomi said. "And you're not touching those children, ever. I won't let you."

Both teenagers smirked now. "What are you going to do to stop us?" LaRue asked. "Other than give us all your DNA, I mean? We'll let you watch us dissect your brother before we render you for parts, though. Graves are so easy to rob."

Took a good look at the girls. Still couldn't see Naomi, but all the other girls now looked worried, but differently than they had before. But the many guns all cocked, which brought my attention back to imminent death.

"You two women, step over near the others," Reid said.

"Um, no thanks. Not into the whole Laser Cage idea."

"Well, you can stand there and be riddled with bullets," LaRue said.

Thought about it. Moved so I was behind Buchanan and therefore directly in the line of fire. "You don't actually want to kill me. Not yet. And I'm not letting you kill my friend."

Amy joined me. "Me either. I'd rather die protecting someone I care about than live like you two do."

"I'd rather you two got into the cage and prolonged your chances of staying alive and being saved," Buchanan said softly.

"Too bad. Not doing it." Reached back and took his hand in one of mine and Amy's in the other. "Better to die like this, anyway. I know how Leventhal there likes to kill his female victims. Going down in a rain of bullets is far, far better."

"Fine," LaRue said. "Kill them all. We can still get their DNA from their dead bodies."

The men with the guns didn't look as if they'd have any issues shooting us all dead. But they never got the chance.

All the guns pointing at us glowed—first golden, then bright red, all in about a second. As the men holding them started to scream, the weapons blew up.

Buchanan pulled both me and Amy down and did the protective huddle, but there was no need—a glowing shield was around the three of us—blood, shrapnel, and body parts hit it and either bounced off or oozed down, but they didn't reach the three of us. The men holding the guns weren't so lucky—they were cut to ribbons.

I could finally see Naomi—her sleeves were pushed up and unlike the others she didn't look worried. She looked angry and determined. She also had a syringe in her hand. And there were at least a dozen more at her feet.

Got a bad feeling in the pit of my stomach. "Mimi, what did you do?"

She looked at me. "What I had to."

CHAPTER 87

NAOMI LOOKED A LITTLE DIFFERENT than the other girls. There was a blue glow all around them from the Laser Cage, but Naomi was glowing a little bit more than the others.

"She got the samples before we realized it, Kitty," Lorraine said, sounding just this side of panicked. Couldn't blame her.

"They were pure," Claudia added, sounding like she was already on the other side of panic. "The street versions are diluted, but what Naomi used isn't."

"Mimi, that wasn't the answer." We had to get adrenaline into her, and fast. But that meant we had to get back to the Embassy, or a regular hospital, because there was nothing in this facility we could trust, even if we could find where they might have normal medical supplies.

"Yes, it was. I can control it." She glared at the Laser Cage and it exploded. "All of you, get out of here."

LaRue and Reid looked at each other, then ran into their room and closed the door. I heard locks being turned. Didn't think they were going to stand a chance against Naomi at the moment.

Our protective shield disappeared. "We need to move, they're calling for reinforcements, I'm sure." I shoved Amy toward the hallway.

Abigail tried to grab her sister, but Naomi was glowing more brightly and Abigail pulled her hand back with a gasp. "Sis . . ."

"Go," Naomi said. She sounded funny, not unclear or slurred, but like she was buzzing, almost as if she was overcharged with electricity. "I can control it. And it'll wear off. It did with Christopher, it will with me. In time." She took a deep breath and let it out. "It's so good to feel . . . everything again."

Adriana dragged Abigail away. "We'll be more help to her if we're out and safe," she said as she followed Amy, who wasn't moving all that fast toward the exit.

Claudia, Lorraine, and Serene didn't look eager to leave, either. I was sure that all of them wanted to help Naomi in some way. Based on Abigail being unable to touch her, though, I was also sure that Naomi was able to not get helped unless she wanted to be. And her expression said she didn't want to be.

There was only one good option. "Malcolm, get everyone out of here."

"Not leaving you, Missus Chief."

I turned to him. "You have to. You're the only one who can actually get the right people on this and I can't do what I have to with all the other girls here." I put my hand on his arm. "I know you want to stay to protect me, I know that's your entire job. And you're damned good at that job. But you're also supposed to protect Jamie and right now, she and the other kids are in danger. No one's expecting this. More computer hacking, more attacks, maybe, but not this."

Buchanan looked at Naomi and back to me. "You're in as much danger of being killed as you are being saved."

"I know. But I have to try to help her, and get us both out of here alive, or I'll never be able to look Chuckie in the face ever again. You know the Teenagers From Hell have called for backup by now. The girls can't get out of here without your help—you know it, I know it, and they know it."

"You're full of it, Missus Chief." He looked like he was going to continue to argue, but instead he jerked a little and nodded his head. "Fine. You be careful." He took my hand, gave it a squeeze, then turned and headed off. "All of you, with me, *now*."

The girls went after him. I looked back at Naomi. She closed her eyes. I counted in my head. In fifteen seconds she spoke. "They're back in the Embassy."

That timed out right for them to have made it back to the bathroom with the power cube in it if they were going at hyperspeed and not stopping to search for things or beat people up along the way. I wasn't leading them, so it was a safe bet they hadn't gotten lost or turned around.

"You can see them there?" She nodded. "Did you make Malcolm go, or just tell him to go in his mind?"

"The latter. I'm not the bad guy, Kitty."

"No, you're just really scary right now, Mimi. Honestly. You need to come with me. We have to get some adrenaline into you, pronto."

"No. I'm ending this. Now."

As she said this, the door was unlocked and flung open, and Reid and LaRue came out, toting some impressively big guns. "Seriously? You two aren't as smart as you like to think you are."

Naomi laughed and the guns exploded, but the kids weren't hurt. Hoped this was because Naomi knew we needed more information from them. "You want to threaten my family and friends? See how *you* like it."

Reid and LaRue were lifted into the air, by nothing as far as I could see, though they were now glowing a bit, too. "Put us down, you bitch!" LaRue shouted.

"It's really stupid to call the incredibly powerful woman holding you a good ways up in the air a bitch, kids. Just saying."

Reid didn't look frightened. "You know, Father said this might happen. That she'd OD. I wish he was here to see it."

Holy crap, the Mastermind had foreseen this? What else was he prepped for? And who the hell was he? We needed him neutralized as if the safety of the world depended upon it, because it did.

"I'm not going to overdose you horrible little creep," Naomi said.

I wasn't so sure of that, but kept it to myself.

Both teenagers started to gasp and their eyes bugged out a bit. Figured Naomi was squeezing them in some way. Whatever way it was, it looked painful. Perhaps she hadn't let the guns kill them not to keep them around for questioning but so she could kill them more slowly later. Like now later.

"Mimi, they have answers we need. We can't kill them."

She turned to me and her eyes were terrifying—open so wide I could see the whites all around her irises, and glowing, just like the rest of her. "I knew you'd say that. 'Don't kill them.' My brother and aunt are dead. Who said 'don't kill *them*'?"

"Um, all of us."

"I mean on their side!"

"Those kinds of things separate us from them, Mimi. It's part of how you know you're a good guy—when you only kill someone because you have to, not because you want to."

She looked back at LaRue and Reid and released the hold on them so they could breathe. Maybe if they'd begged for their lives, or lied and said they were sorry, or just shut the hell up and gasped for air, things would have gone differently.

But they didn't do any of those things.

LaRue smirked. "You know your husband loves her more than he loves you, don't you?"

"And you know he's in on all of this, right?" Reid said quickly. "And always has been."

"He doesn't, he's not, and he never was," I said. "Mimi, they're baiting you because Father really hates Chuckie for some reason. They want you to give in."

"You were his second choice," LaRue taunted. "We all know it."

"How would they know anything about this?" I asked her. "This is just part of their indoctrination."

"Someone knows," Reid said. "Or we wouldn't."

"Second choice, second choice," LaRue said in a singsong voice.

"You won't know anything any more," Naomi snarled.

"Mimi, they know you can read them. They're trying to distract you, to play you, so you don't find out the truth about who Father is, what else they have going on, and all that. We need to question them, and you need to not listen to their lies."

She turned on me. "And *you* need to stop telling me what to do!"

"They must be programmed or indoctrinated or whatever

to self-destruct, like the androids. At least in extreme cases."
Naomi certainly looked like an Extreme Case. She was glowing more brightly and was now floating above the floor.

"Why would we do that?" Reid asked. "We don't want to die. We're just telling her the truth."

"You'd do it because you're confident you'll be brought right back, good as new, with all the old memories and all of the new ones intact." They'd been inside their living quarters longer than just grabbing guns would have indicated. The chances that they'd taken pictures of themselves for download or upload or whatever they called it in their cloning process were high.

"I can't wait to watch her kill you," LaRue said. "When she sees that her husband still loves you more."

"Oh, for God's sake. He does not, you little twerps."

And, maybe if the next few things hadn't happened, things would also have been different.

But happen they did.

CHAPTER 88

BUCHANAN RETURNED, with Jeff and Chuckie in tow. Adriana returned, with White and Gower in tow. And the reinforcements the Crazy Super Twins had called arrived, with lots and lots of firepower in tow.

Vacillated between being glad to see everyone and wishing they'd stayed home. Maybe with Chuckie here he could calm Naomi down. Then again, should someone hurt him, that would undoubtedly flip Naomi over to the side of Kill 'Em All. And I wasn't sure if she'd be selective about the "all."

Naturally the bad guys started shooting, because that was what was expected of them. They seemed unclear on the concept of who to shoot, though, as at least some of the bullets were aimed for the floating teenagers. Perhaps the bad guy reinforcements were freaked out about glowing people floating in the air after bombs had already gone off elsewhere and they were standing on the shredded bodies of their work buddies. Could not imagine why that would throw them.

"Shoot the glowing bitch!" LaRue shrieked, as the rest of us hit the ground and rolled under the body beds. "Bomb her! Blow her up!"

"Bombs," Naomi said, as if she'd just remembered something. My purse was lighter and I saw some small orbs spinning in the air. Great, Naomi had remembered something—that she and I were carrying explosives courtesy of Serene. And no one made better explosives than Serene.

"Kill all of them!" Reid shouted.

"Okay," Naomi said. She sent the bombs into the reinforcements.

"Run!" I shouted to the others. "Serene made those!" Heard Jeff and Gower curse. Yeah, they'd also experienced Serene's explosives firsthand.

I was closest to the reinforcements and, therefore, the bombs, and decided now was the time to run like hell for the other side. Could run on all fours or I could stand up, risk the bullets, and go a hell of a lot faster. Decided to go for living dangerously and left the ground like I was leaving the blocks for a race. I was able to stay low as I zigzagged through the hanging beds. Slammed into Adriana and dragged her along with me.

White and Gower had both grabbed Chuckie, Jeff had Buchanan, and all of us were running for the far end of the room.

"Down!" Jeff bellowed and we all hit the ground, moments before the bombs went off. Hyperspeed, it was probably the best A-C talent going. Why the Flash and Quicksilver weren't considered higher-level heroes was a mystery, really.

The explosions were loud, almost drowning out the screams of the dying. Not quite, though. The body parts splattering throughout the room were a rare treat. The special fluids in the glass tanks, along with the shattered glass, were adding a unique thrill to the whole situation, too.

"Mimi, what are you doing?" Chuckie shouted, sounding horrified.

"Making them pay," Naomi said calmly.

"Don't worry, some of the parts are the pre-clones or whatever we'd call them. That sounds less reassuring said aloud than it did in my head. By the way."

"Of all the commando raids in all the world, why did you have to go on this one?" Jeff asked, as we rolled out of the way of falling bodies and steel girders, because, of course some of the explosion had affected the cables and beds set up, and it was crashing down around us.

"Just lucky, I guess."

The rain of parts, cables, beds, and metal stopped. "I hope you're bringing more reinforcements," Naomi said conversationally. She still had Reid and LaRue held up in the air. "You know, I can see everything. The entire universe. And beyond it, to all the other ones."

"What is she talking about?" Gower asked as he and White held Chuckie down.

Now wasn't the time to explain that multiple universes existed. Now was the time to share that we were well on our way to DEFCON Oh My God. "Dude, she is *not* in her right mind. She's injected at least thirteen syringes full of Surcenthumain Pure. She did it to protect us. But it's, ah, affecting her. Like, for instance, she may now think—"

"Chuck, why did you marry me if you still love Kitty more?"

"That. She may think that."

"Seriously?" Jeff asked. Chuckie looked too shocked to speak.

"Wow, Jeff, the personal growth is impressive and I'm really hoping I get to reward it somewhere in the near future. The two teenagers she's holding up in the air? They're really good at baiting her. Just like we were all in high school with them. Because they know her weakness."

The Mastermind knew us well. He knew Chuckie well. There had to be a clue in there somewhere. Reid and LaRue knew who Father was and I might have been able to trick them into telling me, or giving me enough clues to guess. But that wasn't an option any more.

"Naomi," Jeff shouted, "are you out of your mind?"

"Yes, she is. I keep on saying it, but no one listens. She's higher than anyone has ever been, in the history of the world."

"How can you allow it, Jeff?" Naomi asked, sounding sad.

"Because I know he loves you more," Jeff said. He got up slowly. "Naomi, look at me." She didn't turn. "Look at me," Jeff said, Commander Voice on full.

Naomi turned in the air. "Why?"

"I'm the strongest empath in the galaxy. I can read him. I can read you, too, you know. Your powers are so out of control that the blocks in here can't affect my ability to read you. You know you're not thinking right. Chuck loves you. He loves you as much as I love Kitty, and as much as you love him."

"Why isn't he saying so?" she asked petulantly.

"Because we're not letting him up, in case you try to hurt him," Gower said, as he got to his feet. "You need to stop this, right now. Let those children go."

"No, no, no," I said quickly, as I scrambled to my feet. "They're bad kids. The worst, really. We don't want her to let them go, we just don't want her to kill them. Yet," I added for honesty's sake.

Naomi cocked her head and all of a sudden, all of us were floating in the air in front of her. I could feel her in my mind, so I was sure everyone else could, too.

"Get out of my head, Mimi," I said. "You're not ACE. You don't have the right to do what you're doing. You want to rummage around in heads? Rummage in Reid and LaRue's heads and figure out who Father is."

"ACE . . ." She looked away, but not at anything, more like she was looking off into the distance, or at something only she could see. "I . . . can see ACE. He . . . needs help."

"So do we. We need to know who Father is. All this can stop if we can find the Mastermind, Mimi. You *know* that."

She looked back at all of us, and, once again, I had the hope that we'd all be able to laugh about this somewhere down the line.

Her expression softened as she looked at Chuckie. "I love you."

"I love you, too. Mimi, please put us down, come down, and let's go home," Chuckie said gently. "Please, sweetheart."

"You're afraid of me," she said sadly.

"You're scary right now, Mimi. I told you that earlier. Of course we're all afraid of you."

"I don't mean you, Kitty. I mean Chuck. He's afraid of me."

"I'm afraid of what you've done to yourself," Chuckie said. "I want my wife back, Mimi. Please, sweetheart, we need to get you home so we can get that drug out of your system."

"No!" She dropped us.

Fortunately, she hadn't had us up too high, and also fortunately, Jeff, White, and Gower hit the ground first, so Jeff caught me, Gower caught Chuckie, and White caught Adriana. Buchanan landed, rolled, and came up without missing a beat.

"We could have done what Malcolm did," I said as Jeff put me down.

"Sure you could, baby. We just wanted to be impressive. We also," Jeff said quietly, "need to be ready to run like hell."

"Mimi, we need to help you," Chuckie said, with more than a little desperation in his voice. Yeah, he was Mr. Anti-Drug. Having his wife OD herself willingly was definitely one of the nastiest things to do to him. And the kids had said Father knew she'd do it, too. Meaning this was likely to be part of a long-term plan. Always the way.

"You will *not* take my powers away again!" Naomi was glowing more brightly and she looked, if possible, even angrier and crazier.

"Dude, what is the first rule of Just Say No? It's don't tell the addict you're going to get them clean until they're ready."

"That's not the first rule," Chuckie said, as Naomi looked around and, apparently just for fun, brought down the area where the teenagers had been living. Meaning we weren't going to be able to get any information out of there. "But your point is taken. What the hell are we going to do?"

Buchanan squinted. "I think she's drawing more of the drug into her." He pointed, and sure enough, there was a glittering trail coming down from above and feeding into Naomi's glowing aura.

"I am," Naomi said. Buchanan hadn't been speaking loudly, so either her hearing was also heightened, or she was inside all our minds still, or both. Bet on both, because that was just how our luck ran. "The drug is increasing my powers."

"These aren't your powers," Chuckie said. "These are powers created by a drug that's killing you."

"You wouldn't let me take this before. If you'd really loved me, you would have. What I can do—I could have saved Michael, saved Gladys, saved everyone."

"Mimi, that's the addict in you talking." Maybe telling her the truth would help. At the rate things were going, probably couldn't hurt.

"I'm not an addict. I'm a god."

Oh goody. "You're not a god. You're high. Remember how my mom said she hoped you'd prove her wrong? You promised you would, Mimi. You promised."

She didn't argue.

Pressed this line of thought, in the hopes that it would work. "The Mastermind took your powers, Mimi. Father took them. Find out who he is. Search Reid and LaRue's minds. Find the Mastermind, make all this worth it."

"We have ways of preventing that," Reid said.

"Oh, shut up," Naomi said. And again, I had some hope.

And then LaRue spoke up. "You know, if you did it right, you could bring your brother back. Alive, well, just like he was before he was murdered."

Naomi looked at LaRue. "What do you mean?" she asked. Hopefully.

And I knew then that we'd lost Naomi forever.

CHAPTER 89

BUT I HAD TO TRY. Because maybe I was wrong. "Mimi, they're lying. The only way to bring Michael back would be to clone him, like they already threatened to do. That's not Michael."

"It's really us," Reid said. "And you know it." He grinned at me, his evil, snake-like grin. "You're just as scared of me now as you were when I almost did to you what you deserved in the desert."

"My God, that's Leventhal Reid?" Jeff asked. "How?"

"Cloning. It's the next inevitable Bad Guy Plan phase. The chick's LaRue, too, by the way. 'Cause we're just that kind of lucky."

"Kitty already said their names, Jeff," Chuckie said, voice tight. "Cloning was obvious, based on presumptions from earlier, what we've already seen, and what everyone said. Get with the program. Mimi," he said in a louder voice, "you know they're lying and even if they can bring Michael back, he wouldn't want that."

"How can you say that?" she asked, as she spun toward us. "You don't have the right to tell me what my brother would want. You can't understand what it's like to lose your brother."

"Oh, not the 'only children don't understand our special sibling bond' crap. Trust me, only children form tight bonds. Why the hell do you think Chuckie and I are so close? Why Amy and I are? We understand, trust me. What we're all saying, Mimi, is that we also knew your brother, and there's no way in the world Michael would want you to bring him back from the dead like LaRue's suggesting."

My dream came back to me. Michael wanted to move on, but he wasn't sure that he'd be allowed to go. Because if we held him, brought him back in some way, then what would happen to his soul? These were the kinds of questions I could ask of ACE and the questions I didn't want to ask of Algar.

"I want my brother back!" Naomi was back to looking and sounding completely crazy.

"Stop it," Gower said, voice filled with authority, anger, and fear. "Naomi, stop this right now. This is not how we act, not what we do. We don't become the evil our enemies are."

"Kind of wish you'd grabbed Christopher," I said quietly to Buchanan. "Jeff and Serene didn't addict knowingly or willingly, but he did, and he might get through to her."

"I can go back and get him, I can still see and maybe even reach my return cube point. But I don't know that any of it's going to work. If Reynolds can't get through to her, don't expect anyone else to." He looked around. "We have a bigger issue. I don't know how much longer this facility is going to hold."

Naomi was still ranting and the teenagers were egging her on. "I'd shoot them but I know we want the information they hold," Adriana said. "Kitty, I'm with Mister Buchanan—I think we need to get out of here."

"Not without Naomi."

"I'd like my sister back, too, Naomi," White said calmly, when there was a break in her ranting. "However, that's not the way the world works. People we love die."

"What if I could bring Aunt Terry back?" Naomi said. "Would you want to tell me not to do it?"

White shook his head. "You couldn't bring Terry back. Not really. Any more than those children you're holding are the real LaRue and Leventhal. Oh, I'm sure they *believe* they are," he said quickly as the kids opened their mouths. "But they aren't. Souls don't work like this, Naomi. Once the soul leaves the body, once that tie is severed, it can't come back."

"People see the light and come back all the time," Naomi argued. "Kitty died in childbirth but she came back."

"They do, and she did," White agreed. "But their ties weren't severed. Michael has been dead too long, Terry even longer. I don't know what the children you're holding really are, but I do know that the real LaRue and Leventhal they are not."

"Terry's with ACE, the little bit of her that was left. And Michael could join ACE if—"

"If ACE was back." Naomi looked at me, then she pulled me up into the air, so I was right next to her. We were really high up now. "I see the dream you had, in your mind. Michael said he wanted to go, to leave us?"

"Michael's already left us," I said gently. "He's not alone—Fuzzball is with him. But neither one of them asked that I find a way to bring them back. They asked me to find a way to make everyone let them go."

"I don't want him to go," she said plaintively.

"I know. But what about Paul and Abby? Paul's in danger just by being here, and Abby doesn't want to lose both her brothers and her sister. Jamie doesn't want to lose her godmother. Your parents don't want to lose their daughter. I don't want to lose my friend. Chuckie doesn't want to lose the wife he loves with all his heart."

"But I can protect everyone now."

"It's not worth losing you, the Mimi we all know and love. Not to any of us, I promise you that. Mimi . . . we need to know who the Mastermind is. Whoever Father is, he hates Chuckie. He wants bad things to happen to you because that will break Chuckie's heart."

She looked uncertain. "What if you're wrong? What if . . ." She looked at Chuckie, then back to me. "What if what we think we know is wrong?"

"It's not," I said firmly. "If what we thought was wrong, ACE would have let me know in some way, I know that, for certain. We'll figure it out, I promise. Please, I'm begging you—let's go home, all of us, together. Take the creepy teenagers with us, we'll lock them up and question them. But let's go back and just be us again. Please?"

She looked into my eyes and I saw the Naomi I knew

there again. "I can't. I can see what I have to do." She jerked. "He needs me, right now!"

And with that, she dropped me, Reid, and LaRue, and literally flew up through the ceiling, the glow around her formed into an arrow point as it cut through the building.

CHAPTER 90

I FELL INTO JEFF'S ARMS, which was a relief in so many different ways. "You've still got it."

"Yeah, you make sure I have to practice all the time so I never lose it. Let's get out of here, baby."

He wasn't wrong about wanting to leave—the facility was starting to fall down around us. On the plus side, if we were all buried that would save a lot on funeral costs since we were already so very far underground. Shockingly, didn't find this all that much of a comfort.

Jeff tried to get us to Buchanan, who in turn was trying to get to where I assumed his power cube entry point was. Gower and White were literally dragging Chuckie out of the way of falling chunks of building. Chuckie was staring up at the ceiling where Naomi had gone. I didn't want to contemplate what he was thinking or feeling.

"Kitty!" Adriana had her hand extended near absolutely nothing I could see. She'd come using the power cube gate, too, I assumed, meaning she was probably near her cube entry. "I can get us out! Hurry!"

"Malcolm! Get everyone to Adriana!" My bellowing wasn't up to Jeff's standards, but I made do. Buchanan heard me and ran toward Gower and the others, which was good, because a chunk of concrete hit right where he'd been standing.

White shoved Gower and Chuckie toward Adriana as Jeff headed us for her as well. Caught movement out of the side of my eye—LaRue and Reid were up and running away, toward the hallway. "No, we have to catch them!" I wrenched out of Jeff's arms and took off.

Heard Jeff shouting to the others as I rounded the corner and got into the hallway. The door was open. Well, it was crushed, either by Naomi or by the collapsing building, which was also by Naomi in that sense, and there was a big hole where the door had been. Good enough for Stop the Crazed Clones Work. I sped up.

Heard the pounding of feet behind me. "Where are you going?" Jeff asked, as he caught up to me. "And Richard, why the hell didn't you go with the others?"

"Aside from the fact that I slipped because of the various fluids on the floor you mean? I presume you're going to need me more and I work better with your wife than you do, Jeffrey."

"Wise man probably has a point, Jeff," I said quickly, before Jeff could argue. We were in the giant cave of monolithic mainframes. Amazingly enough, they were all intact and their room wasn't falling apart. Yet. Presumed it was reinforced. Also presumed this wouldn't last.

"Where to?" Jeff asked as we rounded a corner and somehow were facing a wall I hadn't expected. "I ask because this doesn't look like the exit, and breaking through walls down here means we're still underground."

Resisted the urge to curse. "This is a maze. Somewhere on the other side is the exit. We actually have two to choose from, if I can find them. I guarantee the Crazed Super Twins know where the hell they're going. I, on the other hand, suck at mazes. I've been through this in the dark and have no idea how to backtrack. Don't take this the wrong way, Mister White, but we'd have been better off with Malcolm along."

"Not necessarily," White said. "There's more than one way to work a maze, Missus Martini. Jeffrey, if you would be so kind as to help me?"

With that, White leaned against the nearest mainframe to us. Jeff did the same. They both pushed. Heard more explosions. Backtracked a bit and looked around another monolithic mainframe to see a fireball billowing out of the hallway we'd just left.

Decided I could help push and rejoined the men. "We're playing dominoes?"

"Only if it knocks them all down," White said. "Harder, children. Time is of the essence."

"Hadn't noticed," Jeff said, sarcasm knob at eleven and rising.

"On three," White said. "One . . . two . . . three." We all shoved as hard as we could, and the mainframe rocked a little. "Harder . . . again . . . and once more with feeling."

He was right, our last push did the trick and the mainframe went over. It slammed into another, which also went over, and slammed into another, and so on. The slamming sound stopped after about six, though.

White took one of my hands and Jeff took the other. "We'll need to go fast," Jeff said as we all backed up. "They're pretty slick on the outside."

We took off running and went up the side of the first mainframe. It was hard, but Jeff got to the top and dragged me and White along. The next part was tricky, since the boxes were at an angle to each other, like the straightest little mountain range ever. But we were moving at Jeff's fast hyperspeed, meaning that we were able to jump and slide and jump again and keep on going.

"Why didn't Naomi find out who the Mastermind was?" Jeff asked as we reached the last fallen mainframe and he pulled me up onto the top of the next one, which was upright.

"Because she's afraid that she'll discover it's Chuckie."

"Is it?" Jeff asked, as we looked around to determine where to go.

"No. But I can guarantee that Reid and LaRue were thinking of him as the Mastermind when Naomi grabbed us and was digging around in our minds."

"Not that I disagree with your theory, but why are they still trying so hard to make us believe that Charles is the one in charge?" White asked.

"Going to let the Scott Baio joke pass because we're busy. And, as for why, other than that they're really stuck on a theme whether it works or not? The Mastermind hates Chuckie, and he wants him to be the fall guy for all of this. LaRue and Reid said he'd known Naomi would OD, so that means the Mastermind had them ready in case they were captured and questioned."

"Makes sense," Jeff said, pointing toward what I was fairly sure was the far wall. "I think I see the way out. Or it could just be some walls down." Part of why we could see what I hoped was the wall we were looking for was indeed because the building was falling apart and therefore light was coming in from the upper levels and though fallen interior walls.

"Walls down probably are the way out, Jeffrey," White said, as he took the lead and we started running and jumping onto the tops of each mainframe.

We'd just had to separate—White jumped left while Jeff and I jumped right—to avoid a chunk of ceiling that fell onto the mainframe we'd all been on, when something made me turn around. Lights were coming at us from behind. "Are those toy planes?"

"I think they're . . . drones? Small ones, but . . . Uncle Richard! Watch out behind you!"

Jeff's bellowing did two things—alerted White to the new danger which was good, and caused a reverberation that seemed to be the last straw for this area, which was bad, since that meant more ceiling gave way, meaning some of the servers we were hoping to leap onto now either had rubble on them or were down.

The servers were a good fifteen feet tall, the metal they were encased with was slick, it was dark, and we had to jump from server to sever while the room shook and parts of it fell around us. That wasn't so bad. Being shot at by small flying drones while we were doing all of that was the really bad part.

"Down!" Jeff said as he pulled me to the right and a drone whizzed by. I lost my balance and went over the side. Fortunately Jeff had a hold of my hand and he was able to drag me back up.

"Where's Richard?" I didn't see White anywhere.

He'd been a couple servers away from us so we leaped toward where we'd seen him last. We couldn't get onto the actual server because it had taken a direct hit from a big chunk of ceiling and was down.

Made it to the server nearest this one and looked over the edge. White was on top of the downed server, dodging drones.

Jeff got onto his stomach and reached his arm down. "Uncle Richard, jump!"

Decided I needed to help and the best help I could give was to get rid of the drones. Dug around in my purse and pulled out my new Glock, flipped off the safety, and took aim.

Mom had worked with me a lot on both rapid-fire and moving target techniques and I was a really good shot by now. Set my sights on the nearest drone and fired.

Hit it three times and it exploded. Happily the debris didn't hit either Jeff or White.

Did the same with the next two, one of which took five shots to go boom, and one that took four. But three drones down wasn't bad.

Until I looked around and realized two things. One was that there were a lot more than three drones flying around here.

The other was that they were all heading for me.

CHAPTER 91

THE WAY I SAW IT, I had two options. I could try to hit every one of these drones with the few shots left in the clip—and then Jeff, White, and I could be shot to death by the remainder—or I could run and lead the drones away from the others.

I had to jump back toward the drones, but I didn't keep on going that way. I leaped to my left, then turned and headed for what I hoped was the far wall near where we'd first come into this area.

When you're being shot at, running in a serpentine movement is your best bet, because it's a lot harder to hit a target that's moving erratically. This was great in theory and when you were on terra firma, but fifteen feet up and on slick metal requiring all my track and field training, it was a different story.

Jumping from server to server had been a hell of a lot easier when Jeff had been holding my hand. Hadn't realized just how much he'd kept me from slipping until my third jump, which didn't end up my final jump with my going splat at the end only because I was going fast enough that I was able to pretend I was hurdling and land on the next server in line.

However, that meant I'd gone in a straight line for two jumps, and the drone shots were whizzing far too close to me.

Had to dodge to my left to avoid a drone that was attempting a dive bomb, and while I made the jump, I landed in a skid on my left side. I wasn't really hurt, but I also wasn't steady, and I slid toward the edge.

I was mostly over the edge when someone grabbed my purse and spun me around. I was able to grab White's arm and, because of how he was lying on the top of the server, we both actually stayed on it.

"This is reminiscent of Paris," he said.

"I could have officially done without an Operation Confusion flashback. Where's Jeff?"

"Leading the drones away. He's the fastest and I guaranteed I wouldn't let you fall." White helped me to my feet. He kept a hold of my hand. "Shall we, Missus Martini?"

"Absolutely, Mister White."

We took off after Jeff, who was in the distance, doing a great job of dodging, jumping, and moving fast. But there was a whole fleet of little drones after him.

Jeff neared the wall we were heading for and he stopped running in a serpentine fashion. Instead he jumped straight for two servers. The drones clustered behind him.

I was ready to start shooting but I couldn't be sure I wouldn't hit Jeff. This wasn't looking too good when he disappeared.

Managed not to scream, but only because White and I were in the air, jumping between servers when this happened. We landed and White dropped down onto the top of this server, pulling me with him just as all the drones slammed into the wall.

There was an impressive explosion. White waited until the initial debris had flown out, then he had us up and jumping over again. One server before the wall he stopped again. We looked over the edge. Jeff was standing there, looking worried and expectant.

"Right on time," White said cheerfully, as he shoved me off the server.

Managed not to shriek or accidentally pull the trigger of my gun, but both took a lot of self-control. Jeff caught me like a pro, put me down, and waited to catch White, who jumped the moment I was out of Jeff's arms.

"I'd have loved to have known about this whole plan," I

said as I dropped my now-inaugurated Glock back into my purse.

Jeff took one hand, White the other. "There wasn't time," Jeff said with a grin. "Just a reminder that I was the Head of Field for a reason, baby."

"You're the best there is at what you do, Jeff, I know. Now, let's get out of here. I'm almost sure that the wall you just made fall down leads to the bathrooms and one of those bathrooms has a cube gate in it."

Jeff shook his head. "Maybe so, but the damage is too high up and the rest of that wall is still intact. We'll have to get there another way."

"Fantastic. The next section's a maze, too. But the room we entered the facility through also has a cube gate return there, so we could be good."

We headed for the double doors, which, once we reached them, were both locked and standing strong. Fabulous.

"If the doors are locked, where are the people—and I use that term loosely—we're chasing?" White asked.

Waited for an evil laugh or the sound of a cocking gun. There was none. Interesting. Spun around. No one was here. "They got through somehow. Or a server fell on them. But I doubt we were that lucky, so I assume they got out."

"How?" Jeff asked. "Unless they walked out with a key, they didn't have time to grab something before Naomi blew up where they were living."

"They did, actually. They went back in for guns. Maybe they planned ahead." Though it seemed more likely that they'd invoked Evacuation Omega more than grabbed a key. The drones had to have been part of the evacuation procedure. "The drones. Where did the drones come from?"

"No idea," Jeff said. "Behind us is all I've got, and based on what I can see and hear, we don't want to go back."

"Time to break the door down, Jeffrey," White said. "I'll let you try first. I wouldn't want to imply that I don't believe you're strong enough to do it alone."

"You're just too old to handle it," Jeff said as he backed up to run at the door.

"You never used to be so disrespectful when I was the Supreme Pontifex."

"You weren't as mouthy as my wife when you were the Pontifex. I think she's rubbing off on you."

"I'm all kinds of proud. Jeff, do you really want to run at the door at full speed? If it doesn't open you could get hurt."

"If we don't get out, we're all dead. I'll take the risk of shoulder dislocation." Jeff bent over like a linebacker ready to take out the entire offensive line, and charged. Right as the doors opened.

Jeff slammed right into whoever had opened the doors. Showing we weren't completely shocked, White grabbed my hand and we ran after them.

Proving that he'd have broken down the door with ease, Jeff and whoever slammed through at least six walls before they came to a stop in a heap.

"Well, that's one way to get through this part of the maze," I said as we caught up. "Jeff, are you okay?"

"Yeah, baby," he said as he got up. "I had padding."

"Why don't you ask if we're okay?" Christopher snarled, as he put his hand up and Jeff pulled him to his feet. Buchanan was still on the ground. White and I helped him up—it seemed like he needed both of us.

"Malcolm, are you okay?" This earned me Patented Glare #1. "Christopher, you're an A-C, you heal fast. Malcolm's a human and he doesn't."

"I'm okay, Missus Chief. I got the thrill of being sandwiched in between the two of them, so while I got crushed I didn't get battered."

"Some people would like that." This earned me both Patented Glare #2 from Christopher and an annoyed grunt from Jeff.

"I'm not one of them, Missus Chief. Though not being slammed first into the walls is probably why I'm okay."

"Well, I guess that's good. Why are you guys here?"

They both gave me the "really?" look. "Because you two and my dad weren't back yet," Christopher said. "And Buchanan indicated things looked bad here."

"He wasn't wrong," Jeff said, as he grabbed my hand. "Let's get out of here."

"Which gate?" I asked. "Bathroom or the room we originally entered through?"

"We came in via the bathroom," Christopher said.

"And we're closer to the bathrooms now, too, thanks to your husband using the two of us to break through walls," Buchanan said as I grabbed his hand and we took off. "Where are the clones?"

"No idea. We think they made it out."

"We didn't see them, but we didn't have too far to go." Buchanan had us out of the maze and to the elevator lobby door, which was off its hinges. Presumed that was Christopher's doing.

"Should we take the time to search for them?" White asked. "They know things we'd prefer they didn't, and they do have information we need."

We paused at the door of the bathroom with the gate in it. As we did, a loud rumble shook the whole place. It sounded and felt like the sound of thunder when the lightning strike is right next to you.

"The hell with them," Jeff said. "We need to get out of here."

"Link up," Buchanan said, as Jeff grabbed White and White grabbed Christopher.

We were about to enter the bathroom when I looked up. And screamed. Because the ceiling was caving in on us.

Fortunately we were all connected because Christopher took off at Flash Level, as the rubble hit right where Buchanan and I had been standing.

We stopped at the elevator lobby, mostly because its ceiling was still intact. The cubicle section we'd been in was buried. "Now where?" Christopher asked.

"No idea. The elevators go up to the top part of this facility but not out. We could go back to the entry control room, but we didn't find another gate and don't have time to search for another hidden one."

Buchanan shook his head. "I think that area's all down now."

Jeff put his arm around me and pulled me closer, then did the same with Christopher. Christopher followed suit with his father, and White took Buchanan's free hand in his and pulled him closer into our little circle.

Tried to think of appropriate last words. "Love all of you

so much and I really hate that the bad guys are going to get to win."

The ground shook again and as the ceiling fell I noted that there was a golden glow around us.

All of a sudden, we weren't in a collapsing underground facility any more, but in our living room.

We all blinked.

"Are you all in a group huddle for a reason?" Mom asked.

We broke apart to see most of the team and everyone who'd been over at the Gaultier Cloning Facility sitting or standing there.

"Not that I'm complaining, but how the hell did we get out?" Christopher asked.

"Naomi." Looked around, but she wasn't here. Chuckie, who was sitting in between Gower and Abigail, looked at me hopefully. "It had to be Naomi. The way we were pulled out was just like when ACE did it."

Mom sighed. "I should have put my foot down and kept Naomi here."

"Mom, it wasn't your fault. You told her not to go and told me to leave her here. If it's anyone's fault it's mine."

"No," Buchanan said firmly, as Dad walked out with Jamie in his arms. "This wasn't your fault. I was there. She made the choice she felt she had to and she made that choice to protect her friends and family. She overdid it because . . ." he looked at Chuckie, "she was afraid and didn't realize she was giving herself too much."

Chuckie shook his head. "She knew what she was doing," he said quietly, and there was so much sorrow in his voice that I wanted to cry. Held it in, though, because now wasn't the time to lose it completely.

Abigail nodded. "She'd . . . talked to me about it, what it felt like when they gave her the drug. She wasn't afraid of it."

Dad cleared his throat. "Ah, kitten? I think we may have another . . . little problem."

That earned the room's attention. "What's wrong, Dad? Jamie, are you okay?"

Jamie looked at all of us before she spoke. "Fairy Godfather ACE is back," she said. "And Fairy Godfather ACE is *angry*."

CHAPTER 92

WE ALL LOOKED AT GOWER. "Paul, is ACE back?"

Gower shook his head. "He's not here, I can't feel him."

Because ACE cannot be with Paul any more. It was ACE's voice, inside my head.

ACE? You're back? You're okay? We've been so worried about you and didn't know what to do and—

ACE knows. ACE has been where Kitty could not go. Naomi came to free ACE. Naomi came just in time. ACE is grateful, but ACE is also sad. Naomi cannot come home now. Ever again.

Wanted to ask about that, but something else was more urgent. ACE, you sound different. Are you able to be here without being inside Paul?

Yes, but ACE must still have a host. ACE had to make promises in order to return. ACE has . . . broken laws. Laws Kitty cannot understand.

I've talked to Algar, I think I know what you mean, and that you're right in that I probably can't understand fully.

ACE had to promise to interfere less. Naomi did not save Kitty and the others, though Naomi provided the means by freeing ACE. But ACE did not save Kitty and the others, either. There was a long pause.

Then who did save us, ACE, if it wasn't you or Naomi?

Jamie saved Kitty.

Looked at my daughter. She didn't seem to be "there."
ACE, are you . . . inside . . . Jamie?

Yes. If ACE was to return to Kitty, ACE had to agree
to inhabit someone who has no power in this world.
ACE chose Jamie. ACE is sorry, but ACE had to choose
a host who can filter properly.

Interesting choice. Jamie was probably the most powerful
individual on the planet, but if you took "power" to mean
influence within the world, she was less than two years old,
and that meant completely powerless in terms of how the
majority would choose to look at it. ACE had learned as
much from us as we had from him.

I understand. Will it hurt her?

No! ACE would never hurt Jamie! But it will be hard
for Jamie to allow ACE to speak, as Paul used to. Paul
was ready. Jamie . . . Jamie says she is ready, but ACE
does not believe this is true.

And this was also clever. If ACE was in trouble with the
Universal Meddling Elder Gods or something because he'd
interfered, then choosing to inhabit Jamie meant that his
temptations would be fewer.

While we all had asked Gower to channel ACE to ask him
for advice without hesitation, there was no way Jeff and I
were going to do the same with our baby daughter. Asking a
grown man for advice on how to prevent nuclear war or raving lunatics from kidnapping our children was one thing—
asking your toddler who was the potential kidnappee was
quite another.

Check and mate.

ACE is not Kitty's enemy. ACE will never desert
Kitty, but ACE could not inhabit Kitty. It was not . . .
allowed. And ACE knows Kitty has searched for ACE.
ACE has heard Kitty searching for ACE. It gave ACE . . .
hope.

Hope. Is Naomi dead?

Not . . . really. Not as Michael and Fuzzball and
Gladys are dead. ACE has joined them in, at their request. Fuzzball held Michael and Gladys here, waiting
for ACE to return.

Good Poof.

Yes. But Naomi is not alive as Kitty is. Or even as ACE and Algar are. Naomi exists . . . elsewhere.

Did she trade herself for you?

No. ACE would not have allowed that. But what Naomi did to herself means Naomi cannot return to this world as anyone would know her. ACE is sorry. Chuckie will ask, but ACE cannot bring Naomi back to Chuckie or Chuckie to Naomi. Chuckie must stay here, where Chuckie belongs.

It's not fair.

No, it is not. But Naomi made the choice. Freely.

Jamie said you were angry. Is that why? Or are you angry with me for letting it happen?

ACE is angry, yes. But ACE is not angry with Kitty or Jeff or the others. Naomi's choice is not Kitty's triumph or Kitty's fault. ACE is angry that Kitty's enemies have succeeded. ACE is angry that Michael, and Fuzzball, and Gladys are dead and that Naomi can never come back.

ACE is angry that ACE cannot fix what Kitty's enemies have done. ACE cannot tell Kitty what to do or help Kitty. ACE cannot avenge Michael's loss or support Naomi's sacrifice. ACE cannot help Chuckie through this loss, or Caroline, or the others.

I understand.

And ACE is angry that others who do not care about Earth can require ACE to leave ACE's penguins alone without ACE's protection.

I'm sorry we put you into the position of being in trouble with your peers, ACE.

Algar had told me that by helping us ACE had put himself onto the wrong radars and clearly he hadn't exaggerated. The two powerful beings who'd ended up watching over Earth were trapped between the rock of dependency and the hard place of free will, both constrained by their peers or more powerful beings from doing all they wanted to for the billions of human penguins they both watched over.

And yet they were both still here and, in their own ways, both still helping. They'd started out as distant observers and now were actively involved with keeping their favorite penguins alive. They risked for us, even though both of them would probably deny it. They risked themselves to take care of us, because that's what you did for the beings you loved.

No. ACE is not sorry for anything ACE has done to help Kitty or the others. ACE loves ACE's penguins. But right now, all ACE can do is tell Kitty that Kitty thinks right, and, Naomi knows that Kitty thinks right.

Right now. Well, that wasn't permanent, or at least ACE had some kind of plan to work around his new restrictions. Just like Algar had found his ways to work around the restrictions he had in place to protect himself from discovery.

As for my thinking right, took that to mean I was correct and, despite what the bad guys wanted us to think, Chuckie wasn't the Mastermind. It was a small comfort that I could tell him and the others that Naomi knew this before she'd left us. But small comforts were better than none.

Even though you can't do what you have in the past, ACE, I'm glad you're back. I've missed you.

ACE missed Kitty, too. ACE is happy with Jamie. No one can hurt Jamie because ACE is allowed to protect ACE.

Ah. So this was actually ACE's checkmate. I wholeheartedly approved. Thanks, ACE. I swallowed. This is going to be the last time we talk like this, isn't it?

Perhaps. When Jamie sleeps it will be . . . easier for her to allow ACE to interact. When Kitty sleeps it will also be easier.

Great, more weird dreams were in my future. Under the circumstances, I'd deal with them. Well, that's more than we've had for quite a while. You won't talk to me, or anyone else, if it would hurt Jamie, right?

Correct. ACE will not allow anything or anyone to hurt Jamie, including ACE.

Super, that's all any parent can ask. ACE . . . welcome home.

Felt the warmth that meant ACE was hugging me in my mind. Reveled in it because it had been so long.

And then it was gone.

Algar had said we had to be careful of what we wished

for. I'd asked for ACE back, and back he was, but the cost for ACE's return was high, higher than any of us could have guessed, and I knew Algar had known it would be.

Whether the cost was worth it would depend on who you asked. I didn't know, and I figured I might never know. And I couldn't tell anyone. ACE hadn't needed to tell me that, because I knew already.

Where Naomi was now, *what* Naomi was now, wasn't something we were going to get to know. And sharing that she was "somewhere else" wouldn't allow Chuckie, Gower, Abigail, or anyone else to heal. "Somewhere else" meant a search for El Dorado, and that meant focus and energy and more heartbreak, because ACE had said Naomi couldn't come back and he hadn't used any weasel words. He'd said never.

Jamie blinked and looked at me. "Mommy, why are you crying?"

"Because Auntie Mimi is gone, baby."

Jamie opened her mouth, as if she was going to argue. Then she stopped, closed her mouth, and reached for me. I took her out of Dad's arms and held her, while I let myself cry, in part so I wouldn't have to listen to the sounds of other people's tears.

CHAPTER 93

JEFF HAD INSISTED that Mom and Dad and Chuckie all stay in our apartment, versus going home or even down to the guest floor. None of them argued.

Everyone was exhausted emotionally and physically and, heartbroken or not, we all went to bed. Couldn't speak for anyone else, but my sleep was thankfully dreamless. It was also over too quickly.

Chuckie didn't join us for breakfast. "I'm bringing out Charles' parents," Mom said as we finished eating. "They'll be here in a couple of hours. I asked them to pack to stay for a couple of weeks."

"Thanks, Mom. I'll let him know. Soon."

Jeff nudged me. "You should visit Chuck now, baby. Take as long as you need. I'll handle things."

Leaned against him. "You sure? There's a lot that needs handling."

He kissed the top of my head. "I haven't been sidelined into politics all that long. We lose people every day. It's particularly painful right now considering who we've lost, but I learned over twenty years ago that the best thing you can do for the dead is to honor their memory and not let the people who killed them win. And part of how they win is to make us unable to function. So, we'll be functioning."

"Spoken like Commander Martini." I hugged him, then headed for Chuckie's guest room while Dad played with Jamie and Mom and Jeff started discussing strategy.

Knocked softly at Chuckie's door. Didn't get a response. I worried for a moment that he either wasn't there or that something awful had happened to him, so I opened the door.

"Breaking the rules as always, I see," he said. He was dressed. The window had a very wide sill, and he was sitting on it, looking out. He was in profile to me and I'd never seen him look so sad—the sorrow was literally etched into his face.

He was also surrounded by Poofs and Peregrines. The animals looked at me, then turned right back to Chuckie.

"Well, that's part of my charm," I said as I came in and closed the door behind me.

"You know, I wonder if Alexander knew."

"Excuse me?"

"When he sent the Peregrines. His note to Mimi and Abby told them to stay inside the Embassy. Maybe he knew, or Leonidas knew, that they shouldn't be doing active work."

"Dude, your note told you to move in, too. I think they just wanted us all under one roof, *Dynasty* style."

"Maybe."

"Chuckie, I'm—"

"Don't say it." He turned to me. "I know you're sorry, Kitty. Everyone's sorry. For God's sake, *they're* sorry." He indicated the animals. "And it's no more the Poofs or Peregrines fault than it's yours."

"The Poofs and Peregrines didn't lead a commando raid that had a lot more in common with the Iran Hostage Crisis than SEAL Team Six."

"I know you feel responsible, because good leaders always feel responsible for their troops. But you didn't *make* her go."

"No. She wanted to go. Insisted on it, honestly."

"Right. I could have made Mimi stay home. I knew she was up to something. But I didn't want to be that kind of husband, the one who never lets his wife do anything just because he doesn't think it's safe."

"It's not your fault, either."

"No, but I didn't handle it right when it mattered."

"That's not true, either. You did the best you could."

"She thought I was the Mastermind." He looked back out

the window. "When it came down to it, she wasn't sure, and she chose to go to ACE rather than to go to me. And no, you didn't tell us that—I figured it out based on what's going on and where ACE now resides."

"ACE told me she knew the truth before . . ."

"Great. Good to know." He sounded bitter, and angry.

I went behind him and put my arms around him. "She wasn't in her right mind. The clones were playing on all her fears. They did a whole high school number on her. She didn't mean it to hurt you. She didn't look deeply into their minds because she didn't want to discover you weren't the man she loved."

"So she died for nothing, because our enemies are still out there, and they're stronger, we're weaker, and we've gained nothing."

"ACE is back."

"Yeah, he is. And he's in Jamie. It's a brilliant strategic move. And it makes our planet safer again, and protects Jamie and the other children even better than before. But right now, the good of the many isn't outweighing the good of the few for me."

I hugged him. "I know. And I can't blame you for that. And no one does. You're allowed all the stages of grief, you know."

"Yeah? I'll get one day. Today. Tomorrow, for Michael's funeral, I need to be back, the Head of the C.I.A.'s Extra-Terrestrial Division, not a brand new widower."

I hugged him tightly. Widower sounded so sad and so real, and like something that wasn't supposed to happen for decades, not six months into someone's marriage.

Looked out the window to see what he was looking at. The un-Christian Christians and their Club 51 pals were protesting on our street and into the Circle. "Oh. Great. They're back."

"ACE is back to protect people like that."

"No. ACE is back to protect people like us. Or else he wouldn't be in Jamie."

Chuckie leaned his chin on my arm. "I couldn't sleep. At all."

"I'm sure." I kissed the top of his head. "You can sleep today. We'll get by without you. But only for today."

He chuckled morosely. "The animals came in and stayed with me. I think they were worried I was going to jump."

"Were you thinking about it?"

"No." He turned around. "I've never been suicidal since the first day of high school." He shook his head. "My wife believed I was the Mastermind, but you've never believed that for one minute. Why is that?"

I stroked his hair. "Because I've known you since the first day of high school. If you'd wanted to be a diabolical fiend, you'd have started way earlier."

"I suppose so." He closed his eyes, and I pulled him into me. "Why did she choose everything else over me?" His voice broke. "Why wasn't I worth fighting for?"

Thought about how to answer this as he wrapped his arms around my waist and I stroked his hair. "I know she fell in love with you the moment she met you. Lorraine and Claudia told me that about a week after Jeff and I were married all the A-C women got an emotional 'hands off' signal in regard to you. Naomi staked her claim on you early. We both know what drugs do to a person. Mom felt Naomi was already addicted."

"Angela was right again. I don't know why we don't just ask her to run the world. Or just have her tell us what to do every minute of every day."

"Mom wants us to learn it for ourselves so that we can handle things when she's not here." Just like Olga. And Algar. "Free will exists for a reason."

Algar had approved the raid, because if he hadn't, he wouldn't have outfitted us the way he had. So had he always known that Naomi would OD and bring ACE back? Maybe. But if she hadn't, then five of us would have died. Maybe more of us, because the girls only escaped because of Naomi.

ACE had said that because of what Naomi had done she could never return. I doubted the Universal Meddling Elder Gods gave a crap about drugs and addiction any more than they cared about curing cancer or gay marriage. Those little things had to be far beneath them. So what would they care about? Someone getting god-like powers maybe, which Naomi had certainly gotten.

"I don't know that Naomi picked everyone else over you.

But ACE to her is like you to me—the person who was always there to help, to protect, to tell you you weren't crazy. Maybe she thought she could save ACE and then come back to you."

"Maybe. We'll never know. *I'll* never know."

I hugged him and rocked him while the animals clustered even more tightly around us. Did wonder for a moment why none of the Peregrines had shown up during the raid, but presumably they were protecting the kids in the Embassy.

Which begged a question—what were they protecting them from? Or who? "Chuckie, do you think we can trust Mahin?"

"Yes, in part because she has a Poof." He leaned back. "That was random."

"I'm trying to figure out why the animals didn't help. I mean, I know I'd told them to stay here, and the Poofs came when I called them, and I never called for the Peregrines, but before, when the Science Center was under attack, all the animals were here, too."

He gave a half-hearted laugh. "Kitty, it's pretty obvious that, in both instances, they were keeping Jamie and Patrick from going to try to save everyone. Both their mothers were in mortal peril, I'm sure the animals had to use all their powers to keep the kids in the Embassy again last night."

Looked at the animals. They gave me a group "duh" look. "Oh. Okay. Makes sense."

He sighed. "With ACE inside her, you shouldn't have to worry about that any more. ACE can prevent Jamie and the other children from going into an unsafe environment to rescue their parents. And we never want that. If the Mastermind gets Jamie, the bad guys win, permanently."

I blinked. "That's it. That's why Mimi chose ACE. She didn't do it because she didn't love you. She went because she did. You and her family and the kids and everyone else."

"What do you mean?"

"The clones threatened the kids and that's what pushed Mimi over the edge, that's why she shot up—not because we were in danger but because it was likely that they were going to get their hands on the hybrid children. And she went to ACE instead of to you not because she didn't love you, but because without ACE back, there would be no way to protect the children, not really."

"I'm not following how that has anything to do with me. I'm not saying it's not a noble reason, but I'm not seeing the 'me' in this scenario."

"The Mastermind hates *you*. There's something going on between him—and it *is* a him—and you. We determined that last night. So, Mimi went to ACE because if the Mastermind gets Jamie, then he can destroy you, and that is what his goal is."

"But why?"

I was about to say that I had no freaking idea when the com activated. "Excuse me, Chief. I'm sorry to bother you, but Congressman Martini would like you to join him in the conference room, and Mister Reynolds as well, if he's up to it."

"Why, Walt?"

"Certain new . . . events are . . . requiring a discussion of strategy."

Chuckie and I looked at each other. "We'll both be there, Walter," he said.

"I'll let the Congressman know, Mister Reynolds. Chief, your father and Jamie are in the daycare center."

"Thanks, Walt." The com went off. "Think it's about our 'friends' in the street?"

Chuckie shrugged. "Good guess but it could be about anything, really. I have to figure it's important, though, because otherwise I know your husband wouldn't have asked for me to come."

"Yeah. Even so, you can sit this out if you need to, you know."

"No." Chuckie stood up and put his arm around me. "As with everything else in my life, as long as you're still my friend, I can survive it."

I put my arm around his waist and hugged him. "Always."

"Good. Then once more unto the breach, dear friend, once more."

CHAPTER 94

THE POOFS AND PEREGRINES accompanied us downstairs. Chose not to question. Clearly they were all still really worried about Chuckie. Couldn't blame them.

Looking like the Pied Pipers of Poofdom and Peregrineland, we entered the conference room. Alpha and Airborne were in attendance, along with Jeff, Mom, our Embassy staff other than medical, and Cliff Goodman and Evander Horn. Pierre had provided drinks and snacks. Clearly we were going to be here for a while.

"Glad you brought reinforcements," Tim said as the animals settled themselves along the far wall.

"I never walk alone." Realized we were also missing Buchanan, but decided not to ask why because for all I knew he'd just stepped out to use the bathroom. And if he wasn't here then he likely had a really good reason.

Cliff and Horn both gave Chuckie the manly sympathy hugs, then we sat, Chuckie between me and Mom. "So, is this about the love connection between Club Fifty-One and the Church of Hate and Intolerance that's happening outside, or is there more fun we've missed?"

"Mostly them," Cliff said. "We know they're going to protest at Michael's funeral. The church members weren't so bad, but their numbers have increased tenfold by adding in Club Fifty-One. We're concerned about security."

"To the point where the President isn't sure if the funeral should go on as planned," Horn said.

"Colonel Franklin's offered to let us do the floater gate trick again," Reader said. "But while I'm sure plenty of them are stupid enough to fall for it a second time, we can't be sure we'll get all of them. In part because I don't think all of them are out on our street right now."

"The suggestion to call in the National Guard has been offered by more than one Cabinet member, too," Horn added. "Even the Secretary of Transportation agreed."

"Wow, if Langston Whitmore's concerned about our safety, what does that tell us?"

"Prepare for war," Christopher said.

"No," Gower said quietly. "We aren't going to turn my brother's funeral into a military action."

"I agree," Jeff said. "This isn't something we wanted in the first place, but to allow these people to turn the funeral into a reason to create the wars we've just managed to avert isn't the answer."

"You've explained your feelings," Mom said. "But you haven't made a compelling enough case for us to shoot down the idea. The President doesn't want this turned into a slaughter, an assassination, or a riot."

Aha. Jeff had indeed asked us to come down for a good reason. Gower needed support, and he needed it from the only person able to give it in an official capacity. And he wanted Chuckie here to ensure that the three head dudes for the three most important Alphabet Agencies to us were all here to hear it.

"Here's a compelling answer for the President and Cabinet, Mom. We're not allowing the National Guard because our Supreme Pontifex doesn't want it. And if that's not quite good enough, we'll just add a pleasant 'because I said so' and call it good. And yes, this is me speaking as the Head of the American Centaurion Diplomatic Corps."

"I agree," Reader said quickly. "As the Head of Field for Centaurion Division."

"That's our three heads of state making the decision. Is that good enough for the President, Mom?"

She sighed. "It'll have to be. It's not going to do anyone any good if a riot breaks out, and we know they plan to create a situation where a riot will be extremely likely. Having A-Cs do riot control is a bad choice in this situation."

"What about Secret Service?" Horn asked.

Cliff nodded. "They'll be on the scene anyway to protect the President."

Looked to Kevin. "You're our Defense Attaché. What do you think?"

"Speaking in my capacity for American Centaurion, I agree with you. Speaking as a member of the P.T.C.U., I agree with Angela. And I'm not saying that to curry favor with both my superiors. I'm saying it because we're in a delicate position and I'm not convinced any course of action we choose will actually work out as we'd like it to."

"What Kevin said," Tim said. The flyboys all nodded. "Believe me, we understand the emotional reasons you all have for this, but Kitty I think you need to take back that official decree. We're down by four in the bottom of the ninth—it's hard to come back from that."

"Just need to load the bases and hit a grand slam."

"Hard to get four back is all I'm saying, especially when the game hasn't gone your way."

"Four?" Horn asked.

Harlie jumped onto the conference table and mewed. Angrily.

"Yes, four. We lost a Poof in the line of duty, too. Fuzzball's going to be buried with Michael."

"What did the Poof say?" Jeff asked in the resigned tone of a man who's given up asking why he lives in the loony bin but still hopes to see the normal world again one day.

"That the Poofs want to be able to see Fuzzball's service honored. I, ah, don't get the impression they're used to losing Poofs to early deaths. At all." The idea that Harlie and Tenley were the original Poofs Algar had brought with him was strengthened. "They also feel that whatever Paul wants is what Paul should get."

"I'm with Cliff and Vander," Christopher said. "Regardless of the Poofs' opinions. We have no idea if we destroyed all of that drug. Our enemies might already be armed up to our levels. I'd like the National Guard, the Marines, and all the Navy SEALS and Army Rangers, while we're at it."

Serene nodded. "I'm with Tim and Christopher. I think we need to ensure they can't hurt us any more."

"I'm on the side of bringing in the military," Abigail said. "I only have one brother left and I don't want to lose him, and we all know Paul will be the next target."

"Or you will be," Jerry said, voice tight. "Or Kitty." Len and Kyle were clearly backing Jerry's concerns.

"Frankly, everyone around the casket will be a target," Irving said. "I don't know that the National Guard can protect us from all the possibilities."

"It's politically bad to look like the only reason you're not being stoned to death is because the government brought in the military," Doreen countered. "The images from the 1960s of the Flower Children against the National Guard are still used today to show the brutality of stopping peaceful protest with armed force."

"These people aren't peaceful protestors," Amy said. "But Doreen has a point. The media will have a field day with it."

"So, we're a house divided. And you all have good points. Richard, what do you think?"

He sighed. "I think our enemies expected and wanted this—for us to be fearful, for us to be divided about the correct course of action, for the government to feel the need to bring out military to protect us, which sends a bad message. But people being murdered at the ceremony will send a worse message."

"So, fight or flight? Those are our only options?"

Raj cleared his throat. "There may be another way."

CHAPTER 95

I'**D NEVER BEEN IN A FUNERAL PROCESSION,** let alone one like we were putting on. Our limo was in the lead, for a variety of reasons. Reader was driving the hearse and it was in the middle of our procession, for safety. Tim's limo brought up the rear. In between we had an entire fleet of gray limousines doing about five miles an hour down the streets of D.C.

The police had provided what looked like every motorcycle cop in a fifty-mile radius as our escorts. We had four in front, two on either side of every limo, four behind our last limo, and four extras around the hearse.

Because of where we were located in relation to the Arlington Cemetery, we had to take 23rd Street NW down to the National Mall, and then take the Arlington Bridge across the river to the cemetery itself.

There weren't any protestors along most of this section of our route. However, as we reached the circle that took us off of 23rd and onto the Arlington Bridge, there were a lot of people with signs on the grass in the center, behind the Lincoln Memorial. They weren't praising the monument.

"Do we start here?" Jeff asked.

"No," Raj replied. "This is far enough away that the police will handle anything. We're only concerned with those close to the cemetery itself."

"What about everyone lining the bridge?" Kyle asked as we drove onto it and could see it was lined on both sides with protestors screaming at us.

"The police will handle them," Len replied.

"We will, too, shortly," Raj said.

"We could knock them all into the river," Francine suggested.

"Wow, she's really got you down, Kitty," Chuckie said. "But no. We can't harm any of these people, much as we'd all like to."

"It will be fine," Mister Joel Oliver said. "You all need to relax."

Jeff looked around. "Makes you wonder why we bother, doesn't it?" He sounded dejected and defeated.

Held onto my emotions. My being upset hearing Jeff's disappointment and hurt wasn't going to help him in any way. I took his hand and squeezed it. "Are you okay?"

He sighed. "I don't have strong enough blocks for this."

Felt my worry spike despite my desire to remain emotionally calm and cool. "I have the harpoon with me."

"I shouldn't need it, baby, don't worry. At least, as long as I don't have to knock heads, which, per Chuck, we can't do anyway. I can just feel everyone in our processional—they're all hurt, sad, and scared, even the ones who are ready to fight if we have to. And that combined with the concentrated hatred of everyone on the streets is hard to take, that's all."

"Got it," Kyle said. "Tim's car just got onto the bridge and has dropped off our first packages."

"I hope they'll be careful and run like hell if this doesn't work," I said to Raj.

He nodded. "They will."

"I realize troubadours are persuasive," Jeff said, "but I don't like the idea of any of our people out in this mob, let alone an entire team of them, all without guns."

"They all have hyperspeed," Raj said. "And they'll run before they have to fight."

We stopped. "What now?" Jeff asked.

"The entrance to Arlington is completely blocked by protestors," Len said angrily. "They let the motorcycle cops through and then closed it up. I realize we still have plenty of cops with us, but they're in as much danger from this mob as we are. And while I'd like to run these protestors down, I won't."

"All troubadours out," Raj said.

"Everyone ready to run," Kyle said at the same time.

Raj and Kyle were both hooked into their own networks—Kyle had the link to those riding shotgun in each limo, Raj to all of his troubadours.

"Be careful," Jeff said to Francine.

"Gosh, you do care." She winked at me. "I'm touched." She got out and was surrounded quickly, in part because she did look like me and enough people had seen my face in this town to think she might actually be me. Press was here and they started to assist in the mobbing, clearly under the impression Francine was me.

Raj's plan was simple—use the troubadours' natural talent to sway the mob into a more positive frame of mind. It wouldn't work for all of the crowd, but it had the potential to calm down much of it, and since the troubadours all had hyperspeed and A-C strength, they could grab people and run if they had to.

He'd pulled in every troubadour worldwide, and there were a lot of them. Several of the limos in our procession had held only troubadours. The rest were coming from the Embassy via floater gate that landed them inside the limos that were before and behind the hearse.

The troubadours all used hyperspeed to get out of the limos and into the crowds, so no humans saw them do it. They spread out through the crowd.

"Encircling of the cemetery is complete," Raj said shortly. "We have a troubadour agent every fifty feet or less around the grounds and on the bridge."

Our concession to the President was that the police had blocked off public access to the cemetery—if you weren't on the guest list, you weren't getting in. The President's concession to us was that everyone other than those in the American Centaurion procession would be safely inside Arlington before we ever left the Embassy.

We'd asked the police not to physically move the protestors unless they had to in order to let us through. Right now we were still at a dead stop. I couldn't hear them, but I could tell the troubadours were starting to be effective because signs stopped waving in widening circles around them. A few signs were even tossed onto the ground.

Other than around Francine. In addition to the press, she appeared to have scored the most virulent protestors of the bunch, which made sense since she was closest to the entrance to the cemetery. But even so, she was starting to make some headway when the man I recognized as Farley Pecker, aka the Head Asshat of the Church of Intolerance, came up behind her.

He was between Jeff and Christopher in size, so larger than Francine all the way around. He was older, balding with white hair that was puffy on the sides. He had apple cheeks, and when you first looked at him, you didn't realize you were looking into the face of the most intolerant person potentially in the world. I could see Clint Eastwood playing him in a movie, but only if Clint was willing to take the bad guy role.

He shoved Francine, hard, and she stumbled into some people with signs. This didn't look good.

I was supposed to stay in the car, but I was near the door. And I was out of the car in a moment. I shoved him back and away from her while I pulled her away from the people he'd shoved her into at the same time.

"Stop attacking a woman half your size, you horrible man. I realize it's a hard concept for you, but have some respect."

"You're all sinners and Jesus wants you to burn in Hell!" he shouted.

"Aliens should all die!" someone else shared. This opened the floodgates as the usual anti-gay, anti-woman, anti-alien, anti-Jew, anti-black, anti-everything slogans were tossed at us.

Francine and I were back-to-back, me facing the cemetery's entrance and her facing the street and most of the crowd. She began to calmly start reciting the speech Raj had written for all the troubadours. It was all about how America was the land of opportunity, how refugees from the world and the galaxy over came to it as a haven, how America's people were accepting and loving, how the country was founded on tolerance.

Couldn't have proved this last part by anyone nearby, but

it was still a good, touching little speech, appealing to everyone's better instincts. If the Asshat Church and Club 51 members had better instincts, which I wasn't currently prepared to say they did.

Francine's speech was also having no effect on the man in front of me. Not that I'd expected it to.

"God has served justice on your sinful evil," he said. "You all need to die and burn in Hell for the evil you've done."

"I've talked to gods, and they don't like you much."

This earned me some gasps of horror as a tall man in a business suit joined us. He looked nothing like either Leventhal Reid or Howard Taft—he was average size for his height, normal looking, not ugly but not gorgeous, either. But I recognized Reid and Taft in him—there was something about the crazy in his eyes when he looked at Francine and the limos. "I told you, Mister Pecker," he said.

And there was also something familiar about his voice.

"You're aptly named, I can say that. So, who's the head of Club Fifty-One here?" They stared at me, mouths open in shock. "Yeah, I know, how ever did a little Jewish gay-loving and alien-loving girl figure out who this other dude was all by her lonesome? Hard to believe, isn't it? So, since we're now face-to-face while you're threatening me, what's your name? As a warning, if your name's Crotch I'm going to spend the next five minutes laughing my ass off."

He flushed. "My name is one you should learn and tremble before. I'm Harvey Gutermuth."

"Harvey Guttermouth? Wow, that totally fits. Oh, and in case you forgot, we're only supposed to tremble before the Lord. And both of you are definitely not him. Tell you what, you let the cars through, I'll listen to your crap for a while, how about that? So no one gets hurt and all that. And by no one I mean your sad, pathetic, misled followers."

Pecker looked apoplectic—eyes bugged out, face red. Surely someone else had mouthed off to this loser before now, so why I was having this effect I couldn't guess. Just lucky, apparently. Or he had bad gas. Gave it even odds either way.

Pecker opened his mouth, no doubt to blast me with more of his screed.

But Gutermuth put his hand on Pecker's shoulder. "Don't waste words on these, my friend. There's only one way to rid the world of this scourge." He smiled at me, and it was definitely one of those Evil Bad Guy Smiles. He looked around and nodded. Several people with "Kill the Aliens" signs shoved closer.

Which boded.

CHAPTER 96

BEFORE I COULD DECIDE if it was time for me to admit defeat and call in the National Guard—who were literally waiting inside at the Iwo Jima Memorial, because Mom had insisted on one more concession—a group of kids in their late teens or early twenties shoved through the crowd.

"Get away from them!" one of the boys shouted. "They need us here!" he shouted to someone over his shoulder.

One of the girls shoved between me and Pecker and Gutermuth and stood between us in a protective stance, her back to me. I was officially shocked. By the looks on the men's faces, so were they.

"Leave these people alone! You can threaten us, but we're going to make sure they get inside and we're also going to make sure that none of you do."

I put my hand on her shoulder and backed her up just a bit. "They're not above hitting a girl. FYI."

"I'm not above kicking them in the balls, either." She smiled at me over her shoulder. "No, you don't know me, or any of the rest of us. You haven't saved our lives, unless you count when all of you stopped the alien invasion, and we do. The call went out—you aren't here alone."

The kids who'd come with her went behind Pecker and Gutermuth and linked arms. Francine nudged me. "I'm going to join them." She walked over and linked up. Then she started her speech again, the kids next to her nodding along and chiming in.

I was about to mention that though the effort was sweet and very well-intentioned, eight college students weren't going to stop this mob. But before I could, more people shoved through the protestors. Most of them were college aged, but certainly not all. I could definitely spot family groups, too. They didn't say anything, just linked up with the others and started spreading out.

In a rather short time we had a full-on human chain up against the foliage that was the "wall" around Arlington. Once the line was set, the girl who'd been protecting me shouted some orders and she, along with a few more people, created two more chains from the middle of the entrance.

They spread toward the street, then moved as a chain to opposite sides, shoving the protestors out of the way of the cemetery's entrance. It was like watching a non-uniform marching band. And yet there was no way these people had practiced—it was clear that most of them didn't know each other.

Pecker and Gutermuth had managed to avoid the human chain, however, and were blocking the entrance.

I was sure Len was ready to run them down, not that I could blame him. However, that wasn't what the good guys did. I went to the two men. "I'll give you a choice. You can move and let all our cars through without issue, or I'll make you move. The former will allow you some dignity—but I promise that the latter won't."

"We will never move for the likes of you," Pecker bellowed.

"Aliens are beneath us," Gutermuth chimed in. "We will never do as you ask."

"Okey dokey. The No Dignity For You option it is."

One of the many things I'd been practicing was talking to the Poofs and Peregrines in my head. I was getting really damned good at it. And I knew I had all of our Poofs on board because Fuzzball was in Michael's coffin.

So I sent out a request. A rather simple one, all things considered. And, happily, results were immediate.

All the clothing Pecker and Gutermuth were wearing disappeared from their bodies.

They gaped at me. "Wow, you're not aptly named at all,

really, are you?" I said to Pecker. "Well, other than in terms of personality. And you, sir," I said to Gutermuth, "should perhaps consider cutting back on the donuts. Spanx can only do so much, after all. And while imperfections are what make the rest of us fun and interesting, in someone as self-righteous as you are, I think it's only right to demand perfect physical fitness to match your perfect morality and all."

Pecker and Gutermuth tried to cover up and back up into the cemetery, but some of the kids noticed this and the human chain moved fast and blocked them. Meaning everyone could now see both of these dudes standing there butt naked.

While the kids nearest to us started to laugh, the protestors who could see this screamed in horror.

"See how God punishes the wicked?" a voice boomed over the crowd. Not a troubadour's voice, but Oliver's. He had a video camera trained on the scene. "God has exposed them for the charlatans they are! All who follow men such as this are more evil than any other sinner!"

Many of the protestors ran off. Some dropped their signs. Some were laughing. Soon the entire human chain was laughing, so it became hard to tell who wasn't. The press took the opportunity to start snapping pictures and rolling video. Those who weren't doubled over laughing, that is.

Oliver joined me as the rest of the press blocked Pecker and Gutermuth from running off. "Nice choice, Ambassador."

"Thanks. Figured the nonviolent option would be best. Great use of drama on your part, too, MJO."

"Thank you, I wanted to ensure the dramatic. Seeing as I have a direct feed to the major news channels because I was in the car with you and the Congressman, this should be on every news outlet worldwide within the hour, if not sooner."

"You rock. Speaking of my husband, though, how did you keep Jeff in the car?"

"There are two large Poofs inside who shared that we all needed to remain seated with our arms and legs inside the vehicle. Once you had our friends here undressed they allowed me out."

"Ah, good thinking on the Poofs' parts. Think we can get the press to move the sideshow off a bit so the cars can get through?"

"I do." Oliver joined the press mob and spoke to a few of the reporters and camera operators. They started to move toward the side, still not allowing Pecker or Gutermuth to escape.

I waved the limo on, but the door opened and Jeff, Chuckie, and Raj got out. The limo remained stationary. "Why aren't you going in?"

Jeff took my hand. "We can let the President wait a little while. There's something more important we need to do." He walked us to where Francine and the first set of kids to arrive were. "Thank you. For proving that we're still here for the right reasons."

He shook each kid's hand and said the same to each of them. Looked around. Chuckie and Raj were doing the same with the other side of the line.

As I detached from Jeff and followed suit, more of the Diplomatic Mission got out of the limos and did the same, some zipping off via hyperspeed to catch the other sides of the cemetery.

We thanked everyone, even people I was fairly sure had been holding signs not too long ago. But most of the protestors had disappeared or joined the human chain, and that was what the goal had been anyway.

Troubadours advised that the Embassy staff had shaken paws with every single person holding the line and Raj got the rest of us advised and herded back to our cars. Everyone returned to their limos, other than the troubadours, who were going to remain with their new friends on the human chain.

Before I got into my limo I went back to the first kids who were with Francine. "You said a call had gone out. What call?"

The girl who'd shoved between me and the two men threatening me grinned. "Over the Internet. The call's gone out before, but not quite like this. I think it was a hack. We all got the same message—that the haters were protesting this funeral and that decent people needed to show what they stood for."

Made a mental note to ensure we did something nice for Hacker International. And probably Oliver, too, since I figured he'd been in on this with them. "What's your name?"

"Katherine. My friends call me Kathy."

I laughed. "What's your major?"

She grinned. "Criminal Justice. But I'm going to get a law degree after I graduate."

"Why am I not surprised?" Sent another mental message and a business card was in my hand. I gave it to her. "When you're out of school, call me. I guarantee we'll find a job for you." There were more cards in my hand. "And your friends, too." Hey, the kids were all Poof Approved.

"Wow, thank you," Kathy said. "You don't have to do that."

"Yeah, actually, I do." I smiled as I gave the other kids who'd been with her my card. "I'm the Head of Recruitment for a reason, kiddo."

CHAPTER 97

REJOINED JEFF AND THE OTHERS and our procession finally made it through the entrance and into Arlington. It was beautiful, but now that we were inside and past the major problems, all that remained was the funeral. Had to give one thing to the protestors—they'd certainly kept everyone's minds off of the point of the journey.

Michael was going to be buried in the same area as the Challenger and Columbia Memorials, which were near the Memorial Amphitheater. But because of the political brouhaha, the services were going to be held in the Amphitheater itself.

The limos dropped everyone off in front of the Amphitheater and then went to park, keeping a couple of A-Cs with them for faster return. Other than the hearse, which pulled up and stopped. Michael's honor guard got out.

The flyboys were in their dress whites, and Brian, Gower, and Reader were in the Formal Armani Fatigues—black tuxedos, white shirts, with black buttons. Normally it was six pallbearers, but since we'd made it up as we wanted to, White had insisted upon eight.

The rest of the men were in the standard Armani Fatigues. They were, as always, dressed for success. Which was good, because Akiko had about had a heart attack when we'd told her we weren't doing the burka and veil combos for the women any more. The troubadours were also good with fashion design and alterations, though, so they'd been able to help her create more appropriate mourning-wear for the female side of the house.

We women were all in various black ensembles, mostly simple sheaths, and only those who wanted to were wearing black hats with veils. There were flashes of white here and there, mostly gloves, but some other accessories as well.

We really looked like a huge group of penguins, and I wanted to talk to our benevolent observer, but now wasn't the time to try to chat with ACE, since Jamie was undoubtedly awake and this would be a poor time for me to take a nap.

The Amphitheater was, fittingly for Arlington, beautiful—an elliptical building built out of white marble and designed as a mesh of Greek, Roman, and Renaissance styles. It also had a lot of stairs to go up to get inside. Okay, not that many if you weren't carrying anything heavy, but a lot if you were. The wisdom of eight pallbearers became clear to me, especially since we only had one A-C acting as a pallbearer.

The pallbearers lifted the casket—each one of them had a Poof on the shoulder nearest the casket—and walked up the stairs to the entrance. The rest of us followed.

Inside, the Amphitheater resembled an old-fashioned theater—including the slope from the entrance to the stage, and a sectioned colonnade area that curved around from the entrance to the covered stage area at the back—just one that didn't have a roof. And instead of seats it had low, backless marble benches curving to face the semicircular main stage. "Pretty" was the watchword, not necessarily "comfort."

The stage had three levels. The lowest had a stone chair, facing the audience. The second level of the stage had a podium, right behind the stone chair. The third and uppermost level of the stage was a semicircular seating area for what looked to be about a hundred people and an apse in the back. There were American flags hanging from each of the colonnade bay arches, and two more hanging in the apse.

Because of the way the aisles were designed, it was kind of tricky for the pallbearers to maneuver, since they had to enter the amphitheater, walk down the center aisle for a while, then zigzag to the left and back toward the front in order to reach the dais area. Once they were at the front, then they had to go up two sets of stairs to get the casket settled onto the uppermost part of the stage, in front of the people sitting there, which included the President and my parents.

However, the flyboys had served at more than one funeral and, with Hughes in charge, were a well-oiled pallbearing team, and Brian, Gower, and Reader each held up their ends, so to speak.

The lower center seating section was reserved for American Centaurion. The rest of the seats were filled, and the colonnade area had people in a standing-room-only capacity, which included a different set of press, though Oliver was sitting with us.

It was also a bit like my nightmares in that I recognized many who made up the Sea of Faces, and they were all politicians or other bigwigs, though some, like Cliff and Horn, were at least friendly faces. Clearly Oliver's Be There Or Be Square messages had worked on both the good people outside and the maybe-not-all-as-good people in here.

We all filed in after the casket and took our seats, Erika and Stanley Gower going first, with Abigail in between them, all three looking ready to cry at any moment. Gladys' husband, Chuckie and his parents, and Caroline and hers were next, because they were considered part of the Gowers' immediate family.

Because of our rank, Jeff and I were required to go next, with White right after, then the rest of Alpha, Airborne, and the Diplomatic Corps who weren't pallbearers followed. After that, the rest of the Martini and Gower families, and any other A-Cs who'd requested and been granted funeral duty.

The pallbearers put the casket down, then Uncle Mort and Colonel Franklin—who were on the stage with the President and my parents, along with most of the politicians we considered our friends—stood and gave the flyboys an American flag, which they then draped over the casket.

Once the flag was hanging just so on the casket, the flyboys went and spread out behind the audience on the top part of the stage, standing at attention while facing the casket and the rest of the audience. Brian, Gower, and Reader came down and took their seats.

The Vice President went to the podium, and gave a very lovely speech about heroism and sacrifice, reassuring

Michael's parents that he'd been a hero and died a hero. The acoustics were excellent. You could hear the Vice President speaking as easily as the Gowers crying.

Uncle Mort, Colonel Franklin, Senator McMillan, and Senator Armstrong all also spoke. Everyone was relatively brief and had taken some time with their speechwriters, because they were all moving.

Then the President took the podium and gave an even better speech about Michael's heroism and sacrifice that got pretty much the majority in attendance crying if they weren't already.

Finally, though, it was time for the Supreme Pontifex to speak. Because we weren't doing a commando raid concurrently with the funeral any more, we'd cut all the other speeches and delays our side had planned. However, Gower had to speak, because presiding over events such as this was essentially part of his job.

He walked up slowly, shook hands with the President, then took the podium. "I . . ." He cleared his throat. "On behalf of all of American Centaurion, we thank you for coming to honor our dead."

Gower stopped speaking and cleared his throat again. "I'm sorry. This is even more difficult than I'd imagined it would be. I've heard all the kind words, all the praise, and yet, I look at my parents, who've lost their sister, son, and daughter all this past week, and the words just don't . . . mean anything. Because the words can't bring anyone we've lost back."

Tears ran down Gower's face. "We're used to sacrificing. But sometimes that sacrifice seems too hard, too much."

Christopher, who was sitting behind me, leaned forward. "This is going to be a problem," he whispered. "We should have made my dad give this speech, not Paul."

Found myself agreeing. But I was on the end of our row and White was next to Jeff and behind Stanley Gower, with a lot of people blocking his other side. It was going to be awkward to get him out and up onto the stage.

Looked around and caught Doreen's eye. She nodded to me and I was pretty sure mouthed the words "your job." Figured she was crazed by grief, too. Gave her the "you're high" look. Received a Death Glare in return. Apparently Doreen expected me to cowgirl up and actually do something Ambassadorial. Always the way.

She had a point, though, because Gower was floundering and the A-Cs I could see looked worried, my husband among them.

Took a deep breath and got up. I didn't look at anyone, just headed for the stairs up to the podium. As soon as I walked by him, Reader got up and followed me. "You up to this?" he asked me as we started up.

"No, not at all. But Paul's not either."

"Yeah."

Gower was staring at the audience and not speaking when we got up there. Reader put his arm around Gower's waist. "Come on, Paul. Kitty'll take it from here."

Gower looked at me. "You will?" He sounded shocked and confused and I knew Reader absolutely needed to get him out of the spotlight for the moment.

"Sure, Paul. You know, routine. Go where you belong right now, with your family."

Gower nodded and allowed Reader to lead him off the stage. Realized that the acoustics meant everyone had heard this exchange. Oh well. Took another deep breath, let it out, and gave it my best shot.

"I suppose you're all wondering why I called you here."

CHAPTER 98

I WAITED. THANKFULLY, some of the audience chuckled.
Chose to take that as a good sign and forged on.

"I'm not going to apologize for our Supreme Pontifex.
Frankly, when you've lost three family members in about a
week, if you're able to stand and dress yourself I think you
deserve a medal. And I realize that Michael's family is getting that medal. But I want to tell you all that it's not enough."

The chuckles stopped, which was fine.

"Every family who's lost someone to war or terrorism or
any other kind of heroic sacrifice knows that all the medals,
all the accolades for the dead, while nice, aren't the same
thing as having that person back."

Heads in the audience nodded, and not just from the A-C
section.

"But we still carry on, because that's what's expected of
us. Even when the terrorists escape, or get off on a technical-
ity, or flat-out have connections that allow them to waltz out
of a secured holding cell and continue perpetrating their evil,
we carry on. Even if your loved one dies from friendly fire,
you carry on. Even if you've lost your only child or all your
children to war, you carry on. Because that's what we
do—we carry on.

"I'm going to be really honest. We of American Centaurion have all wondered this past week if carrying on was
worth it. I'm sure every person whose career puts them in the
line of fire in some way—police, military, fire, covert or clan-

destine ops, and similar—has wondered at some point if it's worth it. To risk their lives for people who, very often, aren't even the littlest bit grateful."

The policemen who'd escorted us were standing as a group at the entrance. Saw them all nodding. "And yet, they all carry on."

Risked a look at Jeff. He gave me a small nod. Hopefully that meant he approved of what I'd said and where I was going. Oh well, no time like the present to find out.

"Since the world discovered there were aliens living on the planet we've had a lot of haters. Many protests against us. Because we're different. And there have been a couple of groups who were more vocal than the others. I'm sure you know who they are and I'm not going to give them any promotion or acknowledgement by naming them. But they've been cheering about Michael's death. And why? As near as I can tell, because he's an alien and his brother, our religious leader, has the nerve to love and be married to another man. Sorry if that was a spoiler for any of you out there, by the way."

Oh, good, some chuckles were back.

"In the A-C's culture and religion, the sexual orientation of who you love isn't important. Neither is the color of their skin. I guess that makes the A-Cs quite alien in some ways from a lot of humans, more so than their having two hearts. And it certainly makes them more advanced. Oh, they're not perfect, no one is. But they're all smart, and they're all smart enough to know that skin tones and sexual orientation aren't what actually matters about a person. How they live their life is what matters, what they do when faced with evil, what they do when no one's looking."

Chuckie and Caroline were sitting together and, as I looked at them, both gave me the thumbs up sign.

"Michael wanted to go to the stars and that's where he served his country the most. But he also served his country by facing evil and fighting it. He died trying to protect his best friend from being tortured. He died trying to protect his sisters and his aunts from being kidnapped and terrorized. And he died trying to avenge the senseless murder of his loyal pet, an animal that loved him so much it's in the coffin with him, so they can be together forever."

Could spot the animal lovers in the audience—they were wiping their eyes.

"And yet, the people who hate Michael because of his skin color, his brother's sexual orientation, and the fact that he wasn't fully 'human' will tell you that he deserved to die and that he's rotting in Hell.

"Well, I happen to know differently. Michael's not in Hell, he's with his God. And that God isn't here to encourage hate. He's here to encourage us to use our free will to make the world a better place for everyone, not just for a select few who think their way is the only way."

Looked at White. He gave me a small smile. Chose not to look at Christopher lest I get a Patented Glare. I was rolling and wanted to remain that way.

"It's a big universe out there and we're not alone in it, and by now everyone knows that. But I'll tell you, today, we felt very alone. Driving past so many people protesting our very existence, we felt alone, surrounded, outnumbered. And we wondered if it was worth it. We've lost lots of people over the many decades the A-Cs have been on Earth, and there comes a point when you ask yourself if you're done losing. We were at that point today."

All the American Centaurion section was nodding.

"But it's funny. Just when you think things are at their worst, someone can show you that most people aren't like those protestors who hate in the name of God. And we were shown that today."

Thankfully, the A-C section was still nodding.

"They're still outside, and I doubt they can hear me, but there were hundreds of people we've never met before today who came to form a chain to keep the bad people out and let us come here to honor Michael's life and his death.

"And *those* people are why we do this. Because they didn't have to come. It was an inconvenience, and a risk. But they came anyway. Because it was the right thing to do and, at their cores, they're decent people trying to do right in the world and light a candle in the darkness. Just like the A-Cs. And they knew we needed them, just as they've needed us.

"So, to our enemies, I want to say that, despite your best efforts, we're not going anywhere. We will continue to fight you and the evil you perpetrate. You can and will kill more of us, we know that.

"But we will persevere. Because there are more people worthy of our protection and love than there are not. You are in the minority, and we will ensure you stay that way. You can and will throw your worst at us, but know that we will not go quietly and we will not leave the good people of this world at your mercy, any more than they left us."

I looked around at everyone in the Amphitheater. "In a little while we're going to put Michael's body in the ground. Something the A-Cs don't normally do. But they're doing it because it matters to our President and our country that Michael's sacrifice be commemorated in this way. And because we do love this country and world, we've acquiesced.

"Once his body is in the ground, though, you'll all start to forget him, this day, and what he died for. Only we won't forget.

"And I won't actually allow all of you to forget, either. Because Michael is representing every A-C or Centaurion Division agent who's died over the years, unsung and unlamented by most of you.

"He's more than himself now—he's representative of all of our fallen, all our unsung heroes, all our Unknown Soldiers. And he's also the reminder of why we fight and protect—because when we visit his grave, what we'll remember in addition to Michael are the faces of the people who stood against evil and hatred for us to be able to honor him today. We'll see the faces of our brothers and sisters."

CHAPTER 99

I **TURNED TO LEAVE THE PODIUM.** As I did, someone
on the stage started clapping.

I looked over to see my Uncle Mort standing and applauding. The flyboys broke attention and joined him, and then the
rest of the people on the stage followed suit, the President
included. Mom and Dad were both applauding and I was
relieved to see they looked proud as opposed to embarrassed
or horrified.

The President getting to his feet ensured I got a standing
O on the way down. Prayed I wouldn't trip, but before I really had to worry about it Jeff came over and helped me
down.

Since everyone was standing, the pallbearers went back
into action. Well, Brian and the flyboys did. Uncle Mort and
Colonel Franklin took Reader and Gower's places, which,
based on how Gower was doing, was preferable.

They took the casket down and out as they'd come in.
Once they were through the exit, the motorcycle cops started
ushering the attendees out, and in not too long it was just the
press, the people on the stage, and us left.

Press was ushered out, then American Centaurion, since
the Secret Service wanted to take the President and the other
dignitaries out last.

Tim took my elbow. "Got a text from your friends on the
police force while you were orating," he said quietly. "Somehow two sets of men's clothing appeared on the head of the

Bomb Squad's desk. He had them searched and there was a detonator in a pocket. The area around Arlington's being searched right now—bombs have been found, but none have been detonated."

"How did they know to come to Arlington to search?" Jeff asked.

"The pocket with the detonator also held Farley Pecker's wallet."

"Interesting. I assume Gutermuth gave it to him, or even slipped it into his pocket." Good to see the Poofs had totally been on the job.

"The K-9 squad was called because of their close association with us. Officer Melville suggested that Harvey Gutermuth was probably involved. Both men have been found and taken in. Melville said he'd keep me posted."

"Hope they gave them some jumpsuits to wear. Ugly orange ones for preference."

"We can hope," Jeff said. "But I never count on that these days, baby."

"The cops feel your pain, Jeff," Tim said. "Believe me."

Once we were at the gravesite, Gower seemed back under control. He gave a lovely eulogy for Michael, presumably the one he'd planned to give earlier. He also mentioned Naomi and Gladys, saying that Michael's grave would be their memorial as well.

Pierre had brought in dozens of roses, and everyone had one. I took two. As they left, each attendee put a rose onto the coffin. Amy and I went with Caroline. Amy put her rose on without a word.

Caroline stepped up and put her rose on the casket. "Goodbye, Michael. I miss you so much already and I know I'm going to miss you so much more as time goes by."

I hugged her as she started to cry. "Cry all you need, Caro."

But she got herself under control and nodded to me. "I'm okay. Well, as okay as I can be right now. Your turn."

I put both my roses on top of the others. "Michael, be sure you keep all the girls in heaven feeling attractive. I know you're up to it. And Fuzzball, you keep on taking care of him like the good Poof you are."

We moved off so the rest of the family could do the same. As Mom had expected, Nathalie Brewer and Vance Beaumont both came over to express condolences and hug me. Guy Gadoire was with Vance, of course, and did the same. Lillian Culver and Abner Schnekedy were also along but they had the grace to not try to hug me.

Sooner than I'd have expected we were done, and the drivers went to get the limos. Per Raj the troubadours had gone back to the Embassy once the bomb squad had come to investigate and they knew the bombs had been found.

Pierre had an after-funeral buffet set up in the Embassy complex, and all our people and our closer political friends were there. The children were with us now, too, and it was nice to get to carry Jamie around and cuddle her without worrying about what we were going to do next.

Miraculously, for a party we were throwing, no one died. Figured we'd had enough death already and the cosmos had chosen to cut us a break.

The nice thing about parties that take place after a funeral is that the majority don't linger. Even so, by the time we'd gotten everyone out of the Embassy, and then swept for bombs, bugs, and other unsavory things at least three times, it was fairly late.

After we made sure all those sleeping over were tucked away, Mom, Dad, Jeff, Jamie, and I headed upstairs. Once Jamie was in bed and snoozing with all the pets, Mom and Dad hugged and kissed us good night and went to their guest room.

Jeff and I got undressed. "You did great today, baby," Jeff said as I gathered up our clothes. "I didn't want to say too much out in public, in case someone would try to use it against us, but you were amazing."

"Thanks. I just didn't want to see Paul have to suffer through something he wasn't emotionally ready to deal with."

"You were exactly what our Head Diplomat is supposed to be." Jeff kissed me. "And I'm incredibly proud of you."

"I'm always proud of you, so I'm glad I made you proud of me, too." Feeling quite good all things considered, I trotted into the closet, went to the hamper, and tossed our clothes in. "Thank you," I said quietly.

Algar appeared sitting cross-legged on the hamper. "For what?"

"For whatever."

He shook his head. "I didn't do anything. You came up with that speech all by yourself."

"Yeah, well more went on than that."

He shrugged. "Everyone who arrived to help you truly went of their own free will."

"The Poofs did a good job."

"Again, it was their choice."

"You're worried I'm going to worship the Great God Algar and bring the people hunting for you. You can relax—I don't think you're a god."

"You insinuated you did during your run-in with the people exercising the worst kind of free will."

My turn to shrug. "You're pretty amazing, but I know you're not a god. And you know me, I'll say whatever I need to."

He smiled. "I know. Would you like to know the weather forecast?"

This was a new one. "Sure?"

"Quiet, with a strong side of regrouping. I know you don't feel like you were successful, but you've hurt your enemy far more than you know. You'll have some breathing room. Not a lot, but more than you're used to. So use it wisely."

"I was thinking I'd use it to celebrate life and have lots of sex with my husband. Like my King of the Elves likes to recommend. You know, in between all the dedicated work stuff I'm sure you're actually talking about us doing."

Algar laughed and disappeared. In his place was Jeff's fedora.

"What did you say?" Jeff asked as he came into the closet.

I picked up the fedora. "You know, it's been a while since you've worn this."

Jeff grinned, took the hat from me, flipped it onto his head, and picked me up. "Then let's rectify that right away, Ambassador."

"Oh, Congressman Martini, I love how you think."

"YOU HAVE THE RIGHT to remain silent. Anything you say can and will be used against you in a court of law."

"I'd like to say two words—Diplomatic Immunity. Then I'd like to say other words like, I want to call my lawyer, the President, my mom, and a few other people like Officer Melville." The cop helped me up into the paddy wagon.

"That's nice." Of course, he was now actually helping my lawyer into the big metal van. Amy Gaultier-White patted my hand. "You and all the rest get to go to headquarters first, ma'am. Then you can make all those calls you want to make."

"Diplomatic Immunity. We do remember what that means?"

The cop smiled as he helped several other women into the paddy wagon with me. "Yes, ma'am, Ambassador Katt-Martini. We do know."

"I'm the Ambassador for the American Centaurion Diplomatic Mission. My husband is a congressman. And you're risking pissing off a lot of important people."

"Comes with the job, ma'am."

"Why are we being arrested? Since when is arresting diplomats your job? Every woman with me is part of my diplomatic mission." In some way, at any rate. Wasn't sure if I could count the female members of Alpha Team as being part of the Embassy staff. Then again, I was the Ambassador, so I could make those decisions and decide I'd officially instated them as Disturbance Attachés before we left. Minor moral dilemma solved. Major dilemma still not solved.

"You're at the scene of a disturbance, ma'am. Ambassador or not."

"I'll say it again, officer—Diplomatic Immunity."

"Yes, ma'am." The cop gave me the Concerned Officer of the Law look. "You're being moved off the streets for your own protection, ladies."

"Peaceful protest is part of our democracy," Abigail said.

"My husband's going to hear about this," Serene added. "He's an astronaut."

"I'll watch out for falling moon rocks, ma'am," the cop said to her. Wasn't positive, but I was pretty sure he was trying really hard not to laugh. "However, your own protection currently supersedes your immunity."

"Since when?" Amy asked.

"Since now." The cop closed the back doors. Nicely. But still.

"Well," Lorraine said, "at least we're not chained up or handcuffed."

"Speak for yourself," Claudia muttered.

"You tried to hit one of the officers in the face," Lorraine pointed out.

"He was being rude." Claudia looked around. "Can I get out of these now?"

"Sure. You want to break them or have me or Amy pick the lock?"

Lorraine Billings, Claudia Muir, Serene Dwyer, and Abigail Gower were all female A-Cs or, as I called them to myself, Dazzlers. Dazzlers were, to a one, gorgeous, which was par for the A-Cs. They were also all brilliant by human standards, usually focused on medicine, math, and/or science. My girls were also focused on butt kicking.

To a one they looked awed and impressed. "You and Amy have finally learned to pick locks?" Serene asked.

Amy and I both sighed. "Yes, Malcolm's been working on it with us," I shared.

"A lot," Amy added, clearly going for the Full Disclosure option.

Malcolm Buchanan was assigned to be my personal shadow. He was also pretty much the most comprehensively competent dude in covert and clandestine ops imaginable. During Operation Infiltration he'd taught the four Dazzlers with us how to pick locks. Amy and I hadn't done so well with that. So Buchanan had made it a point to ensure that we knew how. Sadly, it hadn't come that easily to either one of us, which was something of an embarrassment, but both Amy and I were proficient lock pickers now.

Amy pulled a metal nail file out of her purse. "Too slow, Kitty." She went to work.

"At least some of us made it," Claudia said as Amy got the cuffs off her and she rubbed her wrists.

The doors opened again and two more women were put in—Doreen Weisman, our last Dazzler on Embassy Duty, and Denise Lewis, who was human but frankly gorgeous enough to pass for alien.

"Diplomatic Immunity!" Doreen shouted. "Do you all understand what that term means?"

The cops smiled, nodded, and shut the doors again. "So much for Claudia's optimism," I said. "I thought you two had gotten away."

"We did, too," Doreen said.

"Someone in the crowd pointed us out," Denise added with more than a trace of bitterness.

The doors opened again and Nurse Magdalena Carter and my sorority roommate and bestie, Carolyn Chase, were both helped inside. "This is supposed to be the land of freedom and opportunity," Nurse Carter said darkly. "Not the land of oppression." She was originally from Paraguay and had joined us during Operation Assassination.

"Senator McMillan is going to hear about this!" Carolyn was the senator's Girl Friday.

"I'm sure he will, miss," the officer said. "From more than just you."

Counted noses. We were missing one person. Sure enough, the doors opened again. Though who was being helped in wasn't on my list of Girls Gone Washington Wild.

"Lucinda? What are you and my daughter doing here?"

Yes indeed, my mother-in-law was there, carrying my daughter, Jamie. Two officers helped them in, with a third standing behind to catch them if Lucinda lost her balance.

"Thank you so much," she said to the officers. "You're all too kind, and I just want you to know how much we appreciate all the good work you do and long hours you put in."

She got very friendly smiles from the cops. "You're very welcome, ma'am. You and the little lady be sure to sit down so you don't lose your balance." The doors shut again.

"Mommy, this is so much fun! Gran'ma Luci said we could come watch you work!" Jamie bounced over to me for hugs and kisses.

Happily gave out the necessary snuggles, then handed Jamie to Amy for more of the same. "Lucinda, what part of 'you and Jamie stay at the Embassy' didn't come through clearly?"

"No part of it, Kitty," she said as she settled herself in between Doreen and Serene, opposite Amy. "I just thought it would be fun for Jamie to see what you girls were up to."

Lorraine and Amy both nudged me. "I think Kitty just wanted to be sure you and Jamie didn't get hurt," Amy said as she finished loving on Jamie and handed her to Abigail. "And I have to agree. Are you alright?"

"Oh, yes, Amy dear, we're both fine. It was quite exciting, all the chanting and jumping up and down."

Managed to keep my mouth shut but only by grinding my teeth. Abigail hugged Jamie then passed her on to Carolyn.

"You do realize it's a political protest?" Serene asked, radiating innocence. While my first impression of Serene, during Operation Drug Addict, was that she was a crazy loon, my second, third, fourth, and fifth impressions of her were Innocence on the Hoof.

However, I'd learned there was a lot more to Serene than most of us ever saw. Right now, for example, I had a feeling she was asking because she knew I couldn't do so without snarling, and she was doing it in such a way as to not upset Lucinda.

And it worked, of course. Lucinda patted Serene's knee. "Oh, yes, dear, I know. It's part of how our great host country works, and it's important for Jamie to see that, to see how her father is a part of something so much bigger than himself."

"Jeff's always been a part of something bigger than himself," I pointed out.

"Yes, Kitty, but Jamie couldn't go to active situations with her father, now could she?"

Regardless of Amy and Lorraine's nudging, Doreen and Serene's wide-eyed "shut up, shut up" stares, and what I could feel radiating from the rest of the girls—that I needed to keep my mouth shut—I couldn't stop myself. "Um, have you been paying attention to anything that's gone on since Jamie was born?"

Fortunately, before Lucinda could reply and I could gain more Bad Daughter-In-Law Points, the doors opened again. And, just like the last time, who was being shoved into the paddy wagon with us wasn't anyone I was expecting.

Lillian Culver was helped inside. "Thank you, officers, that will be all."

"Yes, ma'am. Do you need anything else?" the officer who'd been doing most of the talking asked. Unlike with Lucinda, where he'd clearly been happy to help, or with me and the others, where he'd been trying not to laugh, right now he seemed very controlled and official. Presumed he knew exactly who Culver was.

"No, no, we're all good here now." Lillian turned to me and smiled widely. She was a top lobbyist, *the* top for most of the big defense contractors, meaning she was incredibly powerful and influential in this town—the epitome of a Washington insider. And, as seemed to be the "thing" here, she had "her color," which happened to be red.

Culver was an attractive enough woman, until you looked at her just long enough. Then you realized she was all bones and angles, with a very wide mouth her bright red lipstick really emphasized. I called her Joker Jaws to myself for a reason.

Right now, I was getting the Joker's smug "I've trapped Batman and all his cronies" look from Culver. Couldn't wait to hear what she wanted.

But before Culver spoke, the doors opened yet again. "Good grief, it's like a Marx Brothers film in here. We're about to be at standing room only."

Culver laughed and reached her hand down. "Nathalie, you're here, too?"

Representative Nathalie Gagnon-Brewer was helped in by the officers and Culver. "Thanks, Lillian. Kitty, I'm glad I caught up with all of you." She was a French expatriate, a former international fashion model, and a widow. Her husband, Edmund, had been a representative from California, and he'd been murdered during Operation Sherlock. As with Jeff, the President had asked Nathalie to take over her husband's seat in Congress. And as with Jeff, considering the state of the union and the world after Operation Destruction—when Earth had gotten to learn, in a really big way, that we weren't alone in the cosmos—Nathalie had said yes.

"Wait for me, wait for me," a man called before the cops could close our now very full paddy wagon up again. Vance Beaumont climbed inside. "Thanks, guys, appreciate you holding the car for me," he said to the officers.

They nodded and closed the doors behind him. "Vance, what are you doing here?" I asked.

Vance was married to Guy Gadoire, who was to the tobacco industry what Culver was to defense. Vance spent his days thumbing through *GQ* and dressing accordingly, throwing lavish parties, and hanging around.

Despite all of this, I'd come to realize he had a functioning brain he liked to keep hidden, and he was actually a better friend to me now than I'd have ever thought when we first met. Same with Nathalie, of course. And while Culver and I couldn't be called friends, thanks to my "uncles" the top assassins, she and I had a good working relationship where she didn't try to push me into making bad decisions for American Centaurion too often and I returned the favor by not threatening to "call home" too often.

"I thought this was a woman's rally against the anti-alien Presidential candidate," Lucinda added as Vance jumped the line and took Jamie from Nathalie—who'd just barely gotten her from Carolyn—to give her a quick "airplane flight" she loved, if her squealing with joy was any indication.

Vance gave Jamie a kiss, handed her off to Culver, and shrugged. "I have the wife role in my relationship, in case you missed that key point, and, also in case you didn't notice, the Cleary-Maurer ticket is also anti-gay."

"And anti-woman," Nathalie added. "They aren't pro minorities, either."

Shocking me to my core, Culver both cuddled Jamie—who didn't scream in horror but instead cuddled back—and nodded. "They need to be stopped."

"Wait, what? Lillian, are you saying you were here as part of the protest?"

Culver shrugged, gave Jamie a kiss, and handed her over to Doreen. "Yes. I'm a woman, in case you didn't notice, and I'm not excited about what Cleary and Maurer both stand for."

"They stand for hate," Lucinda said calmly as Jamie clambered from Doreen and over Lucinda to get to Serene. "And, as such, they need to be opposed." She looked right at me. "And our young women need to see that their role models are so opposing."

"Fine, fine, yes, I noticed everything and yes, I'll stop complaining about Jamie being here." Stood up and hugged my mother-in-law. "I just don't want either one of you getting hurt, that's all."

She hugged me back. "I know. I may have been a housewife more than a career woman, but trust me—no one will touch a hair on one of my grandchildren's heads and live to talk about it."

"So," Claudia said as she took Jamie from Serene, "do we think Adriana made it without getting nabbed, or do you think she's in a different arrest vehicle?"

"And, since we have two who were out of the Embassy against orders," I gave Lucinda the hairy eyeball, "where's Mahin?"

Before anyone could reply, the back doors opened once again. Two more men joined us—Len and Kyle, my official driver and bodyguard. They'd both played football for USC, but they weren't causing the cops any problems. "Thanks," Kyle said as the cops once again closed our doors. He stayed by the doors, blocking both entrance and exit.

Len nodded to everyone as he worked his way forward. As he reached the front of the holding area, car doors slammed—they were clearly the doors to our particular car. "Everyone, please keep your seats," Len said. He took Jamie from Lorraine, and handed her to me.

"Hey, I just got her," Lorraine said.

"Sorry." He didn't sound sorry. Len pounded twice on the metal separating the cab from the rest of us, and the paddy wagon lurched off. We drove for about thirty seconds and came to a screeching halt.

The doors opened yet again, and two more people joined us. Tito Hernandez, our Embassy doctor, and Mahin Sherazi, who'd joined up with us during Operation Infiltration. Tito was literally dragging Mahin aboard.

"A little help?" he asked Kyle, who reached down, grabbed the back of Mahin's shirt, and lifted her into the back.

She was shouting in Farsi. I didn't speak her native tongue, but it was pretty clear that she wasn't saying nice things.

Kyle and Tito got the doors closed, Len did his hand slam on metal thing, and we took off, this time at a much faster rate of speed. Sirens were going off around us—clearly we had at least one police car as an escort, maybe two. Maybe more.

"So, what's going on?" I asked Len. "And I'd really like an answer. Starting with what you, Kyle, and Tito are doing here in the first place. And why you all happily leaped into the paddy wagon with us instead of, oh, I'm just spitballing here, getting us *out*."

He sighed. "You weren't supposed to go to this thing without me and Kyle."

"It was, despite us having four men in here, supposed to be a women only thing. Hence why we left the men at home. Or thought we did. Mahin, you were supposed to stay home, too."

She tossed her hair out of her face. "I went with Lucinda and Jamie."

"Shocker."

"Mahin is part of our family, too," Lucinda said calmly. "And I brought Doctor Hernandez, Len, and Kyle along with us to protect Jamie."

"Wow, check and mate. Good one. Look, I appreciate the

arrest solidarity, but didn't it occur to anyone that some of you staying out of jail might be helpful?"

Culver cleared her throat. "Ah, Kitty? I don't think we're actually being arrested."

"No? Then why are we in a police riot van?"

"For our safety," Lucinda said. "That's what the nice officers said."

Got a bad feeling. "Look, you all realize that we've been herded into a metal van and are being taken God knows where by God knows who, right? And that the local police have been infiltrated and impersonated before, usually by people wanting to perpetrate a great deal of malice aforethought on us? Remember? Anyone?"

The car came to a stop, the doors to the cab opened and closed, then the doors to our section opened yet again.

Had to admit—I really wasn't expecting to be where we were or see who was standing there, though it shouldn't have surprised me all that much.

Gini Koch lives in Hell's Orientation Area (aka Phoenix, Arizona), works her butt off (sadly, not literally) by day, and writes by night with the rest of the beautiful people. She lives with her awesome husband, three dogs (aka The Canine Death Squad), and two cats (aka The Killer Kitties). She has one very wonderful and spoiled daughter, who will still tell you she's not as spoiled as the pets (and she'd be right).

When she's not writing, Gini spends her time cracking wise, staring at pictures of good-looking leading men for "inspiration," teaching her pets to "bring it," and driving her husband insane asking, "Have I told you about this story idea yet?" She listens to every kind of music 24/7 (from Lifehouse to Pitbull and everything in between, particularly Aerosmith) and is a proud comics geek-girl willing to discuss at any time why Wolverine is the best superhero ever (even if Deadpool does get all the best lines). Because she wasn't busy enough, she's added on featured guest columnist and reviewer for Slice of SciFi and It's Comic Book Day.

You can reach Gini via her website (www.ginikoch.com), email (gini@ginikoch.com), Twitter (@GiniKoch), Facebook (facebook.com/Gini.Koch), Facebook Fan Page (Hairspray and Rock 'n' Roll), or her Official Fan Site, the Alien Collective Virtual HQ (http://aliencollectivehq.com/).

Gini Koch
The Alien *Novels*

To Order Call: 1-800-788-6262
www.dawbooks.com